THE WINDMILL YEARS

The Windmill Years

Vicky Martin

Heywood Books

© Vicky Martin 1978

First published in Great Britain 1978
by Macdonald & Jane's

ISBN 1 85481 005 7

This edition published 1989 by
Heywood Books Limited
55 Clissold Crescent
London N16 9AR

Printed in Great Britain by
Cox & Wyman Ltd, Reading

This book is sold subject to the condition that
it shall not, by way of trade or otherwise,
be lent, resold, hired out, or otherwise circulated
without the publisher's prior consent in any
form of binding or cover other than that
in which it is published and without a similar
condition including this condition being imposed
on the subsequent purchaser.

CHAPTER ONE

Even now, at the height of summer, stillness came to the last studio shortly after 4.30. Perched at the back of the building, a large converted attic, it lay under the shadows of other roofs and the light was not good enough to continue working much after four o'clock. As the time was realized, there would be a sudden surge of noise. People would begin to stretch and to talk eagerly after the silence of the two-hour work period, to collect their things together and to stack drawing boards. More and more sounds. Feet against the wooden floor and down the stairs, sporadic bursts of laughter, names called. And then, gradually, like a clumsy machine, the art school would begin to quieten and shut down. The stairs became deserted and night prematurely occupied the empty studios. In the front of the building work might well continue but here, at the back, unless a lecture was scheduled, it would become absolutely quiet.

Anna Hayward, sitting alone in the deserted east studio, tilted her head a little to listen to the aeroplane go over. She heard it every afternoon at 4.45 as she sat in the quiet, one of the few who never wanted to go home. She was unable and unwilling to shut off the day's work in a matter of moments and move on to the interest of the evening. Anna disliked evenings. Her life was lived entirely in the daytime and she wanted to prolong it. Especially a day like today. She watched the light seep from the vast arched windows. She heard them calling, 'Good-bye... Good night.' from the street three floors below, as she tapped her pencil lightly against the wooden donkey she sat on and studied the life drawing still pinned to her board.

It surprised her that she had had no premonition this morning as she came into the studio of anything but a normal day. It seemed extraordinary that something so good could happen to her with no warning at all. She had pushed the swing door open at 9.20 and seen the model, Joanne, already arranged on the faded chaise longue, her body dabbed pink where the heat from the electric fires touched her. Anna loved life drawing, found it totally absorbing. It required the most intense concentration, especially when drawing Joanne with her sad, ravaged face and her hair, as red as Anna's, twisted into a wiry mound on the top of her head. Joanne's stomach was as soft and wrinkled as a fine leather glove and almost as impossible to draw. The flesh concealed the form. 'Well, it's the babies that do it to you,' she told them in the morning tea-break, a pathetic little figure in her quilted nylon dressing-gown. 'They ruin your muscles, especially the stomach muscles. Never go back, they don't, not to what they were.'

Anna listened with no idea that, at 11.15, just as they should have been settling down again for the late morning period, Hilary would come panting up to the studio and single out ten of them and shepherd them down into the holy atmosphere of Richard Cannon's office, that Richard Cannon would tell them with very little emotion in his voice that they had been chosen, would be staying on, had survived to become second year!

'Second year,' Anna said and pride shivered through her and a stab of intense joy made her laugh aloud, hug her knees, bunch herself tight. For the other nine it was exciting enough. They were all keen and first year meant nothing, merely an extension of being 'good at art' at school, but those who survived into their second year could begin to take themselves seriously. For Anna it was not just exciting, it was a lifeline. It was happiness too intense and too new to be left alone. She needed to stay where she was, savouring it . . .

She looked up, suddenly and uneasily, as the studio door opened and then she relaxed because she saw it was Pym. Anna was not the only one who hovered in the evenings.

'Thought you'd be here,' he said in his soft Scottish voice, and he came and stood behind her, bending to put his hands on her shoulders and tucking them under her hair. Anna did not flinch. So gradually, so gently, had he taken to touching her that she had not had a chance to be afraid of the contact with another body. A male body. Over her head, Pym studied her drawing.

'I like it but you've exaggerated the face . . . the eyes are too big, too dramatic. It weakens it. Spoils it.'

'She had such a sad face, Pym. I wanted to show how it was. Too many children and too little sleep.'

'Well then, paint her portrait!' he said impatiently, coming round to sit in front of Anna. 'Paint her stupid, weak, brown-eyed face. Sad like a cow. You could feel the effort that thinking was for her. Sometimes I could hear the machinery of her brain grinding and scraping . . . life bewilders her. She obviously tries to work it out by going to bed with a lot of different men and is then surprised and a little hurt when the kids come! Paint her if you want to, but not in life class. Draw the body, Anna. That's what matters!'

Whenever he finished speaking, especially if he were feeling provocative, he would hold his face still and wait. Marvellous face, Anna had thought, again and again, thin and mobile, the eyes set deeply and tilted up at the outside corners. A wide and wicked mouth. A face that would recur, generation after generation, and belong to the men who were alert and involved. Pym MacDonald, entitled to criticize because his talent had already set him apart.

'I don't agree,' Anna said primly and then let the subject drop. She had learnt in her first days here, when she began to know Pym or rather when he began to know her because Anna never approached anyone first, that she was no match for him. It had been Pym who had addressed her in the quiet evening stretches when they found themselves the only two occupants of this deserted studio, Pym who nudged aside the barriers of her shyness by simply ignoring it, by asking her questions that had to be answered, by talking to her even if she rarely talked to him. And when she finally felt at ease with him, she discovered that he could argue her into the ground and that he loved to argue. In class, especially in Michael Miller's class, he would contest any criticism made of his work, defending each mark he put down, each piece of colour if colour were involved, with a fierce pleasure. Although he was a slight man, shorter than Anna, his aggressive masculinity soothed her. It was reassuring that she could at least have Pym for a friend, that he gave her a small piece of his life that he allowed no one else. These sessions in the evening lull were very precious.

Being a shy girl, when she did speak the words came tumbling out, chasing one another. 'Do you remember, Pym, the first morning? How we came in and stood on the edge of that big lost group of people and envied the ones who obviously knew their way around and had paint stains on their jeans?'

'I remember Hilary,' Pym said, leaning back. 'She stood in the middle with her list and her timetables.' He mimicked. 'No, I can't come to the telephone. Tell them to ring back after eleven. Don't they know what it's like on the first morning of a new year? What's your name? Anna what? Hayward? Group C. Middle studio at eleven. Here's a timetable. You're with that lot over there!'

Anna laughed but his words reminded her of the way Hilary's sharp eyes had flicked over her body, making her crouch more deeply inside herself as Hilary saw how fat she was. She moved her thoughts to something else. 'And gradually we all made our way up to the coffee bar and, like the innocents we were, totally unwarned, drank cups of that filth that comes out of the Dalek pretending to be coffee! And we hung around and the brave ones started conversations and friendships and hatreds and jealousies and others, like me, said nothing.'

'What I remember most about the first day was the inflated price of beer in that effete pub where we lunched because we hadn't found any of the cheaper places. And sitting and listening to Hilary and Michael and all the fourth-year lot in their self-assured corner, swapping gossip about the summer holiday and talking about us as if we were completely deaf . . .' He leaned forward, forearms resting on his knees. 'But why this sudden burst of nostalgia, Anna? Isn't it rather soon?'

She shook her head and her face was transformed for a moment by her shy smile. 'It's just that I love it here so much. But I haven't dared to admit it until now. Now I know I am safe for another year at least. I feel I belong here and I've never felt that about anywhere in my life. Never at school, never in my family . . . What's so extraordinary is that I dreaded the thought of coming to London. I was terrified. I thought my life had been scrunched up like an old envelope, and thrown away. And instead, I found myself here. And I love it. I love it from the moment I push through those swing doors into the chaos of the hall and fight my way into the girls' cloakroom and try to hang up my coat; and all through the struggle to settle down and make myself concentrate until the deep work period comes and I push myself down into the concentration, like pressing my hands into clay; all through the day until it ends and I sit with this tired, satisfied feeling.'

'You're lucky then. My day ends with a sense of frustrated disappointment. It's not how hard you work, Anna, it's what you have to show for it at the end that counts.'

She ignored him, needing to let her enthusiasm run. 'I love the intense revelations in the coffee bar and the secrecy of the cloakroom. It has green doors with things scratched on them. Someone has written I love Pym MacDonald just above the roller towel holder . . .'

Pym gave a short burst of laughter and took a handful of her hair, tugging it affectionately. 'There must be something behind all this sentimentality. Something more than mere pleasure at being accepted to stay on?'

Gently she took her head back, out of his reach. 'Yes, there is . . .' She wanted to tell him but it was hard to choose the words. 'I've decided to go and see my father, Pym.' She made her hands into a church steeple. 'It's a great relief to me. I've been worrying about it on and off ever since we came here. Whether to see him or not! It's easy for Linden, because she is always *absolutely* sure about everything. As far as she's concerned, he might as well be dead. They were close, you see, before he left. She hates him now . . . But he never felt much for me and I was always apologetic about myself. Linden and I were country children, Pym. Bicycles and pony children. He took our lives and shook them to bits and we were expected to accept it. Suddenly we were living in a flat, one of two hundred. Four huge blocks, sides of a square, with a little garden in the middle like a joke. Tiled halls and margarine-coloured paint and a lift in a wire cage. Nowhere to go on a nice evening or at weekends to lie and think without being watched by someone. Nothing to pick and bring home and stick in a jam jar and try to draw. There isn't even any way of telling if it's winter or summer except by watching what they plant in the flower-beds or seeing how many leaves there are on the plane trees. In the beginning I hated him too. If it hadn't been for Holland Park I would have gone completely mad – but the odd thing is, after a year, not only have we survived, we are all quite happy! My mother is all right. Linden loves it. And I have this place. It's so ironic, Pym, that out of his selfishness comes all this . . .'

'And you want to go and tell him that?'

She nodded, and tucked her thick hair behind her ears, revealing a high white forehead. 'God knows why. You know what I'm like. I'll get there and then say nothing. We have never been close. It's just that I can't bear to think I will never see him again and I do have a reason tonight for visiting him. So I will!'

Pym nodded, grinding the cigarette under his foot. 'I hope it won't disappoint you if the meeting is a failure.'

Anna stood up. 'No, I won't be disappointed. I'm too happy tonight. Besides, all the meetings I have ever had with my father have been failures.'

She gathered her pencils and unpinned the drawing. She stacked her board against the wall and followed Pym down the stairs.

There were islands of activity in the quiet of the big Victorian building which housed the Cannon School of Art. The coffee bar was alive, a room too small for its purpose, its walls lined with benches and notice boards and in one corner the science-fiction shape of the coffee machine which Pym had christened the Dalek. 'With this coffee we will exterminate you!' The lithograph room was still humming and clattering. And Hilary Parker's office, half way down the last flight of stairs to the hall, had the door half open. It was a blend of village shop and pedlar's van and courtroom. It smelt of the small cigars she had smoked constantly during the nine years she had been Richard Cannon's secretary, organizing the Cannon School of Art, bullying, mothering, and making life miserable for the few unfortunate students she took a dislike to.

Founded in 1879 as a drawing academy, the Cannon had been taken over by its namesake, grandson of the founder, in 1955. But nowadays half the fees were paid by the G.L.C. and not the mothers of young ladies with talent. It was small but its reputation was impressive and competition was fierce. From Hilary's office, students could buy pencils and putty rubbers, fragile sticks of charcoal wrapped in tissue paper and drawing pins. In Hilary's office, people were chosen and discarded and final lists made. She dispensed frightening sarcasm, aspirin, sticking plaster and great sheets of white paper on which to draw future masterpieces and dreams. In the evenings, always the last to leave, she made her way home to a flat in Wimbledon. There had been a husband once, Pym said. 'But he didn't last.'

Anna paused by the telephone box in the hall. She pulled her address book from her bag and looked up her father's number . . . She had entered it not under H for Hayward but under F. It seemed strange, to look up his number. It made her hesitate. But the triumph still carried her and, after a few moments, she dialled his number.

'Hallo?' His voice had become unfamiliar. It had more life in it than she remembered. 'Hallo? Who is it?'

'It's Anna.'

'Anna!' He said her name with deep surprise. 'Well, well.' Hearty now. 'How are you?'

'Fine. I was wondering if I could come and see you . . .'

'Of course you can come and see me.' He laughed, playing the father role rather badly after a couple of years without practice. 'We'd love to see you. Come round now. Come for a drink.'

'All right. It will take me about half an hour.'

'Fine . . . see you around five thirty.'

He had sounded, Anna thought as she put the telephone down, as if she were a casual acquaintance, just passing through. But then, Anna and her father had never enjoyed one another.

Anna made her way to the bus stop, a large strange figure in jeans and plimsolls and a long loose shirt which exaggerated, rather than concealed, the bulk of her body. Her red hair lay on her shoulders and down her back like a cape.

'Night, Anna,' Pym said, passing behind her, touching her arm. She turned to look at him and he blew a kiss and walked on, up towards Notting Hill Gate and Paddington. Pym had a place now. Two rooms and a shared bath. And he had Jane, a tall, black American girl whose loud laughter rocked the class. A flamboyant extrovert, as definite as Pym, she competed with him, fought with him, arrived with him in the morning but left without him around four o'clock each afternoon to do the tedious things which went, she said, with loving someone. 'I do the shopping and the cleaning and he just rolls home when he's hungry . . .' Yet she said it in such a docile, affectionate tone that she must like it like that, Anna thought.

'Good night, Pym.' She watched him go, watched his springy step, hands in his pockets. She envied Jane her possession, if only temporarily, of such strong life force.

All through Anna, deep to her core, was a longing to be linked with someone. A man. She was incomplete, she felt. Parallel with this longing, and equally strong, was a craving to be thin. She stood, now, thinking: *When I am second year, I will not eat so much. I shall work instead. Work and work. I shall probably forget about food for days on end . . . I could start dieting now. Or tomorrow, after I've weighed myself!'* Anna had a special technique for standing on the scales, with her weight all on one foot and leaning backwards a little. It made them read a few pounds less. When dieting, she converted her weight from stones into pounds. It seemed more of an achievement to drop from 174 pounds to 169 than from 12 stone 6 to 12 stone 1! But Anna's diets were rarely successful for more than a few weeks. They were extreme and short-lived.

For a week, perhaps ten days, she would exist on apples and yoghurt and then some small failure, some pain, would drive her to buy doughnuts, éclairs, bars of chocolate which she ate secretly all at once and the guilt that came after would make her buy more.

Her bus came, and Anna went upstairs, finding a seat by the window. She enjoyed buses. She made a hole in the dusty window and looked down on the cars and the people, threshing about in the rush hour. As she watched she thought of her father, wondering if she was doing the right thing in going to see him. Opening it all up again.

It had been her sister Linden all those months ago, almost in a previous existence it seemed to Anna now, who had come to find her on a mild May afternoon to tell her. Linden had searched the various corners of the big garden until she was bored and when she finally found Anna she folded her arms and looked down and said, without bothering to soften the words, 'We have to move to London, Anna.'

Anna, lying on her stomach on the short grass, drawing a daisy, had rolled over. Now, in this grumbling bus, she could still see Linden's expression, hear the words, feel the disbelief and then the hollow sickness in her stomach as she realized Linden was not playing. These things were branded into her memory.

'We are moving to London, Anna, because we can't afford to stay on here. Not now . . .'

Linden, always Linden, first to everything. First to be born and first with the news. Centre of the stage, wearing the spotlight as easily as she wears her clothes. And then me. Anna. Plodding in her wake like some grotesque mid-day shadow. Dull and faithful as a winter coat. My life is speckled and stained with her entrances and exits, her laughter and her rage and the things she has made me aware of.'

Pictures flicked through Anna's mind. Linden learning ballet, light and strong in a white tunic. Anna, stiff and stilted, two classes lower, wearing an airtex shirt tucked into navy knickers; Linden running, linking her arm through some friend's arm and bending her head to whisper a secret; Linden angry, tossing her plaits, lifting her chin and never afraid to let her anger show, to let the feelings spill. Linden acting, borrowing, taking.

'How can we live in London? We live here.'

'Haven't you realized what has been happening between Mum and him?' Linden's voice had been flat and impatient. 'They're separating. This place is far too big for the three of us and, anyway, he can't afford it and a flat for himself and his new friend!' She spat out the words. 'Don't try and pretend you haven't realized!'

But I hadn't, Anna thought. It had seemed to her then, looking up into Linden's scorn, as it frequently seemed to her now, that she inhabited a different world from them all. A world linked by words but not by understanding.

'Isn't he happy with Mum?'

'Obviously not. But it's hardly sudden, is it? He's been away so much recently.' For one moment Linden's mouth wavered. She had missed him very much. She had always been his girl, his favourite. Then the rage replaced the pain. 'We all thought it was work . . . That's what he said, but he lied!' Suddenly she had crouched down, as if needing to get closer to the ground. She tore up short blades of grass with her fingers. 'I suppose it's the classic mid-forties thing. She's been his secretary for three years. She's called Tracey. It's so pathetic. So insulting and ordinary. He wants us to go and meet her, but I shall never go!' She had raised her head, looking straight at Anna, her huge hazel eyes opened so wide there was white all round the irises. 'Never!'

'Are they getting divorced?' The panic had been cold in Anna then. Ice-cold. This was her place, the old red brick house on the edge of a Gloucestershire village, with its stuffy attics and wild garden and decaying greenhouse.

'All I know is that he's moving out. And we're selling this place and getting a flat in London.'

'Well, should *I* see him, Linden?'

Linden wasn't listening. Her mood had changed. She lay on her back, arms folded under her head, a little smile on her mouth. At nineteen she was bored with life in this little place, bored with the boy-friends she tolerated in strict rotation. Her conquests had all been empty victories. She looked at the sky. 'I would have gone soon, anyway. Time for me to get on with life. I shall learn to cook properly. Brilliantly. I shall get myself a very good job. Mum will work too and she'll be OK. She has Aunt Prue living in London and she'll make friends if she tries. She may even re-marry. She looks good enough. And you can go to some art school or other. That's what you want, isn't it? And get thin!'

It had been obvious to Anna that Linden and her mother had discussed the whole subject in detail as they discussed everything, sitting together on the swing seat on summer evenings, rocking and talking, or round the kitchen table on colder nights, drinking cups of tea. They were two women from the same mould.

'Is she very unhappy?'

'No, at the moment I don't think she is.' However shamelessly she might arrange her own beliefs about herself, Linden was shrewd in her judgment of others, especially those she knew well. 'He's been away a lot. She has learned to live without him, even to be happy without him. It's just the psychological thing of realizing he is going permanently. At the moment she sees herself as a tragic deserted figure ... You know how she's always been, full of stories about herself, full of romances. Her real life, as she thinks, was concentrated into the few brief years before she married. Once she married, once she settled on her great love, and achieved her ambition at the early age of twenty-two, what was left? Suddenly she has a reason to re-live all that time and she has us to think about and plan for. She says she will hate selling this house but she's damned if he's having the dining-room table or the glass. She's enraged, you see, because he's been living with this Tracey, secretly, for months. I'm sure she was always keener on sex than he was so it's doubly ironic that, having toned down her own feelings to suit him, he should up and leave her like this! I mean, I can't believe he finds a great intellectual soul mate in this Tracey. It has to be physical! Anyway, her anger will carry her for a while but when it wears off . . .'

Linden stretched her arms expressively towards the sky and Anna shivered, thinking how callously Linden scattered the secrets that Veronica must have confided in all those talking sessions.

'We will have far more opportunity in London,' Linden had said, sitting up abruptly.

'But I must see him again, just once or twice. Don't you think I should?' In her fear, Anna slipped back into childhood. She could have been ten years younger than Linden, not two.

'No. You should not see him.'

Despite Linden's vehemence, Anna had worried about it through the tangled months which followed when they sold their house and moved to Oakfield Court on the Kensington High Street side of Holland Park. She had watched her mother struggling to make herself a new life as a single woman and, at first, failing. For twenty-two years, Veronica Hayward had been the lesser half of a pair. Her married years had so eaten her away there was scarcely enough of her left to cope on her own.

'She is like someone getting over a stroke,' Linden said, 'learning to use new parts of her brain and of herself.'

As Linden predicted, her mother's anger wore off and was replaced by a patient, 'he'll come to his senses' role which enraged Linden. 'It is escapism, nothing more. You don't want him! You don't need him! Stop living in the past.' Driven by Linden's strength, Veronica got herself a job in Kensington High Street.

Perhaps, Anna thought, *Linden doesn't notice how much Mum is drinking now. Or perhaps she thinks she needs it!* When she concentrated on Veronica, Anna felt only hatred for her father and thought Linden was right. They should cut themselves off completely. But then she would feel again this underlying craving to visit him, just once, as if to round him off in her mind.

It was all right for Linden. Easy for her, really. She had her hatred to make her sure and she belongs in London anyway.

The very first time they came to look round this flat in Oakfield Court, Linden had been the one who questioned the estate agent, who opened doors and cupboards, who chose it really. She had walked into the big bedroom at the front, which had a commanding view of the miserable little garden and much the best cupboards and announced, 'This will be my room. I like this flat, Mum. I think we should have it!'

They did have it. And Linden enrolled herself in a Cordon Bleu cooking course and began in early September, making friends easily among the girls she learned with. They slaved away in the hot kitchens in batches of ten, their hair tucked neatly into white chefs' caps, and they copied out endless recipes on to index cards. After a month, Linden had her waist-length hair cut into a short, blonde, silky cap, which made the impact of her face doubly startling. A face with high cheekbones and a small, strong chin, a long neck, and those enormous speckled eyes. Linden met brothers and friends of the girls she cooked with and within three months of her arrival in London it was unusual for her to be at home in the evening.

Anna had picked, from the bedrooms which were left, a room at the back of the block. The light was better here. She had a view of the narrow road which ran along behind the flats, of dustbins and garages and the undignified backs of some rather smart mews houses. How she had loathed it in those first weeks, she remembered, and how she had loathed him for causing it!

It was only Holland Park that saved her from absolute misery in the beginning. August was warm and dry that year and the long summer had tired the park. It was over-used, the grass thin, the trees shabby, but Anna lived in it. She walked through it, she sat and drew in it, she took her easel and painted and came to know it. She knew each segment and she knew the faces of the people who used it. For long stretches she would lie on her back and look up at the blue sky, as clean a blue as the sky over her home, as she still thought of Gloucestershire, and almost as comforting.

And then it was 26th September and Anna was presented with the great unexpected gift of the Cannon. After the first few nervous days she allowed herself to sink into the work and fascination. The Cannon contained Pym and other people who would become her friends. It was, quite simply, the best thing that had ever happened to her.

And it's going on. For at least another year! The excitement made her move in her seat. At last she had answered for herself the 'Should I see him?' question. She would see him because she wanted to.

I will tell him that I am happy at the Cannon although the rest of London still makes me uneasy. That Linden is completely at home, and Mother has her job and spends her evenings exactly as she spent them before. With jig-saws and gin and bitter-lemon and bridge. She folded her hands. *I'll tell him, in case he hasn't realized at the advanced age of forty-seven, that life is a bewildering and back-handed business and that all our contentment is due to his betrayal, as Linden calls it!*

The flat was near South Kensington. Two tall white houses had been knocked into one and converted into flats. Anna pushed open the front door and went into the hall. She ignored the small lift and began to walk up the stairs, wanting to delay the actual moment of confrontation and also trying to use up some calories.

Douglas Hayward was a small man. He liked his world to be populated with small attractive women. He had been proud of Linden. She had belonged. Veronica still belonged but she had become obsolete, ousted by Tracey's youth and determination. Anna knew she had never been satisfactory. Even now, on his doorstep, hardly connected with his life at all, she felt apologetic about herself. She believed that her height and solidity somehow offended him. Since she had achieved her present height of five foot ten and her present weight of twelve stone five pounds, she sensed that he did not like standing by her. In the last few years they had talked, if at all, from opposite ends of the room.

Anna pressed the bell.

Tracey opened the door. She was small, as Anna had known she would be, and blonde with a fringe that touched her eyelashes. She smiled, showing big white teeth. 'Come in, Anna. I'm Tracey. Pleased to meet you.'

'How do you do,' Anna said, disconcerted by Tracey's jeans and T-shirt and freckles. She had expected far more glamour.

'Darling!' Not being able to bring himself to lean up and kiss her, Douglas took her hands and swung them out and in, out and in. He smiled. 'It's good to see you.'

Reclaiming her hands, Anna caught a glimpse of Tracey's amazed face and saw her wondering how a man as small, good-looking and compact as Douglas Hayward could have produced a monster like herself. She wanted to laugh. She wanted to say, 'You should meet Linden. She's quite normal!' but she didn't. She sat down, hunching her shoulders forward to try and look smaller. She hated to be studied by a stranger. Tracey stared. Douglas offered a drink. There was silence.

Anna began to talk in a rush, about how happy they all were, how good things were, until she realized she was sounding thankful that he had left them and lapsed, abruptly, into an embarrassed silence. She sipped the sherry he had pressed on her. She thought, '*He looks silly like that with his hair combed forward. It makes him look older, not younger . . . Why does she want him? There are so many men in the world, what could she possibly want with my father?*'

For half an hour she sat and sipped and listened while Douglas struggled to keep the conversation going and Tracey smiled. Anna found herself unable to tell him any of the things she had come to tell him. Now she was here, she didn't want to confide her joy at being accepted for a second year to this virtual stranger and certainly not in front of Tracey. For half an hour she sat and watched Tracey and Douglas trying not to touch each other while she was there. Then, when she could stand it no longer, she finished her sherry in one eye-watering gulp and pushed up the cuff of her shirt as if she wore a watch.

'Is that the time?'

They all played the game.

'Don't go yet, Anna.'

'Won't you stay and have something to eat?'

'No. Really, it's very kind of you but I have to go out later,' Anna lied.

'Well, come again soon, darling. And bring Linden.'

'Yes.' She stood up.

Tracey went and opened the door and Anna backed out. All three of them said good-bye repeatedly to cover up the marked lack of kissing and Tracey and Douglas stood in the doorway, still not touching, until Anna disappeared round the bend in the stairs. She had the distinct feeling that the moment they closed the door they would burst out laughing.

CHAPTER TWO

It was just before five o'clock when Linden Hayward walked up a few shallow steps and into the hall of an imposing block of flats behind the Ritz Hotel. It was very cool after the heat of Piccadilly, after the dust and struggle of a summer's afternoon in London with tourists and wandering shoppers. She crossed the big, carpeted hall, impressed by the magnificent display of fresh flowers on a console table, by the tall looking-glass. She smiled at the uniformed porter.

'I've come to see Mrs Carroll.'

He directed her down a wide passage painted a calming and expensive green and Linden paused outside a solid and panelled front door. She checked her watch. She was exactly on time. She didn't want to seem that eager, that young and anxious, so she leaned against the wall to let a few minutes go by.

Linden Hayward, organized as she was, had lately been experiencing sudden bursts of impatience about her life, the feeling that she was dangling in space and hadn't yet started. One of these moods had attacked her that morning as she struggled to whip up a Genoise sponge in the stifling heat of a ground-floor kitchen in Hans Crescent. At eleven o'clock, thankfully sipping a cold drink, Linden had stopped to read the notice board in the hall and her eye rested on the neat card. A Mrs Robert Carroll was looking for a cook for the weekdays. A living-out job with an intriguing address in Piccadilly. It was dated that morning. Impulsively, Linden unpinned the card and went into the phone box. She found money in the big pocket of her apron, composed herself for a moment, and dialled the number.

The voice that answered told her Mrs Carroll was in the country that day. Linden explained who she was and asked for the country number, giving her voice the kind of authoritative impatience which obviously impressed the woman on the other end of the telephone. A number in Sussex. Linden dialled the nine-figure number and waited.

'Hallo?'

'Mrs Carroll?'

'Yes.'

'My name is Linden Hayward. I'm a student at the Jennifer Jackson School of Cookery and I've just read your advertisement on our notice board. I would like to come and see you.'

'Well, Miss Hayward, I am anxious to employ someone as soon as possible. However, I hadn't planned to come to London today.'

'Oh dear,' Linden said, making her voice worried. 'Because I have provisionally accepted another job. It's just that Piccadilly would suit me so much better. But if I can't see you this afternoon . . .'

There was a silence. 'Just a moment and I'll see what I can arrange. In fact, I think I'd better telephone you back at one o'clock.'

'Thank you very much. The number is. . . .'

'I have the number. I have employed several girls from Miss Jackson before. That is why I will try to see you this afternoon if it is possible. I know how quickly you find yourselves positions.'

When Mrs Carroll rang back at one o'clock and Linden was summoned into Miss Jackson's office to take the call, the interview was arranged for five that afternoon. Linden then replaced the card on the notice board. Miss Jackson had said, 'I think you two will suit each other perfectly.'

Linden checked her watch again. Five past. She moved forward and pressed the bell. The brass on the door shone. As Linden studied it the door swung inwards. A woman in her fifties, immaculately dressed, stood and considered Linden for a long moment and then gave her a careful smile. Not, Linden thought, a woman who cared if you liked her or not.

'Miss Hayward? Do come in.'

As Linden stepped into an inner hall she said, 'I'm Marietta Carroll. Come through to the drawing-room. We'll talk in there.'

Linden followed the slender back, taking down in mental shorthand the first feel of the place. The mellow wood of an antique chest-of-drawers; double doors into a large drawing-room; tall windows overlooking Green Park; a cabinet, lit from the inside, containing a dozen or so fragile Oriental-looking bowls and vases; twin sofas, chintz-covered, and huge china lamps.

'Do sit down.' Marietta Carroll settled herself on one of the sofas and Linden took an armchair. 'When you telephoned this morning, I had no intention of coming to London today. But I spoke to Miss Jackson and she praised you so highly, I *had* to come and meet you.'

Linden smiled politely.

'As I mentioned, I have had several girls from your school before– I hope you are not insulted that I call it a school – and they have all been excellent. I have a very nice woman in the country but I need someone here to look after us in the week. Unfortunately my last girl has just got married – you girls all get married so young!'

Linden sat with her hands folded in her lap. She thought how clever this woman was to cut her grey hair so dramatically short. It was extremely unusual on a woman of this age, showing the shape of the head and the bones in the face. A beautiful head, Linden thought. She was not nervous. If she did not get this job there would be other opportunities and, as yet, she was not sure she wanted to work here. She let the silence run as she looked round the room. She turned her head sideways, towards the open french windows ... Linden fully appreciated each part of herself and it was automatic now for her to seek out such situations as this, to sit with her head against some framing light and then turn, slowly, as she did now, to let the impact of her face touch the onlooker gradually.

'What a lovely room!' she said when she looked back at the older woman.

Marietta came out of her thoughts. 'Thank you. A little later I will show you the dining-room and the kitchen. The kitchen is upstairs, I'm afraid, and rather small. In theory these are service flats. But I believe our kitchen is very well equipped which makes up for the lack of space.' She paused, troubled by this girl who seemed so at ease, who sat in the chair as if she had been in the room many times. A narrow, long-legged girl, built on the same lines as Marietta herself, she wore one of the long skirts so many girls were wearing that summer, a cotton scarf knotted round her neck, a long-sleeved T-shirt. She looked lovely. Passionately interested in clothes herself, Marietta admired success in other women rather than resenting it. And yet she was disturbed by this girl. Perhaps, she thought, it was the unusual self-possession.

'How old are you, Miss Hayward?'

'Please call me Linden. I'm nearly twenty-one.'

'Linden,' Marietta repeated. 'It suits you.' She sat forward in the chair. 'Now, let me tell you about the job in as much detail as I can and then you can tell me if you feel confident that it is what you want and that you can fulfil it. I understand you take your examination at the end of this month. I say this because, having been without a cook for the past four weeks, I am most anxious to find someone quickly. I asked Miss Jackson if I could put an advertisement on your board a month ago but she said it was too soon – nearer the examination you would be free for interviews. She is very exact!'

'Your card went up yesterday,' Linden said coolly. 'Which was when I had my other interview...' She was not so sure now that the rival job had been such a good idea. Marietta was watching her shrewdly.

'When could you begin?'

'If I pass, and I'm confident that I will, I could start at the beginning of August. However, I would rather have a short break. Just a couple of weeks. I think it would be so much better if I came to my first job fresh, don't you? I had planned to spend two weeks in Cornwall with my Great Aunt. My sister and I go there every summer.' When she finished speaking, Linden made her face demure but interested. She had just made up her mind that she would like to work here.

Marietta smiled. She was beginning to feel out-manoeuvred. 'You know, Miss Jackson was so flattering that I am almost prepared to wait for you.' She stood up, disconcerting Linden. 'Will you excuse me for a moment? I had an appointment in the country this afternoon which I postponed to come to London. I have to discover which day they have altered it to and I think they close at five-thirty.'

She left the room and through the open door into the hall Linden heard her speaking on the telephone. Marietta Carroll spoke with a curious word formation and very slowly. There was no trace of a foreign accent but perhaps, Linden thought, it had been eradicated by many years in England. She certainly didn't look or sound wholly English. While she was waiting, Linden went and peered into the illuminated cabinet, almost touching the glass with her nose as she stared at the delicate and beautifully painted bowls inside.

'They are lovely, aren't they?' Marietta said, returning. 'I am always so glad my husband chose to collect Chinese porcelain rather than beer mugs or stamps!'

Linden laughed, for the first time allowing herself to be natural.

'Now, come upstairs and see the kitchen and then we will discuss all the important details.' Marietta led the way. As they passed the dining-room she pushed open the door, allowing Linden to look in. A large white parrot in a cage in one corner gave a harsh squawk when he saw them, dipped his beak into his seed and scattered it on the carpet.

'That is Icarus,' Marietta said. 'The only other occupant besides Robert and myself and a lot more trouble to feed than either of us. My son Oliver gave him to me – and named him.'

Linden had the distinct impression that the bird was a present Marietta would happily have done without.

When Anna left her father's flat she walked for a while, hands in the pockets of her jeans, feeling rather lost. She wandered into a tobacconist's and bought a large bar of fruit and nut chocolate, breaking off the squares one by one and feeding them into her mouth. And because she found herself near South Kensington tube station, she bought a ticket to Notting Hill Gate, intending to get out there and walk home through Holland Park.

It had become something of a ritual, this nightly walk home. She needed the twenty minutes that it took to adjust from the interest and exhilaration of a day's work at the Cannon to the bleak and empty evening. She walked regardless of the weather, needing to see trees and grass, to move through the series of little gardens the park was made of and the occasional open spaces, to watch dogs and squirrels, to walk the formal flower gardens in summer and in autumn to wade the drifts of crunching leaves.

Tonight she went slowly past Holland Park School and under her feet, on this summer evening, the pavements were dusty. The noises of London were muffled and remote here. Anna passed, as she did each evening, lovers and old ladies with their dogs and children who were out too late, flitting guiltily through the evening like giant moths. She felt safe in the park, camouflaged in winter by the darkness and her duffle coat and now, in summer, by this long loose shirt or a cotton kaftan and a shawl. The walk calmed her. The peace lasted until she reached Oakfield Court where she lived.

When she let herself in, Anna went straight to the kitchen. She preferred it to any other room in the flat. It was large and unmodernized with a built-in dresser and an impractical low, white china sink. A clothes airer hung from the ceiling by a complicated arrangement of ropes. Only the walls didn't belong. They were a startling bright yellow painted by Anna one week-end in a fit of despair. And on the blank wall above the door a mural, only half finished, of Noah's ark.

Linden sat at the big wooden table in a cotton dressing-gown. She had washed her hair and drops of water trickled down her neck and made damp patches on her collar.

'You're late.'

Anna said nothing. She didn't want to confess. Not yet.

'I've just got myself a job!' Linden said, looking pleased. 'D'you want some peppermint tea? I've just made it.'

'I hate it,' Anna said ungraciously. She plodded to the dresser and unhooked a mug. She always moved more heavily when Linden was watching her. 'What sort of job?' she asked, spooning in instant coffee and sugar.

'Well, what do you think? Computer programming?' Linden was grinning. She wore her good moods, all her moods, very obviously at home. 'It's a cooking job, of course. Provided I pass the exam, which I'm sure I will.'

Anna sat down with her cup of coffee, stiff with sugar like a workman's brew. Her hand moved, stealthily, towards the biscuit tin.

'It's a very, very smart place,' Linden said. 'What an estate agent would call a maisonette, I think. They pinned up the details on the board this morning and as soon as I read them I rang up and I went for an interview this afternoon. Apparently she's had quite a few girls from our place.' Linden sipped the transparent tea. 'Funny woman. Not amusing funny. Odd funny. Very smartly thin with those stick-like upper-class legs and pointed knee bones when she sits down.

'Her name is Mrs Robert Carroll. She has two sons but neither of them lives there, a house in the country and a voice like a foreign queen. She extracted a potted history of my life from me and I could feel her slotting me into some social category or other but I'm not sure which. I contemplated dropping pass words, muttering, "Table napkin, table napkin, table napkin."'

Anna ate biscuits steadily. 'Do you want to work there?'

'Yes, I do. I need a job, Anna. I must get on. I want my own money. I loathe living on his hand-outs. Most of the girls I cook with are just filling in time or making themselves marriageable. We're a strange little group. The dim, pretty daughters of well-off families. Only mine is not so well-off as theirs are. Do you know, Anna, that out of the ten of us in my group I am the only virgin? We were talking about it at lunch today. I admit they are an attractive lot and stupid with it, but even so they must be pretty typical. Which makes me unusual! After my birthday, I may well be the only twenty-one-year-old female virgin in London.' A wide smile spread over her face. 'Just think what I have to offer my lucky millionaire when I meet him! I shall gaze into his eyes and say, "I have *saved* myself for you." I shall not mention the fact that I wouldn't go to bed with any of these creatures I go out with if they were the last men on earth!'

'No one has ever wanted to go to bed with me,' Anna said flatly, chewing.

'How do you know? You never talk to men. These things are not entirely communicated by telepathy and electric shocks, you know! Anyway you're too fat!' She snatched the biscuit tin away. 'Why do you eat so much?'

Anna swallowed her mouthful guiltily. She thought about it for a few moments. 'I think it has something to do with you looking like you do and me looking like this! And of course I come from a broken home!'

Linden stood up, irritably, carrying the tin out of reach. 'The only reason you look like you do is because you never stop eating. Your face isn't bad but no one can see it sandwiched between your hair and your chins!'

Anna flinched. 'Why the hell don't you leave me alone! Go

and dress up for Geoffrey or whoever it is you're not sleeping with tonight!'

When she spoke again, Linden's voice held an uncharacteristic softness. 'Anna, I never mean to go on at you but the way you are so humble about being fat, as if it was an act of God, not something entirely your own fault, just drives me crazy. We ought to care about each other. No one else cares much!'

'Well, actually I am getting thinner,' Anna said, with dignity.

'I know you are. That's why I go mad when I see you sitting and eating and eating without thinking! You haven't really got double chins.'

They exchanged wary smiles.

'I must go and change. I am, as you so elegantly put it, not sleeping with Geoffrey tonight and Mum is spending the evening with Aunt Prue.' She paused in the doorway, wanting to leave on a friendly note. 'Did they let you know, at the Cannon, if you can stay on?'

Anna hesitated. 'Yes,' she said eventually. 'I can. Another year at least!'

'Good.' Linden was genuinely pleased. 'That's what you wanted, wasn't it?'

'Yes.' Anna turned in her chair so that she was looking at her sister. 'And I was so happy about it that I wanted to see him.' Neither of them could refer to Douglas as anything but "him". 'So I rang him and I went round for a drink and I met that Tracey and I told him all about us and how, in some crazy way, what he did has turned out well for all of us!'

Linden narrowed her eyes. Anna could feel her searching for words that would really hurt.

'Didn't you feel just a tiny little bit disloyal? Didn't you mention the fact that although everything has turned out so well, as you put it, your mother has to get herself through each evening by drinking half a bottle of gin? She isn't happy, Anna! Or haven't you noticed?'

'I didn't feel disloyal. I felt uncomfortable. I said none of the things I went to say. But I needed to see him, just once, and I'm glad I have!'

Linden curled her lip in disgust and shrugged. But she didn't leave. She fought her curiosity for some moments but in the end she had to ask.

'What was she like?'

Anna turned back to the table. 'Beautiful. A wistful, strangely sensitive face. Great dark eyes – pools of mystery and promise, a sensual mouth, odd in such a vulnerable little face.'

'Rubbish!' Linden interrupted.

'Well, you go and see for yourself, if you want to know what she's like.'

'I shall never do that! Never!' Linden made a magnificent exit and Anna crossed the kitchen and carried the biscuit tin back to the table.

CHAPTER THREE

Freddie Monroe was driving fast because he was late and also because he enjoyed the intense concentration which driving at speed demanded. It relaxed him to have his mind fully occupied with the car and the roads, to seek out opportunities to overtake and let the car's blunt nose push through the traffic. The car was a source of continual pleasure to him, a 3.8 Jaguar, five years' old now but superbly cared for. It expressed, in terms of performance and looks and the interior smell of real leather, everything that Freddie thought a car should be. Even now, irritated as he was, cornered as he felt himself to be, hurrying to make an appointment which had been forced on to the end of an overcrowded day, the car could calm him. He had also cultivated, in the past few years, the attitude of accepting situations he could not alter. It saved a great deal of useless struggle. This appointment was one of those situations.

Freddie was on his way to value the collection of a certain Robert Carroll, a personal friend of one of Granbury's directors.

'I'd like you to go, Freddie,' Tim Granbury had said. 'I know it's a fairly important collection and if he does decide to sell, obviously we'd like to be the ones to handle the auction. I told him we'd send our expert. The house is near Lewes, in Sussex. Nice day out for you.' He grinned, a round, amiable man in his late fifties. 'He suggested some time early next week. Pick a day that suits and I'll ring him.'

'Tuesday is usually fairly quiet.'

'Right. Tuesday it shall be!'

On Tuesday morning, around eleven, the appointment was suddenly cancelled and, without Freddie's knowledge, altered to this Thursday afternoon, the last afternoon of the week Freddie would have chosen. It would take him at least another hour he estimated. He wouldn't be back in London till seven-thirty at the earliest! As if there wasn't enough going on in his life already . . .

The July afternoon was glorious, the sky a flat soft blue, the gardens all alight with flowers. He saw none of it. For the last few months, Freddie Monroe had been entirely wrapped up in himself.

For ten years, Freddie had worked at Granbury and Company, one of London's largest auction houses. His speciality was Chinese porcelain. He was an unlikely man to be so obsessed with the fragile beauty of ceramics. A tall, powerful man of twenty-eight with a round, strong face and thick, brown hair. A man determined to go a long way but not sure how to begin. Until a year ago. Until the summer of 1970 when he noticed the first Japanese dealers, sitting patiently at Granbury's summer sale of Chinese porcelain and works of art. Over the months that followed, he saw more and more Japanese dealers.

'Obvious, really,' Tim Granbury said. 'Once the Japanese relaxed their exchange controls last year, the dealers who are interested find the whole world open to them.'

They came for the Chinese porcelain, which they prized so highly, and they came especially to London because the prices in London were, by their standards, absurdly low. In the middle of all this sat Frederick Peter Monroe, his brain crammed with knowledge and pulsating with the brilliantly simple idea of buying investment collections of this porcelain which was going to become more and more sought after. The overwhelming Japanese interest would push prices through the roof! But no one seemed to realize it yet, or if they did, they didn't see the opportunity it presented. Freddie at first played with the idea as a theory but the more he thought about it, the more interesting it became. He thought about it until it seemed his brain worked on its own, elaborating, perfecting; sleep and food became incidentals; frustration began to build up in him and he now found he could think of nothing but this idea. It was a once-in-a-lifetime situation but he was unable to take advantage of it because he did not possess sufficient money for the first stage.

Freddie was no stranger to frustration. As a child he had been trapped in a way of life that maddened him. He was a restless only child, a cuckoo, born with an instinctive appreciation of beautiful things which his parents misunderstood and distrusted. His father, forty-two when Freddie was born and a builder all his life, could not understand Freddie's conviction that there was far more to life than this neat little council estate, and the prospect of a good job, a wife, two children, the hoped-for car. The fact that his son wanted to work with antiques made John Monroe acutely uncomfortable. He didn't consider it a man's employment . . .

When, at fifteen, Freddie walked out of school and got himself a job as a general dogsbody in an antique shop in the middle of Reading, John Monroe adopted an angry silence. When, at eighteen, Freddie left for London, both he and his parents secretly sighed with relief, free to go their own utterly different ways. But still, it made Freddie feel guilty and a little sad that he saw them so rarely, that he moved now in a circle of people they would distrust and probably dislike. He had taken a girl home for the weekend once. He wouldn't do that again in a hurry! Freddie was still a man on the outside – for most of his life he had felt himself to be marking time, waiting for his opening, poised. Like a child pacing round a glass-walled sweet shop with no door.

A week ago, as he let himself out of the uninspiring flat he rented in Battersea, he heard the telephone ring. He was early so he unlocked the door and went in again to answer it.

'Frederick?' It was his mother, her voice timid.

'Hallo, Mum.'

'Sorry to disturb you so early, dear, but . . . well, I was wondering if you could do me a favour? Well, not me so much as Sheila Pierce. D'you remember her? Used to live in Clifton Lane . . . Her husband was in the police, worked in the East for a long time. Well, she's on her own now and she's having trouble, you know, with money, and she's got these two little bowls he bought her when they were in Hong Kong and she wondered if they were worth selling and I said perhaps you wouldn't mind taking a look at them for her and just seeing if they're worth anything or not.' She paused for a breath. 'She only lives in Fulham.'

Freddie said 'yes' because the favour would quieten, for a while, the guilt his mother's voice on the telephone always started in him. Her timidity seemed, somehow, a criticism of himself.

The house in Fulham was small and stuffy. He sipped a cup

of tea he didn't want, looking round and seeing nothing of interest and wondering how quickly he could get out. The old lady talked and talked, obviously lonely, her voice lurching from one subject to another with a panicky speed, lest Freddie should slip in a 'Well . . . it's getting late,' or a 'Mrs Pierce, I think I'd better be on my way.' She heard a lot of that. But eventually she paused and said, 'Now, Frederick, I'll show you my little bowls,' and she left the room and came back with two of the most beautiful blue and white Yuan dynasty bowls he had ever seen.

Thinking of that moment now, Freddie laughed aloud. The sharp bark of his laughter filled the car. *Of course*, he had thought, *they can't be genuine*. He held them one by one and his heart thumped in the steady way he always reacted to something absolutely right. They were genuine. As he sat in that little sitting-room, the whole of Freddie's idea began to fall, at last, into a definite order. There was no question of ethics involved. He knew exactly who would buy these and how much he would pay and that was the beginning.

When he finally spoke, he made his rich voice casual and kind. When he wanted to, Freddie could talk with such charm he made his listener feel the only person in the world. 'These are certainly worth selling. They could fetch anything between –' and he paused, as if thinking, and let her hang there, mouth a little open – 'well, between fifteen hundred and two thousand pounds each, at auction. If the right people are there! However, I would very much like them for my own collection. Would you consider selling them to me? I would offer three thousand five hundred for the pair. You might get more at auction but . . .'

She was overwhelmed. Knowing he could have got them for five hundred, Freddie felt no guilt at all. He believed in fate, in timing, in patterns. But, above all, he believed in grabbing the chance when it came, making the opening for yourself if you could. 'Perhaps you'd like a couple of weeks to think it over? Or show them to someone else, to get another opinion?'

'I wouldn't dream of it. It's far more than I thought they were worth and, besides, I'm so happy to think you will keep them and they will be loved! They've always been loved!' She laughed, coyly. She thought, *After all, after all their worries, he's turned out all right. He's not nearly such an aggressive young man as a lot of people said he was.*

'It should have been so bloody easy,' Freddie said aloud, winding down the car window and throwing out his cigarette. 'I go to Whitman, I offer him the pair for five thousand and suggest that I obtain some more pieces, build up a collection for him as an investment. I leave Granbury's. I am launched!' He was holding the wheel so tightly his knuckles were white. 'But Whitman is in New York for a couple of weeks and I cannot get my hands on three and a half thousand!' He laughed again. The irony was that, in a couple of years, the sum he now found so out of reach would appear trivial! But his bank manager had been unhelpful. Freddie had never saved anything. He rented his flat. He spent a great deal of money living the kind of life, with the kind of women, and eating in the kind of places he had come to feel at home in. His friends became rather vague when approached for a loan. In the last two days, Freddie had been reduced to wondering how much his father had put away . . .

It was nearly 4.30 when Freddie turned his car between the stone gate-posts of Pyecomb Manor and drove up the curving drive. He saw magnolia trees, green lawns, white doves and the dignified white façade of a large Georgian house. It was one of the loveliest houses he'd ever seen. For a moment he was a child again, lying in his bedroom with a pencil and paper and drawing up his master-plan. The things that he wanted from life.

He got out of the car and slammed the door, sweating and rather tired, which was unusual for Freddie. As he crossed the gravel he put on his jacket, straightened his tie and his hair. He rang the bell.

The double doors in the porch were open and through the large, flagged hall, Freddie heard piano music, elaborate jazz, tangling itself and then unwinding, a river of sound. As no one appeared to have heard the bell he stepped into the hall and went towards the music, turning left into an enormous sky-blue drawing-room where a man sat playing a grand piano. A labrador lay at his feet. As Freddie paused in the doorway it lifted its head and barked twice without enthusiasm.

Oliver Carroll stopped playing abruptly. He swung round on his stool, swore under his breath and then stood up and attempted a smile.

'Hallo. You're from Granbury's, are you? Sorry I didn't hear you arrive.'

'That's okay.' Freddie looked at this tall young man with untidy brown hair in jeans and a T-shirt, and oddly incongruous lace-up city shoes.

'If you don't mind my saying so, you don't look like a porcelain expert,' Oliver said.

Freddie laughed. 'The long black moustache and the pekinese up the sleeve come later!' He went towards Oliver with his bouncy step, holding out his hand. 'I'm Freddie Monroe – you are Mr Carroll's son?'

'Yes. Oliver.' They shook hands. 'My mother was going to be here on Tuesday to see you but she had to go to London suddenly to interview someone. And then they made the appointment for this afternoon which she decided she couldn't do either, for some equally vital reason, so I've come down from London to show you the stuff. Come to think of it, it would have been far simpler if I'd interviewed the cook in London on Tuesday and she'd stayed here to see you!' He smiled. 'Anyway, it's all over there – all those cases.' He said it without much interest. 'Look, would you like coffee or a beer or something?'

'A beer would be nice.'

'Yes. I think I'll join you. I haven't had breakfast yet!' He frowned. 'By the way, the burglar alarms are all off and I've put the key in the first case. It fits them all.'

'Thank you.' Freddie crossed the room, turned the key and opened the door. Then he paused for a moment and he felt himself slow down. Peace invaded him as he reverently lifted, from its ebony stand, a delicate jar. He cradled it in his hands. 'Prunus mume,' he said.

Oliver felt some comment was necessary. 'Pretty, isn't it? What exactly is it meant to be, that pattern?'

'Early flowering plum.' Freddie's deep voice caressed the words. 'Painted on a blue ground which is meant to represent cracked ice. These jars were often given as New Year presents and the Chinese New Year coincides with spring. Hence the blossom and the breaking ice! Very logical and very beautiful.' He could hardly bear to put it down. He half turned to Oliver Carroll. 'You know, I would rather own one of these . . .' and then he let the sentence die because there was nothing in his life to bargain with.

'It never ceases to amaze me,' Oliver said, 'the way people are moved by such an enormous variety of things. Quite honestly, that pot does nothing for me!'

'It might raise some money for you if you were to sell it,' Freddie said dryly.

'Yes. Is it true there is beginning to be some interest in this stuff? My father seems to have got wind of something and he's a shrewd old boy!'

'He's very well-informed this time.' Freddie turned back to the case, not wanting to elaborate, but he looked round and watched Oliver leave the room with his curious untidy walk. Freddie got out his notebook and pen and began to write but when Oliver returned with two pint mugs of beer and put them down on a low table in front of a sofa, Freddie left the porcelain for a moment and came to sit down.

He drank deeply. 'God, that's good!' He put the glass down. 'You work in London?' he asked Oliver.

'Yes.' Oliver leaned back, feet crossed at the ankle, glass resting on his stomach. 'I play in a jazz club. Billy's Basement. Maybe you've heard of it? I'm the piano bit of a trio. We're the regulars there. I've been doing it for about six months now.' He smiled. 'Do you know anything about my family? About the great Carroll Empire?'

'A little.'

'Then perhaps you'll understand that my family, especially my father and my elder brother, are not awfully impressed by my choice of career.' Oliver tried to make the words light but his voice betrayed an underlying bitterness. 'I spent a couple of years in Australia and I know they hoped I'd come bouncing back, ready and eager to start at the bottom like James did. When I said I intended to play the piano for a li.ing . . .' He laughed. Then he sat forward, suddenly afraid he was saying too much to a stranger. 'They are moved by ambition and money,' he explained simply. 'Not music!'

'Well, there's nothing to stop you having business interests on the side, is there?' Freddie said, lighting a cigarette and offering the packet to Oliver as an afterthought.

Oliver took one. 'Thanks.' He dipped his head into the lighter Freddie held out. 'No, I suppose there isn't.' His tone made it obvious that the idea had never occurred to him.

'Is your father intending to sell the collection?'

Oliver shook his head. 'I don't think so. He's suddenly realized what all these bits and pieces can be worth.' He stared, morosely, at his feet. 'God, these shoes are uncomfortable! When my mother rang me at two o'clock and commanded that I hurry down here, these were the first pair I dragged out from under the bed! My family all have the amazing idea that, because I work in the evenings, from eleven till four or five some mornings, my days are empty and boring and therefore entirely at their disposal. It never occurs to my mother that I might need to sleep. Or to practise!' He drained his glass.

'Perhaps it suits them better not to realize,' Freddie said sympathetically, putting himself carefully on Oliver's side. He stood up.

'No, I don't think it's that,' Oliver said truthfully. 'It's just that they are unable to take me seriously.' He watched Freddie walk back to the cases of porcelain, wondering why he was admitting this to a complete stranger. But there was something about this man that made him easy to talk to and Oliver seldom allowed himself the luxury of saying what he felt. 'Look, do you mind if I go on playing? I take my music far too seriously, to compensate for their lack of interest I suppose, and I do need to play in the afternoons.'

'I shall enjoy it.'

Oliver Carroll went back to the piano, and his fingers began to coax out *That Old Black Magic* in a series of velvety chords.

Freddie worked his way systematically from case to case and shelf to shelf, at times totally absorbed in some piece of particular beauty, at times letting his brain prowl round the problem of Sheila Pierce and the Yuan bowls and a backer. Freddie's idea of a partner was someone who would not interfere at all, a man wrapped up in his own, totally different field and merely astute and interested enough to provide the initial capital. At some point during the next hour he noticed that Oliver Carroll stopped playing, got up and left the room. When Freddie placed the last bowl back on its stand and locked the last case it was just after six. He took the key back to the first cabinet, wanting to take out and hold, once again, the exquisite jar he had started with.

'All finished?' Oliver said, coming through the french windows, a pair of plimsolls on his feet now. The dog followed him.

'Yes. I'm just having a last look at this. It is really lovely.'

'Who buys these things, apart from the odd eccentric collector like my father?'

'The Japanese,' Freddie said carefully, turning to face Oliver.

'Haven't they got enough at home?'

'Not at the kind of price they want to pay, the low prices they can pick up items for in London especially. At the moment.' He put the prunus mume jar back and locked the cabinet. He held out the key to Oliver. 'If your father is wise, although working for Granbury's perhaps I shouldn't be saying it, he'll hang on to this lot very carefully for a while. I've been in this business for ten years now and I can honestly say this is the first time I can tell you with absolute certainty that prices are going to rise and rise. They have to . . . the Japanese interest is bound to make them soar.'

He paused. 'Look, I must ask you not to repeat this because I am hoping to act on it but I could buy you a collection of porcelain, purely as an investment, and guarantee that in twelve months the value will have doubled. Barring a third world war, of course!' He showed no trace of the excitement he felt as he saw the interest grow in Oliver Carroll's face.

'Are you serious?'

'Absolutely.'

'You could buy a collection for me?'

'Not just for you.' Freddie's brain was working like a machine. *Why not? Why not try this boy? Easy to handle . . . definite risk of course. He could mention it to his father who might, in turn, express disapproval to Tim Granbury. That could be embarrassing . . . Hell. No risk, no game!*'

'If I can find myself some sound financial backing, I shall start an investment service, buying collections for a selected number of people. I've thought it over quite carefully and I think a dozen clients to begin with, in this country. At the moment the collections would certainly be of Chinese porcelain but as the market alters one must be prepared to switch.'

'What a fascinating idea!' Oliver frowned. 'Seriously, is

there money to be made in this game?'

'A hell of a lot,' Freddie said. 'One hell of a lot!' He lit a cigarette and discarded the half empty packet on the chair beside him. The gesture fascinated Oliver. Freddie sat down.

'To be quite honest,' and he smiled, 'it's rather a relief to talk about it all. I find myself in the most extraordinary position. I probably know as much about Chinese porcelain as anyone in Europe. I definitely know as much about the international art market, having worked at Granbury's for ten years. I know half a dozen people who will jump at this idea if it is suggested to them in a professional way and I also know of two bowls I can pick up for three thousand five hundred pounds tomorrow and sell for five or six thousand at auction next month.' He was leaning forward, his round, brown eyes utterly sincere.

Oliver took a cigarette from Freddie's abandoned packet. 'Well, why not buy them for yourself and set the ball rolling?'

'Strange as it may seem to you,' Freddie said simply. 'I don't have three thousand five hundred pounds.'

No one like this hard, talkative man with his air of unshakeable confidence had ever discussed an idea of this nature with Oliver before. It was assumed by his family and circle of close friends that his lack of academic success, and the fact that he chose to make his living as a jazz pianist, signified a definite simplicity. To a certain extent it was his own fault, partly the image he handed out, but it was also largely due to James.

Nearly six years older than Oliver, James Carroll had always turned his ability to reason quickly and his obvious intelligence to good use. He was a man who had succeeded outstandingly in everything he had done so far. He had never understood Oliver. They had reached a stage now when, if Oliver did venture an opinion, at a dinner party or a family Sunday lunch, on anything outside his own sphere, James would receive it with a patronizing kindness he might equally well adopt if discussing the stock market with his grandmother.

In the silence of this big room Oliver suddenly had an enchanting mental picture of James, of all of them, when he let it slip he was connected with a highly successful business venture. He lined them up in his mind and impressed them for the first time in his life.

'Look, Mr Monroe . . . Freddie . . . would you be prepared to tell me more about this idea? I mean, if I said I could be seriously interested in putting up some money?' He smiled, shyly, the words seeming to him rather absurd.

Freddie leaned back. 'Well, yes, I would. To be honest, time is running out. Other people are going to have the same idea pretty soon.' He shrugged expressively. 'I could show you my estimates and outline the whole idea in detail but I have to ask you to assure me that if, at the end of it, you aren't prepared to put up the money you will keep absolutely quiet until I have the opportunity to put the idea to someone else. Fair enough?'

'Yes. Of course.' Again Oliver had a delicious vision of James's face. 'When shall we meet?'

Freddie got up. 'Tomorrow. Come to lunch with me . . . Friday is a quiet day. Can you make it about twelve thirty? There's a little Italian restaurant near Harrods we could go to.'

'Right.' Oliver stood too.

'I'll have the car anyway, so I might as well pick you up. What's your address?'

'Twenty-seven Peterstone Mews. And if I don't answer the bell first time, ring and shout like hell. When we have two or three late sessions running I sometimes find it impossible to wake up.'

'Don't worry, I could wake the dead if I thought they were interested in my idea.' Freddie laughed.

They crossed the hall together and once in the porch they shook hands.

'Would you tell your father from me I'll have this lot typed up and in the post as soon as possible. Oh, and I'd rather you didn't mention any of this other to anyone just yet, Oliver. Until I leave Granbury's, I could find myself in a rather embarrassing position.'

'Of course. See you tomorrow then.' Oliver watched Freddie march across the gravel and swing himself into his car. He gave a brief salute through the open window and started the engine. Oliver bent and fondled his dog thinking, wryly, that Freddie Monroe was just the sort of man he should have been.

As he turned out of the gates Freddie resisted the impulse to toot his horn. He knew it was vital that he present an image of a serious, trustworthy man. He wanted Oliver Carroll to think of Freddie Monroe as a man in a fortunate position with a hell of a good idea.

CHAPTER FOUR

Linden began to work for Marietta Carroll on 20th August. As she had predicted, she passed the examination with no difficulty. She also had her way about the holiday, two weeks in Cornwall in her Great Aunt's small house. Veronica didn't go. She had decided to take her holiday later in the year. It was just Anna and Linden, given these two weeks almost as a reprieve from real life. The holiday was out of sequence, the last holiday of childhood coming very late. The weather was lovely and they swam and surfed and lay in the sun, achieving a level of friendship that was unusual. They ignored all outsiders. They wanted nothing of other people at all. On the last Sunday they shared the seven-hour drive back to London and on the Monday Linden began work.

Each morning, she left the flat with Veronica at ten to nine, walking down Melbury Road, talking with her mother until they reached the estate agents in Kensington High Street where Veronica worked. Gradually the days stacked into weeks. Linden loved the routine. She felt she was at last engaged in the adult part of her life after far too long training. Faces at the tube station became familiar as did the face of the man who sold her a newspaper each afternoon, the doormen at the Ritz and the grey-suited army who strolled Jermyn Street between twelve and two on their way to drink somewhere.

Each morning she would let herself into the Carrolls' flat, liking the coolness and the quiet after the activity of the street. A small shiver of pleasure touched her at the thought of the day ahead. She would open the double doors to the drawing-room and wake up that lovely room, pulling back the curtains, opening one tall window. Light came in an avalanche. From the dining-room, Icarus squawked eagerly, waiting to be uncovered.

In the kitchen, Linden made fresh coffee and waited until Marietta came rustling down the passage. She was the only woman Linden had ever met who wore genuine négligés. Marietta would say 'Good morning', and make a little conversation about the weather or the shopping or lunch, and then disappear, with her coffee, to dress.

At home, Linden talked about the Carrolls a great deal. They were interesting because they were quite new, obviously rich and therefore exotic. Linden talked about them until they became a serial that ran each weekday between the time that she got home in the late afternoon and went out again in the evening. The outlines she sketched in the beginning were gradually coloured with detail. In Veronica and Anna she had two eager listeners both, for the moment, very much on the sidelines of life.

'Marietta is a difficult woman to get to know. Some days, like today, she talks to me a lot but at other times she is quite cold and rather bossy, as if she is afraid I am getting too close. I think she is bored. A lot of women friends come and she goes out a lot. I don't think she likes her friends much, though.'

Anna laughed.

'Well,' Linden qualified, 'I get the impression that the only people who matter are her husband Robert and the elder son.'

At first the male Carrolls were guessed at from the silver-framed photographs on Marietta's dressing-table. 'Her husband looks as if he must have been Army at one time. Nice, English face. Tidy little grey moustache. I know he has travelled a great deal especially in the East. And one of the sons, the eldest – James, I think – is very like her. Very attractive in a cold way. Straight dark eyebrows. He runs the family business with his father. I gather it's cosmetics. She asked me if I used them. The Coral range she called them. Then she said, "No. They would be too old for you. Perhaps you have heard of our Celandine collection? They are younger products."'

'Well, of course I know Carroll Cosmetics,' Veronica said. 'I have used them quite frequently. What does the younger son do?'

'Ah. Oliver. The face in the photograph is much younger, gentler. Harder to describe. I gather he has taken a long time to settle. He spent some time in Australia but now he works as a jazz pianist in some London club. She talks about him rather carefully, the way you talk about Anna, Mum!'

Both Anna and Veronica looked up sharply.

Linden described the flat as 'Quite perfect. Like an interior decorator's shop window. Each painting under its own little light. All the furniture with the velvety look of antique wood. Of course, the kitchen is on another floor to the dining-room so everything has to be carried up and down on trays. I'm getting good at carrying trays. I've developed a leaning-back sort of walk like waitresses have.' Linden poured herself a cup of tea. Her audience still sat listening. 'Best of all I like shopping for her. She has accounts everywhere. Jackson's and Fortnum's and Harrods.'

'How old is she?' Veronica asked. She had covered the kitchen table with a new jig-saw. They were an obsession with her now. The bigger the better. Thousands of cardboard fragments, waiting to be arranged into a whole and perfect picture. Order from chaos.

'Very hard to say exactly. In her fifties but I don't know which end. The eldest son is twenty-eight if that helps. And the cleaning woman tells me Marietta is half Italian, which explains the way she talks and the négligés.'

'And neither son married?' Veronica said.

'No.' Linden winked at Anna. 'I couldn't make up my mind which to have at first but I really think I'll go for Oliver. A little young perhaps but more interesting. Less conventional.' She placed a piece of jig-saw deftly in position. 'Funny to think I've been there nearly a month and never set eyes on any of the men! I suppose Oliver sleeps all day if he works in the evenings and James and his father are away at the moment on some business trip. New York, I think she said. Actually, it's better not to meet them. They will turn out to be just as dull as everyone else when they're real!'

Throughout her short adult life, Linden had picked and chosen from the men she had met and had never yet wanted anyone. It amused her considerably that James Carroll's photograph interested her so much. What she said about choosing Oliver was untrue. It was the elder brother's self-contained face she said a silent good morning to as she collected the empty tea cup from beside Marietta's bed. A face that showed nothing of the man behind. Although she laughed at herself and would have admitted it to no one, she missed that face over the week-end. And when, one damp Thursday morning at the beginning of October, Marietta came into the kitchen unusually early and said, 'Linden, I have a family lunch party today. Would you go shopping for me, please?', Linden felt a definite excitement.

'The boys always tease me about the frailty of lunch here so I thought perhaps some large steaks – and could you make an English pudding? For a joke, but they will like it. A suet pudding?' She moved around the small kitchen, obviously pleased. 'My husband and James arrived home last night. Oliver is coming too, if he wakes up! I have an appointment with my hairdresser at eleven. Oliver might arrive before I get back, so could you explain, please? He is always either early or late!' She paused, wondering why she talked to this girl so much. 'I will be back at twelve-thirty.'

Oliver Carroll hesitated outside the front door. He yawned. He pushed his hands through his hair and pulled his sweater down and made his face ready for his mother. She had asked him to lunch in a tone that he knew he couldn't refuse. Nice to see his father again. But surely she could have made it dinner, not lunch?

'Of course I'll come. But I do see quite a lot of James, Mother. Living in the same house, you know, we bump into each other now and again.'

'But you never come to Pyecomb now, Oliver. I want you all under one roof.'

Pyecomb, he had thought. Even the name made him homesick. He loved the place. He had been born there, deep in the Sussex countryside. He loved every inch. 'I'd love to come down more often. But usually I don't finish until four on Sunday morning. And Sunday evening you all come back to London.'

Marietta had not answered. She never expressed an opinion about his job.

Oliver rang the bell. As the door opened he began to step forward, ready to kiss his mother, and found himself, instead, confronted by one of the most striking looking girls he had ever seen. She wore a cotton apron.

'Have the Carrolls moved or is it the wrong flat?'

Linden laughed. 'I'm the new cook. Mrs Carroll isn't back

from the hairdresser's yet.' She closed the door behind Oliver as he came into the hall.

'I'm Oliver Carroll. I'm the younger one. The other one!' He held out his hand. He was bigger than she had expected, younger, shyer. A gentle face.

'Linden Hayward. Can I make you some coffee?'

'I'd love some. I don't think I've been to bed at all. Some nights we just slip into the right mood and we go on and on. We stopped at five this morning. And when I got home I was so exhilarated I sat down to play some more and James came stamping down the stairs!' Oliver laughed. 'He'd just got to sleep. Fighting the jet lag, you know. For some reason he didn't appreciate my playing.'

'I'll bring the coffee down,' Linden said.

'Can't I come up?' He tucked his hands into his pockets. 'If it will annoy you I will stay down here but that drawing-room always feels like a headmaster's study to me!'

He followed Linden up the stairs. He came into the little kitchen and sat on one of the stools, favourably impressed by the size of the steaks. The fact that he was so tired somehow lessened his normal shyness. 'How long have you been working here?'

'A month now.'

'Where do you live?'

She smiled, handing him coffee in a fragile cup.

'Why do you smile?' Oliver said.

'Because I spend a lot of time telling my family about this place and all of you. Now you ask me about myself.'

'Tell me. Have you a big family?'

'No. My parents are separated. I live with my mother and my sister. My mother works as a receptionist. My sister Anna is at an art school. It's surprising because no one in my family before has ever been able to draw anything and yet Anna appears to be really rather good!'

'Perhaps she needed something of her own.' Oliver spooned sugar into his cup. 'Like me. Playing the piano for a living! My family can hardly bring themselves to talk about it. Especially with that great hungry company waiting for me. I wonder how long I can keep out of it!' He was talking to himself. He drank some coffee. 'How do you know your sister is good?'

'Well, I don't really. It's just this mural she's done in our bathroom at the flat. I think it's fantastic!'

Oliver let his eyes rest on Linden. The nape of her neck, narrow and concave like a small boy's. Narrow and strong. He wanted her to turn back again so that he could see her face. 'Will she do paintings for other people? Could I come and see it? The bathroom at the mews is white and dull. I spend a lot of time in there. I'd love to have a painting on the wall.'

'I can hear the front door,' Linden interrupted. 'I expect it's your mother.'

Oliver stood up, taking his cup. 'Better go down . . . see you later.' He paused in the doorway. 'I do mean it. About the mural.'

Shortly after he went down, James and Robert Carroll must have arrived. The place seemed full of voices and laughter. It was unusual. Linden felt that the rooms resented such frivolity. At 1.30 she put the avocado pears on the dining-room table and then knocked on the double doors to the drawing-room. She opened them both and stepped in. For a moment she stood quite still, letting them see her. Then she said, 'Lunch is ready, Mrs Carroll.'

'Linden, my dear, come and meet my husband and my son James. It seems extraordinary that you have been here over a month and your paths have not crossed. Oliver you have met, earlier, I think.'

'Yes.' Linden stepped into the room. She came forward and held out her hand to the older man. She wore her small smile. She moved the smile to Oliver. Last of all she let her eyes come to James. His hand was cold and firm. His smile as careful as her own.

When Linden carried in the steaks, the atmosphere in the dining-room was quite different. She had the distinct impression that voices had been raised before she came in. For her benefit all conversation stopped. They commented politely on the avocados. As she left, she heard Robert Carroll saying, 'Look, Oliver. I have no intention of interfering in your life but what future can you possibly have playing the piano?'

When the bell in the kitchen rang, about twenty minutes later, she carried down the suet pudding. It looked splendid, golden and fluffy on top. It was received with a great deal of reluctant laughter.

'You see,' Marietta said, 'how different lunch is around here now! So you must both come at least once a week.'

'Linden's sister paints, you know,' Oliver said suddenly, as if he had been silent for a long time. 'I thought it would be a good idea if we had something painted on the wall in our bathroom, James. Liven the place up.'

James looked politely surprised. He met Linden's eyes. She could feel his interest.

'Perhaps,' she said quietly, 'you had better come and see what she has done in our flat before you decide; you might hate it!'

'Yes. Good idea. Can I come this evening?' Oliver said.

'Of course.' She put cream on the table. Her eyes touched James again, questioning. 'Would you have time to come this evening, Mr Carroll? I think you should both approve before asking Anna. Her paintings are very dramatic!'

Marietta laughed. 'My dear, you must call them James and Oliver. They are far too pleased with themselves already without having someone as pretty as you fussing over them.'

'I'd like to come,' James said.

'And afterwards, Linden, you must come out and have dinner with me. It's only fair . . . you've cooked enough meals in a month to deserve one in return!' Oliver's eyes danced. It was obvious there was a conflict in progress that Linden knew nothing of.

'Thank you,' she said with a smile. 'I'd like that.'

She picked up her tray and closed the door. In the kitchen she clenched her hands in triumph. *If I dare, there is nothing I can't do. Nothing I can't have!'*

It was raining. Big, slow drops of rain dented the puddles in Holland Park. Anna ran through puddles, looking up at the tumbling grey sky and feeling rain on her face, rain on her hands. She ran under the trees and out of the wrought-iron gates into the street of tall, dignified houses. Light spilt from between their heavy curtains on to their neat autumn gardens. She could smell wet earth and late roses. Rows of lights in Oakfield Court made the buildings look like a giant computer, ticking away, processing the life forms inside. 'I am happy.' Anna jumped a puddle. 'I am.' she said to the deserted streets, 'extremely happy. I have a place to work, to absorb me until seven in the evening. People to talk to and lunch with. But best of all, far, far the most exciting thing, is that he bothers to shout at me. Again and again!'

He was new this autumn term, this first term of Anna's second year, a skeletal coil of energy with a revolutionary and rather cruel way of teaching. He singled out anyone he thought interesting and made their lives miserable. Pushing and pushing, perhaps for a whole week. At first it had been, obviously, Pym. But Pym could cope with him, relished the battle in fact because he respected the man and admired his work. Then it was Martha Holland who was dreamy and brilliant and immune. She went her own quiet way. She listened politely to the tirades and then ignored them. And then, suddenly, this week it was Anna. Three days running he had destroyed her in life class. Each day he became more vitriolic.

'Anna,' he said, that morning, 'I'd like you to tell me what it is you are attempting to draw?' His voice was soft and deceptively friendly but he looked, not at her face, but at the paper in front of her. 'Do you really think you are making an honest attempt to put that woman's arm down on this piece of paper?'

'Well . . .'

'Well, what? Surely you can understand the question? Is this really the best you can do or has your mind been wandering again?' Still soft, his voice was, but menacing now, hinting at the rage or frustration or whatever it was inside him that caused him to care so much. He stared down at Anna and in her panic she saw that he had broken his glasses and Sellotaped them at one side.

She was aware of the attention of the whole class now, in the dead silence. Aware, too, of a wave of sympathy but not enough sympathy to make them intervene.

'I have tried . . .' she said softly.

'But not very hard! You haven't bothered to look at the model, have you, Anna? We might as well sit a sack of potatoes in that chair as far as you are concerned because this . . . this effort . . . is drawn purely from your imagination!' He stabbed his pencil into her drawing again and again. She felt it was her that he stabbed. The words hurt her physically. 'I see you have a cliché that you keep in your head. Human arm equals shoulder, elbow, forearm, wrist, hand. Put a bend in the elbows. Fingers are difficult. Won't do fingers. Just a bit of fuzzy pencil work. Now, that's finished! Lunch time!' He took his eyes from the drawing and they bored into Anna. 'Joanne's arm is unique!' he shouted. 'It is unlike any other arm in the world!' Joanne looked alarmed. Anna felt herself begin to swell with internal tears. 'It's no good drawing pretty pictures out of your head in my class. You're wasting my time and your own. I want you to draw that woman's arm. I don't care how small a piece you draw but this time look at the model. I want to see some form!'

Just as she knew she couldn't take any more of this, he swung away, leaving her cringing, crumpled, eyes blurred with tears as she took the drawing pins out and attached a clean piece of paper from underneath. Her hands shook. She stared at the paper. It was as pathetically blank and eager to please as she was herself. She needed so desperately to please. . .

She must succeed because this was all she had, her only reason for being different, justifying the way she edged through the world in her big, shy body, justifying all the evenings she spent alone in the flat while Linden and all other unattached females explored the intricate world of sex and London and night. Having only this, only her days, she had to believe she would achieve something at the Cannon. She didn't want to rock the world with her paintings but she wanted desperately to be considered serious. Even in Veronica's world where to be 'plain' and 'without sex appeal' was to be as good as dead, people with talent could be redeemed.

He had just destroyed Anna's lifeline. She raised her eyes. He was two people away from her now, talking with little interest to a small Swedish girl. The sight of him terrified her all over again. His words repeated in her head. . . Sobbing, suddenly Anna stood up and grabbed her bag and lurched out. The studio door slammed behind her.

She couldn't leave. She couldn't bring herself to go into the street. Instead she huddled in the deserted coffee bar. Absolute desolation filled her. She had no idea of time. She was surprised when people began to drift in. She realized it must be nearly one o'clock. Members of her class either maintained a tactful silence or asked her if she was coming to lunch. When she shook her head, they left her. She wondered that Pym had not come to find her, help her. She crouched lower.

'Anna, where are you?' It was Michael Miller, shouldering his way into the room, seeing her in her corner. 'I've been looking for you everywhere!'

There was a small burst of laughter. Michael occupied a unique position at the Cannon, because of his age and his take-it-or-leave-it teaching and his shameless flitting from girl to girl. He sat down by Anna, surprising her deeply. He had hardly spoken to her outside class before. But now, looking sideways at him, nervously, she had the full treatment. The slow, lovable smile, touching the corners of his grey eyes, the corners of his mouth; the boyish hand in the hair. 'I hear, from my sources, that Bony has been giving you the treatment this week.'

Anna shrugged. 'Not specially. He does it to everyone . . .'

'But you most of all at the moment.' Michael leant forward and looked into her face. 'You mustn't take it so badly, Anna. You're here to learn and he can teach. Believe me, he wouldn't bother to make your life hell if he didn't think you were worth it. I know he overdoes it but that's the way he is. It drives him mad to see people not using themselves fully, half-concentrating. We've talked about it a lot, over this last month. I've worked with him before at the Central.'

'I don't mind,' Anna lied.

'You do!' Pym stood in front of her, arms folded. 'You quiver with terror like a rabbit whenever he comes near you.'

'You must tell him what you think.' Michael said. 'Tell him what you're trying to do. Stand up to him, Anna. If you're scared you won't learn from him.'

'He's pretty hard to answer,' Pym said.

'But he gets results!' Michael stood up and fed a five-pence piece into the Dalek. 'How hard do you really work in my class? Nice, chatty mornings, I know. Bit of a rest, really. But nothing as exciting as the results Bony gets with his terror campaign. No one is on their mettle.' He lifted the plastic cup to his lips and sipped and grimaced. 'God, someone must have crawled into that thing and died!' He put the cup down. 'Anyway, I don't want to hear any more about you walking out of class, Anna! I've talked to Bony about you. We discussed that little painting you did for the end of first year and we were both impressed by it. Really. So don't waste your time being scared. Listen to him. You keep your eye on her for me, Pym!' He winked and jokingly kicked the Dalek as he went out.

Pym sat in the space Michael had left next to Anna, putting his arm along her shoulder and playing with her hair. Her heart thumped.

'Well, well . . . what about that "little painting" bit?' He pulled cigarettes from his shirt pocket and shook the packet with his left hand. He took a cigarette out with his lips. 'Want one, Anna?'

'No, thank you. You told him, did you?'

'Yes, I did.'

'Is it true, about him and Bony, about them talking over my painting?'

'Of course it's true!' Pym took his arm from behind her head to strike a match. He laughed. 'I know you're very lovable, Anna, but not even for you is Michael going out of his way to concoct encouraging stories. It's hard to believe but these people who move God-like among us, supposedly teaching, are really mere humans! And they must talk among themselves and presumably sometimes they talk about us.' He made his voice deep and rich like Michael's. 'That fat girl with the orange hair can really say something, Bony!'

Anna jerked her head to stare at him.

'It's true. It's true that you're fat and it's true that you're good, Anna. You can paint. Why don't you look at *yourself* instead of some distorted image you hide behind? Mmmm?' His face was gentle. 'It's not a crime to be fat, you know.'

She leant against Pym, dropping her head on to his shoulder for a moment in an extraordinarily relaxed gesture. Happiness burst through her, softening her. Pym, surprised and touched, turned his head and put a small kiss on the end of her nose.

Anna stayed in the coffee bar for a long time, that evening, absorbing what had happened. In class that afternoon Bony had cruised round behind her like a shark, looking over her shoulder and muttering, 'Better. A little better,' and then cruising on. Now, when all round her people were hurrying to join evening classes or to go home, she sat and tried to accept that it was true. That she had potential. Tried to believe it strongly enough so that she wouldn't need constant reassurance and proof. Odd to realize that the way she felt about life – that everyone else mingled happily and understood and she lurked on the outside, looking on, misunderstanding and bewildered – might help her to paint.

That "little painting" was of the river and the grey sky. Cranes and barges, muddy browns and greens, painted in such a lonely mood that the feeling somehow came through. Joy took hold of her. She told herself she had a reason for spending four years here. She would succeed. That she might be pathetically young for her age and aggressively virginal and awkward but she had a reason. Anna stayed in the coffee bar till well after six. She smoked a cigarette that someone gave her and refused a banana; she talked to two new students, two brothers, telling them the name of the wood-yard where they could buy hardboard to paint on. Then someone began to draw her . . . out of the corner of her eye she saw the movements of head and hand and sat politely still until he had finished. Outside the sky was heavy with rain. The clock chimed once for 6.30 and her lethargy vanished. She sprang up. She ran down the stairs, snatched her coat, swung out into the rain. Oh God, she was happy tonight!

As soon as she opened the front door and stepped into the hall, Anna sensed that there were other people in the flat. There was music coming from the sitting-room. Soft, unusual music. Not Veronica's Sinatra or Linden's folk singers. Something sophisticated. And voices, too many voices, coming from the sitting-room when, normally at this time, the kitchen was the meeting-place. Anna began to move cautiously across the hall, wishing she had come in more quietly.

Veronica looked round the sitting-room door. 'Anna. . .' Her voice was a little too loud, her face slightly unnatural. 'I'm so glad you're back, darling. Come and meet Linden's friends.' She pounced, taking Anna's arm, bringing Anna into the room.

Anna was wet and flustered, still a little dazed by the events of the morning. She was not ready for these people. The room was very tidy. A fire in the grate. Drinks on a tray and the ice bucket out. Linden in a long dress. Three strange people. Two men. One girl.

Anna always felt a different species from her mother, from Linden, but tonight she was surprised that she could understand Linden when she spoke.

'This is my brilliant sister, Anna. Creator of murals of genius!' Linden laughed. 'Sarah Field. James and Oliver Carroll.'

Despite herself, despite her unwillingness and her wet hair and the feeling that she didn't belong at all, Anna was intrigued to meet these men in the flesh. She sat down on the arm of a chair. How had Linden achieved this coup?

'After suffering just one of my lunches – only one, Oliver insists that I go out with him and taste real food!' Linden's eyes danced as Oliver denied it.

James, the elder one Anna thought, the good-looking one with a smile that touched the left side of his mouth more than his right, said; 'We came to meet you, Anna.'

'I've brought them to see your mural.' Linden had poured a large gin and tonic and she crossed the room and put it into Anna's hand. She gave a huge wink. 'I told them, quite honestly, that you are brilliant and extremely expensive but, occasionally, if you really like someone you will paint a mural as a commission! They have this blank white wall, you see. . .' All the time she spoke she looked at Anna, her eyes shining, saying: 'Well?'

'It's terribly good. Your boats and sailors thing.' It was the strange girl who spoke. Sarah.

'Would you be willing to paint something for us, Anna?' James said. 'Would you have time?'

Anna shrugged. 'If you like.'

'Darling, you could sound a little more keen,' Veronica put in.

Anna flushed. 'Well, I haven't had much time to think and I haven't seen the room. I don't know if I'm keen or not.'

Linden stood by the fireplace, her eyes resting on James. Strange to see the photograph living and breathing. His voice was very deep, very English. A lovely voice. Funny, she hadn't thought about that. *This morning I left this flat knowing neither of*

49

them. Now, here they are. Just because I dared, followed Oliver's lead and asked them. There James sits, with that secret face. . . How interested is he? He is not coming on to dinner afterwards. He is committed, this evening, to this Sarah girl. Still, he had very little notice. Oliver she hardly considered.

Anna took a sip from the drink Linden had poured her. It was far too strong. *How brave of Linden,* Anna thought, *to bring them here . . . suppose there had been no gin? Suppose Mum had been in one of her jig-sawing frenzies, covering the floor with similar pieces? But it wouldn't bother Linden. She would re-categorize herself as coming from an eccentric but well-bred family. She would carry it off.* Anna looked cautiously from brother to brother, instinctively more attracted by Oliver's gentle face and more solid body. He sat in silence, watching Linden.

The girl Sarah was suggesting that they could tile their bathroom, from floor to ceiling. 'One can get fabulous tiles now.'

Rather unkind, Anna thought, disliking her.

'How long have you been at your art school?' James asked her. He was quite relaxed, but his voice was without interest: he was being polite.

'I'm second year.'

'And will you come and inspect the blank white wall in our bathroom? You could give us an estimate, perhaps.'

Either he was laughing at her or he was making an attempt to treat her on a business basis to flatter her. Either way, Anna needed to get out. 'I'll come and see it.' She stood up. 'If you'll excuse me a minute . . . I got wet, coming home.' She put her drink down carefully as a sign that she was coming back.

But she didn't go back. In her bedroom she hung her coat behind the door. She went to the dressing table to brush her hair. The rain had stained it dark brown, her white skin was whipped pink. She looked down at her jeans, gum boots, despair welling up in her. She sat on the bed until she heard signs of their departure. Only then did she wander into the hall, stopping in the shadows by the kitchen door.

They were putting on coats and saying polite things to Veronica. James spotted Anna. 'That's agreed then, Anna. Come round any week day and look. Oliver is always there, sleeping or strumming!'

Anna nodded. She looked at Linden, at James, at Oliver. The

prodigal Oliver. As overshadowed as she was, perhaps? She felt a sudden interesting sympathy with him. Good-byes were scattered and the front door closed.

Veronica moved back into the sitting-room and looked out of the side of a curtain. 'Lovely car . . . they're going to some cocktail party, I think. Oliver has to be at his club at eleven so they'll eat quite early.' Veronica moved to the tray of drinks and filled her glass. Half gin. Half bitter-lemon. She had been to the hairdresser at lunchtime. Her hair was a grey meringue, her small face aged by too much eye-make up. 'They really seem quite keen to have something painted by you.' She had had too many drinks to hide the surprise she felt. 'Do try and do something less harrowing than the one we have. I don't mind the galleons or the guns. It's those drowning Spanish sailors. They depress me. Their faces are so agonized!'

'People do look agonized when they're drowning.'

'Well, you don't have to be so literal. Anyway, you've never seen anyone drown, have you?'

Anna shook her head, thinking: *If Linden didn't live here, we would never talk at all. We have nothing to say to each other, Mum and I.*

'There are sausages in the fridge,' Veronica said, disconcertingly. 'I'm playing bridge at Prue's. I think I'll walk.' She fiddled in her handbag. She finished her drink and smiled vaguely at Anna. 'What a good-looking man James is!'

When Veronica had left, the flat was very quiet. The fire settled down on to itself. Anna turned off the lights and opened the curtains. The square was damp and dark with occasional people, street lights wearing misted collars. She put on a record. Joni Mitchell. She lay on the sofa.

Why did Linden bring them here? To involve me? To pull me into her life? Or am I useful for once? She cleverly avoids me being an embarrassment by casting me in this arty role! Anna put her hands on her stomach. She was abruptly overwhelmed with loneliness, thinking of Linden skirmishing in some noisy party. Overwhelmed by her inability to form a relationship with a man. *It's not just because I'm fat. A lot of successful people are even fatter and I won't always look like this, will I?*

Occasionally Anna had caught a glimpse of herself in a stranger's glass and it was like a premonition. For one moment she would see herself as she could be and then her mind would censor the image and she saw only her size. She wouldn't count her hair or the pale grey eyes. Black-lashed. Hawk eyes, Linden called them. Witch's eyes, Pym had once said . . . No, it wasn't her looks. It was the raw wound of her shyness which made her uncomfortable to be with, difficult to talk to, awkward in everyday situations which most people coped with easily.

At least I have my work to hold on to! Anna went into the kitchen and began to prepare herself a large meal.

CHAPTER FIVE

In the east studio, Anna's studio as she always thought of it, they were waiting for a lecture. Donkeys and easels were pushed back, chairs and benches arranged in rows and the slide projector in position. The white screen waited patiently. An upended dais formed a temporary desk. After the usual struggle the brown blinds had been lowered to blot out the October night and the light from tall street lamps which would otherwise flood the room. There was a lot of smoke in the air, a lot of talk, and Anna sat between Pym and Martha Holland, hands round her knees, chin on her hands, wishing she hadn't agreed to go with Linden, after this lecture, to Oliver Carroll's house.

'You've been stalling for nearly two weeks, Anna. It's getting embarrassing for me . . . he keeps ringing up and asking when you'll come. I know you're not doing anything on Wednesday, which is the day he suggested, because you never do anything! So I'll pick you up at seven-thirty, after the lecture. I haven't forgotten that – and we'll go round and you can at least look. Then, if you don't want to do it, for God's sake just say so!'

Anna sighed. Wednesday had been the best evening for her all this term. There was always a lecture from 5 o'clock until 7 o'clock and by the time there had been questions and discussions it would be past 7.30 when she finally left, fitting herself into the safe dark evening. She would be home around 8 o'clock and by then it was quite respectable, she felt, to bath, eat, watch television or go to bed. It was one evening out of the week she wasn't ashamed of. One evening she could usually look forward to. But not tonight!

Richard Cannon, soul of the school, picked his way to the front of the room, stepping over feet which strayed untidily into the gangway between the rows of chairs, and coughing several times to show his disapproval of the smoke. A tall, gaunt man, he was a strict vegetarian, a non-smoker, a teetotaler. 'Such bad luck to go through all that and *still* be so unhealthy,' Pym remarked each time Richard was ill. Hilary held her usual position, just behind Richard Cannon, hovering and adoring.

He stood in front of the screen. He held up his hands for quiet and then folded them, tucking them under his armpits and dipping his head as he thought what to say.

'Good evening, all of you. I want to tell you a little about the man who is coming to talk to us this evening. He's rather late, but that's not the only thing I want to tell you . . .' He paused while laughter flickered. 'He's going to speak tonight about something a little outside our usual subject range. Frederick Monroe works at Granbury's, the auctioneers. He is what they call an expert which means that, in his chosen field, he knows a very great deal. He is the man they come to for opinions and valuations and classification for cataloguing. His field is ceramics. His speciality is Chinese porcelain. Now, in case any of you are fidgeting, let me tell you that I've heard Freddie speak before and he is fascinating. He has a huge knowledge of the whole history of porcelain and, believe me, it's a pretty interesting story! By the way, have any of you noticed the prices that are beginning to be paid for this kind of thing at auction? They write up most major sales in the *Times* and I've been reading the reports with interest.' He smiled. 'I happen to own a small incense burner . . .'

In Kensington High Street, Freddie was caught in a five o'clock soup of cars and buses and pedestrians, all paralysed for the moment in the October twilight. He knew he was going to be late for the lecture but as there was nothing he could do about it, he put it from his mind and used this enforced pause to slow down.

He had always been an extrovert but just lately he was aware that he sometimes overdid it. Like an actor who could not stop playing a particularly absorbing part. *And yet*, he thought *it's all coming right!* Excitement tightened him. It seemed that the more he released his flamboyant personality, the more he let the strength and confidence which he felt come to the surface and show, the more he gained.

It was nearly three and a half months since that afternoon at Pyecomb when he met Oliver Carroll. In that time, Freddie's life had altered dramatically. Taking stock now he found it seemed unreal. He had left Granbury's a month ago, deciding he must commit himself entirely to Monroe Investments. His flat was now an office. Neatly-labelled brown folders, one for each of his eight carefully nurtured clients, were gradually growing fatter. And all this from one lunch with Oliver. After all it had proved so ridiculously easy . . . Above all this, Freddie almost had his hands on the premises he needed! He would then be fully launched.

He was late, now, because he had visited Oliver half an hour previously. He hadn't telephoned first because he found Oliver quite impossible to deal with on the telephone. Freddie had stopped outside the house in Peterstone Mews and rang the bell. The silence from inside the house was discouraging. He needed to see Oliver. He felt impatient and exhilarated. He wanted to see him now! But Freddie had turned to leave when the door finally opened.

'Oh, it's you,' Oliver said. 'Sorry I was so long. I was washing-up and I dropped a glass when you rang.'

'Washing-up?' Freddie said, incredulously, picking his way over the heaps of paper on the floor. He was aware of the conflict between Oliver and James over the state of the house and the three stages the house went through each day. In the afternoons it was Oliver's to create whatever chaos he chose. In the evenings James wanted order. In the mornings, a woman came to make the beds and hoover.

'You know what washing-up is,' Oliver said, irritably, and Freddie could sense he was in one of his maddeningly withdrawn moods. 'I've got some people coming this evening and I suddenly find myself agreeing with James and being ashamed of the place!' He relented and smiled. 'Make yourself a coffee if you want but don't untidy the kitchen!'

'She must be someone special,' Freddie said, playing along and concealing his impatience. He boiled the kettle and made two mugs of coffee, glancing at his watch. 4.30. He grimaced and took the coffees into the living-room just as Oliver lost interest in his cleaning and sat down at the piano.

'Oliver, I've had the most amazing piece of luck.' Freddie handed him a coffee, longing to say, 'For God's sake concentrate!' and slam the lid of the piano down on the tune Oliver began to pick out with his right hand. 'You know how we've been saying we need a much better base than my flat, well . . . I've found somewhere. In Brook Street. A whole building with a shop, a store-room and two floors above. And, what's more, it goes with an established company. The building has a ten-year lease and although it's a bit run-down at the moment, structurally it's sound. It belongs to a man called Sam Jones. I've known him for years.'

'And he's selling up?'

'Yes. He's up the spout in a big way and extremely anxious for cash. So anxious that he's letting the whole thing go at a very low price.' Freddie laughed. 'He wants to go to Devon and buy a cottage.'

'How much does he want?' Oliver said, picturing an imposing building. An outward visual sign of success.

'The whole set-up, the company, this building with a ten-year lease, is thirty five thousand pounds. Of course the rates are high but if anything disastrous should happen to us, it will be an asset we can easily dispose of and certainly for more than Sam is asking. In my opinion it's well worth it!'

Oliver's fingers still pursued the tune. 'How much have we in the kitty?'

Freddie unzipped his briefcase. He came and stood by Oliver, casually flicking through pieces of paper as if he didn't know every figure by heart. 'That last commission from Hartley has made us look pretty healthy but we would need another ten thousand pounds. If you don't want to commit that much I am sure that, on these figures, I could borrow the money from my bank.' Freddie had learned, that first day he took Oliver to lunch, that however loudly he might disclaim any interest in the world his father and brother inhabited, Oliver responded to the proper terms. He had grown up in a world of finance and he understood the language even if he didn't choose to speak it. 'If you do put in another ten thousand I still think you are getting a pretty impressive return on your invested capital. However, what about letting your brother give the whole thing a look-over?'

In the beginning, this particular ploy of Freddie's had worked superbly. At the mention of James's name, Oliver had flared up like a schoolboy and agreed to anything. But now he was wiser. He met Freddie's eyes. 'That isn't necessary. It is my money to invest in whatever I want. Anyway . . .' – and he hesitated unhappily – 'I'm afraid James is distinctly hostile to the whole idea. I let it out the wrong way. I was stupid, looking back on it, but he's so bloody patronizing sometimes and I just couldn't resist telling him about it all. He went very quiet. Sooner or later you two must meet and argue it out!' Oliver frowned, unhappy at the thought. 'Besides, as I pointed out to James, the only other time in my life I asked him for advice was about a year after I left school. I have a friend who had just inherited a boatyard in Wales. Pembrokeshire. He wanted me to go in with him and I was very keen. James told me it was a bloody silly idea and said I knew nothing about boats, which I didn't. But it was a lovely place . . . James showed me a lot of stuff about how boat-builders were always going bankrupt and I took his advice and went to Australia instead. About nine months after, they began servicing the supply ships which go to the big oil tankers. They have doubled the size of the yard now.'

'So the mighty James can be wrong,' Freddie said, filing the information away.

'Once in a blue moon.' Oliver stood up. 'I think you're right. We do need a base and an impressive one . . . lots of white paint and thick carpet. When can I come and see it?'

Freddie tucked his papers away. 'Well, not now because I have to give a lecture. Tomorrow afternoon?' He looked at his watch. 'God, I'd better move. Shall I ring you in the morning?'

'Yes . . . but not too early!'

Freddie laughed. 'Okay. Lunch time.' He put his hand briefly on Oliver's shoulder in a gesture of farewell and triumph. Freddie was a man who liked to touch people. He made his way to the door. 'I was going to give up lecturing when I left Granbury's but then it occurred to me that the more people who are interested in our subject, the better. Got to keep talking up the market! 'Bye, Oliver . . .'

As the door closed, Oliver had closed his eyes. He felt himself being pulled into the centre of a very intricate circle. His feelings were mixed. In one way it delighted him to be involved. Suddenly he was the focus of Freddie's attention, consulted, considered, courted almost . . . *It must irritate him like hell that someone as useless as myself is the source of the money he needs!* Attention from James, too, since Oliver had been stung into mentioning the whole thing. James was curious and disapproving. He would have relayed the whole thing to Robert and Marietta, Oliver knew. His hoped-for triumph, beating them at their own game, had not quite turned out as he had envisaged. *But it will!* Oliver thought. *It will!* Still he did not look forward to the meeting between Freddie and James. He knew his brother very well and the few months of association with Freddie had tempered Oliver's original hero-worship. He still admired the man enormously, admired his courage and the way he pushed and his burning ambition but he recognized, alongside this, Freddie's unscrupulousness. When James and Freddie met ... As always, Oliver dived into his music, losing himself in it, escaping into it, subconsciously hoping that when he concentrated on the real world again, things might have changed!

At last Freddie got through the Church Street traffic lights. He put his foot down, screaming round the corners in this narrow street, up towards Notting Hill Gate. He needed a short burst of speed to show the world his exhilaration. He thought briefly of James Carroll — Freddie rather looked forward to meeting James. He was not afraid of him because he knew he had done Oliver nothing but good. Then he put it all from his mind as he pulled up outside the rambling Victorian building which stood out oddly in this street of small white houses. He slammed his car door, strode into the hall and began to run up the stairs to the studio where they normally held lectures.

'I have been trying for the last two years,' Richard Cannon was saying,' to persuade Freddie Monroe to write a book, to commit to paper some of the enormous store of knowledge he carries in his head.'

There was a stir by the door and heads turned as Freddie seemed to burst into the room. He paused, getting his breath back, looking round and taking in a first general picture of the room before he moved forward to shake Richard Cannon's hand and apologize for being late. He swung his shoulders out of his overcoat, which Hilary took for him. Anna stared at this thick-set man with his broad face and rather wild brown hair. A lion of a man, she thought.

'Good evening.' His voice was rich with the traces of an accent running through it. North country? 'I must apologize to you all for keeping you waiting. I expect Richard has told you a lot of flattering things, to fill in time, and I shall spend the next couple of hours disappointing you! However, the advantage of a subject like mine is that there can't be many of you who will jump up and shout "Rubbish!".'

There was laughter. They settled more comfortably into their seats. They liked him now and they wanted him to be interesting. Their mood reached out to Freddie and as he felt it, he relaxed. He began to enjoy himself.

He is a frightening man, Anna thought. *Fascinating and frightening . . . not a man to be across the room from. You should be up close to him, sheltering by him. Protected.* Then she shook her head violently to get rid of the absurd imagery.

The lights were turned down and Freddie stood at an improvised desk with a page of notes in front of him. 'I'm going to begin with a brief history of porcelain. It's strong stuff. Wars, rebel hordes sweeping down and destroying everything. Emperors. There will be a lot of Emperors! But first a couple of points. . . You may wonder why, in describing porcelain, so many of the terms used are European. The reason for this is that the first serious study was carried out by a Frenchman. Famille Rose . . . Famille Vert . . .'

He was a very good speaker. He loved it, he drew strength from their attention, and tonight, full of excitement, he was quite fascinating. In the light which spilt from the screen his face was hypnotic. He made the subject live. He made the Emperors real people, giving them such character that, although their names were difficult, somehow it was possible to remember which was which. 'The centre of the porcelain industry in 17th-century China was the town of Chin te Chen . . .'

Anna sat with her hands locked round her knees, mesmerized by him, by his voice and the pictures he spun in the dark room and slides which sprang disconcertingly on to the screen; delicate bowls and dishes and bottles and jars. Time ceased for her. It passed in one swift stroke. When she became aware that he had finished speaking and that everyone was clapping and that the lights were on, she blinked, bewildered and disorientated. She had been so deeply involved. It was a shock to become aware of the room again, of other people, of movement and the silence because the projector's constant background hum was stilled.

'Questions,' he said, coming round from behind his desk. 'Has anybody got anything to ask or are you sick of the whole subject?'

Anna moved in her seat. She wanted, desperately, to ask a question . . . she wanted to ask something startlingly intelligent so that he would notice her and single her out with his eyes. Amazed at her own courage she put up her hand. Her heart beat with deep, full beats. She searched herself for a question but all she really wanted to ask was the history of the man himself. He would not look her way. He acknowledged hands from the left and right, the back of the room, the front; he talked to Richard Cannon, to Hilary. In desperation Anna stood up, unfolding herself, her hand still raised.

'Yes?' Suddenly he was looking at her, paralysing her.

Anna swallowed. She was conscious that everyone watched her. The room was silent and expectant.

'You have a question?' he said, seeing a girl with orange hair, round-eyed and fat, hand poised in mid-air. She stood out from the sea of ordinary faces like a pumpkin in a cabbage field.

The silence stretched until a few seconds became a lifetime and she waited for him to ridicule her, make a joke of her, which would have been in keeping with his hard face. But instead he smiled, isolating Anna from the room and the people and making it possible for her to speak.

'It doesn't matter. It wasn't a good question anyway.'

Laughter rose in a great surge so that it seemed to Anna the roof would burst off and leave them all staring up stupidly at the stars. Colour burst into her cheeks and she sat down.

Freddie waited until there was quiet. He looked at this strange girl, met her eyes, saw the extent of her embarrassment and her vulnerability. In his present mood of triumph he was touched with pity for her. 'Why don't you ask it anyway?' he said gently.

'Well,' Anna muttered, 'I wanted to know about you. How you got to be an expert?'

'I'm glad someone asked! I thought this was going to be one of those unsatisfactory evenings when I don't get a chance to talk about myself!' He paused. 'I came to London at eighteen, knowing only what two years as general dogsbody in a small antique shop in Reading had taught me. That wasn't much. I presented myself on Granbury's doorstep and for some reason they took me on. I became what is known as a learner porter. At the end of my first year the only thing I was expert in was moving furniture. I carried things about, from one room to another, for sales. I read and listened and picked up what I could and eventually I graduated into cataloguing. I had always been interested in ceramics and so I concentrated on them. I should think, though, it would be far more difficult to get in through the back door now, as I did, than it was ten years ago.' He stopped and gave Anna a smile which she received with delight.

There were a few more questions and then Richard Cannon said some closing words. The slides went back in the box. Frederick Monroe went back into his overcoat and he and Richard moved towards the door.

'He was an interesting man,' Pym said. 'So unlikely to be involved in such a delicate subject. Tough and pushing. More of a salesman.'

'I thought he was magnificent,' a girl said vehemently.

'Typical. Just the sort of man you silly bitches like. Nasty piece of work. Virile and unsubtle and . . . look at Anna!' He laughed and ruffled her hair. 'She's besotted!'

'Don't be silly.'

'But I'm jealous of that expression. Why don't you look like that when you think of me?'

The room emptied. People called good night to one another.

'I'll put this lot away if you like, Hilly,' Pym said, and he stayed where he was and offered Anna a cigarette. She took it because she wanted to respond to the gesture and because she wanted a reason to sit for a little while. The match flared. The room was empty. Pym's eyes touched hers and she looked away, withdrawing.

He smiled and edged up close, putting an arm round her. 'Jane has gone home to Mummy for three whole weeks, Anna. Wanna fix dinna, as she puts it?'

'I wish I could but I have to go somewhere with my sister tonight.'

'Why? Why do you have to go?'

'Well, it's all fixed,' Anna said unhappily. 'It's a painting job.' She said this with embarrassment. It was thought very presumptuous by other students to accept outside commissions at this stage. 'Only a bathroom . . . She feels sorry for me, I think. She goes out a lot and I don't. She has always been different, always looked good. Even as a child she looked good in school uniform! You know the type?'

'Not enough of them, unfortunately.' Pym watched her shrewdly with narrowed eyes. 'Go on.'

'There isn't much else. I think it's useful for her if I do it. Linden is a great layer of plans. She's a strong person . . .' Anna found, to her deep surprise, that having once started to talk about Linden, a subject she had never broached before, the words were beginning to come on their own. As if they had been waiting to come out for months or years. 'She has set it all up. She has fixed this evening and I'm going with her to see this bathroom I'm supposed to paint the mural in. I don't want to do it but I think, if I don't at least go to look, she will be furious.'

'So what?' Pym said. 'Let her be furious. Think of yourself. You don't want to do it? Don't do it!'

'You don't understand. It will be better if I do what she wants.'

'I see.' He stood up, looking down at Anna. 'Underneath it all, you long to be like her, don't you? You want to be a success socially. You really believe that some night a wand will wave and you will be transformed into a carbon copy of this sister of yours, twittering your way through endless trivial evenings or holding hands with some amazingly boring guy with money and a sports car. That's what you dream of, isn't it, Anna? Groping under the table in a bistro. That's what little girls dreams are made of, isn't it? Trivial, tiny little dreams. How marvellous to ask so little of life!'

He put out his hands, catching Anna's arms above the elbows and pulling her to her feet. His strength surprised her but she came quickly, not wanting him to feel the weight of her body. She avoided his eyes, conscious only that she was taller than he was, dipping her head. When he kissed her mouth, gently and with great confidence, she swung away, wild with embarrassment.

'Leave me alone, Pym! You don't understand anything about me. Go and torment someone else. Pull the wings off some of the flies.' She sat down, away from him, dropping her head on to her knees.

He came and sat in front of her so that their knees touched. He put his hands each side of her head, lifting it up. 'I'm sorry, Anna. Come on. Tell me about it . . .'

'Why should I trot out my inferiority complex for you to play with later?' Her voice shook.

'You know I wouldn't do that. Just tell me why you are so afraid of people.'

Her anger faded. His gentle, curious mood was irresistible. The attention was so irresistible. She turned her head sideways, cheek on one hand and sighed. 'I don't know, Pym. I wish I understood myself. I never feel at ease with people. I crave their attention and then when I get it, I am humiliated. Like tonight . . . I feel they pity me. All my life I've felt big and plain in a family where it mattered that you were small and pretty. So I tried to be good. To please everyone. To reassure myself that if I couldn't be beautiful or clever I could at least be obliging.'

Her hands shook and she clasped them together. 'Over and over again there would be aunts or cousins visiting. 'Haven't the girls grown, Veronica? Linden has the family look. So like you.' And then a pause and my mother saying, 'Anna paints, you know.' They made it so obvious that I had failed by the standards they had. My mother and Linden speak the same language. They talk about everything. They laugh about men. Linden can say, 'You know how it is when they look at you and you just sense the interest? You know they want to approach.' And Mother says, 'Yes.' But I don't! I don't know what the hell they're talking about! It's as if the whole world is full of people recognizing secret sexual messages that I don't even realize are being passed!' Her voice was low and desperate. She stopped abruptly when she realized Pym was laughing.

'You're not supposed to laugh, damn you! I've just told you things I've never told anyone and you laugh. You should be sympathetic. You try living in this world as a twelve-stone female lump!'

'Oh, Anna . . .' He stopped laughing. He leaned forward and put his forehead against hers. 'Anna, Anna. It isn't like you think. You haven't started, that's all. Sex has nothing to do with weight or messages or being born with your eyes open or big breasts! There aren't rules and exams and standards. Either you do it or you don't. That's your choice. Once you start you'll probably wonder what all the fuss is about.' He smiled and his face was so close to hers that it was blurred.

She pulled her head away. 'I think it matters much more than you say.'

He let his breath out in a long sigh. 'You're such a sitting duck. I can't bear to think what might happen to you . . . Of course the first time matters. Something to be thought about. Probably won't mean a lot to you but it should be with someone you care for. This sister and mother team you grew up with sounds terrifying! Childhood fascinates me. There are no distractions in a child's world and memories are being laid down all the time. Happiness dangles on such delicate threads.'

Anna smiled. 'I can't imagine you as a child, Pym. You must have always been like this.'

'I can't imagine you as an adult!' He looked serious. 'Well, come on. It's quite obvious I have to take you in hand, Anna. For your own good!' His slanted eyes danced and he reached out his hand and put it against one of her big round breasts. Stilling her. Making her flicker inside with surprise.

'You don't mean . . . ?'

'Yes, I do. Come back and cook supper for me and I'll tell you about how it is up North where the nights are long and cold!'

'But I couldn't! Not just like that.'

'Why the hell not? It's your body, isn't it? It's not your mother's or your sister's! It's yours. Do what you want with it. Start using it a little . . .'

His mood invaded her, started in her first tentative responses, tightened her with a courage she didn't think she had. She was suddenly delighted. She stood up and laughed and helped him fold the projector, coil the wire, put it in the cupboard. They turned out lights and ran down the stairs, thumping past Hilary's office.

Hilary jumped when she saw them. 'I thought you two had gone long ago!'

Pym winked and Anna heard herself laugh with a laugh that

had never come from her throat before. They started down the last few stairs into the hall.

And then the street door opened. Linden came in and the street light came with her, like an aura, outlining her and displaying her.

Anna felt Pym stiffen. As Linden stepped forward towards them, Anna looked at her objectively and knew the impression that face would have on a stranger and the appeal a man like Pym would feel. A man who loved women anyway.

'Hallo. I'm Linden. Anna's sister.' She held out her hand, open and warm and expecting to be liked.

'This is Pym,' Anna said dully, feeling a complicated range of emotions. Jealousy first, scalding like nausea, and certainty that she would not go with him now. She felt caught out, like a petty shop-lifter, trying to sneak away with a life for herself. With an evening for herself. *Not allowed, Anna! Not allowed!* And yet she also felt a perverse pride that Linden and she were connected at all.

'I'll get my coat, Linden,' she muttered. In the cloakroom she switched on the lights and gripped one of the basins with both hands. Her face swam before her as if the mirror were one of those distorting fairground glasses. She began to wash her hands, meticulously, each finger in turn, scrubbing the nails. When she had finished she washed round the basin in one of her desperate attempts to get God on her side by being good . . . But God, it seemed, was bored with good fat people. Anna pulled on her duffle coat and buried her hands deep in its comforting pockets. As she made her way back to the hall, she thought, *Perhaps there has been a miracle. Pym has told her I'm going with him . . . told her for me that I don't want any of this mural.*

'What have you been doing?' Linden laughed. 'Come on. We're late already.'

Pym took his eyes, reluctantly, from Linden's face and looked at Anna. For the past five minutes he had not given her a thought. He had forgotten her existence. Now he frowned, remembering. 'Look . . .'

But Anna pushed her way into the street as he started speaking, letting the door that swung shut behind her say good night.

'Good night Pym,' Linden said, opening the street door again. She paused for a second, looking over her shoulder.

Anna heard her ask, 'What's your real name?'
In over a year it had never occurred to Anna to ask.
'Alexander,' he said.

CHAPTER SIX

A large white bathroom. A long wall above the bath, tiled for a couple of feet and then blank. One big window with a white Venetian blind. White bath, white basin, white lavatory. *The whole room is like a blank canvas*, Anna thought, as interest grew in her against her will, competing with the dull misery which had occupied her ever since leaving the Cannon.

'Well?' Oliver sat unceremoniously on the closed lavatory. 'Does it inspire you?'

She looked at him cautiously. It was hard to know if he was joking or serious. His rather flat, quiet voice contrasted oddly with the smile that followed the words. Anna decided that he was, in fact, quite disinterested and that the whole idea was merely an attempt to humour and get close to Linden.

'It would look better with some colour in here,' she said. 'What exactly did you want me to paint?'

'The wall,' Oliver said carefully.

'I know that. I meant, what should I put in the mural? What subject?'

He had been looking past her into the narrow upstairs landing, listening to the sounds of Linden in the kitchen below, as if to reassure himself that she was still there. He collected his thoughts with difficulty. 'Well, I rather hoped *you* would think of something. Aeroplanes? Hot air balloons? Horses? What do you like painting best?'

Anna stared at him. A straightforward face, she thought. Very misleading. His eyes were such a dark blue they appeared almost black. His obvious disinterest depressed her. She thought for a moment, seriously, about painting in here. 'Mermaids,' she said. 'It's not a very original idea but it could look very good. I could do them with long curling tails and great festoons of hair and shells and seaweed. Curling things everywhere. Waves and rocks, combs in their hands.'

He stood up. 'That's settled then.' His abruptness killed her short-lived enthusiasm. He came past Anna, a solid man, a few inches taller than she was. His eagerness to go downstairs was obvious and, perversely, Anna wanted to delay him.

'Suppose you don't like it?'

He paused and looked back at her. 'You shouldn't say that. Where's your confidence in yourself?'

'I have none.'

'Well –' he shrugged – 'if we hate it you could paint over it. Make it white again. We'll be no worse off. But I'm sure we'll like it and of course we'll pay you anyway.' He began to look restless and awkward. 'What should we pay you, Anna? Would you like to be paid now, before you begin?'

Anna made a small uneasy gesture with her hands. 'No. Let me see how long it takes. I don't know what to ask . . .' She met his eyes. 'To be honest, whatever Linden says, I've never done a mural for other people before. I didn't want to do this. I didn't bother to think about it because I was going to make some excuse. Say the room wasn't suitable or I didn't have time. But now I've seen it, I don't mind doing it.'

He faced her, arms folded. 'That is exactly the way I run my life. It is inevitably disastrous. Much better to say "no" right off.'

'I never can.'

'Nor can I.'

They smiled at one another.

'When should I start?' Anna said, in a quite different tone, at last talking to him like a human being. 'I would like to do it fairly soon because this is a quiet month at the Cannon. I could come in the late afternoons, except Wednesday which is lecture day.'

'Fine. Start tomorrow if you want. I work here every afternoon but I'll give you a key anyway, just in case I'm not in.'

'I won't disturb you?'

'Are you a very noisy painter?' he said, over his shoulder, starting down the stairs.

This time she did laugh, whether he meant her to or not. 'I'm incredibly quiet. I'll come tomorrow then, above five.'

'Fine. In fact, I'll be the one who will disturb you, I expect. I hope you're not allergic to jazz. If I'm not playing it, I'm listening to tapes and hero-worshipping. Usually Oscar Peterson.' He disappeared, two at a time, down the spiral stairs.

Anna stayed where she was for a moment and then she moved stealthily along the short passage and looked round the first open door. This small house was furnished and decorated too cleverly for men on their own. She suspected Marietta Carroll had organized it. The bedroom she looked into first was a big room, with hessian walls and curtains of a lovely dull orange. An immaculately tidy room with a discreet double bed. A wall of cupboards and real scales. Hunting prints on the walls. No character obvious except control. James's room, she knew. Correct, very cold, very tidy.

Feeling like Goldilocks, she moved on to the next bedroom. The bed was rumpled where someone had sat on it to telephone. Drawers were open, their contents spilling out; a heap of clothes on the chair; odd shoes covering the floor of the open cupboard; the window-sill was heaped with magazines and dusty books and beside the bed, in the place where he obviously emptied his pockets each night, coins and matches and a crumpled handkerchief. On the floor, under the window, were a pile of large books which intrigued Anna. She stepped into the room. It smelt nice. A dressing-gown hung behind the door and she touched it, wanting, as she always did when she saw a man's dressing-gown, to put it on, shrink into it. She crouched and read the cover of the top book. *Chinese Porcelain, the Blue and White*. The other four were all about ceramics.

'Anna.'

Linden's voice made her jump and drove the odd coincidence from her mind.

'Yes.'

'Come and eat. I've scrambled some eggs.'

Anna went carefully down the stairs, running her hand down the curving banister, looking at the huge piano which dominated the room although it was pushed against the wall. Sitting-room and dining-room were all in one with a kitchen at the back partitioned off by white louvred doors. In the kitchen end, Linden and Oliver sat on high stools at a peninsular unit which divided the kitchen. There was salad and three plates of scrambled egg. French bread and a cheese board. There was also a bottle of white wine.

'Wine and scrambled egg,' Linden said, as Anna got on to her stool. 'You've so much money, you Carrolls.'

'Well, someone worked hard for it,' Oliver said good-naturedly, pulling the cork from the bottle, 'even if it wasn't me!'

As Anna picked up her knife and fork, a hunger raged through her, which made her hands shake. Hunger like a fire. Hunger that Linden would never feel. Hunger that Anna fed with food whereas it needed to be fed with people and understanding and peace. She ate for a while in complete silence, totally absorbed, and then she was suddenly afraid that she appeared revolting, the way she was cramming the food in. She looked at the others. She looked down at the rounded outward bulge of her stomach. She put down her knife and fork.

Linden had been doing all the talking. She was good at keeping up a comfortable, social flow. She had eaten half her food and she now lost interest, pushing the plate away. It fascinated Anna the way she could leave food uneaten on her plate.

'Well, what's this mural to be then?' Linden asked.

'Mermaids,' Oliver said quietly. His eyes rested on Linden most of the time. Occasionally he forced himself to look somewhere else.

'Will James like mermaids?'

Perhaps, Anna thought, *he doesn't notice how often she brings James into the conversation, how much she asks about him? Or perhaps conditioned by a lifetime of being Oliver in a world in which James is more admired has made him very aware of Linden's tactics, however graceful. We are like her two glove puppets, Oliver and I!*

'I don't think James will mind as long as it doesn't put him off his morning routine,' Oliver finished carefully as he refilled their glasses.

Anna ate thick chunks of cheese on french bread, elbows on the table, enjoying the wine, and her mind slipped away from this room where she felt she wasn't required and crept the dark streets to the ugly house Pym lived in. In her imagination she walked the three flights of stairs and rapped on the door. She pictured him reading, or drinking beer from a can while he made toast, or eating mandarin oranges from the tin with a fork. She wondered what would have happened if she had gone with him, if they had spent five minutes less at the Cannon and slipped out before Linden had come. Would she and Pym have talked and nothing more? Or if they had made love, would he have been repelled by her large white body? And, if she ceased to be a virgin, would it change anything? Would she gain some confidence, find life easier? She dreamed that they had and she would. The wine was beginning to make her happy. Oliver pulled the cork from a second bottle, put on a cassette of George Shearing and explained it enthusiastically, offered Anna a Gauloise.

She took it. She liked the smell of the smoke but it was harsh in her throat.

'You must be mad to smoke those things,' Linden was saying, gathering plates expertly and putting the coffee pot on the stove. 'You're killing yourselves!'

How amazing, Anna thought, *to be so confident and optimistic about the future that you bother to conserve yourself*!

'I think you're right,' Oliver was saying. 'A couple of years ago I couldn't have cared less. But now I feel mortal!' He held his glass with both hands. 'A close friend of mine died last month . . .' He left the sentence but it had said what he wanted it to. He had the gift of making one small sentence express a great deal. But people seldom listened.

There was a slowness and a seriousness creeping into the evening which made Anna uneasy. She felt she shouldn't be there. She felt in the way. Terribly in the way. She slid off her stool.

'Would you mind if I went now? I promised Pym I'd drop something in this evening . . .'

Linden lifted her head sharply. 'Don't go yet. I'll clear this lot and then come with you.' Her eyes commanded, 'Stay!'

'Well, I'll come back and pick you up in about an hour.'

'I'll take you home, Linden,' Oliver said. Gratitude sparkled in his eyes as he stood up. 'You'll come tomorrow then, Anna? About five?'

'Yes.' She pushed her arms into her coat and Linden took the car keys from her bag and threw them on to the sofa. 'See you later, Linden. Good-bye, Oliver.'

Oh, it was lovely to get out into the street, into the sharp cold night with a big white moon, to slip into the familiar little box of a car, the ancient mini Veronica had driven for five years, and start the engine and chug out of the mews, out into the noise and the lights and the life of London. Anna drove towards Paddington, towards Pym's house. When she reached his street she parked outside and sat for a while, wondering if she should go up and see him, remembering the things he had said and the way he had looked at Linden. Eventually it seemed the way he had looked at Linden was more important than anything else. Humiliation replaced curiosity and she wanted to put distance between herself and Pym. She drove home much too fast.

'Are you awake? Anna? Are you awake?'

Anna struggled upwards out of the active darkness of her sleep. 'I am now . . . what time is it?' She pulled herself into a sitting position and Linden flopped on to the end of the bed. The light from the passage hurt Anna's eyes.

'I felt like talking. You don't mind, do you?'

'Not now that I'm awake. What time is it?'

'I don't know. For God's sake, stop bleating on like a bloody speaking clock!'

Anna laughed, weakly, thinking how typical of Linden to burst in, wake her in the middle of the night and then snap because she dare to ask the time.

'Well?' Linden said.

'Well what?' Anna yawned hugely.

'Oliver's nice, isn't he? Why the hell did you rush off?'

'I didn't exactly rush off.'

'It seemed as though you did.'

'Well, I had to see Pym,' Anna lied. 'Anyway, Oliver obviously thinks you're marvellous and I didn't want to sit there, gooseberrying!'

'Well, I wish you had stayed! You knew that I wanted you to stay!' Linden traced, with one finger, the pattern on the quilt. 'It's all a little awkward. I don't want Oliver to think I'm marvellous.'

'James?'

'Yes.'

'Why?'

'Because he's far more suitable. And he interests me. The way he is so controlled. He's terribly clever. Oliver talks about him a lot if encouraged, with a kind of resigned admiration and occasional bursts of fury. That house excited me. I looked for James's things. I pictured him in the kitchen. Oliver said that every evening when he gets in he makes himself a sandwich. Always ham. Isn't that odd? The same, every night. And then he baths and goes out to dinner with some woman or to friends or takes out some business people. Always the same. Just like a machine.' She fidgeted her hands together. 'I'd like to disrupt him. It would be a challenge. He seems hardly to notice me when he comes to see his mother, which is interesting in itself. He's so polite to me. Tonight, after you'd gone, I was busy thinking up things to say in case James came in. All the time Oliver was going on and on about this marvellous scheme he's involved in and how he will make a fortune and how James will be amazed, he was moving down the sofa towards me, ready to snuggle up and I was poised to make it all appear quite harmless if James came in. Anyway, I don't want to hurt Ollie . . .'

'I'm sure it's happened before,' Anna said dryly.

'But he's so . . . so unscheming. I went with him to the club he works at. That's why I am so late. We got there about eleven and he introduced me to the fellow who plays the drums and the other one. Double bass player. It's rather nice in a scruffy way. People sit at little tables and drink and there's a small dance floor. There's a girl who sings, too. A very pretty girl. Can't remember her name. A bounding bosom and big brown eyes. She sat on the piano. She has an incredible voice. Oliver thinks she'll be discovered soon. I must say, she did seem too good for the place. I stayed for about an hour and half and people came to talk to me but eventually I couldn't stand the smoke or the noise, so I wrote Ollie a note and gave it to the barman to give him and slipped out. I don't think he minded. He seemed to have sunk into a dream world, leaning over the piano, eyes half closed . . .' She sat up straight. 'He's a nice boy, Anna. He didn't pester me to sleep with him. He treated me as if I was too precious to be concerned with such an animal idea. Just a few gentle kisses.'

Anna rolled over violently, pulling the quilt up to her head. 'I'm tired.'

'All right,' Linden said comfortably, standing up and going to the door. 'But what I really woke you up to tell you was that I've persuaded Ollie to give a dinner party. I said I'd cook it if he provided the house and the food. And you're specially invited. Oliver insisted.'

'You mean you persuaded him!'

'No, really. He suggested it. He wants you to come because he has someone he wants you to meet.'

'And James, I suppose, will be there?'

'Of course! Anna, you must come . . . you must go out more.'

'I do go out!' Anna surged upright, voice furious. 'I go out with my friends from the Cannon! I don't want to come to your party.'

'Please come, Anna.' Linden's voice was suddenly very quiet, almost pathetic. 'Please be there. I want you to be there. It helps me. All this matters to me so much, Anna. I'm twenty-one. I must use what I have now. I really want him, Anna. I know you think I'm hard and pushing, but I'm realistic, that's all. I believe in picking a man for a lot of good reasons . . .' She gesticulated down the hall. 'She married for love!' For a moment her face was a blend of scorn and pity.

Searching Linden's face for some clever and totally false role, Anna could find, in the light from the passage, only a nervous honesty.

'I never thought anything worried you. You seem so sure.'

'I know I have potential. I can use people but that isn't to say I won't use them for their own good. I'm not going to waste myself. I need someone like James. I would be good for him. Please come.' She was very narrow in the doorway, like a small boy with her cropped head. 'Please?'

Anna sighed.

'Will you? Will you? Will you?' Like when they were children, Linden dancing round their father, spilling out a river of pleas and never refused.

'When is it? I might be busy.'

They laughed together, quite suddenly and at exactly the same second. The laughter grew, semi-hysterical, like a tickled child and it changed the night into a dark secret, something to be got up into. They went into the kitchen and Linden made cocoa and plans.

'You can have Oliver.'

'I don't want your cast-offs.' But Anna spoke amiably, letting herself go with Linden's dream. Her bare feet curled, protesting against the cold of the linoleum.

'He's not mine,' Linden said. 'I am nothing like the person he thinks I am. He'll realize that. There is a lot to Oliver . . . he won't be happy with someone like me.' She sat down opposite Anna, putting a mug in front of each of them. She shivered her shoulders and closed her hands, bare, ringless hands, round the warmth of the mug. 'Life waits to be stepped into, doesn't it, Anna? Think how it will be five years from now. I wonder what we'll be doing?'

'You, I imagine, will have got your way exactly. You'll be the rich and stunning Mrs James Carroll, guiding your husband into politics perhaps. And I shall be a famous painter. A recluse. Intriguing. Thin . . .'

Linden laughed. 'Skinny even?'

'Skinny.' Anna said the beautiful word with relish and then dipped her lips into the hot sweet cocoa. She thought wryly that it was good to be Linden's friend. If you did what she said, if you played her game, she could set your life shining and spinning.

CHAPTER SEVEN

Although it was the last thing she had expected, Anna found that she came to enjoy her afternoons at Peterstone Mews. Having somewhere definite to go at five o'clock rearranged her whole day and she would anticipate the time when she would pack up and go, at various stages of the morning and afternoon, and feel a pleasant excitement. This mural put an end, temporarily, to those evening pauses with Pym and Anna was glad of a break. For the moment he embarrassed her. She felt she had been absurdly open with him and he, in turn, had dismissed her at the first glimpse of Linden. She tried to avoid him. It made him laugh and he threw paper darts at her with messages written on them. She would crumple them, furiously, but later, when no one was looking, smooth them out and read them. *Forgive me, for I know not what it is that I am supposed to have done!* Or *I love you when you look angry and sulky, like a big red thundercloud!* Although he outwardly took little notice of Anna's withdrawal, there was a definite change in their relationship. Pym was working even harder than before, sensing the end of the year, the need to achieve something. He was more argumentative than ever.

The first afternoon that she went to the mews, the pockets of her duffle coat bulging and two large baskets weighing her down, Anna paused on the doorstep. She was unwilling to touch the immaculate brass knocker. Even out here, in the cobbled street that ran between the white houses with their big garage doors, she could hear Oliver playing. It was some lovely, embellished version of an old tune. She stood, frowning, until the name suddenly came into her head. *Stormy Weather,* she thought, listening while the music danced playfully around the melody and then settled down and became sombre, calm, so that she could imagine the girl Linden had spoken of, singing. Anna waited until the music paused before she knocked.

'Hallo, Anna,' he said, looking younger than ever in a T-shirt and patched blue jeans. 'I was just going to make some coffee

. . . would you like some? Or tea? I could make tea if you'd rather.'

'Coffee would be fine.' The room was unrecognizable, strewn with pieces of paper, music, magazines, newspapers, catalogues. Anna stepped carefully towards the kitchen.

'It's instant. Okay? I can't bother with the beans. James is always grinding them and mucking about but the end result tastes just the same to me. I don't really taste it at all: it's just a hot drink!'

'You wouldn't say that if you'd ever drunk the stuff which trickles out of the coffee machine at the Cannon. It has an evil, tinny sort of smell. It tastes as if the plastic cups have dissolved in it.'

Oliver laughed, looking at her with a gentle curiosity, as if surprised that she could make him laugh. 'Milk?'

'Yes and two sugar, please,' she said defiantly. And she took the striped mug and her baskets and made her way carefully up the spiral stairs.

In the bathroom she put her coffee on the window-sill and took off her coat. She leaned against the wall, wondering how to begin. At home, unworried, she had filled the bath with newspaper and started splashing paint on the wall. But here, she thought she should prepare a preliminary sketch, work out the colours first, prime the wall, check which paint would best resist the steam. Get real dust sheets. For a moment she was scared and she wished, passionately, that she had brought Pym.

The music began again downstairs. Two or three false starts and then it seemed to gather strength and confidence and run away on its own. It flowed up the stairs. Anna slid down, sitting cross-legged, her mind wandering, lulled by the music, her coffee and the mural forgotten. There was a pause and then he began something quite different, classical, slow and sad and built of oval sounds. She knew little about classical music and she had no idea of the composer but for nearly an hour she sat and listened, feeling utterly peaceful. It was obvious that Oliver had forgotten all about her. Occasionally, when he made a mistake, he would swear. He talked to himself quite frequently, encouraging or castigating or exploding with exasperation. 'No . . . no. Christ, that's hopeless!'

A particularly violent outburst stirred Anna from her trance and she got up, rather guiltily, and began to map out, in pencil on the white wall, the idea she had sketched out that morning in the coffee break. As she became engrossed, she became braver, suggesting with sweeping lines one tall mermaid at the front with curling tail. She worked, with the light on, for almost an hour, hearing but taking little notice of the door, of voices. Until the voices became raised and so angry they stopped her working . . .

'I know it's your money, Oliver, but I wish to God you'd talk to someone about this whole idea. Not necessarily to me. We know nothing about this man. Talk to your tax men. Or the solicitor. I know you've got a good legal document but what the hell use is that if this fellow Monroe goes bust? The whole business rests on his assumed knowledge. I know Father has made over thirty thousand pounds to you and it was readily realizable cash before you gave half of it to Monroe. What income will you get from him? Okay, so eventually you'll inherit a slice of the business but that will be in shares which may well have dropped in value and the family hasn't got that many shares anyway! Are you really telling me you will be able to live comfortably on what you earn playing the piano and what little unearned income is left after you've paid tax on it? What do you really know about this man Monroe?'

'He has worked for Granbury's. That should tell you something!'

'I don't doubt his knowledge. Used car salesmen have a lot of knowledge: it's the way they use it.'

'So what do you doubt, as you put it? My ability to manage my own life? Is that what you doubt? It's such a ridiculous word, James!'

James laughed. 'I'm sorry, Ollie. I don't mean to interfere. It's your life and your money but it's just that I can't help feeling money is my line and music is yours. I wish you'd let me go into the whole idea in detail. And I'd like to meet this man.' There was the sound of ice in a glass, of a drink being poured. Anna found it quite impossible not to listen. The voices filled the small house. 'Are you going to let me meet him soon or is he to be hidden until he's made you a millionaire?'

'You'll meet him at this party Linden's cooking. But I don't expect you will like him. In fact, I am sure you'll dislike him because he is an extrovert. He goes after what he wants in a totally different way from you, James.'

'I don't want to like the bloody man,' James snapped. 'I want to be able to trust him. And I don't want him to make a fool of you, Oliver.'

'Mind your own damn business. Or businesses!'

At this point, Anna very quietly closed the bathroom door. But perhaps they heard and remembered her. The voices dropped. In a little while the music began again. Thinking she had been in the house long enough, she gathered up her things and put on her coat. She went down the stairs as quietly as she could, murmuring good-bye to Oliver, hoping James wouldn't emerge from the kitchen, and escaped into the street.

It took her over a week to gather the courage to start painting. She primed the wall. She did a water-colour version to help her. She bought pots of paint and brushes and eventually, on the second Thursday, she began cautiously filling in flat areas of colour. As she worked she sang softly, letting her voice join in with songs she knew when Oliver played them, happy with these hours from five until seven. She was quite at home in the house now, answering the telephone if Oliver was out and writing notes in her neat handwriting on the pad by the telephone. James was never home before seven, usually arriving just as Anna left. Occasionally he arrived while she was still working and she would hear him go to the kitchen, make his sandwich, pour his drink.

Once he came up the stairs in a deliberate attempt to speak to her. Her first panicky terror of him was fading, although the fact that Linden could dare to want him underlined clearly in Anna's mind the gulf between Linden and herself. Anna decided he was not terrifying, he was merely reserved and he thought before he said anything. Not for James the remark, the spontaneous remark, which might be hilariously funny or acutely embarrassing. He thought first. Then he spoke. He gave the impression of being always preoccupied. He stood in the doorway of the bathroom and looked at the mural for a long time before he spoke. None of this, 'lovely, lovely,' while looking out of the window. He studied the mural, ate his sandwich, loosened his tie and said eventually, 'Why do you give equal importance to the figures and the background? Is it deliberate? You want that flatness, do you?'

His question was disconcerting. Anna thought and frowned. 'Yes, I think I do. I want it to work abstractly, in areas of colour and shape, regardless of the figures.'

'Why don't you finish one piece first? You seem to work all over.'

'I know . . . I'm not quite sure enough of what I want to finish one part at a time.'

James gave her his crooked smile. 'I like it very much. Will it be done in time for Oliver's dinner party? It appears to be a major social landmark! Terrible if the bathroom wasn't up to it!'

'I hope it will be finished . . . it should be. Although I'm enjoying it so much now I must be careful not to spin it out.' When she left that evening she felt sufficiently at ease with James to call good-bye to him.

The following afternoon, Anna could hardly wait to get back to it, to get on with the painting. She bustled through the living-room when Oliver let her in, refusing a coffee, taking the stairs two at a time. She threw her coat down and began to work at once. Oliver's music washed over her. She hummed happily. This place was almost like a second home to her now.

When the doorbell rang it pierced Oliver's music, Anna's concentration. She heard voices, a man's and a woman's and, wary after the last scene she had overheard, she closed the bathroom door. She worked steadily for an hour, growing more and more excited over the painting, until she realized she was tired and it must be nearly seven and they might want to bath. She washed her hands, and because it was Friday she felt she should tidy up. She folded the dust sheet and put it in the cupboard under the basin and then, with her coat and her baskets and a bag of wet brushes, she started slowly down the stairs.

To the people sitting below, as she slowly revealed herself, feet first, Anna must have looked very strange. Plimsoles, jeans frayed round the bottoms, a vast shirt over a polo-necked sweater. Her hair was bound out of the way with a scarf she had tied bandage-like round her forehead. Marietta Carroll had never needed to learn tact. When she was young, shyness had made her abrupt. Now, in her fifties, she no longer cared if her habit of speaking her mind was disconcerting.

'Good Lord, who are you?' she said.

Anna took in the two strangers, guessed they were Oliver's parents and did not want this meeting.

'Mother, this is Anna Hayward. Linden's sister. I told you she was doing a painting for us.'

'Linden's sister! Are you really the sister of my dainty little Linden?' Marietta laughed. She was sitting on the sofa, thin legs wound round one another, back straight. Her face was proud and rather appealing, Anna thought, hating her.

'Don't look so horrified. Was I very rude? I'm sorry, my dear. I was startled by you. This careless Oliver never told me there was anyone in the house!' She smiled, charmingly, waiting for a gracious response.

'It's quite all right. I'm used to surprising people,' Anna said, hurt and angry, looking from one to another. Oliver, intensely embarrassed. Marietta, amused. The other man, obviously Oliver's father, medium-sized and in his early sixties with a high, clever forehead.

'How do you do, Anna,' he said, taking control of the situation and filling the heavy silence. He held out his hand and Anna was obliged to put down her baskets, shake it. 'What a very talented family you are! My name is Robert Carroll. I'm Oliver's father. I'd very much like to see this mural.'

'Well, it's not finished, of course . . .'

'I realize that.' Deep voice, like James. He took cigarettes from his pocket and offered them to Anna before lighting one.

Marietta made an angry noise. 'Robert, you shouldn't!'

He winked at Anna and started up the stairs.

'Do have a drink, Anna,' Oliver said and it would have been so ungracious to refuse that she felt she had to accept. She asked for a sherry and sipped it politely while Marietta questioned her, but when she estimated that a decent interval had passed, when Robert Carroll had come carefully down the stairs and said he liked the mural and the sherry had been sipped away, Anna stood up and made an excuse and thankfully left. She had meant to ask Oliver if she should come in over the weekend. She didn't remember until she was almost home and she didn't want to telephone so she decided to leave it until Monday.

On the Monday afternoon, Oliver started apologizing as

soon as Anna let herself in. 'Anna, I'm so sorry about the other night. About my mother.' His voice was shy. 'She is often like that. It drives me mad, her tactlessness . . . and she cross-examines! James does it too. They like to know all the facts about a person. It never occurs to them that they sound extremely rude.'

'It really doesn't matter. I should have coughed before I came down or stamped my feet. I am often too quiet . . . Linden says I sneak about but I don't do it consciously. I think it's just that I hate drawing attention to myself. And I was concentrating so hard upstairs . . . I was listening to your music.'

'Talk about a captive audience! Do you like what you hear?'

'I know nothing about music. Real music, that is. It is alien to my family. Linden and I buy pop stuff sometimes, I love Joni Mitchell. But yours is quite different. It surrounds me, like a cloud of sound and it's so alive. I'm beginning to think I should always paint to music.' She stopped, pushing back her hair, afraid that she sounded too intense. 'Except that you keep saying "Sod it" and "Bugger" when you go wrong. That's a bit of a let-down.'

Oliver threw back his head and laughed, delightedly. 'God. Do I? I had no idea.' There was a small pause and Anna got the impression he would have liked to touch her in some way to express his relief and his laughter. But he became shy again. 'Anna, come and have a coffee. I've bought you something as a peace offering. I notice you often come with a brown paper bag. Look, doughnuts, as an apology for my terrible mother!'

'I love doughnuts,' she said quietly. 'Thank you very much.'

He shrugged. 'Listen, I won't be around for a few afternoons. We'll be rehearsing at the club. And Linden rang and said she'd come in one afternoon to talk about the party, so when you see her, ask her to come Friday, will you? I'll definitely be in then.'

Three quiet afternoons, letting herself into the deserted house, liking the feel of the place. And on each afternoon there was an offering for Anna in the kitchen on a plate. An éclair, a piece of cheese-cake, a flapjack. She could not resist them although, as she ate them, she realized with surprise that she had not been buying so much for herself recently. She worked in the bathroom, watching, almost with awe, the way the mural grew. It seemed to have a mind of its own now. It was coming so right. It was going to be far the best thing she had ever done!

On Friday, Oliver was there again, looking up as she let herself in and smiling. 'Hallo, Anna. I was hoping you'd come soon. It feels like tea-break time!'

'I'd like a coffee but, Oliver, you shouldn't buy these cakes for me.'

'Don't you like them?' He looked very concerned. 'Linden said you were always eating cakes. I thought . . .'

Anna took off her coat. 'She was being nasty about how fat I am! Oliver,' she explained patiently, 'Linden can be nasty, you know, however angelic she looks.'

'She doesn't look angelic. She looks absolutely beautiful! Her face is far too alive to be angelic . . . and a few doughnuts aren't going to make a lot of difference, are they?' He seemed hurt out of all proportion to the incident.

'No, they're not,' Anna admitted unhappily. 'And I do enjoy them, Ollie. I just wish I didn't!'

The doorbell rang. It was Linden, springing in when Oliver opened the door. 'God, it's cold!'

'Is it?' Oliver's face lit up when he saw her. He closed the door and leaned on it as if he would like to keep her in his house for ever.

'Bitter . . . Hallo, Anna. Eating again, I see!' She took off her hat and coat. 'I've really come to ask about this party, Oliver. How many people and what shall we feed them on? You know it's a week today? I had a good idea about using turkey, before everyone is sick of it. I tried out a recipe last week. A fricassé, with cream and wine.'

'Sounds delicious. I really don't mind. There are ten people coming.' He looked at Anna. 'You are included. You will come, won't you, Anna? I particularly want you to meet a friend of mine. The man I'm in business with. He is in the art world too!'

'A year and a term at art school and two bathroom walls haven't really dented the art world yet, Oliver. He may not have heard of me!'

'But you will come?' Oliver insisted, smiling.

'All right.'

'You are so gracious!' Linden said. 'Am I allowed to look at it?'

'If you want.'

'I like watching it grow.' Oliver sat down. 'It's like a serial, the way it changes every day. I'm sorry that a weekend is about to happen! Two boring days of baths with nothing new to see!'

Linden paused at the bottom of the stairs. 'Why don't you go home on Sunday? Your mother is expecting you. I've been making an enormous steak and kidney pie for her to take home. Apparently your Mrs McKay has flu.'

'I have to work Saturday night ... maybe I'll go Sunday morning. I don't know.' His voice said he did not like Linden in league with his mother.

'Is James going?' Linden asked vaguely. 'Does he go most weekends?'

'Yes. He says he likes to unwind but he can only stand the quiet for two days at a time. James thrives in London. The pace suits him.'

'Your mother says he works extremely hard.'

'Like a robot! A brilliant robot. Since he became managing director just over two years ago C.C. has flourished. The Kingston factory has doubled in size. They've brought out this whole range of men's cosmetics, whatever they are! Bath oils. Aftershaves. Pre-shaves. In between shaves. A little factory in France.' Oliver got up and strode to the fridge, taking out a beer and drinking from the triangular hole on the top of the can. 'Do either of you want a drink?'

'No, thank you,' Linden said, for both of them. 'He must have been very young when he was made managing director.'

'Yes. I suppose he was. But he's always seemed old to me. Five years is a big gap. James had always perfected everything before I had had a chance to learn the basic rules.' Oliver's voice took on a reluctant pride. 'He does the job bloody well!'

'Couldn't you?' Linden asked. 'If you bothered?'

'No, I don't think I could. Anyway, I have no desire to. I'm happy with my life as it is.'

For the last three days, Anna worked desperately hard to finish the mural. It was a good thing, she told herself, to have a deadline. She painted the detail of faces, neatened edges, softened the sky. And on the day before Oliver's party, she stood back and wiped her hands on her painting shirt and decided it was finished. She climbed out of the bath, went into the passage and then walked back into the bathroom, trying to see the mural as if for the first time. However hard she looked for fault, it filled her with a deep satisfaction and pride. And she needed, very badly, to show it to someone whose opinion she valued and that meant Pym.

Anna was alone in the house. Ignoring the coolness with which she had treated Pym over the past few weeks, she went into Oliver's bedroom and rang the Cannon. Someone passing the phone box in the hall said they would try and find him. Anna waited, listening to the sounds of feet, people calling and laughing, little jigsaw pieces of conversation as they passed the waiting telephone. At last Pym's voice.

'Hallo?'

'Pym? It's me. Anna.'

'Hallo, Anna. What's wrong?'

'Nothing. Nothing's wrong. Are you busy?'

'No. At this particular moment I'm on the phone.'

'You know what I mean. Will you come and see my mural? I want you to see it, just once. I'm so pleased with it. Can you come now?'

'Yes, I'll come!' He filled his voice with mock resignation. 'But where are you?'

'Twenty-seven Peterstone Mews. Off Queens Gate. Will you miss evening class?' she asked.

'For you, Anna, anything!'

'Quite a place,' he said, when Anna let him in about twenty minutes later. He wiped his feet on the doormat with exaggerated care. 'Your boy-friend's pad?'

'Not mine. Linden's. Do you want to take off your coat?' She felt suddenly shy with Pym and he sensed it and teased her, handing his coat to her in solemn silence, standing, hands together.

'It's upstairs,' Anna said. 'And listen, Pym, if you don't like it, don't go on about it. Don't elaborate on the faults.'

Laughing, he followed her. 'I see . . . just drop everything and come round and look at my painting and give your opinion but be sure it's a good opinion.'

'It's in there.' She hovered outside the bathroom door while he went in. For a few moments he said nothing. Then he looked over his shoulder at her. 'Not bad at all. In fact, it's about the best thing you've done. Very brave for you. Very confident. Except that rock at the front. Couldn't you make it softer? More speckly. Like a bird's egg?'

As he said it, she knew he was right. She went past him and picked up a brush.

'You've worked hard on this, haven't you?' Pym stood in the doorway. 'You ought to bring Bony to see it.'

The doorbell rang, interrupting him.

'I'll get it.' Pym leaped down the spiral stairs and crossed the ground-floor room. He swung the door inwards . . . Linden was on the doorstep, a large brown paper bag in her arms, the Mini behind her with boot and doors open as if it had exploded.

'Hallo.' She smiled, apparently quite unperturbed to find him here.

She was the last person in the world he had expected to see but the only person who could have silenced him. He stood absolutely still, blocking the doorway, smiling at her, and then he took the bag from her. He put it on the kitchen table and went to the car where Linden was struggling to remove a cardboard box from the tiny boot.

'It's terribly heavy . . . it's got the turkey in, amongst other things.' She moved aside to let him lift it. 'Can you manage? Oh, thank you. I'll bring the rest.' She slammed the car doors and followed him into the house. Putting the box down on the now crowded kitchen table, Pym watched her come across the room, seeing in this better light that she really was as lovely as he had thought before. His eyes settled on her face. Still he hadn't spoken.

'That's the lot. Thank you . . . Pym.' A fractional pause before she said his name, as if she had to think to remember it.

'I came to see Anna's mural,' he said.

She nodded, rather surprised by the effect he was having on her, making her feel nervous. She was seldom nervous. She forced herself to be deliberately bright, busy. 'Let's have some coffee. I'm sure Ollie won't mind our helping ourselves. I'm cooking this dinner for him tomorrow and I thought I'd try and get most of it organized tonight. But of course you don't know Ollie, do you? Is Anna upstairs? Is it good, her thing?'

Ignoring all previous questions he said, 'Come and see it before you do anything else. Come and show some interest for a change!' and he caught hold of her wrist and pulled her gently towards the stairs. The contact surprised them both. A shock wave, as if their bodies were already well aware of an attraction their minds chose to ignore. Linden pulled her hand away sharply and went ahead of him up the stairs.

Anna was washing brushes. She turned when she heard them and as Linden came in and Pym leaned in the doorway, Anna clearly felt the tension between them. Linden studied the mural. 'You're extraordinarily good, aren't you?' she said with surprise in her voice.

Anna shrugged but she loved the praise.

In the kitchen they sat and drank coffee and Linden talked a great deal. Pym was unusually silent, stirring his coffee and watching the swirling patterns his spoon made. He would look up at Linden, down to the cup again. When he finally began to drink his coffee he found it unpleasantly cool.

'Must check through this list before I begin . . . Butter, flour, white wine for cooking, parsley, mushrooms, lettuce.'

'I think I must go now,' he interrupted her, got off his stool.

'Shall I run you back?' Anna asked.

He shook his head. 'I rather like taking my time. I'll see you tomorrow, Anna.' He tugged her hair affectionately. 'I'm proud of you. Your mural's great!' He tucked his hand into the pockets of his old canvas jacket, lowering his head a little and looking at Linden from the top of his slanted eyes. 'Good-bye, Linden.'

' 'Bye,' she said, her voice deliberately vague. But her eyes followed him and rested on the door after he had gone.

CHAPTER EIGHT

The following evening, Linden came into Anna's room just after 6.30. She was wearing a long velvet pinafore dress and a white silk shirt and she fiddled with the cuffs, turning them up and down, occupying the space in front of Anna's long mirror as she leaned forward to check her eye make-up.

'What are you going to wear?' she asked Anna, without taking her eyes from the reflection of her own face. She stood back a little and lifted the dress to examine her shoes, turned and looked over her shoulder at her back view. Anna had never seen Linden so unsure of her appearance. Watching her, Anna decided she had never before seen Linden demonstrate any hesitation over clothes at all. Did this evening matter so much? To Anna it was just another ordeal in the long series of things that had to be lived through.

'I shall wear my black dress, of course!' Anna said. It had been an unnecessary question of Linden's as Anna had only the one thing to wear in the evening. Her uniform, the way a sweater and jeans were her uniform for the day. The black dress was a long, tent-like garment. It was made of a light jersey, embroidered round the neck and cuffs and hem. At the moment it hung against her wall on a wire hanger looking like a great black parachute.

At last Linden seemed satisfied with herself. She turned her scrutiny to Anna who sat on her bed in her pants and bra, trying vainly to do something about her nails.

Anna hated Linden's stare and she gave up her nails and climbed into the black dress. She was, definitely, a little thinner. The dress reminded Linden of a drying umbrella but she said nothing. She had decided on a new campaign to boost Anna's confidence.

Veronica came and leaned in the open door and Anna looked at the two faces and was catapulted back six years...

She had been thirteen. She and Linden had been asked to some party and Anna was hiding upstairs, the dread pulsing through her like pain. The door had opened and she had looked up to see Veronica. Her mother's face had worn, then, the expression it held now, all these years later. A blend of bewilderment and pity.

'What is it, Anna? Don't you want to go? Why aren't you ready?'

'I am ready but I don't want to go.'

'But you're wearing white socks . . . you can't go to a party at your age in white socks! We bought you some tights when we bought the new shoes, didn't we? Why are you crying? Your eyes will go red and puffy.'

Veronica was never angry. Just impatient. No time for Anna. No time to unravel. Anna's plainness distressed her so. Her children were dolls to her. Girl dolls to dress and watch and encourage. Only Anna couldn't and wouldn't. Anna could not form words in her brain to make the explanation. She still couldn't have said if allowed, 'Give me more time. Don't make me go and compete and fail again. Don't make me wear these shoes so that I am taller than anyone else and this dress I bulge out of. No one will dance with me . . .' But of course she had gone, as she would go now. She had gone and stood in an awkward row until girls on either side of her were claimed. And when it seemed that everyone else was talking or dancing she had gone upstairs, slowly and with dignity, and hidden in a bedroom, counting the china horses on the mantelpiece until it was time to go home.

'We really must get you a new dress, now that you're a little thinner,' Veronica said, slurring the words slightly. 'Something more . . . more . . . and your hair, Anna. Couldn't you do something with it? On top of that dress you look like a . . . like . . .' She began to laugh, at first quietly and then doubling over with the laughter. 'Like a marquee!'

It was Linden who flushed. 'I like that dress,' she snapped, and she pulled at Anna's arm. 'Come on, Anna . . . Night, Mum!' She swept Anna down the passage and Veronica's laughter followed them. 'She's drunk!'

'She doesn't know what it's like to go shopping,' Anna said, between tight lips, taking her coat from the hook and following Linden out of the flat. 'Dragging from shop to shop. The sneering, pitying faces of girls who serve you, secure little tens and twelves and fourteens, watching while I struggle to cram myself into a eighteen. Staring as if I come from outer space. I hate the communal changing rooms, full of little, skinny girls, all flat and bra-less, while I hunch my shoulders to try and hide my huge bosom!'

They ran through the hall and out to the car. Linden slammed her door, starting the engine as Anna climbed into the passenger side. 'For God's sake, don't get in a state about it now . . . just keep on dieting if you mind so much!' She pulled out into Melbury Road. 'Anyway, your bosom's the best bit of you. If you like that sort of thing, and a lot of men do. . .'

'Maybe it's all right out of clothes but crammed inside a dress or a sweater it turns into a bolster. No waist. No shape. It's so unfair!'

'Stop it!' Linden almost shouted, rounding on Anna.

Anna shrank back, startled.

'You look very nice. Now stop all the drama. . .' Suddenly she smiled. 'That's my role, the drama, isn't it? Can't have two of us at it! And this car is completely out of petrol. Why don't you ever put any in?' She swung into the Blue Star garage and smiled appealing out of the window. 'Two gallons, please, two star. And we're in a terrible hurry.'

'I never put any petrol in because I never get to use the car,' Anna said flatly but she felt better. The outburst had driven her nervousness away. It was as if she only had a certain amount of fear in her and this evening's ration had just been spent.

James opened the door, immaculate in a velvet jacket. 'Good evening.' He stood aside to let them pass with a slight flourish, like a conjuror, Anna thought. In fact she felt like a conjuror's rabbit, suddenly pulled from the safety and peace of a top hat, bewildered and blinking.

The room looked very tidy. Linden had come in earlier and laid the table and arranged flowers. Glasses and decanters and bottles on a trolley. The whole place perfectly organized, immaculate and yet lacking something. *Perhaps*, Anna thought, *it is because there are no bits and pieces. Everything was bought at one time, to match everything else. There are none of the accidents which make a room beautiful. Or is it just that I prefer it with*

Oliver's litter everywhere?'

Linden swung smoothly into action, tying on a big white apron and not betraying the slightest hint of the tension she was feeling.

'What can I get you to drink, Linden?' James leaned into the kitchen.

'I'd like a whisky, please. Lots of ice and water.' She loved the way he said her name, emphasizing the first syllable but it disturbed her that he did not watch her more. She was used to their eyes. 'Is Oliver here?'

'Just! He got back ten minutes ago . . . And Anna? What will you drink?'

'Gin and tonic, please.' She stood awkwardly, holding the drink which James gave her, and sipping it occasionally. James positioned himself between the two of them, rather like a referee at a tennis match, turning his head to speak to them in turn. Anna found his good manners made her formal in return but she no longer found him frightening.

'Your mural is a great success,' he said. 'I must admit I was rather doubtful in the beginning but Ollie does have a knack about these things . . . It makes the room! Having no artistic sense at all, I find it amazing that you know what colour to put next to what. That big blonde mermaid is fascinating!'

Anna murmured, always uneasy when praised. It was obvious to her that James was going to try and make this evening a success for Oliver. She thought: *Why does he have to make it so obvious he is trying?* She wondered whether to go and help Linden or keep out of the way. Usually Linden hated help – she called it interference, and James was in the kitchen now, leaning against the room divider, head bent as he talked to Linden. Anna didn't want to spoil anything!

From upstairs came muffled swearing. Then Oliver's voice. 'James, can I borrow a shirt?'

'Yes, if you must,' James called back. 'Why the hell don't you put yours out for Mrs Baker? You're here all day.'

'I'm asleep when she comes!'

When he came running down the stairs, Oliver looked freshly scrubbed, his hair still wet. He acknowledged Anna with a smile and went into the kitchen to see Linden. When he reappeared, he poured himself a large whisky and scooped a

cigarette from the box by Anna. 'I thought I'd never get away
. . . there's a visiting quartet this week, luckily, hence the time
off, but we had to rehearse for next Tuesday. And then my car
played up. I'm going to sell it and get something small and reliable.'

'Like our Mini!' Linden emerged, slightly flushed from the
heat of the kitchen, starting her sentence at Oliver but turning
her eyes to James half way through. 'It's very old but it never
breaks down. The only time it stops is when Anna forgets to put
petrol in it!'

Anna said nothing. She was quite used to being featured in
Linden's conversation in this way. The talk turned to cars, to
James's Aston Martin and Oliver's jeep, and as Oliver's friends
began to arrive they were drawn in too. They all seemed to care
passionately about their cars . . . A couple called Tom and
Lizzie raved about their Peugeot; a man with corrugated hair,
who stood very straight and was a stockbroker, drove an NSU; a
bony girl with great giraffe eyes rode a motor bike. Another
girl, rounder, blonde, sexier, chattier: Annabel. Her brother
John. Both owned Minis.

'And Anna is a painter,' Oliver said suddenly, bored with
talk of cars. 'You must all come and see the bathroom and if you
like it, perhaps you can put your names down on her waiting
list!' He smiled at Anna apologetically. He led the way upstairs
and they trooped after him. Linden went back to the kitchen
and James followed her to refill the ice bucket.

Anna, sitting alone and rather uncomfortably on the arm of
the sofa, sighed very quietly. Just a long breath, really. She felt
she had nothing in common with these people. She knew no one
they knew. She didn't know how to talk to them and she didn't
want to talk much. She had thought better of Oliver; that he
might have invited some people from his club . . . but of course
this entire evening was arranged merely to satisfy Linden. He
probably asked the first people who came into his head. The
guests were necessary, like furniture!

The doorbell rang. One long, important peal and two small
rings. Anna looked round. No one appeared to take any notice
so she got up and went to the door. When she saw the man on
the step she made a small, startled sound.

He came in, frowning as he saw her, and Anna closed the

door and registered again this absurd fear which he started in her. She said nothing. He would not have remembered.

'The Cannon,' he said, snapping his fingers, pleased. 'The girl with the red hair and the urgent question, jumping up and down, and when I said, "What is it?" you said, "Nothing" or "Go home" or some similar put-down!' He laughed, taking off his coat. 'What's your name?'

'Anna.'

'Hallo, Freddie!' Oliver led his troup down the spiral stairs like the Pied Piper and the empty room was suddenly crowded. 'This is Freddie Monroe.' Oliver introduced him proudly, rather touchingly, as a child might introduce an older friend. They drew round Freddie in a loose circle, curious. He was something new.

'You have some clever scheme for making money out of pots?'

'No, pots of money!'

'Are you going to make Ollie rich?'

'Ollie can't do real work!'

And James came forward, sliding between them with the whisky Freddie had asked for. 'I'm James . . . Oliver's brother. I've been looking forward to meeting you.'

Freddie smiled. 'I'm flattered.' The two men measured each other. In this room of upper-class voices, Freddie's accent had become more marked, as if he needed to show his difference and his strength.

'I'm very eager to hear about your investment scheme. Oliver is rather vague about the details.'

Freddie raised an eyebrow. 'Really? Perhaps . . . Look, would you rather I didn't discuss it, Oliver?'

'No, of course not,' Oliver said unhappily.

'Well, what exactly do you do?' Lizzie was asking.

'We buy antique porcelain for clients. And sell it.'

'Isn't it a little more complicated than that?' James said.

'A little.'

There was the distinct trace of tension in the room, laughter a little false. Feeling it, intrigued by it, watching James and Freddie backing, mentally, into their respective corners and Oliver taking the role of unwilling referee, Anna was glad for the first time that she had come. And while they all waited for

Freddie to elaborate, he suddenly turned, detaching himself from the group and approaching Anna, where she sat on the arm of the sofa. He took her hand and kissed it. 'Life is full of co-incidence . . .'

'I'm amazed that you remember me.'

'You stood out. That's one of life's great arts, to stand out. In a sea of ordinary restrained faces there was yours. Bursting to speak. As if you had a mouthful. And then you froze on me.'

'I was scared.'

'I know you were.' His round brown eyes, exactly the colour of his hair, Anna noticed, held her as they had in that lecture. 'How do you know these people?'

'I was going to ask you . . .'

'Why? Are you surprised that a man of my obviously humble background should be here?'

'I don't think there is anything humble about you!' She felt cornered by him. The fear made her honest, made her voice matter-of-fact. 'Anyway, you are utterly at home here. Far more than I am.' This man's presence changed her, woke her. She dragged her eyes away and scanned the room, wondering if the other women felt it. Or was it just herself? Intercepting curious glances, she knew the others did feel it too.

'It's far more of a coincidence than you know. Do you remember how late I was for that lecture at the Cannon? Leaving poor old Richard to waffle on while you waited for me?' He leaned against the wall, looking down at her as she sat so uncomfortably on the sofa arm. 'You don't look any smaller sitting down, you know. You just look uncomfortable!' Anna flushed, but she stayed where she was. 'Do you know what had made me so late? I'd been here, seeing Ollie. I'd found us some ideal premises. We have been operating from my flat and it is awkward.' He took a cigarette from his packet and then put it on the mantelpiece. 'This new place is perfect.' He inhaled smoke and raised his voice. 'I meant to tell you, Oliver. We're all signed and sealed. Possession before Christmas.'

Watching Freddie intently, Anna saw the way his fingers moved against the mantelpiece, drumming a restless pattern. The way he stood, the way he held his glass and spoke and his expression all demonstrated supreme relaxation and confidence. *But he is nervous*, she realized with deep surprise. *How can a man, who can command the attention of two hundred students for two hours, be nervous of anything? This must matter very much to him for some reason.* As she looked up, thinking this, he looked down at her and a violent feeling shook her. It was quite new to her. A form of recognition, brushing aside the slow and painful first stages of conversation. She felt she knew him.

'Where is this shop?' James had strolled over, outwardly friendly.

'Brook Street. It's a perfect area from our point of view. Discreetly impressive. Four floors. A big basement store-room, ground-floor showroom, a first floor with a kitchen and a room I shall use as an office. Up top are a couple of bedrooms and a bathroom. I shall live there, I think. The lease on my present flat expires at the end of the year and it never hurts to live over the shop!'

'The rates must be enormous in that area!'

Oliver had been hovering. Now he broke in. 'Of course they are. But we're dealing with large sums of money. We can't sell the kind of thing Freddie knows about from a stall in the Portobello Road!'

James smiled with his lop-sided mouth. 'Yes. Well, it's because the sums of money are so large that I'm so curious! I understand you've . . . left Granbury's?'

'Yes. I had thought of staying, on a part-time basis, to help them out, but I just can't make the time any more. The response to our idea has been extraordinary. . . . Another thing, Ollie. I've written to your cousin as you suggested.'

James looked surprised. 'Which cousin?'

'Carlos Stephano,' Oliver said. 'You probably don't know, as you aren't interested in these things, but he is quite a well-known collector! In fact –' Oliver laughed to the room in general – 'my parents met when my father went to see his collection and my mother was staying in his house! Carlos has been a collector since the 'thirties and I thought he might want to enlarge his collection, or take advantage of the prices, and the demand, and sell.'

It irritated James unbearably to hear Oliver talk like this, like a parrot, he thought, uttering lines learned off by heart. 'I don't think it's a good idea to involve any more of the family!'

'Are you all ready for dinner?' Linden's voice, firm and clear, cut into the triangle of the three men, broke it. She put the last two bowls of vichysoisse soup on the table and lit the candles. 'Because I'm ready for you!'

Freddie raised an eyebrow at James's retreating back. 'The tycoon doesn't seem to like me. Or trust me.'

'It's not you,' Oliver said, his voice low and angry. 'It is simply because I am involved. James has a deep-rooted suspicion of my common sense!'

Impulsively, Anna reached out and touched Oliver's hand, hating to see it all go wrong for him. He gave her a brief smile.

'Don't worry. He'll get used to the idea,' Freddie said calmly.

For a moment both Oliver and Anna looked at Freddie, trusting his confidence, taking strength from him.

The table had a white cloth, silver candlesticks, flowers in the centre in a low bowl. Linden sat between Oliver and James. She had turned off the lamps as the ten of them drew round the table and sat down, drawing themselves closer into the area of candlelight, quiet for a moment in the primitive way people fall silent before they eat. Linden often felt they were subconsciously missing the saying of grace. Then the ritual silence passed and they fidgeted and shook out table napkins and looked up, pretending to be pleasantly surprised when James filled their glasses with white wine.

'Now,' Freddie said to Anna, 'tell me the rest of your name and how you come to be here.' He relaxed into his chair and winked at her as he spread his table napkin on his lap.

'Hayward. Anna Hayward.'

'You don't seem to fit in.' He made it a definite compliment.

'Linden is my sister . . . she works for Oliver's mother. I think they asked me because Linden suggested it.'

Freddie's eyes moved from Anna to Linden, paused and came back to Anna. 'Yes, I imagine people do go out of their way to please her. No one would believe you are sisters!'

Few people, except Marietta Carroll, had said it so bluntly.

Anna had the answer ready, the careless answer to cover the hurt. 'Linden is older. She took the best bits.'

'You mind a lot, don't you?' he said, frowning. Somehow, it seemed to Anna, he had closed the room off, isolated the two of them. 'You must be very young. The world only needs so much window-dressing. I'll tell you a secret, Anna. Most people are incapable of forming an opinion about new people they meet. Hand them a character, something credible, something they want, and they'll think of you like that for ever more!' He hunched his shoulders as if he were tired.

'Why don't you eat something?' Anna asked him.

He looked down at the bowl of soup and smiled. 'I forgot. We have to pretend to be here to eat, don't we?'

'Yes. Do you often forget to eat?'

'Yes.'

She laughed. 'I just can't imagine being like that. I live from one meal to the next snack . . . food is everything to me!' It surprised her that she could talk to him so easily. Somehow he had broken through the barrier in her which interfered between thought and speech.

'You are like Oliver. You remind me of Oliver a few months ago, when I started to make him think about being successful. I had to bully him a little into doing himself, and me, a huge favour. It's hard for Oliver to think of himself as anything but a bumbling failure but one day – ' and Freddie's voice dropped – 'one day he'll be able to tell that bastard James where to get off.'

'You're going to sell the stuff you talked to us about?'

'Yes. In a city cluttered with pretentious rubbish and Victorian bric à brac we are specialists. We sell knowledge. At the moment antiques and antique porcelain in particular are a good investment.' He paused, seeing that Anna stared in fascination at his untouched soup. He smiled and took a mouthful. 'I see you are determined I shall not make a social exhibition of myself.'

'How did you meet Oliver?'

'I went to Pyecomb to value his father's collection!' For a moment Freddie was silent. 'The odd thing is, in a roundabout way, it's all due to your sister that Ollie and I met. She started it all . . . well, that's not absolutely true. It really began in Japan in 'sixty-nine. But you've heard it all before!'

'I haven't,' James said, across the table. 'And I'd be most interested to hear about it.'

Freddie shrugged. 'In that case I had better give my lecture again. I could have brought the slides if I'd known . . . I was just saying that in nineteen sixty-nine Japan relaxed her exchange controls. The Japanese have always had cultural links with

China and Chinese art, especially ceramics, have always been highly valued. When the controls were relaxed, a few Japanese dealers began buying porcelain in London at what they considered to be rock-bottom prices. Word got around. Now, perhaps eighty per cent of a sale will go to Japan. Everyone is bringing forward pieces to sell. Values are going up and up and a few of us realized the investment opportunities. We aren't the only ones, you know. But we are the most organized, I hope!'

'So you have the knowledge and Oliver supplies the odd contact and the. . . .' said James.

'The money,' Freddie interrupted James bluntly. 'And with Brook Street we shall have a good façade and somewhere for people who are thinking of the idea to come and look and talk. So if any of you are bored with your shares. . . .'

There was laughter all round the table. Beside her, Anna felt Freddie relax as they laughed. He finished his soup and sat back a little. He was not sure how to approach James and it bothered him. He discarded the idea of assuming humility, appealing for advice. Too late for that. Perhaps total disinterest in James was the best course? He began to talk to Annabel on his other side.

Linden rose and gathered soup bowls and after a moment's hesitation, Anna got up to help her. In the kitchen Linden had salad in two large wooden bowls, rice and her turkey fricassé in the oven; a dish of sautéed mushrooms with almonds and parsley. As she put the food on to the plates, Anna took them to the table and distributed them. Oliver circled, filling glasses, and for a while there was another of the ritual pauses. Not until everyone was seated again did the conversation start. The talk was general and good-natured. There was laughter and admiration for the food.

Linden was beautiful in the candlelight. It caressed her face, giving her a dignity and perfection she would assume at twenty-five or twenty-six. She could feel her beauty in the way the others looked at her. She was satisfied with this evening she had created and she was enjoying herself because she intended to be happy. She tried to be happy all the time. Sometimes it was hard work but she found that, normally, once she took the initiative, people would respond to her mood. She loved to feel them respond. Men *and* women. To feel her charm affect them and change them. She had learned her art as a small child, realizing that as she made people smile, made them happy, she received adoration in return. It disturbed her if people were restless and unhappy. That was why she could never forgive her father. He had shaken things and untidied their world and made it, if only temporarily, a sad and ugly place. It was better now, apart from Veronica's 'lapses', but still Anna was . . . Linden looked at her sister. Anna nagged at her so. *Look at her now, lost in herself, all wrapped up in her fear and her fat. What does she think about? Why doesn't she try and talk to them, feel them out, dip into them? Is it Pym she wants?*

A small, quite unexpected spurt of fear touched Linden. She didn't want to think about him. Anna was welcome to him . . . And then she looked at her sister again and was surprised to see Anna laughing, head tilted back, as if woken from a sleep. Anna laughing with Freddie Monroe!

Linden jumped as she realized James had spoken to her.

'I'm sorry, James. I was just taking stock.' She knew that her trick of speaking her thoughts appealed to people, flattering them as if she were entrusting them with secrets. 'I was just being satisfied with it all. Self-satisfied, I suppose!' She gave him a little smile.

'I was asking how old you are, Linden?'

'Twenty-one.'

'That's what I thought my mother said. So where did you learn your self-possession?'

'I was born calm.' She had a trick of parting her lips, at first in the centre and then letting her mouth widen into a slow smile which made James sit forward.

'And yet you don't seem dulled, as so many girls in London are. Tired of everything. Bored!'

He had never spoken personally to her in the odd times they had found themselves alone in his parents' flat. Strange, she thought, that here, surrounded by people, he should begin it. 'Well, I've only been in London just over a year. I think it has a lot to do with your basic personality. I am quite determined to be happy.'

'Can it be arranged like that? Forced like that?'

'I think so. It is important to have plans, to have routines.'

'If I take you to dinner somewhere, quieter than this, will you outline your entire strategy for me? I think, perhaps, we could learn something from you at C.C.'

She laughed, eyes dancing. 'Worker-contentment, you mean? The Linden Hayward Thesis for life!'

'Well, it seems to do amazing things for you,' James said quietly.

'This food is delicious,' Freddie deliberately broke in. 'But I am sorry to say, Linden, that having achieved perfection, you have nowhere to go but down!'

She hesitated, reading correctly the traces of an insult in his tone and wondering why. Did he think she belonged with James? 'Oh, I have a long way to go yet!' She tilted back her head and laughed. She held all their attention.

James, used to evaluating people and situations through the opinions of others around him before taking a decision, looked at the expressions on the faces of the people round this table. They were all warm, admiring, enchanted.

All except Freddie. 'Have you ever played the childish, but revealing, game, Linden, where each person is compared, by others who know him or her, to a bird?'

'Yes. We played it as *very* small children. And I know you are longing to tell me what I am. What am I, Freddie?'

He sat back in his chair. 'A hawk. A small one. A kestrel!'

'And you, Freddie, are a jackdaw!'

'No. An owl!' Lizzie said. 'And Oliver is an ostrich or a robin or a duck.'

'And Tom and Lizzie are a pair of turtle doves!'

'And Anna?'

'A penguin.'

'A pigeon.'

'No, no,' Freddie said, genuinely laughing for the first time, gathering all their attention with his rich voice. 'Anna is still an egg!' His eyes held her, slowing and stilling her as the laughter rolled round the table. Warmth between them, deep and frightening warmth which Anna had never felt before. Very quietly he said, 'Egg, come for a drink when this rigmarole is over, will you?' and didn't wait for an answer, taking her acceptance from her face.

From that point on Freddie dominated the table, swinging into his role as funny man and winning them all against their wills. The evening reached a plateau. There was peace and the wine made them more interested, more interesting. Conversations became intense and quieter. Linden produced oranges in a caramel sauce, a chocolate mousse, Brie and Camembert.

And later, when she put a tray of coffee on the low glass table and James began assembling brandy glasses, they all left the table and moved back to sit on the sofa and chairs and on the floor. There was smoke in the room. Oliver sat down at the piano and began to play unobtrusively until he was lost in the music and forgot them all, even Linden. And Freddie came and sat down by James, taking the initiative, and they talked intently and coldly, digging out the foundations of a deep and lasting distrust.

When she wasn't looking at Freddie, Anna watched Oliver, and listened to his music, thinking that his face was sad when he wasn't making an effort to talk to people.

Linden came across to Anna, bending her head and saying quietly, 'I'm going upstairs for a moment . . .' It was a command and Anna rose obediently and followed. Linden went into James's bedroom and when Anna came in, half-closed the door.

She moved up to the square mirror, looking at herself, talking to Anna from the looking-glass. 'He has noticed me. He wants me to have dinner with him. He is so solemn, it fascinates me. He says he must square it with Ollie first. 'She wrapped her arms round herself, turning to Anna. 'I love the layers of it all, the intricacies. . . .'

'Pym says it is trivial. He says we have trivial, tiny dreams about who we will go out with and hold hands with and sleep with!'

'Well, Pym is absolutely wrong! Life is a game, Anna, and you might as well try and win it. Sitting on the edge, saying how meaningless the whole thing is, gets you nowhere!'

She spun round on her heels. 'Isn't that Freddie extraordinary? Terribly pushy . . .'

Anna hunted words for her thoughts. 'I think he makes all the other men seem only half alive.'

'He looks like a boxer. James doesn't trust him, does he? He thinks Oliver is committing far too much money. So does Robert Carroll. I heard them talking about it a couple of days ago. They are worried. Anyway, how do *you* know him, Anna?' There was a flat curiosity in her voice. Her tone said it was not possible for this man, who was interesting, if extremely undesirable, to find Anna attractive. 'He's talked to you for most of the evening.'

'I expect he feels sorry for me,' Anna said, her voice acid. 'He wants me to go on and have a drink with him.'

'Go on? Now? Afterwards?'

'Yes.' She couldn't keep the triumph from her face. To 'go on' was something Linden was always doing.

Linden raised an eyebrow. 'Well, you see? I told you you would enjoy it.'

'I don't enjoy it or not enjoy it! I just feel out of place. It's so odd to gather people up and dress them up and sit them at a beautiful table and give them all this exotic food, pretending it's like this every night when everyone knows most evenings they eat scrambled eggs on trays in front of the telly.'

'Don't be so superior! It's no odder than anything else. It makes a change, as they say.' But she didn't go on. She didn't round on Anna and cut her to pieces, as she was capable of doing, for daring to denigrate her evening. Instead she said, 'Don't let him have you, Anna. Not just like that. Not just for something to do later on.'

Anna stared but she couldn't answer because Annabel came in, followed by the other girls, full of laughter, flopping on to James's bed, praising the dinner, saying they felt fat, asking for the loo.

CHAPTER NINE

Anna sat by Freddie in silence, her hands on the seat each side of her. *Nice car*, she thought, liking the smell of leather and the wooden dashboard.

'What are you thinking, Anna?'

'That I like your car.'

'So do I.' He thrust the cigarette lighter into its socket. 'Are there some Disque Bleu in the dashboard compartment?'

'You left your cigarettes at Oliver's house. I saw you throw them on the dining-room table.'

'There should be some more!'

She found a packet with four cigarettes in and lit one for Freddie and one for herself.

'Don't you want to know where we are going?' Freddie said, turning to look at her.

She shook her head and smiled. 'I have a friend, at the Cannon, and he says that I am too lacking in curiosity ever to succeed as a painter.'

'Is it true?'

'I don't know yet.'

Freddie parked in a small side street off the Kings Road and he got out and came round to Anna's side of the car, opening and closing the door for her, and his old-fashioned good manners surprised her. He put his arm along her shoulders, steering her towards a doorway and downstairs towards music and semi-darkness, past a crowded little bar and along the edges of a dance floor to a table in the corner. Several people waved at Freddie. Almost before they sat down, a waiter appeared.

'Good evening, Mr Monroe.'

'Hallo, George. What do you want to drink, Anna? A brandy?'

She nodded.

'I think I'll have Armagnac.'

They sat for a little while, lost in their separate thoughts. The loud music made speech unnecessary. Anna looked round, pleased that she could sit with him like this, in silence, without feeling she had to search for something to say.

'Come and dance with me,' Freddie said. He had been watching her for the last few moments, watching the way she studied the room, the way she played with her drink. He stood up and she followed him on to the crowded floor.

He pulled her close to him, ignoring the other bodies which moved so busily, and the music slowed as if to please him. Anna put her face against his, absorbing the smell of him, the wide, hard feel of him. She wanted to press herself into him. His hands moved against her neck, her back, sometimes he pulled away a little, looking into her face. Time did not exist for her. She would have stayed forever in the sounds and the darkness, oblivious of people and life outside, if, eventually, when the girl at the discothèque put on a loud, clapping, almost insulting record, Freddie hadn't indicated with a light pressure on her arm that they should sit down again. To be with him filled Anna with an overwhelming pride.

At the table he leaned towards her. 'Now, explain a few things to me, Anna. I want to know how the land lies with James and Linden and Oliver. Who does what and with which and to whom, as the old limerick goes?'

'No one does anything to anyone.'

'Yet!'

'But Oliver is . . . intrigued, fascinated, stunned, whatever words you like, with Linden.'

'And Linden, shrewd girl, feels James would be more her scene?'

Anna paused, feeling that she wanted to defend Linden from the sarcasm in Freddie's voice and yet wanting to speak the absolute truth. She trusted Freddie. Her instincts told her that he was an irresistible force and his energy, even now when it was late and he was gentle, was obvious, beating inside him like his heart.

'James interests her. He is so organized and outwardly cold. She is used to being fussed over. She is bored with that, I suppose. She finds his reserve intriguing. Also he is important. Linden plans things, thinks things through. She says she would be good for him. She says' -- and Anna laughed -- ''she'd like to disrupt him!''

'Oh, the biting uncertainty of it all!' His voice was thickly sarcastic. 'But at least she appreciates how little time any of us has. At least she tries. For that I respect her. But she is wrong about James. He would waste her. Dehydrate her.' Freddie finished his drink and put out his cigarette. 'I'm tired, Anna. Come on, let's go home!'

'Linden said I wasn't to let you have me, just like that . . . just for something to do later on!'

Freddie burst out laughing. 'You make quite a team, you two! But she's wrong about you. I've seen hundreds of girls, hovering as you are, neither child nor woman, holding on to their virginity as if they were strippers!'

'I've never held on to mine. Nobody wanted it! And everyone is born a virgin. It's not a crime. It's like laughing at someone for being a certain age.'

'Anna, my love, I'm not laughing at you. I'm much too tired to sleep with anyone but I like your company. Come home with me and we'll have a coffee and talk for a bit. There are very few women I can talk to.' As he stood up he was surprised to realize it was true.

Anna went with him up the stairs, into the damp night, into his car. He slammed his door but he made no move to start the engine. He looked across at Anna, put an arm along her shoulders. 'What do you want, Anna? An Oliver or a James? Or no one but yourself and your own life? Or someone like me?' He kissed her between the words. 'Pushy . . . successful . . .'

'Unbelievably modest!'

'Unbelievably honest. At least to myself about myself!' He ran his finger along her upper lip, tucking it into the little dent at the corners of her mouth, running it along her lower lip. 'There are millions of experts in the world, my love, experts on malarial mosquitoes and rainfall and Romans. You name it, somewhere there's an expert on it. I had the sense to pick a subject which will make me very, very rich!' He laughed and pulled away from her, starting the car. He lapsed into some private thoughts and Anna watched him, sensing that he was a man without fear of embarrassment. Not a man you could shame. It must give him, she thought, an extraordinary advantage.

His flat was small and rather depressing and it was obvious that he was moving out. In the living-room were tea chests and one large packing case. Heaps of old newspapers. As they came in, the telephone rang and Freddie said, 'Make us a coffee, love,' and sprawled on the only armchair. He picked up the receiver. 'Hallo?'

Anna found mugs, instant coffee, sugar but not milk. The kitchen was bare and rather sordid. No one had bothered to clean it recently. She watched Freddie through the open door, trying to assume a relaxed expression in case he looked up, while inside the sheer joy of being with him threatened to make her laugh like a maniac. As always, when she was happy, she made great vows to God. *I shall never eat chocolate again. Or take sugar in anything. Or eat potatoes . . . Who rings him at two in the morning? A woman, obviously.*

As she carried in the mugs of black coffee, she saw Freddie getting angry. His voice became cold, frightening. 'Look, this is a waste of my time and yours and I know you have to be awake half the night working but I don't! I need sleep.'

Anna put the cups down with exaggerated care and Freddie looked at her and made his mouth into a kiss. Whatever it was that he transmitted generated excitement all through her unaroused body. But behind that excitement her mind functioned clearly. *In this one evening I have seen all the sides of him, seen him nervous, angry, cold, gentle, laughing. I shall not be able to pretend I didn't know how he could be.*

'You're repeating yourself again. I'll ring you in the morning. Good night!' He put the receiver down and sprang to his feet, circling his shoulders wearily, swooping for his coffee. He made no attempt to explain the telephone conversation and Anna did not ask.

'Come on . . .' He stretched down his hand, to where she sat on the floor. 'Come and calm me down, talk to me. There's nowhere to sit in here and I'm too old to lie on the floor! As she stood up, he laughed at her expression. His anger had vanished and he touched her forehead with his lips.

She followed him into a small, cold bedroom. A double bed, a chest of drawers, a chair. He didn't switch on the light and the room was semi-dark, lit only by left-over light from the sitting-room. Freddie put his coffee down and kicked off his shoes and came to Anna, taking her coffee away, gathering her hair and pushing it over her shoulders.

'Well, Fatty, let's have a look at you!' He began to take off her clothes and she stood, stiffly, like a child, obediently lifting her arms to help him. She had no idea what to do, what expression to wear, whether to smile or talk. Her instincts, totally inexperienced on this level, appeared dead. And so she did nothing. When she was naked, she was surprised to find she was not scared of his scrutiny. She watched him throw off his own clothes, get into bed and hold up the sheet for her. 'Come on. You'll freeze out there.'

'So that's why you took off my clothes,' she said, and she found she could laugh as she got into bed beside him, moved up against him and felt for the first time in her life the surprising warmth of skin and a man's body, touching her, against her, around her.

Freddie hugged her, smiled at her, talking softly. 'See how nice it is? Isn't it nice if I touch you, Anna? Do you like this?' His voice, soft as his hands, moved over her, exploring, showing her herself. 'I want to save you up for later, keep you as a birthday treat.' His face in her hair, his hands taking great bunches of her hair. 'Why do you appeal to me so much? You have no motives. You just stand there, waiting for life to happen to you . . . waiting to be happy or unhappy . . . Why don't you ask more? Shall I happen to you, Anna?'

'Yes,' she whispered, thinking: *All my life I will remember the feel of his voice against my face and this cold little room.* She felt she was being touched by two people, Freddie outside and someone inside too. The combination was overwhelming. There was no time but eventually she became aware of a change in Freddie, that he gathered himself up, controlled himself and kissed her and then put his arm under her shoulders. He lay and stared at the ceiling. He didn't want the responsibility of sleeping with her at this stage. He began to talk, almost to himself, about his life and his plans.

'I spent a lot of time watching people of my own age during the years I worked in Reading for Tenacia. The place was like a large rock pool, a typical minature world. I watched my contemporaries, watched their lives freezing in their late teens. Barely out of childhood and yet they were finished because not one of them had a plan. They floundered about, enjoying the money they could earn, having real sex at last instead of the elaborate fantasies of the last few years, believing all the stuff the advertisements told them. Even the best of them were drugged by it all. By the time they got over it, it was too late. They were married, encumbered, trapped at a low level. Not for me. I made a list, all those years ago, of the things I wanted out of life. I realized I was starting with nothing but I thought, if I had a clearly defined plan, I would be way ahead of the average man of my age. I have been lucky, too, and I have worked extremely hard. I expected good luck. I demanded it, in fact!'

'Meeting Oliver, that was your good luck?' she asked but she knew it was true.

'Yes. But if not Oliver, I would have found someone else. I was getting intensely frustrated, though ... And then that extraordinary morning. For some reason I can't understand I can recall that whole day in the most minute detail. I was late getting up. I had no time for coffee and when I went into the garage opposite, where I rent a space for the car, it suddenly reminded me of a church my mother used to take me to as a child. I remember that the window-boxes, with all the dead flowers in, depressed me; that I tried to hide my anger when Tim Granbury told me he had made the appointment in Lewes; that I was low on petrol and stopped at a garage somewhere in the country and was served by a very pretty girl in white dungarees. Everything had softened and become greener as I left London. Have you seen Pyecomb?'

'No.'

'It's quite a shock. A real house, in every sense of the word, and amongst all that dignity and splendour, Oliver, playing his piano, scruffy as usual and furious at being ordered down there, furious with himself for not being able to tell his mother to go to hell!' Freddie laughed. He leaned up on one elbow. 'I'd better take you home, before you know more about me than I know myself! Are you a spy, for James?'

'I don't want to go home!'

'Well, I can't keep you here,' he said, his voice suddenly bored.

She hated to get up, to dress, to feel her body separated from his warmth; it was an effort for her to go down to his car, into the cold darkness of the early morning; she hated the journey home, taking her further and further from his flat; when he stopped his car in Oakfield Court she shut her eyes and pretended they were still driving. Anywhere.

'Here you are, Anna. Home and almost untouched. You can face them all with a clear conscience tomorrow!' He didn't get out of the car. He put his hands each side of her face and kissed her. 'Thank you for your company. Happy Christmas, Anna.'

'But it's only the sixth!'

'Well, I won't see you between now and the New Year!'

She had been weaving intricate dreams of her life with him, seeing him every day, every night. His words hurt her as if he had hit her. 'But why? Have I done something wrong? I would have slept with you, if you'd wanted . . .'

He shook his head. 'It's hard to believe there are still girls like you being born! Anna, I am in the process of moving house, establishing a business, getting my entire life re-organized and Oliver's too! I haven't time. Anyway, what's your hurry? You're not going away, are you?'

She shook her head.

'Good . . . Come and see me at Brook Street if you want but I warn you, if I'm busy, you won't like me! If not, I'll ring you when things have calmed down.'

There was nothing else she could say. He leaned over her, opening the passenger door and Anna got out, pulling her coat tightly round her and standing forlornly on the pavement, watching him drive away.

He saw her in his driving mirror. He shook his head and smiled and then yawned. *Funny, funny girl. A child, really* . . . And yet she had intrigued and entertained him. If he had time, he thought, he would like to see more of her, sleep with her and watch her change. It was refreshing not to come up against the usual façade, the assumed world-weariness. What had she said? 'Have I done something wrong? I would have slept with you if you'd wanted.' He laughed softly, the words touching him. Once before he had known a girl like that. . . . Remembering, he smiled again and then he put his thoughts back on to Brook Street, back to the sale in ten days and back to real life!

CHAPTER TEN

Freddie did not acknowledge Christmas at all. He had no time for religion, no time for the great commercial feast. It had always annoyed him the way the holiday was so drawn out but this year, intensely busy as he was, the traffic and the herds of Christmas shoppers irritated him unbearably. He worked, in those last weeks of 1971, from seven o'clock in the morning until ten or eleven at night. He was determined to have Brook Street functioning by the new year. Although it was merely a psychological date, it was something definite to aim for. He nagged the decorators constantly. He had his own belongings moved into the bare top floors of Brook Street and he searched for a girl to act as a combination of secretary and saleswoman. He interviewed dozens of girls. He was offering a high salary, and he was extremely fussy. He wanted a pretty girl with enough charm to keep an impatient client happy if he was delayed or merely stalling, a good typist who could spell and think for herself. Two weeks before Christmas he found Penny Dimmock. He liked her at once. She was blonde with an impressive bosom and she said she could start the following Monday. From that first morning they began a comfortable flirtation which both knew would lead nowhere.

Freddie moved into Brook Street on 14th December. Two days later there was an important sale at Sotheby's. Freddie viewed on the Tuesday afternoon, circling the main pieces, outwardly showing no interest at all. He picked up a very mediocre vase bearing the reign marks of Chia Ch'ing. Beside him, Maisie Hunter, a familiar face at all major auctions, raised an eyebrow.

'Surely not . . .?'

'Morning, Maisie.' He smiled at the enormous woman. She was as tall as he was. She wore a fur hat and on the top of her heavy-jowled face it looked like short, crazy hair. 'I don't always buy for millionaires, unlike you.'

She laughed. 'But you do buy consistently, Freddie!' She too picked up a very ordinary bowl. They both knew the pieces they would be competing for the following morning. Freddie marked his catalogue. He looked round, taking in the familiar faces, relishing the thought of the sale. Freddie loved the tension, loved the contest. And tomorrow, bidding for a wealthy American woman whom Tim Granbury had put him in touch with, he could afford to go sky-high.

'See you tomorrow, Freddie,' Maisie Hunter said as he left.

Freddie ran down the stairs and out into a cold and crowded Bond Street. He walked briskly to Brook Street, looking at his building and feeling a wave of pride and excitement. He let himself in, irritated to see that the painters had left when it was only just after five o'clock, then the telephone began to ring.

'Freddie?' It was Oliver.

'Yes.'

'Guess who's in town? My cousin, Carlos Stephano! He just rang me. He's at the Dorchester for four days. On Saturday he flies to Rome and he won't be around again till March or April. He asked if we'd like to go in for a drink tomorrow evening at about seven?'

'Fine. Shall we meet there?'

'Yes. I'll be in the hotel, downstairs, at seven. I'll wait there for you.'

'Good. There's a major sale tomorrow morning. Do you think he'd like to come along?'

'I don't know. Maybe he's going anyway but I'll mention it. It's Sotheby's, isn't it? Eleven?'

'Yes.'

The following morning, everything went right for Freddie. He outmanoeuvred Maisie Hunter and came away with the four best pieces that had been offered. Two for Mrs Hull, the wealthy American client. Two for Freddie Monroe, to perch tantalizingly in the window at Brook Street and proclaim to the entire world the quality of merchandise that Monroe Antiques dealt in. He spent the afternoon on the telephone, again successfully, and when at ten to seven that evening he swung into the Dorchester Hotel and began to look round for Oliver, he was elated and confident.

There was, of course, no sign of Oliver. Freddie sat down in one of the large armchairs, crossed his legs and lit a cigarette, watching as he waited the constant and amazingly varied stream of people who came in and out of the hotel.

Oliver had spent the afternoon Christmas shopping. He had wandered from shop to crowded shop, repelled by the haste and the hard sell and yet longing to buy presents that would please people. He loved Christmas. It still held a childish appeal for him. He could relive, if he let himself, the anticipation, the thrill of that dark lumpy stocking at the end of the bed. He loved the service in the village church, the carols and the clusters of people between the graves on Christmas morning, wishing each other well. If his life was merely a calendar, and he sometimes believed it was, then Christmas was the hinge on which each year pivoted.

When he had bought his presents, he took them home and wrapped them in silver paper and red ribbon and then piled them back into his car. He knew his mother was leaving for the country the next morning and he wanted her to take them all to Pyecomb, to join the heap under the tree in the hall.

Linden let him in. In the eight days since the dinner party, she had seen him only once. He had taken her to lunch on the previous Saturday, as a thank-you, he said, and because neither of them had anything to do. Linden, in the process of establishing herself with James, the memory of the evening with him stored in her mind in minute detail, had been a little withdrawn. The lunch was not a success. Eventually Oliver had asked the question which had been burning in his throat. 'Did you enjoy your evening with James?'

'Very much,' she had answered smoothly, having expected the question.

'He asked me if I minded that he was taking you out . . . wasn't that nice of him? Quite out of character. He actually pretended I had some small claim on you.'

'Well, I was your friend first.' She knew she sounded absurd, schoolgirlish, and was angry with herself.

Oliver put his elbows on the table. 'And his friend last?'

'Ollie . . .' She put her hand over his. 'Don't use this and me to build up a big drama. I want to go out with as many people as I can.' Her voice was gentle.

Now, as she held the door open for him, they both remembered that conversation. She smiled. It appeared that she was delighted to see him but he knew, now, that the smile was automatic, for postman or dustman or king. 'You look like Father Christmas with that lot,' she said. 'Did you know I was spending Christmas with you?'

'No.' His face lit up for a moment.

'Well, apparently your Mrs Thing . . . McKay . . . is still ill.'

Oliver stood quite still, arms still full of his parcels. 'I bought these round to go down with my mother. Is she in?'

'No. What's the matter, Oliver?'

'I always get like this about buying presents.' He smiled, laughing at himself. 'I want so much to give people things they will adore . . . presents that will make their faces light up. And I never, never succeed. It depresses me. I know you will hate what I have bought for you. I wish you weren't going to be there! I shall hate to watch you and James getting closer.'

'Will James be there?' she said, her innocence so convincing that Oliver stared at her.

'Of course he will be there!'

'Why "of course"? I know he has friends of his own.'

Oliver stacked his parcels on the hall table. 'Not really. He has women. He has men he plays squash with, men he sometimes goes racing with, men he drinks with. James does not have one whole all-round friend because he has never given anyone enough time!'

'Then he must be very lonely,' she said softly, meeting Oliver's eyes, letting him see that there was no way of making her deviate.

Oliver went back to the door. 'I must go. I have to see Freddie at seven.' And then he moved back to her, very quickly, and put his mouth on hers. 'I don't mean any of it. You will make my Christmas!'

It was nearly 7.15 when Oliver hurried into the Dorchester, seeing Freddie at once, coming towards him. 'Sorry . . .'

'I hardly recognized you,' Freddie said dryly, looking at Oliver's grey suit, his tie. 'I didn't know you had a real suit, Ollie!'

'It took a bit of finding! We'd better go on up – he has a suite on the sixth floor.' In the lift Oliver stood, head bent, hands deep in his pockets. 'I haven't seen the old boy for years. Not that he's that old. My mother's contemporary, I think . . . He probably won't recognize me. I was sixteen the last time he came to Pyecomb to stay.'

'Somehow I don't think you will have changed all that much,' Freddie laughed. He followed Oliver down the wide corridor.

Carlos Stephano was in his late fifties. His mother and Marietta's had been first cousins and there was a family likeness between them. They had the same narrow build, a similar nose. 'Oliver, how very, very nice to see you!' His accent was thick and romantic, his hair white and his face very brown. He looked exactly like Freddie's mental picture. 'It is such a long time since we last met. And this must be Mr Monroe. I am delighted to meet you.'

He drew them into the large sitting-room. 'Do sit down, both of you. What can I get you to drink? Oliver, you must tell me all the family news. How is your mother first of all?'

'Very well.' Oliver relaxed. He had forgotten the man's warmth, the outward charm. He took a gin and tonic and one of Freddie's cigarettes and for a while they talked about the family. Freddie sat, legs crossed, patiently, his eyes travelling the room, trying to work out what it must cost to stay here for even four days.

'And so, when you are not playing your piano, you now have this business interest with Mr Monroe?' He stood by the fireplace, by the tall vase of flowers. 'I did not realize you had inherited your father's passion, Oliver.'

'Well, I haven't, Carlos. It's all Freddie's idea, really – he was with Granbury's, you know.'

'Yes, I do know. But I was not aware, until you mentioned it in your letter, about the current interest in Chinese porcelain. I have reduced my collection considerably over the past ten years. It seems I have made a mistake!'

'Well, it's a mistake it is not too late to rectify,' Freddie said. 'I was lucky enough to buy something this morning that I want you to see.' He opened his briefcase. He took out a small, cloth-wrapped bundle. 'I hope you don't mind my taking advantage of your experience?'

'Not at all.' Stephano crossed the room to where Freddie sat and took the object from him. 'Exquisite.' He carried it to the large lamp. He took glasses from the pocket of his jacket. 'And this is bought as an investment? Not merely for its beauty?'

'Yes. A lot of people are suddenly becoming aware of the . . . beauty . . . as you put it!' Freddie laughed. *Gently*, he thought. *This man will not be hurried. Cautious from instinct and habit.*

Carlos laughed too. 'What good taste the world is developing! This was the sale you mentioned on the telephone, Oliver? In fact, towards the end, I was there. At the back somewhere. I must admit that I thought at first you were exaggerating the interest in your letter, Oliver. I was quite wrong. There was a tension, an excitement in the room which surprised me. But the prices seemed high. Are you telling me, Mr Monroe, that they will go higher?'

Freddie drank deeply from his glass. 'Last summer, when Oliver and I first met, I told him I could buy him a collection as an investment and that the value would double within twelve months. In fact I was over-cautious. They have already doubled and they will do so again and again because these things are still selling for way below their value.'

Carlos shrugged. 'But what is their value? To me, maybe, this is worth a great deal of money but . . .'

'To the Japanese, it is worth far more. They would take that home to a rabid market. They have started an erruption of interest. A snowball, to mix metaphors.'

'I see.' He handed the dish back to Freddie. 'I wonder if you would both stay and have dinner with me here? We could have something sent up, and talk a little more. Perhaps I should think of building up my collection once again . . .'

'I should be delighted to stay,' Freddie said.

Oliver nodded. 'Fine, but I shall have to leave at about nine-thirty.' He laughed. 'I have to change, for work, you see.'

He settled down with his second drink. He listened to Freddie talking with a candour and a humility which he had never used before. And yet the confidence was there.

Freddie knew that Carlos Stephano was cautious in the way rich men are often cautious, convinced that the world is full of people waiting to relieve them of their money. Waiting to cheat, to reduce them to their own level. From his outward expression, despite the polite interest, it appeared he had dismissed the idea before it was fully explained. But as Freddie talked, he watched Carlos's expression grow less and less withdrawn.

When they ate, they talked of other things.

'I cannot believe it is nearly nineteen hundred and seventy-two,' Carlos Stephano said. 'But perhaps the time does not go so quickly for you? I shall be glad to go home. I have travelled so much this year. Too much.'

I have travelled, too, Freddie thought. He flicked back through the year, as through the pages of a diary. The thought of a new year filled him with exhilaration. And for some strange reason, Anna's face moved through his mind.

CHAPTER ELEVEN

Spring came absurdly early to Holland Park, doggedly invading the small enclosures, the trees and the flower-beds. Stubby crocuses pushed up through the earth and opened, purple and yellow and white. Squirrels were busy. There was a certain smell in the air in the evenings, a smell of warmer air and memories of previous summers.

Despite her scorn because she thought that spring in the city was a fragmented thing, not all-enveloping as in the country, Anna was elated by it, woken by it. She was happy to be back at the Cannon again with work to hold her. The short Christmas break had been depressing and she had missed Linden – missed the bite and the laughter. Anna spent a lot of her Christmas holiday at the window, like a child on a wet afternoon, making patterns on the glass with her finger, patterns in her head about Freddie. She had spent hours choosing a card for him, agonizing over the wording inside, over what she should write, posting it not too early and not too late. There was no acknowledgement. Nothing from him but silence but it didn't worry her unduly. She needed him, real or unreal. He filled an emptiness. She dreamed round him and she was convinced that, in time, she would see him again.

Prue, Veronica's sister, spent Christmas with them, bustling in with a cardboard box full of mince pies and cheeses and wine and a Christmas cake. 'I never have enough time to cook all the rest of the year. On holiday, I love cooking!' she told Anna.

Anna liked her aunt. She was so unlike Veronica! She was solid, with a brisk walk and flat-heeled shoes. Her hair, once as red as Anna's, was flecked with greys and browns, her hands freckled. Prue and Veronica were different physically, emotionally, mentally. They lived out their respective roles, scoring off one another constantly but quite happily. Veronica, the younger sister, prettier and sillier. Prue, dowdy, sensible, far, far cleverer. She had worked in the foreign office for thirty years. There had been a man once but he had been married and the relationship died out as gradually as it had built up. Prue was content, unlike Veronica, with her neat and solitary life.

'Anna, you're bored,' Veronica said, again and again, 'stuck here with us! You should be out with your friends.' She underlined Anna's failure. She made Anna feel it over and over again, turned her from her window, forced her to go out, hide in her bedroom, in the kitchen.

'She's all right,' Prue said. 'Leave her alone, Roni! Why shouldn't she have a rest? Holidays are for doing what you want. Don't nag her!'

'I don't nag. I'm just sorry she should waste time. They are so precious, those few years when you are young.'

Anna stared at them, her mother and her aunt, wondering if she and Linden would some day sit like this, the fierce caring gone from their lives, lived through and half forgotten.

'Did you know,' she said suddenly, 'how it would be for you? When you were like Linden and I – what did you think would happen?'

They stared at her, putting down their glasses.

'Good God!' Prue said. 'I can't remember being young. I was thinner, I suppose, and shyer. That's all.'

Veronica's eyes had filled with tears. She stood up unsteadily, filling her wine glass, leaving the room, one hand trailing theatrically behind her.

'Take no notice,' Prue said, looking at Anna's expression. 'She has always enjoyed making exits.'

Anna sat down, comfortably, crossing her ankles. 'You are so different,' she said.

Prue had laughed. 'Not quite as different as you and Linden!'

Prue stayed a week and when she left there was one silent day until Linden came back, bursting with things to tell them, pacing the room as she described Pyecomb, the tree, the church, the turkey; the people who came and went; Oliver and James.

When she came to James she spoke more quietly with a satisfaction in her voice, thinking of the long dining-room table. Linden had been one of the family over Christmas, a difficult role to perform from the work point of view, emerging flushed from the kitchen to run upstairs to the room she was sleeping in, a grey-green room with tall windows, and brush her hair and cool her face and change before running down again to eat. But she was glad to do it. She sat at the table with them, rehearsing how it would be, later on, when she was with James. She watched him a lot, listened to him, studied him. His still face fascinated her. He was without spontaneity, but he could be warm. With his mother he was warm. And sometimes Linden would look up and find he was watching her and he would smile very slowly, as if surprised at the things he was feeling.

Anna worked extremely hard in those first weeks of the new year, working alongside Pym, the easy relationship between them re-established. Bony had suggested to his group that they concentrate on movement, speed and change this term. Anna and Pym took to spending their lunch hours in Holland Park children's playground. On the warmer days, or cold days with sun, the small children would be there, excavating the sand pit while their mothers talked; learner-walkers, swaying unsteadily like tiny drunks; three-year-olds, having earnest conversations and sudden violent fights; confident four-year-olds, running and shouting and jumping. There was an afternoon in late February when the playground was crowded and Pym and Anna stayed on into the afternoon working in silence, trying to put down the speed, the enchanting head-bent concentration of children talking and thinking. They drew until a sudden cold wind activated the mothers. They came out of their gossip and began to wrap up their children and take them home.

Pym straightened his shoulders. 'Silly women – why do they have to take them away? A bit of wind will do them good!' He opened his hands in exasperation. 'I haven't finished . . .'

'It's freezing, Pym.' Anna laughed. 'You hate children, don't you?'

'Yes, I do. They interrupt and lessen things. They are like keeping rabbits or guinea pigs. I shall never have any.'

'Suppose you get married?' Anna shut her sketch book, stood up and buttoned her coat. 'Will you ever get married?'

'Is this a proposal?' He laughed, turning up his collar, tucking his arm through Anna's as they began to walk. 'I'll buy you a coffee . . . Yes, I think I will. I have reluctantly decided there are some women I would be prepared to marry. Exceptional women, of course. If it mattered enough to her, then I would!'

'And if she wanted children?'

'We will just have to fight it out. Interesting battle,' he said, almost to himself.

'You sound as if you know her already...' As she said it, she thought of Pym belonging wholly to someone else, and hated the idea. She still relied heavily on his friendship and on his attention.

He was silent as they went into the restaurant. When they were sitting down, warming their hands round white china cups of weak coffee, he said: 'Anna, I've got the opportunity to draw some dancers rehearsing. The Royal Ballet. I know a man who knows one of them. They're going to be at the Duke of York Barracks all next week and they don't mind a couple of people watching, if we keep quiet.' He heaped sugar into his cup. 'Do you want to come?'

'I'd love to... will Bony give us the week to spend as we want?'

'Yes, of course he will. It ties in perfectly with his movement thing. I'll ask him this afternoon.'

They were by far the best drawings Anna had ever done. Even those first quick sketches on the Monday morning shocked her, excited her. The speed of the dancers and the way they stood about, resting, feet turned out, heads bent, or leaned against the wall, exhausted. They wore thick woollen leg warmers, the girls with their hair scraped back, flat chests showing every rib. Tiny girls, strong and sweating, and men with lumpy muscles, turning and throwing their bodies, and all the time striving to hide the effort and the stretching and the difficulty and the pain. A tinny piano, the dancers grouping and re-grouping, the thump of feet on the wooden floor. Anna was fascinated, totally absorbed, lost in it.

Strangely enough, Pym lost interest. After that first long day, when he felt he had, to a certain extent, conquered the obvious technical difficulty, it seemed to him too much the same. On the Tuesday morning he grew more and more restless and eventually, at twelve, he whispered to Anna that he had had enough. 'I'm going to take the afternoon off. Coming?'

She shook her head. 'No, I think I'll stay.'

'See you,' Pym said, gathering his things and waiting for a break in the dancing before he made his way out.

He crossed the paved yard and went into the Kings Road. He looked with little interest at the shoals of self-consciously dressed people who strayed in and out of the boutiques. He bought himself some apples at a fruit stall and bit into one, running between the cars, coming into Sloane Square. And as he crossed into the centre of the square, he saw Linden, standing at a bus stop with a shopping basket. He stood quite still for a few moments and then ran forward, leaping dangerously through the cars, pushing his way past people until he stood beside her.

'Can I carry that for you?' He said it awkwardly, the cliché sticking in his throat. But he knew he wanted more than the typical passing-in-the-street encounter.

She looked round, surprise on her face. 'Hallo, Alexander.'

'Don't call me that,' he said sharply.

She raised her eyebrows. 'Start again. Hallo, Pym!'

'Hallo.' He put out his hand to take the basket from her. 'I feel it is such a nice day I want to be generous, helpful.'

'You have enough stuff of your own to carry.' She kept her fingers on the handle.

'I can put my stuff in your basket!' He took it from her. He wanted to smile and laugh. No reason except her face. 'Where are you going? Can I come?'

'I'm just going back to work. Piccadilly. I've been doing some shopping for Mrs Carroll – she's the mother of the man Anna did the mural for. I. . . .'

'I know,' he interrupted. 'I know everything about you. Can I come? Just for the ride?'

'If you really want to. If you've nothing better to do!'

The bus came and Linden went upstairs and right to the front, as if to discourage him. She sat by the window and Pym sat down beside her and his thigh lay against her. They both moved a little away from the other. The bus crept forward, hesitating at a zebra crossing, and then moving towards Knightsbridge.

'I think about you all the time,' Pym said flatly, into the silence which hung between them.

She said nothing. The calm which she took for granted, the

endless, easy answers to turn away unwanted attention, had suddenly vanished. He smelled of paint and smoke and soap. She looked at his hands, long-fingered, holding the basket on his lap. Thick wrists for such a slight man. Golden-haired, sticking out from the frayed cuffs of a denim shirt. She could not look at him. Linden, made of confidence, could not lift her head and turn her eyes. Dared not.

'I don't want to. I don't want to take any notice of you because I feel it's so bloody for Anna. Everybody wants you, don't they? Every second of every day you underline Anna's opinion of herself! I am really fond of her . . . .' His voice had grown angry. 'It would be better for her if you were removed. Taken away all together!'

She was recovering herself. 'Murdered, you mean?'

'No, I was thinking of something more extreme!'

'What is more extreme than death?'

'Marriage!'

She laughed. 'Well, I hope to be married some day!'

'To me?'

She couldn't laugh at that. The words were ludicrous but the tension between them, seeping into her, made laughter impossible. She was not prepared for the feeling or for him. She had not thought to see him again. She groped for her self-possession.

'Surely Anna has told you about me? How grasping and scheming I am? Planning and bullying, hanging out for a rich husband!'

'You're just playing. You know you are too exquisite to be wasted. You know you are special, don't you? Anna knows it too. That's her trouble.' He smiled. 'Luckily, I am special too!'

'Really? And what makes you special?'

He shrugged. 'I made myself what I am . . . What time do you finish work?'

'Five.'

He nodded. 'I'll come and meet you. I can show you where I live. I live in squalor. I offer you far more of a challenge than some ordinary, eligible, boring, desirable man.'

'You talk balls most of the time, don't you?'

Pym shouted with laughter, putting his arm along her shoulder as the stiffness between them vanished. 'I didn't think you could talk like a human being! I thought you were an animated doll! What a relief! We shall be able to make each other laugh when we're not in bed.'

She shrugged her shoulders automatically from under his arm, her defensive roll well practised, but it felt unnatural. She could shrug off his arm but she could not turn off the unwanted but definite current between them which surprised her so deeply.

At the Carrolls' front door, Pym put down the basket. Linden found her key.

'I'll be here at five,' he said.

She said nothing. She let herself in, turned, looked at him and frowned. 'I don't know that I'll be here.' She closed the door.

The flat was very quiet. Marietta had gone out for lunch. Linden went up to the kitchen and prepared a light evening meal for them, cold chicken in mayonnaise, a salad. A bowl of fruit. She set it out in the dining-room and cleared the kitchen. She made herself a coffee. It was just after two. She put ice in the bucket, sliced a lemon, carried down glasses and she had finished. She took her coffee and went into Marietta's bedroom, sitting on the stool by the dressing-table and studying James's photograph.

She knew that James was interested in her now. She had had dinner with him twice since Christmas. On both occasions there had been other couples present but James had shown a deliberate possessiveness which Linden loved. She had played up to it, sitting in his car until he came to let her out, waiting to be helped with her coat, waiting to be included when he talked of people she didn't know. She knew he was a gradual man. It would be no wild affair. It would be slow and build and build . . . She shivered her shoulders, thinking of his solemn mouth when he kissed her good night. She found the lack of emotion fascinating. She was used to being grabbed at, handled, subtly or unsubtly, as a matter of course.

'I shall be away for a couple of weeks, Linden. I'm going to Europe.' He took her face in his hands, as if committing it to memory. 'When I get back, we must see more of each other. Would you like that?'

'Yes. I would!'

She stood up, walking restlessly to the window and looking

out over Green Park. *We are suited, James and I. I would fit into his way of life. I would be invaluable to him. I could organize a social life for him, see the world with him . . . This may be the last generation able to enjoy wealth. I would have beautiful clothes. I would be stretched.* Little unasked-for moments of Pym kept coming to her, making her tremble with a high-pitched nervousness. She turned and wandered downstairs, picking up books, ashtrays, idly arranging cushions, wishing that she smoked or drank or had some way of lessening the tension. *I should be able to get on with Marietta, although no woman who marries James will have an easy time with her! I can make it all work out.* Still her stomach churned with anticipation. *God, some ridiculous art student friend of Anna's offers to walk me back to his sordid little flat and my heart races. It's pathetic.*

She would not go with Pym. She wrote a note for Marietta, saying that she felt unwell and had left a little early. It was just after three. She would go now, long before Pym came back. He would be annoyed when he found she had left, think her rude and dismiss her from his mind. That was how she wanted it. She pulled on her jacket and tied the scarf over her hair. She opened the front door, stepped out and virtually fell over Pym!

He had been there for two hours, waiting, thinking, sitting cross-legged and eating his apples until he heard someone come down the corridor, or voices. Then he would jump up and stand, as if he had just rung the bell and was waiting for the door to be opened.

He stared at Linden's amazed face. 'I think I am flattered that you are trying to avoid me!'

She didn't bother to deny it. 'Have you been there all the time?'

'Yes.'

'But why?'

He took her hand, carefully, to see how she would react. She let her hand lie in his, docile, curled. 'Because I wanted to stay here. There was nothing I wanted to do more. I stayed here and thought about you, on the other side of that door, doing things! Now, come on . . .'

He gave her arm a gentle pull and she went with him, down the long green corridor.

'Let's walk for a bit,' Pym said, tucking his arm through hers. 'And talk. I'll tell you about myself. You need to know about me. I am twenty-two years old. I was born in Scotland, near Perth, and my father died when I was six or seven. My mother re-married. I have two half-sisters. My family is happy, normal. I go home to see them regularly. I came to London because I won a scholarship to the Cannon. I sat for it because I wanted to see the South, live here for a while. My stepfather is in local government, with the water board. My mother is a good cook. She will be shy when you first meet her . . .'

'Is she coming to London?'

'Some day. Or we'll go to Perth.'

'You're completely mad!'

'I do have an aunt. She lives in Dorset. It's a lovely cottage. We'll go and stay there.'

Linden snatched her hand away. 'Look, I'm sorry, but I haven't time to come with you now.'

They had stopped walking. Pym faced her, stood in front of her, took both her hands and lifted them up to his mouth. 'Please,' he said.

You couldn't call it a flat, Linden thought coldly, a little breathless after the four flights of stairs, as Pym unlocked the peeling door, flinging it open with a flourish, standing aside and ushering her in. She went in very cautiously, uneasily. She stood just inside the doorway. A room with two big, dusty, uncurtained windows. A bare floor. In one corner a bed with a bright striped rug, in another corner a sleeping bag. Everywhere, on the window-sills, on the floor, all over the table, pieces of paper, tubes and tins of paint, jars of brushes, pencils, empty milk bottles. Three big cushions to sit on. An easel by the windows.

'The bathroom is down the hall. The kitchen is in here.' She looked through an open door into a small room with a little fridge, a sink, a baby Belling. Cupboards, shelves and two enormous saucepans. 'I cook a lot of spaghetti.' Pym opened one of the large windows in the bigger room and light and noise came in and sunbeams full of dust.

'Four floors up! Traffic is muffled, isn't it?' He faced her, arms folded. 'Can you smell the lilac?'

'It's much too early for lilac.'

'I can smell it anyway. I think it's the landlady's bath oil.'

He came across to her, taking her hands. He kissed each side of her mouth. Then he drew back and with his feet he pushed the three big cushions together and pulled at her arm. 'Come and sit down. Jane bought these. I should tell you about Jane. Will you stay here, let me draw you for a bit?'

'All right.' She felt she was reacting like Anna, lost, wanting very much to get out but wanting, also, to stay. She sat down. Pym put one arm round her neck, rocking her gently from side to side. He said her name, over and over again. And then, afraid that she might leave, he sprang to his feet, uncovered paper, pinned it to a board, sat cross-legged a few feet from her and began to draw.

'What shall I do?'

'Sit still and talk.'

'I thought you knew everything about me?'

'Only the side Anna knows. One half.' His head moved up and down, looking at her face, at the paper, at her face. The sun came in the big windows. Pym got up, walked to her and gently took the scarf off her hair. He stood looking down at her and put his hand against her face. Then he went back to his drawing.

Linden leaned herself more comfortably against the wall. She seldom sat on the floor. Sounds came in the open window. Cars, voices, the occasional angry horn. In the room was silence. It was easy for her to stay still. She sat with her face expressionless but her mind was frenzied, mocking herself . . . *What are you doing here? Whatever it is you feel for him is exactly what you despise in your mother. This weak, mindless giving in to the first deep emotions, clinging, like a jellyfish, giving up everything for what is basically an instinctive sexual response. He is ridiculous. Ridiculous. Only a face, that's all. He pretends he knows about me, that he has some special knowledge of me. It's crap. It's a bluff. He knows nothing.*

She stood up suddenly and Pym swore.

'Sit down!'

'No, I'm going now. I've wasted enough time here. I've seen how horrible your flat is. I'm sorry for you.'

He went and stood with his back against the door. 'I shall not let you go until you say you'll have lunch with me tomorrow. A picnic. In the park. I make good sandwiches. Don't argue. I love arguing. I could stand here all afternoon.'

She hovered between fury and laughter. The laughter won.

'How do you get away with being so . . .? You're ridiculous! A picnic in February!' She went up to him and he put his arms round her and moved her in circles, round and round in a crazy lurching dance. He kissed her face and neck and ears and chin and nose and eyelids, he said her name over and over again.

He insisted on going home with her. It was six when she let herself into the flat. *Three hours*, she thought. *What did I do with them?* She ran herself a bath and took off her clothes. This evening she was having dinner with one of the grey-suited faces. She found her own name ringing in her head, over and over again. It woke her several times in the night from involved and rather frightening dreams, the voice repeating, 'Linden, Linden, Linden.' And in her dreams she shouted, 'Go away!'

By the following morning, she had decided not to see him. She would telephone him at the Cannon, explaining that she had to work at lunch time. It was impossible . . .

'Linden,' Marietta said, 'as I'm going out for lunch today and we are also out this evening, don't feel you have to stay later than you need. Go home early if you want to.'

'Thank you,' Linden said, wondering if Pym always had fate on his side. Not, of course, that Linden was influenced by fate.

When she answered the door, just after one o'clock he was standing and smiling with a large brown paper bag under one arm. He was still for a few moments. The deliberate blankness of her face made him temporarily unsure of himself. Then he moved forward, kissing her cheek. 'Well? Are you coming?' he asked quietly.

She was unable to refuse him face to face like this. His happiness and determination carried her too. It was extraordinary for Linden to be so docile but she let it happen, telling herself she could stop any time she chose. For one afternoon only she would let herself respond to the attraction, share the exhilaration, live with him in the simple happy circle he seemed able to create around them. But the afternoon became evening and still she was with him, eating in a small bistro, listening for hours as he talked and planned . . . 'And on Friday evening we'll catch the six fifteen to Dorset. We can get a taxi to the cottage. It's not that far from the station. My aunt will be away but she is happy for us to stay there. There is a lot of food, she said!'

On Friday afternoon Linden came home and packed and

wrote a note which she left on the kitchen table. She was still letting it happen and for the first time in her life she was unable to explain her actions to herself. But she wanted to go with him. Anna? She shut her small case and pushed the thought of Anna from her mind.

The station was crowded with commuters and week-end travellers and the train was very full. Eventually they found two seats, opposite one another. Pym talked most of the way, leaning forward to touch her hand or her knee, oblivious of the other occupants. Two hours later they got out into a cold February night and an almost deserted station. It was well after eight o'clock and they were lucky to find the solitary taxi parked outside. The journey lasted fifteen minutes and at last Pym was as quiet as Linden. He wished they had arrived in daylight. He wanted her to see the beauty of the country, the first view of the little cottage.

When they arrived he paid the driver and took a key from under a flower-pot. He unlocked the front door and switched on a light. Linden followed him in and behind her the car retreated, leaving them in total silence. The room was white and beamed and pretty with a big fireplace and rose-patterned curtains. Pym put a match to the expertly laid fire and it crackled into life. He crouched in front of it, pretending to watch it, needing a few moments to lose his shyness.

Linden moved around the room, laying her coat and knitted hat on a chair, looking at things.

'Drink?' Pym asked.

'Yes, please.'

He stood up and arched his back. 'Funny. I've wanted this to happen for so long and now it has I feel . . . paralysed. Not ready for you. Almost afraid.'

She shrugged, unhelpfully, willing him to disappoint or repel her, to make it easy for her to dismiss him later. She took the whisky he poured. 'It's a pretty cottage,' she said, primly.

Neither of their moods survived long. They ate soup and toast and cheese and drank some red wine and the tension vanished. They sprawled on the big, soft sofa and drank coffee and Pym moved his fingers gently against her face and neck, turning her head to kiss her.

Tenderness filled her, softness towards him, a longing to

touch him, love him, surprise him. She explored his face in turn with her fingers and her lips and they stayed in the room until the fire folded down on to itself and it was almost dark. They went upstairs then into a cold bedroom. A double bed with a dip in the middle which rolled them together from the start. Making love to him seemed to Linden, natural and right. She wanted to as she had never wanted to before, loving his slight strong body and the way it seemed to fit her own perfectly.

Pym said, 'We've wasted so much time . . . I knew, I told you that, from the first moment I saw you. We've wasted nearly six months. If we both live to be ninety in perfect health and are never separated for a day, I shall always regret those wasted months.'

She laughed. She shivered as he touched her again, letting her body respond. Perhaps, after all, this was what she wanted? But hours later, in the stillness of the early morning, she watched Pym sleep. She thought how different his face was with his eyes shut and his mouth in one still line. And she knew she wasn't sure of anything.

On Friday, armed with her ballet drawings and bursting to display them, Anna searched the Cannon for Pym. He had not come to the barracks since the Tuesday morning. Anna had had a strange, solitary week, getting home around seven each evening and going straight to her room, staring at the drawings, making colour notes for paintings. She had not seen Linden apart from the odd contact at breakfast.

'Where is Pym?' she asked Hilary.

'He hasn't been in all week. I thought he was doing something with you?'

'No. How odd!' She ran downstairs and in the hall she almost collided with Bony.

She muttered 'Good morning', eager to get to the telephone and ring Pym's house to see if his landlady, the Hag as he called her, would look for him. Perhaps he was ill?

'I'm glad to see you, Anna,' Bony said. 'I wanted to have a look at how you have spent your week.'

She opened the flat case in which she carried drawings and went with him into the good light of the bottom studio. His silence as he leafed through was very flattering. At last he said, 'These are good, Anna.' He discussed them with her for five minutes, advising her to go back and use the last morning, complete her ideas. There was no way she could refuse. Anyway, she was thrilled and flattered by his interest and she forgot Pym and went out to catch a bus down to Sloane Square, to spend one more day drawing the dancers.

Anna got home at six and found the flat deserted. In the kitchen, on the dresser, was a note written in Linden's neat, round handwriting. *To whom it may concern. I've gone away for the week-end. To Dorset. No telephone number I'll be back Sunday evening. Linden.* Anna shrugged and made herself coffee, littering the room with her coat and drawings, bag and scarf. She heard Veronica come in and looked up as her mother bustled into the kitchen.

'No Linden?'

'She's gone away for the week-end. Very mysteriously . . .' Anna held out the note.

'I'm glad she hasn't taken the car. I simply have to go and see Granny tomorrow, Anna. I thought I'd spend Saturday night with her . . . Will you come? You don't want to stay here alone, do you?'

'Well . . . I'd love to see her. But there is this painting I want to do. It's all fresh in my head.'

'It was her eightieth birthday last week.'

'I could write a letter for you to take.'

'She asks about you and Linden.'

'I'll come next time.' Anna was screwing herself up inside, fighting the picture her mother painted of the frail, lonely old woman. In fact, her grandmother was active, bossy and difficult.

'Well, if you really must stay . . .'

'I would rather.' Already her mind was painting, figures in the shadows, the squares of light from the big windows and the way they touched the dancers and the floor.

She painted for the whole week-end, filling the flat with loud music when the quiet oppressed her, stopping exhausted on Saturday evening and telephoning Pym's home. No answer. Anna tried again at ten and the Hag answered and said it was too late for calls to her lodgers and put down the telephone. Anna went back to the film she was watching on the television, an ancient love story which made her cry, quite comfortably, and made her envious for the time the film portrayed when emotions had seemed so simple.

Veronica got back on Sunday afternoon, depressed after two days with her mother. 'Oh, Anna, she has deteriorated . . She repeated herself. She never used to do that. And she asked about your father constantly. Almost as if she knew I was hedging. I didn't want to talk about it.' She took ice from the fridge and made herself a strong drink. 'I think I'll have a bath and go to bed early. I find driving such an ordeal now!'

It was nearly ten when Linden arrived home. Anna, in the kitchen, heard the front door, heard two voices and a long, long silence. Her curiosity was aroused. When the silence had lasted a good five minutes, Anna couldn't stand it any longer and she went and looked into the hall.

Only Linden, leaning against the closed front door, her eyes shut, her head thrown back. Hearing Anna, she opened her eyes. 'Hallo.' There was something very strange about the attitude of her body, and her voice.

'Do you want some coffee? I've just boiled the kettle,' Anna said.

'Okay.' Linden came into the kitchen, sat at the table. Anna made a second mug of coffee, uneasy, putting it in front of Linden and sitting down on her own side of the table.

'Linden's face was very pale, her eyes huge, glittering. She was staring at her hands and moving her fingers as if she were playing some musical scale on the piano. She had learned for a couple of years. Expressions came and went, a smile catching her mouth sometimes and just as it seemed she would let herself go with the tender thoughts that smile expressed, she would pull herself away, frown, clench her hands.

'I adore him, Anna,' she said at last. 'And he loves me. And he is the exact opposite of everything I have ever wanted in a man. He cares about none of the things that matter to me. More than that, he despises most of them or simply never considers them. And yet he only has to touch me, less than that, look at me . . .' She met Anna's eyes. 'I let him make love to me. Or rather, it was quite mutual. We made love . . .'

Anna knew she was not required to speak. She wouldn't have known what to say, anyway.

'I never thought I would feel like that. I never wanted to be so close to anyone before. With him it's impossible not to be . . . nowhere else to go. It seemed absurd, indecent, not to make love to him. All this time in London I've been playing, knowing when a man wanted me and enjoying the power I felt.' She laughed. 'I liked to sit across a table from a man and pretend not to know what he wanted, to ignore the carefully thought-out little touches, the hints, the way they turn the conversation to sex. And if I liked him enough, I'd go home with him, anticipating how he would be, catagorizing him according to technique. I had this image of myself, laughing at them in my head, holding myself aloof. The more I played with them, the more infatuated they became!' There was genuine bewilderment on her face and she dropped her chin into her cupped hands and her expression changed completely. 'But with Pym . . .'

'Pym?' The word was torn from Anna, harsh with shock. 'I thought you were talking about James!'

'Of course not! I would never be so stupid with James!' Her voice was normal again. 'I met Pym in Sloane Square last Tuesday. At the bus stop. And in the afternoon he took me to see his flat, although you can't call it a flat really.' She was quiet for a moment, remembering the impact of those little rooms. She remembered her disbelief and the strength and thinness of his body and his freckled arms . . . but, no, that was Dorset . . . she was so confused by him. 'There are no rituals with him. No games. In the evenings last week we talked, he drew me, and Friday afternoon we caught a train. It's a tiny cottage on the side of a hill. It belongs to his aunt but she was away. Sheep with black faces and icy water and springy mossy grass and rain. And Pym . . .' She dropped her head into her hands and began to cry.

Anna's throat was closing up. 'But he is my friend!' Her voice was jerky. 'I can talk to him. He minds about me! But after you have had him, I will remind him of you and he won't want to be near me! You will take him away!'

Linden was deep in her own tears. Anna had not seen her cry since she was a small child. Tears were Anna's thing. Private explosions of frustration, of secret rage, were Anna's, not

Linden's. Anna watched for a few moments and could not bear it. She went and stood behind Linden, hovering, her hand above Linden's shoulders but unable to touch her. They never touched each other.

'I didn't mean that,' Anna said. 'Why are you crying? If Pym loved me I would be so happy . . . if anybody loved me!'

Linden lifted a wet and angry face, swinging to look at Anna, eyes narrowing.

'He is not what I want!' she hissed.

Anna shrank back to her own side of the table.

'He is far too young for me! I don't want him. Oh, God, how can I get the days to pass quickly? I want to forget this. I want to leap on a great step so that I can look back and laugh at him. And myself. He talks of marriage . . . marriage! I don't know him! He says he wants no children, that must be clear from the start. He talks and he talks. He talks so much, doesn't he, Anna?' Her face and voice softened. She folded her arms low as if she cradled a baby. 'I never thought I had such feelings in me. I am afraid.'

There was a great sickening envy all through Anna, threatening to choke her. Envy that she did not feel things as Linden did, that no man would ever stir her to these extremes. And, conversely, she was full of a childish curiosity and wanted to ask, 'What was it like with him? How did it feel? What did he do first? And next and next? How many times? Where did you sleep with him?' And then she realized that it was Pym, Pym, Linden had spoken of, sat now and thought of and curled herself against and shrank from. Loved? *Traitor. Traitor!*'

Linden looked up at her sister. 'Anna, I'm sorry if . . .'

'Linden?' It was Veronica, drawn by their voices, in her pink quilted dressing-gown. 'Did you have a nice time? Your note was so mysterious?'

Linden smiled quite calmly. 'I had a lovely time.'

'Now I'm awake, I'm going to have some tea.'

'Yes, I'd love a cup. This coffee is far too strong, Anna!' Linden stood up, going to the sink, pouring the coffee away. Her voice was quite normal. She stroked away the remains of the tears.

Anna went towards the door, pausing to look back at Linden and her mother, watching them edge together. Knowing

Linden would talk and Veronica would give satisfaction and drink up details and grow misty-eyed. There was doubt in Anna then. She could not decide if Linden really felt things or if it was all just something she thought was necessary. Part of the script....

'Well, who is this man you were with?' Veronica was saying. 'I haven't even heard of him.'

'Well, he's no one really!'

CHAPTER TWELVE

Freddie woke up when the sun, falling through the skylight in the sloping roof of his bedroom, spread itself flat on the white wall and the increased light intruded into his sleep. He stretched his way out of sleep, blinked and folded thick arms behind his head. He lay for a few moments, warm and content with his room and his life and his healthy male body. And the excitement which waited for him each morning shivered through him. He sat up and yawned. It was after 7.30. He was later than usual. He could not afford to over-sleep. He would not let success slip away through some trivial mistake of laziness or inattention. A world-shaking disaster, that was different. An event over which he had no control could strip him of everything and it would at least be tolerable afterwards. But there must be no mistake of his own making. People – they were the unknown quantity, to be studied, manipulated, slid forward, like pieces in a chess game.

He got out of bed and went to the bathroom and showered. He shaved, singing a little song, registering pleasure in this building that surrounded him. He loved the obvious age of it, the feeling of thick walls round him, solid wooden doors and deep skirting boards. The sash windows were a little twisted in their frames, some of the doors hanging a little crooked on their hinges and all the floors creaked. He loved it all – solidity, permanence, age. He splashed his face with Eau Savage and went back to his bedroom to choose, carefully, what he would wear today. The first of March! This morning Carlos Stephano was coming to Brook Street with a friend.

Two weeks ago, Freddie had written to Stephano again, as he had requested, because Freddie had managed to purchase a particularly fine bowl which he knew Stephano would appreciate. Freddie was being so careful, so gradual . . . Stephano wrote back. Yes, he would be most interested to see the bowl and he had a friend who would be accompanying him to London and would also be interested to meet Freddie. With the bowl, Freddie planned to show Stephano a press cutting of a sale in New York where an almost identical item had fetched £2000 more! He pulled on a clean shirt, whistling to himself.

In the kitchen, he plugged in his kettle before running down two more flights of stairs to collect his newspapers. Every morning he breakfasted on *The Financial Times*. Each week-end he read *The Investors Chronicle*. He had a game he played with himself, an elaborate fantasy, when he imagined himself confronting James Carroll and defeating James purely on facts. He pictured that long, impassive face growing flushed, ragged and angry. Childish, but he enjoyed it. However, it bothered Freddie that he disliked the man so intensely. They had, after all, met only once, at Oliver's party, and yet he felt James's influence, felt his distrust, in everything Oliver did and said. He disliked James for his extreme caution and his absolute conviction that Freddie must be unsound, if not dishonest, because his field was artistic. He disliked James's personal coldness and the maddening patronage with which he treated Oliver.

Freddie drank his coffee at the kitchen table. He could never eat anything at breakfast.

March the first. Freddie sat back. *Two months into 1972. What have I achieved? What have I forgotten?* He was reasonably satisfied with Brook Street and his neat brown files of clients and collections. To add Stephano would be a triumph, but there was something nagging at the back of his mind. A loose end. Irritating as a dripping tap. Something he wanted to do and had forgotten?

That girl, he thought suddenly, remembering the Christmas card. *Big, plump girl with a head full of originality. Quiet. Soft, white body. Only half grown-up. She could be useful, connected as she was with the Carrolls. Maybe the sister will pull it off and marry James.* Thinking of Linden, Freddie smiled and registered a kind of respect that he rarely felt for a woman. Not that he thought them mentally inferior. He had known women who were far superior intellectually to himself but they nearly always had a flaw. An emotional crack which made their judgement a hit or miss affair. They were subjective. They would abandon careers, or alter direction or simply stop dead in their tracks for a man. Freddie could not imagine himself changing the minutest portion of his life unwillingly for any woman! But

Linden Hayward, in the short time he had watched her and talked to her, had impressed him. Not that she was particularly clever but she was shrewd in the way Freddie himself was shrewd, standing back from people, asking, 'How can they help me? What can I get from them?' She thought ahead. She cared enough to push. She was strong. *But I doubt if she's strong enough to bend James Carroll into the kind of man she wants!*

He heard Penny come in. He went to the stairs and called down to her, asking if she wanted coffee.

'Yes, please. Not too strong!'

He smiled. She was at the moment involved in an intense love affair which brought her in heavy-eyed in the mornings. He put on his jacket, made a coffee and carried it down. It was just before nine o'clock.

Penny was sitting at her desk and Freddie bent and kissed the nape of her neck, put down the coffee and picked up his post.

'You're getting familiar, Mr Monroe!'

He grinned. It was a comfortable morning ritual. 'Today, for a change, you'll have to work!' he said. 'Stephano's coming round with some mate of his. Could you slip out and get a bottle of whisky, in case they hang on till midday? And some nice, dry sherry. And some flowers. Do you think you could stick them in a vase upstairs?'

'You're really pushing the boat out.' She sipped the coffee and grimaced. 'What kind of flowers?'

'Don't ask me,' Freddie said. 'Something expensive looking – you can take them home with you afterwards.' He gave her two five-pound notes. 'Thanks.'

The first of March, Anna thought, settling herself into class life, unpacking pencils and pinning up paper. She was huddled into an unusual corner, hoping very much that Pym wouldn't come or that, if he did, he would be on the far side of the room. Anna had slept very badly, which was unusual for her, restlessly moving from one shallow dream of Linden and Pym to the next. She didn't want to see him, think about him. But of course he came and he put his easel next to her.

He tugged at her hair, gently. 'Hallo, you.'

Anna was not capable of acting. Looking at him she felt

intensely sad and she wished he would go away. Whatever it was she had drawn from him in the past, she could no longer take. How could she tell him things, knowing he might take them to Linden? How much already had he laughed with Linden? No, that was unfair. She sat in silence, head bent.

'Anna, are you angry with me? Because I didn't tell you last week. It was all so sudden.'

She lifted a blank face but her eyes were angry and miserable. 'I have no claim on you. Why should I care what you do?'

'Don't be so silly. You know I've been after you for years!' He sat behind Anna, on the back of her donkey. 'I wish to God she was nothing to do with you! I'd like to talk to you about it but I know you are sick of hearing about her.' He touched Anna's arm. 'Can't I love you both? Anna?'

'Ssshhh. . . .'

'I won't ssshhh.'

She tried to smile, turning a little. 'I can't help how I feel, Pym.' Looking into his face she was suddenly scared for him, remembering things Linden had said. 'What will you do?'

'Do?' He spread his hands. 'Nothing . . . just everything in my power to get her to come and live with me, marry me, whatever she wants. I am obsessed with her. I can't stop thinking about her. That extraordinary sense of humour, exhibitionism almost, under the control and the prim exterior.' He saw Anna dip her head. He stood up. He threw his arms wide. 'I am a man in love . . . you fools. Insensitive fools!'

'Shut up!'

'Throw that maniac out!'

'Look, Pym, if it's RADA you want you're in the wrong building!'

Anna wished he would move. It was impossible for her to concentrate. All she could feel was his intense happiness, pouring out of him, in the tapping of his foot and his sudden smiles.

Gradually, through the day, she became more used to the idea. It no longer seemed terrible – just overwhelmingly sad, underlining Linden's constant, effortless victories. By four o'clock, Anna was tired and she couldn't face the thought of staying any longer. She didn't want to find herself alone with Pym. She didn't want coffee and she didn't want company. She fetched her coat and pushed at the swing door and went into the street, blinking with surprise. She had not expected this gentle spring afternoon. She had somehow thought the world outside would match the damp sadness of her mood. But there was warmth and sunshine. She didn't want to go home. She wandered up to Notting Hill Gate and the shops were full of summer clothes and light, bright shoes. A flower shop full of daffodils, their yellow faces leaning forward imploringly towards the glass.

I suppose, if it really happens between Linden and Pym, it will mean he will be around for ever. But she was still so shaken by it. Almost automatically she began to walk along the Bayswater Road . . . 'Come and see me at Brook Street if you get impatient,' he had said. She had gone over and over that evening in incredible detail until now she wasn't sure what she actually remembered and what she had invented and dreamed. Had he really said that? Had he taken notice of her? Had he? Would he? Surprised at her own daring she walked doggedly onwards, undoing her coat, letting the wind lift her hair. A bus paused near her and she jumped on to it and rode down to Marble Arch. Then walked again, down Park Lane, her feet moving more slowly now. *It will be just another shattering disappointment. It's stupid to go today, feeling like this, as sad as this.* But she went, at first walking down Brook Street as swiftly as she could, looking straight ahead towards Grosvenor Square, then turning and walking back more slowly. This time she saw the shop and crossed the road. She looked at the fragile pieces of porcelain in the window and tried to feel something for them, to form an opinion. The interior of the shop was smart and sophisticated, chocolate brown. A blonde girl sat and typed with flying hands. Anna drew back, lacking the courage to go in. She looked up at the floors above, wondering if he was there.

'Well, what do you think?'

She jumped, violently, and stared at Freddie. His face was exactly as she remembered it and yet it was a shock. Although she had hoped to see him, she was not prepared, not dressed, her face not ready. As usual she had only half thought about it. An instinct had made her come.

'Do you like the pieces in the window?' he said.

'Not really.'

'Come on in and see the rest of it.' He pushed the door open and Anna hesitated for a moment and then went in. She hovered as Freddie walked across to the girl at the desk.

'Hallo, Pen . . . all well? Penny, this is Anna Hayward, a friend of mine. Come on up, Anna.' He went through a door at the back of the showroom and up a flight of stairs. They were steep with a polished wooden banister. At the top they led straight into a big, white-painted room. A desk, bookshelves, a low sofa, upright chairs, a table against the wall. Freddie threw down his briefcase. 'Cuppa tea?'

'Yes, I'd like one.' She put down her basket and slowly took off her coat. 'Shall I make it?'

'Thanks.' He sat down behind the desk. 'Kitchen's through that door there.'

After a short search she found tea in a tin, milk and sugar. Tidier and cleaner than the last kitchen. She wondered, without being able to smile, if she would continue to see him so rarely that each time he would have a new kitchen. There was a packet of digestive biscuits on the small kitchen table but she didn't want one. Not here. She made the tea in a brown enamel pot and carried it through on a tray, concentrating carefully so that she didn't spill it.

He had been thinking so deeply that he had forgotten her. He looked up, surprised for a second, and then smiled. And it hit her all over again.

How simple! she thought. *I came to see him because I wanted to see him. Now I am here, he doesn't mind.*

'Like it?' Freddie said, making a gesture to include the room, the whole building, but not taking his eyes off her face. 'You're thinner!'

'I think it's very smart . . . Am I thinner? Really?'

'Yes. And what else? How are you? How is your sister? Oliver has not mentioned her for weeks.'

'No, well, he wouldn't. She sees James now.' Anna poured tea. 'Milk? Sugar?'

'No sugar. Funny day! I'd forgotten how you make me feel. You're very soothing, do you know that? I said I'd ring you, didn't I? There wasn't any time?'

He leaned forward, elbows on his desk. 'I've had a very good day, Anna . . . will you have dinner with me to celebrate? Or do you want to play games and be insulted because I haven't approached you before?'

Her stomach leapt with a wild, childish hope. 'I'm not insulted. I knew you were busy. You said you would be.' She lifted her chin. 'I was busy too, until today.' She dropped her eyes and thought of Pym, mentally wrapping him in tissue paper, putting him away.

Freddie moved his eyes up and down her body. 'You'll have to start dressing better,' he said flatly. He looked at his watch. 'It's not quite five. Come on. We'll go and buy you a dress.'

'Don't be silly.'

'Come on. I feel generous! And I won't take you out in that black thing you wore last time. Come on, woman.' He picked her coat off a chair and threw it at her, hustling her down the stairs, into the street, walking so fast they were almost running as they turned into Bond Street and crossed the road to Fenwick's.

'The other shops are too old for you. And too expensive for me.' He walked her through the various departments until they came to the dresses. He eyed her. 'What size are you? Still a couple of stone too fat.'

'Sixteen. Size sixteen,' Anna said humbly.

He flicked down a rail of dresses and kaftans. Beautiful colours, high necks, full sleeves and deep buttoned cuffs. 'Try on this, and this.'

She took them, silently, amazed and embarrassed and yet delighted. She went into a small curtained changing room, slipping off her coat and sweater and jeans and trembling, terrified that Freddie might wrench back the curtain and expose her, white and huge in her substantial underclothes. The first dress was deep green and navy, and turquoise and black and a kind of grey brown. Silk. It looked marvellous on her, skimming over the bulges, taking the bolster look from her bosom. She could not believe the reflection. She stared, expecting it to dissolve like a mirage.

Timidly, she pulled back the curtain to show him, her cheeks bright pink. He was talking to two sales girls and Anna felt their curiosity.

'Great. Have that one,' Freddie said.

'I haven't tried the other yet.'

'Well, it couldn't look better. Really, you look lovely.' His voice dropped as if he realized how embarrassed she was feeling. 'Have you got shoes that will do?'

She nodded, amazed at the extent of his involvement, expecting, at any moment, to be asked if she needed tights. She took off the dress and when she emerged from her cubicle, back in the duffle coat, Freddie wrote a cheque. The dress was packed in a large carrier bag and handed to her. He propelled her into the street.

'Can you find your own way home, Anna? I want to go into Sotheby's. I'll pick you up about eight. Okay?'

She nodded. He turned and walked away, leaving her staring after him, clutching the paper bag and her basket and remembering the last time she had stood on the pavement and watched him go.

Anna crept into the flat and ran down to her bedroom to hide the bag and the dress, afraid of questions. She got into the bathroom before Linden even came home and when Linden pushed open the door, waving her hands at the steam, she was annoyed to find the bath occupied. 'Hurry up, Anna.'

But Anna didn't hurry. She lay in the hot, silky water. She washed her hair. She scrubbed her body all over. She wandered down to her bedroom, leaving wet prints, and lay on her bed until her damp, heavy hair made her get up and crouch in front of the electric fan heater, brushing it dry. Her hair reached her waist now. Newly-washed, it had every shade of red and orange and copper. *Wasted on me, really*, she thought. She dressed with elaborate care, enjoying the whole female ritual intensely. At last she allowed herself to put on the dress. She was afraid that, in the shop, some clever lighting or trick mirror would have made it look far better than here, in her own brutal looking glass. But she was wrong. The dress still held its magic.

'Anna . . .' Linden burst in and then paused, staring. 'God, where did you get that? It looks marvellous on you.' There was a deep surprise in her voice. 'Turn round!' She came forward and touched the silk. 'Those colours are beautiful on you. You look much thinner . . . But your hair ruins everything. You must let me do something with it!'

'What?' Anna said cautiously but she was overwhelmed by

the genuine admiration in Linden's face.

'Sit down!' Linden commanded. She gathered up the mass of hair and brushed it and twisted it into a great silky knot at the back of Anna's head, against the nape of her neck. She told Anna to hold it while she went to Veronica for pins. Anna sat, arms aching, waiting until Linden came back and pinned and pulled and at last said, 'Yes. Look at that.'

'It's quite nice.'

'It goes with the dress . . . you can see the collar and the shoulders and it makes your neck look long. Actually, your neck is quite long, but I'd never noticed before.' She gave a little, quick step of satisfaction. 'Now tell me where you are going?' Their eyes met in Anna's mirror and Anna saw that Linden was wearing Veronica's diamond earrings. A long dress, cut low at the back. She turned the question round.

'Where are you going, Linden? Isn't that rather smart for Pym?'

Linden swung away. 'James, not Pym. It's some charity ball thing. It was arranged before he went away. Pym understands!' She paused, her back to Anna. 'Look, all those things I said last night . . . I was tired. I didn't mean them. Forget it, will you?'

The doorbell rang and Linden moved calmly down the hall and let James in. They had not seen each other for over two weeks. He bent to kiss her cheek. Each time he didn't see her for a while, he forgot how lovely she was. He followed her into the sitting-room where Veronica was crouched over a new 5,000-piece puzzle of the Armada. She glanced round and sat back on her heels, pushing her hair back from her forehead.

'Good evening, James.' She looked at James and Linden, side by side, and her mind framed them, married them. 'Did you have a good time in . . . wherever you were?'

'Very good, thank you. Very satisfactory.' He approached her. 'Those things must take months, Mrs Hayward.'

'Do call me Veronica.' She picked up her empty glass from the floor beside her. 'Fill me up, will you, Linden, when you're pouring James a drink?'

'Whisky, James?'

He nodded. He stood by the fireplace, one arm resting on the mantelpiece. He gave Veronica his polite attention and his conversation but his eyes went back, again and again, to Linden.

She seemed different tonight. Withdrawn. It intrigued him. She had always seemed, in the past, a little too ready to listen to him, flatter him with her attention and her charm but tonight she was dreaming, pausing with the whisky bottle in her hand as she looked out towards the tiny garden. She was experiencing a longing to be somewhere else which was so strong it stilled her completely for a few moments.

Veronica got up, rather stiffly, and carried her empty glass to the small round table. 'Linden is asleep . . . Yes, these puzzles do take months but I find them so absorbing! Something to do in the evenings when I'm on my own.'

Linden made an effort. She carried James his drink and stood by him, asking him about Germany, about France, remembering carefully the places he had said he would visit, discussing the differences in the cosmetic market in England and Italy. But she was glad when James said it was time to leave.

'Shall we walk down, James? That lift is so slow.'

'Yes, of course, if you'd rather.' He tucked his arm through hers. They heard the sound of hurried feet and on the first floor landing they were surprised to see Freddie bounding into view, taking the stairs two at a time.

He paused, smiled broadly. 'Evening, Linden. Evening, James,' and then went past them. Standing where they were for a moment, James and Linden stared back at his disappearing figure.

'So that's who she's dressed up for,' Linden said, raising an eyebrow. 'How unlikely!'

They went on down.

'Do you like him?' James said carefully. 'Personally, I cannot stand the man. I'm quite convinced he's far too sharp to be wholly honest. Oliver worships the ground he walks on.'

'I don't know what I think about him but I know he doesn't like me.' Linden laughed. 'What on earth can he see in Anna?'

'From the little I know of Freddie Monroe it's more likely that he feels she will be useful!' James shut his car door very hard indeed.

CHAPTER THIRTEEN

They knew Freddie in the restaurant, a small, smart place off Walton Street with pink table cloths and candles. They showed him to a table in the corner and asked what Anna would drink. They knew, apparently, what Freddie would drink. She asked for whisky. She took little glances at Freddie all the time, little excursions into him, deciding that he looked tired and that he dressed very well but rather flamboyantly. His relaxation and his confidence built a castle round her, there was no need to be unduly aware of herself. If she bored him he would tell her. She felt she had no responsibility except to enjoy herself. She drank some whisky and it warmed and freed her.

Freddie picked up the hand which Anna had left lying hopefully on the table. Her hands did not match her body. They were long-fingered with delicate wrists. Freddie opened her hand, turned it over, looked into the palm. 'I always notice hands . . . yours are very appealing. Gentle hands. Your sister's are square and strong and rather masculine. Very strange on such a delicate body. You look lovely, Anna. You know that, don't you? Can you feel the admiration of people who look at you?'

She laughed. 'I think that's exaggerating it a bit. But it's a beautiful dress. Thank you for it. I'm sure I shouldn't have let you buy it. Isn't it against the rules?'

'What has your mother been telling you? If you accept anything other than chocolates or flowers you will be branded a whore?' He laughed, emptied his glass and looked round for the waiter.

'Two more whiskeys, please.' He opened his menu. 'I came here with Oliver, the day we started it all.' His mind zigzagged. 'Thank God I'm an only child,' he said, almost to himself.

'Why do you say that?'

'You, of all people, shouldn't need to ask. Brothers and sisters warp each other's lives. They compete from the start. They need to impress each other. Look at Oliver and James. You and Linden.'

'But, in other ways, you gain a lot. Linden and I are at least always there for the other.'

'If you had no sister, you'd have a friend to fill the gap. It would be a cleaner, more useful relationship which you could use when you needed it and get away from when you felt the competition was too hot. Anyway, what are we going to eat?'

They ordered lasagne and steak tartare and salad. And Freddie talked about Stephano, about the man's caution, about the friend he brought. 'A woman. I was expecting a man.' They drank a lot of red wine and Freddie smoked after the steak was eaten. 'I trust you, Anna, not to repeat all these things. In fact, I know you won't.'

His confidence was well founded. She was his. And in a way she did not yet understand, for the moment he was hers.

'Tell me something about yourself, Anna.'

'Nothing has happened to me.'

He smiled. 'So nothing has happened to you. I could happen to you if I have time.'

'If I have time, too!'

He laughed. 'I think you might just fit me in!'

The restaurant and Freddie and the wine and food, which she hardly noticed, enclosed her and gave her for the first time in her life the feeling that she was one half of a pair. Freddie invaded her completely. She could not stand back. She remembered her first instinct about him, fear of him, and now found it absurd. He was so gentle.

'I could tell you about my home. In Gloucestershire. I loved it very much. I still dream about it, at least once a week. In colour. Would you like to hear about that?'

'Yes. I love to watch you talking. To watch your mouth.'

She talked until she was hoarse, telling him everything that came into her head, talking through three cups of coffee and a large glass of brandy, talking until at last she became aware that the waiters were restless, that everyone else had gone. She looked round and blinked, surprised.

Freddie asked for the bill. He said, 'Well, where shall we go now, Anna? Do you want to come home with me? I should tell you I'm not tired tonight.' His eyes danced at her. 'Do you want to come home with me?' he said again, very quietly.

'Yes.'

This time she was not afraid of him seeing her naked. She had told him so much. He had penetrated something far more secret than her body. She was curious and eager for him. There was no question of waiting. She remembered what Linden had said . . . 'It felt indecent not to make love.'

Freddie was in his best mood, elated by the success of the day, built up by Anna's round-eyed attention. He felt a genuine affection for her, almost a possessiveness. He made love to her with great care and tenderness and also considerable authority. 'No . . . not like that, with your mouth like a fish. Kiss me like a woman, Anna, not a child.'

She was deeply surprised. Surprise was the strongest thing she felt. Surprised to feel him inside her, at the weight of his body, the tension and the darkness. Too much to register at once. Feelings in her, breaking loose and bursting like bubbles of air from under water. His deep voice, encouraging. It was always Freddie who was making love to her. He imprinted his personality on the darkness. Freddie, no disembodied set of hands, no anonymous body. She did not have an orgasm. Neither of them expected her to. She fell asleep against him and Freddie lay on his back, one arm beneath her, putting off the moment when he must get up and take her home.

She woke because Freddie stirred beside her. For a moment she was lost and scared, amazed to feel the body beside her. Naked, warm body. She moved cautiously and Freddie yawned and rolled over and enveloped her.

'I didn't mean to go to sleep.' He put his heavy head against her shoulder and the gesture affected her more than anything he had done previously. 'We must get up. I must take you home.'

'I don't want to go home.'

'I don't want to get up and take you but I can't believe you are in the habit of staying out all night and I don't want to start a panic. I don't want to be greeted by your mother screaming "Rapist" at me.'

Anna laughed. Then Freddie rolled away from her and switched on his lamp and she was suddenly terrified that she looked awful. Hair dishevelled, make-up smeared, fat and white and horrible. She got out of bed and turned away from him, looking for her clothes. Freddie pulled on his pants and shirt and then he touched Anna's shoulders, turning her round to face him. Both of them, half-dressed, barefoot, standing very close to each other. Anna thought how wonderful he looked with wild hair and a sleepy face. Impulsively, she put her arms round him, hugging him, and then standing back to look at him again, to try and believe it had happened.

He thought she looked like a child, heavy-lidded, soft-skinned, plump, with all that long hair. He thought he would feel like hell in the morning. He breathed in deeply, put his arms round her, face in her hair.

They said very little in the car. Four-thirty in the morning but London was not sleepy. Outside her flat Freddie leaned to kiss her, yawned, said: 'Good night, Anna, or good morning.'

'Happy Easter?'

'No, not this time, I'll ring you tomorrow.'

Anna slept until 12 o'clock. She was aware that Veronica came in, around 8.30, to say that she and Linden were leaving for work. Anna acknowledged this with a grunt and then sank back into sleep. She was woken a second time by the telephone and thought *Freddie* and almost fell out of bed in her eagerness to answer it.

'Hallo?'

'Happy birthday. Want to have lunch with me?'

'Yes. But I've only just woken up . . . I'm not dressed.'

'Never mind.'

'What time is it? Where shall I meet you?'

'I'll collect you at twelve-thirty. That gives you half an hour! I have to drive down to Henley.'

'Freddie, I don't have to be smart, do I? I have no smart clothes. Just jeans.'

'Just jeans will do very nicely.'

It is happening to me, Anna thought, putting the telephone down very carefully as if he lived in it. Joy pulsing through her with every heart beat and a nervousness in her stomach at the thought of seeing him. Perhaps the feeling would have gone. *God, what can I wear*? and she rummaged through

Linden's drawers and through her mother's and at last found a shirt of Veronica's and a long navy sweater with a knitted belt. No thought of the Cannon. No thought of the work she had sworn to devote her life to. Nothing but Freddie.

He came at exactly 12.30. In the daylight she was stricken for a moment with an overwhelming embarrassment. He read it in her face and he kissed her. 'Don't look like that. It's a lovely day!' He drove much too fast down the M4 and they had lunch at The Compleat Angler and watched the river and the weir. They drove into Henley and Anna sat and waited patiently in the car while Freddie disappeared into an immense mock Tudor palace to discuss a forthcoming auction with 'the loaded Mrs Hull'. Anna waited patiently and happily. She didn't want the radio. She wanted nothing but her thoughts and they were all of Freddie.

CHAPTER FOURTEEN

Although she had waited for so long and anticipated in such detail, love caught Anna unawares. She was stunned into an instant and total acceptance. She had no idea of using time to measure the strength of the relationship. She loved Freddie. She was overflowing with all the love she had never been able to place before. She believed that this was her destiny, to be linked with this forceful, tender, gentle, generous, extrovert and ambitious man. Her head was full of misty love poems. Freddie cared only for Shakespeare, the big speeches, which he was fond of shouting in a deep Churchillian voice, pacing the room and waving his arms. Then he would stop and turn and look at her and cross the room and envelop her, sweep her off her feet, scaring and delighting her with his strength.

I have a lover, Anna thought, again and again. *I am no longer a virgin. Men look at me differently. I have joined a group that most of the world belongs to. I belong. I understand!* If it was at night that she thought these things, in the darkness, she would get up and turn on the light and examine herself minutely, and would be disappointed to find so little outward change. But mentally she was rearranged. Her state of mind made work difficult but she was immune to Bony's rages and Pym's raised eyebrows. When she did work, the results were intense, as if she was seeing the world more clearly and from a different angle.

On some days she didn't go to the Cannon at all. She stayed at home and dreamed and waited for the telephone or the sudden unexpected peal on the doorbell. It was enough to fill a day, to wait like that. Waiting had become a positive occupation because if he did come, or telephone, she would experience such happiness and peace and relief; she could not bear to risk missing him. Now her life was lived for the evenings and Freddie. The days, which previously had been all important, were merely pauses.

Through those months of spring, life in the flat in Oakfield Court was entirely changed. Anna and Linden, each wrapped up in an extremely intense period of their lives, were blind to the other's state of mind. Only Veronica saw it all, the recipient of confidences, loving the excitement, always ready to listen. She saw the great change in Anna and although she couldn't bring herself to like Freddie, she was grateful to him for Anna's happiness. He had somehow taken away the panic, the desperate shyness which hid a longing for attention. It was as if Anna told herself, 'Freddie wants me. Me! I am the person he wants to be with in the evenings, the one he talks to about Stephano and Maisie Hunter and Mrs Hull, about the market, about sales; he likes the way I look. He makes love to me.' Over and over again she told herself and as she began to believe this, others did too. Other men noticed Anna. She was a little thinner but it was more than that. It seemed that her striking hair and the flamboyant clothes which she wore under Freddie's skilful direction and the witch eyes, looking out at the world with some courage now, had organized themselves, become the outer skin of a whole and interesting person. Even attractive!

March, April, May, Freddie, Freddie, Freddie, steadily climbing his ladder, steadily increasing his profits. He was content to see Anna. He enjoyed her. She played no games. She told him she had no one else to go out with. She would be ready at a moment's notice if he rang her. She was convenient, humble, fresh and clean and he relished the bite of her intelligence and the way she remembered the names of men and women he was involved with. She suited Freddie in these months of spring, when everything was going perfectly, when Oliver was docile and the market rose and Freddie's confidence grew, layer on layer.

When Freddie took Anna out, they always went back to Brook Street afterwards and they would make love. In the early morning he would get up and take her home. Although he complained, for the moment he rather liked this immature relationship. It was new for him. In the past women had moved in, stayed, moved out. It made her different.

Anna was pleased that he wanted her and proud of his strong male body but the actual process of love-making did not affect her deeply. She was still too busy exploring him as a person, shrewdly mapping out the will to succeed which ran through him like his spine, seeing how he forgot anything inconvenient, could be ruthless one minute and sentimental the next. Occasions mattered to him. And memories. She came to know and interpret his various smiles, the way his voice altered on the telephone. Sex was just a part of him and so new to her she didn't pretend. She answered Freddie with an honesty that disturbed him. Freddie had always prided himself on his knowledge of women and their responses, his subtlety and success in bed. Sometimes Anna's calmness angered him and he demanded to know what she felt, what she liked.

'But I like everything. Just being with you. Close to you.'

Freddie made an exasperated sound, telling himself he should not expect a child to act and respond like a woman . . . And yet she was not all child. Freddie lay on his back, arms folded under his head. 'Oliver came to see me last night, about nine, with some crazy scheme for making battery-operated shopping baskets. On wheels!' Freddie laughed aloud. 'Dolly trolleys, he wants to call them. He thinks we should take some of the profit and set up a small manufacturing company; I'm afraid I was rude. I told him we were building an investment company and it was all going very nicely and the last thing we wanted was to waste time and money on some crazy scheme. It's not the first time he's done it! Sometimes his mental age seems to be about fourteen.'

'No, it isn't,' Anna said. 'Can't you see? You've involved him in an exciting world but he cannot contribute much because you have all the knowledge. So even if you are making him a lot of money, he cannot tell himself that he is succeeding. He tries to think up something of his own. He . . .'

Freddie put a hand over her mouth. 'All right, all right. Spare me the analysis. Most people would be quite content to have money made for them!' *And fortunately*, Freddie thought, *Oliver does not press the point that he has absolute financial control!*

'But Oliver is not interested in money for its own sake!'

'Then he must be more stupid than I thought!' Freddie swung himself out of bed. For a moment he thought about the previous evening. Oliver had not come alone. He had brought a girl with him. A small girl with a white skin and black eyes and a big mouth. 'Rachel,' Oliver had said. 'From the club.' She had held out her hand to Freddie and their eyes met and they both registered interest.

Quite suddenly Freddie felt uneasy. He was letting Anna come too close, relaxing too much with her. He began to feel cornered. He turned and looked at her.

'Freddie, do you think you could pick me up from the Cannon tomorrow, at about seven-thirty, after the lecture? It would be such a help. We've been sorting out the lockers and files and I have a year's work to bring home and Linden wants the car.' She watched him with a comfortable little smile on her face. She was fitting him, he felt, into a cliché.

He stood up. 'I'm sorry. Tomorrow's out,' he said flatly.

'Oh, why? Freddie, don't be so mean.'

'Anna, if you don't take that ridiculous patient look off your face, I think I shall hit you. I am not your damn chauffeur!'

'Go to hell!' Anna stood up, surprising him, the new-found confidence giving her courage. She would argue now but she wanted Freddie to win. She expected him to turn on her with a blend of sarcasm and anger and make her feel safe. But instead he lit a cigarette and looked at her with a bored disinterest.

Anna was terrified – she understood that expression. It said, 'On my terms, Anna!' She sprang up and went to him.

'I don't care. I'll leave the stuff there. It's been there a year. It can stay another week. Or until I can get Mini.'

Freddie was gracious in victory, resting his arms on her shoulders. 'Anna . . .' He shrugged. 'I've done the boy-friend bit, and I'm just not interested. I really am busy tomorrow. And all this taking you home is getting a bit tiring.'

She put her face against him. She had nothing to say. She told herself she must never, never again, try to use him as Linden used her men.

Pym put himself constantly in Linden's way, reading clearly in her reluctance to see him and her bewildering changes of mood that she was torn. He acted purely by instinct. He felt that Linden was essential to him and therefore he would do everything in his power to see her and make her accept him. He telephoned her at work, constantly asking her to have a drink with him, or coffee, or just to walk; he questioned Anna to find out Linden's every move, when she saw James, when she saw other men. There was a graph in his mind on which he plotted his chances . . . Sometimes, when Linden was in one of her crazy moods, especially when he had her in his flat, he could believe that she would eventually accept him. He talked even more than before, desperately dragging James and the whole situation into the open. 'I know you hate to give up the idea of James and all that he stands for. You have been indoctrinated by your mother . . .'

'You are utterly wrong. I have been indoctrinated but not to look for success and money and security. I have been told, again and again, that love is everything!' Linden was half drunk. They had consumed two bottles of harsh, cheap wine. They seemed to tighten each other into highly emotional moods and she needed to spill the nervous energy which the alcohol and Pym had created in her. She stood up, draping herself in a blanket, holding her wine glass in one affected hand. Her voice was, for the moment, Veronica's.

'Oh, my God, when I look back . . . the pity of it all. So easy now, to understand. But at the time. Don't waste your life, Linden. Look at yourself. Lucky girl, you are young and beautiful. You have everything for this short time in your life. Make the most of it! You must live this time and remember. You will never live so intensely again. The memories you store when you are young are twice as bright. Pour me another glass of wine, my darling. Oh, when I think back . . . A woman's life is nothing without love.' Linden stopped abruptly, letting her hand fall, spilling wine. The blanket slid down her naked body and lay round her feet. 'Stupid, weak, alcoholic . . . She still loves him. She'd have him back tomorrow. I listen and I pity her because she is forty-five and faded and alone and she wants nothing from life but him!' She stooped and retrieved the blanket. 'You are like her, Pym. You want to build your life round one person.'

He shook his head. He lay on the cushions, weight on one elbow, almost hypnotized by her. When he spoke his voice was husky. 'I don't want to . . . I have no choice. Also, in one way your mother is right. You have a far greater chance of happiness if you love a lot.'

'Rubbish!' She swung round and crouched to his level. 'Happiness is success. Achieving your ambitions is happiness! Happiness is making your life into something real and definite and substantial, not lying back, flabbily experiencing emotions and orgasms and love. You won't be happy, Pym.'

'Why not?'

'Why are you being so placid all of a sudden? Why do you just lie there, questioning me? Why don't you shout back like you normally do?'

'Why should I? You are quite happy contradicting yourself!' He sat up smiling, speaking with a confidence he didn't feel. 'You know, underneath, that you want to be with me. No one else will do for you. I don't know why we belong together, but we do. And sooner or later you'll admit it. And I'll wait until you do. I'll wait years if necessary because I have no choice.'

She came and lay down beside him, spreading the blanket over the two of them, whispering, 'I wish one or other of you were dead. Then I wouldn't have to think . . .'

'I'm not going to die until I'm ninety. I had my palm read.' He put his arms round her, pulling her towards him so that their bodies touched all the way down; she made no attempt to hold herself away from him. She put her mouth on his. A sudden triumph made him tremble. He believed he was winning. He had no idea that the more he pushed Linden, the more he confronted her, the more she took refuge with James.

Linden actually sought James out now. She took the initiative in a way she had never done in her life before. He found the change intriguing. Underneath his cool exterior, James Carroll believed himself to be a romantic man. There were traces of Oliver's shyness in him, too, but they were well trodden down. In the beginning he had found Linden so dazzling that he had been unwilling to involve himself with such confidence but now, changed as she was, quieter, troubled about something, she appealed to him far more.

James disliked extroverts. It was one of the reasons he so disliked Freddie Monroe. It was basically unhealthy, James thought, to be constantly on display. It showed weakness. In the beginning he had thought Linden too flamboyant, her self-confidence rather frightening in one so young. James had not bothered to understand many women. There had not been time. Women had always wanted to be with James – they were successful only if they asked as little of him as he asked of them and no more. But with Linden, he began to feel differently. Now she seemed to want to be with him, to be quiet with him. She waited, obviously nervous, at the end of an evening until he mentioned the next time and then she would relax. She telephoned him just to talk. To ask 'How are you?' She seemed to need him and, for the first time, James enjoyed the feeling of being needed by someone other than his mother.

James had made no attempt to sleep with her. He was not sure why, especially as through March and April, he found himself shedding the two or three regular women he went out with. They had begun to seem unnecessary, almost coarse. Too open, too dull. Linden made most other women seem shallow and pale. He asked her to come to Austria with him, at Easter, for a week's skiing. She accepted but she hesitated before saying yes. James booked them separate rooms. He was beginning to think of her as considerably younger than himself, innocent under the façade. After all, she couldn't help the effect she had on men. It was born in her. It didn't necessarily mean she used it. As if underlining his opinion, Linden made no attempt to flirt with him. Instead, she seemed to be watching him constantly. Assessing him, judging him, choosing? The holiday was a success. There were eight of them in the party. Linden fitted beautifully amongst his friends. She came home very sunburned. She was beginning to feel safe.

'I see James is nurturing this one,' his friends were saying. 'Well, I suppose we all have to go, sooner or later.'

'How very nice,' Robert Carroll said, turning and looking across the bedroom at Marietta, 'to wake up and see that lovely face every day.'

She raised her eyes from the newspaper. 'What face? What are you talking about?'

He laughed. 'I am doing just what I always accuse you of doing. Carrying on a conversation with myself and then expecting you to understand . . . I was thinking of Linden.'

Marietta laid the newspaper down. 'I didn't think you'd noticed.'

'I didn't think you would take it so calmly. Surely you were hoping for some ancient debt-ridden title?'

She smiled at him, not bothering to deny it. 'One cannot have everything! I do long for James to marry . . . I must be getting old. I want to be a grandmother, Robert. And my heart has sunk so many times, when it seemed he would choose one of those huge, long-limbed aggressive-looking girls he has cared for in the past. Models or whatever they call themselves. I am surprised at myself but I would far rather have Linden. She has such character.'

'And she's intelligent and she can laugh.' Robert stood by the window, drinking his coffee. He was dressed, except for the jacket of his suit, which he would put on when he had finished his coffee. His head throbbed gently. His blood pressure was high and the pills he took to counteract this made it impossible for him to drink alcohol. It depressed him more than he would admit. He did not need to drink but he had enjoyed it all his life. Wine at lunch. A Bloody Mary or two before dinner. Whisky when he was tired. He sighed, wondering why old age and all that came with it should be the reward of a lifetime spent working hard, using his brain and opportunity and the little money he had started with, to build up a vast and successful business complex. Now James could cope with it all. Why, just when Robert could be sitting back, enjoying life, had his body chosen to let him down? *Have I left it too late?* he thought.

Watching him, Marietta knew the gist of his thoughts. Outwardly her face was calm. Inside she was desperately afraid. Robert was her life. He had been, on and off, for thirty-six years. James was a constant source of pride and joy. Oliver she had never found easy although she had struggled not to let it show. But Robert was everything . . . she watched him put his hand to his temples. He looked so tired. Robert, whose energy had been notorious. He was only sixty-two. A young man still. She couldn't bear to see him standing like that, eyes closed, looking old.

'Robert,' she said sharply.

'Yes?'

'Does your head ache?'

'A little.' He came to the bed and stooped to kiss her forehead. 'I'll see you at about one.'

She watched him go out, heard the front door close. She

looked down at her hands. Strange that these hands, almost an old woman's hands, should have appeared ... only a little while ago her hands had been white, supple, and free from these veins. *It seems then*, she thought, leaning her head back against the pillow, *there is never a time when you can sit back. You come through the early times, the difficulties, the other people who interfere and divert and attract, you come through all that and at last you are ready to sit back and enjoy one another's company, content to love one man, but only to find so much more is asked of you. You find that this man you have built your life around may require that you go on alone. Go on to what?* She shivered. This lovely room, this whole comfortable life which enveloped her, seemed suddenly fragile and meaningless, mere wrapping paper. She swung her legs out of bed. She heard the click of a key in the door with pleasure and relief and turned her thoughts, thankfully, to Linden and James.

Anna was waiting for Freddie, sprawled in a chair in the sitting-room of the flat and trying to sit still. She hadn't seen him for eight days ... He had flown to Italy to stay with Carlos Stephano for a few days; the few days had grown into a week. A week in which Anna began to realize the extent of her dependence and how much she missed Freddie. She had worked every weekday at the Cannon, until eight or nine at night. It had been a beautiful week – almost summer. Today in the lunch hour she had sat on the pavement with Pym and others in a long row, eating ice-creams, faces tilted up to the May sunshine. A few weeks into the summer term, settled down but still eager, they leaned against the solid brick front of the building and talked, and people walking down the pavements smiled and stepped tolerantly over their out-stretched legs as if they were always there. It was that sort of day.

Pym had finished his choc ice and closed his eyes. 'She's seeing him tonight, isn't she, Anna?'

'Who? What?' Anna pretended not to understand.

'Linden. Seeing James. He's taking her somewhere. She said he was taking her out on Thursday ... I often ring her when she's working. I like to hear her sounding awkward and furtive. I like to think he might be there, standing by her.'

'Sadist!'

'Not at all.' He felt optimistic. It was probably the sun, he thought dryly, but he liked the feeling. 'I am going to make her understand that it is essential that we are together. She still plays with the idea of him, of his life, but this week-end she is coming to Dorset with me and after that it will be all right.'

'Pym . . .'

'I've bought a car, Anna. It's an ancient Volkswagen but it goes. Slowly. We will have a long, long drive and we will talk. I shall fill the back seat with bottles of plonk and paper, to draw her on. I cannot quite get her. I must have her face. Just in case . . . I shall come to your flat at seven tomorrow and pick her up. After this week-end it will be all right.' He opened his eyes, turned to look at Anna.

His face was thinner, she thought. 'Pym. You mustn't . . .'

'Don't you tell me what I must or must not do!' he snapped, angry that she would not fit in with his mood. At once he was sorry. He put his arm round her shoulders. 'I worry enough for two of us, Anna. You don't have to warn me.'

Oh, Pym, Anna thought now, in the quiet of the sitting-room hugging her knees, scared for him. *Why did you have to meet her?*

She looked up, as Linden came in . . . surprised as if she had conjured Linden out of her thoughts. Linden wore a pleated skirt and very high-heeled shoes. She looked crisp and smart and daytime.

'Anna, I'm going to the Carrolls. For the week-end. I promised Marietta I'd cook for them down there. Mrs McKay and husband are away for two weeks. James is driving me down tonight . . . Marietta had made other arrangements but they fell through. She suddenly asked me. Today. I couldn't refuse.' She was twisting the long shoulder strap of her bag with her hands.

'You can't go!' Anna crouched into her chair. 'Pym . . .'

'Never mind about him. Just explain, tomorrow, that I have gone. I warned him I might have to go.'

'You explain! You do it . . . telephone him . . . I won't! He thinks you are going to Dorset with him.'

'Does he tell you everything?' Linden's face was furious. 'I wish to God he'd leave me alone. All right! Don't mention it. Let him turn up here and find I've gone. Perhaps that will finish it, once and for all.'

'He's bought a car. For you! To take you to Dorset in. A slow car. So you can talk!'

'Don't be so ridiculous.' Linden paced nervously, backwards and forwards. She came to the window and jerked back the curtain, searching for James's car. 'He is a child!'

'Who is?' Veronica came in, face alive, ready for excitement.

'Pym. He is driving me mad!' She closed her eyes and his face came into her mind. Last night she had rolled away from him, out of his bed, as he talked of Dorset, shouting, "Leave me alone! Alone!"' 'Why doesn't he stop hounding me? Anyway, I'm going with James and that's all there is to say.'

She stayed by the window, watching, and when she saw James she picked up a small case, called good-bye and ran down the stairs, meeting him on the ground floor, taking his hand, clutching at him as if to make sure he was really there. Impulsively, unusual for James, he kissed her as he took her case.

'Anna,' Veronica said, inhabiting Linden's place by the window, watching them drive off, 'tell me about Pym.'

'You've met him.'

'But what is he like?'

'I can't describe him. He is brilliant. Out of the whole lot of us he is probably the only one with enough originality to succeed as a straight artist. Given reasonable luck. He is already attracting attention. He paints so . . .' She broke off, knowing Veronica would not understand if she lapsed into Cannon jargon. 'He's difficult in some ways. Argumentative but fascinating. He looks into people, cares about them. If Linden has him she will be happy ever after, and extremely poor!'

'To be poor is not a crime,' Veronica said, dreamily. 'It is humiliating and it takes a lot of the joy from life but we were happier, your father and I, in the beginning, when we were struggling.'

'I don't understand you. What do you want for Linden?'

'Later, when you were born, we were through the worst. He was on the way up. Less money worries. He began to travel, on business. I had you two to think about. I had money to spend on clothes for us. Women friends to lunch, a little car for myself. Bridge. Busy in my own way, not realizing I was lonely. Filling in my life.' She was talking to herself, not to Anna, her darkly pencilled eyebrows raised, her mouth, lipsticked into theatrical

160

points, her eyes over made-up. She stroked the skin of her throat upwards with one hand.

Such pity filled Anna that she felt tears in her eyes. She could not bear the creases in her mother's face, the way her eyes were beginning to be hooded by the folds of her eyelids. She looked at her mother and knew that Veronica was about to look old. She had got it all wrong and there was no more time.

'Divorce him. Start again. Look for someone else. Linden will marry and I am unsatisfactory. I won't be able to confide as she does. You can't spend the next thirty years waiting for him.'

Veronica looked at Anna with surprise. 'Why should I divorce him?'

'He's been living with her for almost two years!'

'Two years! He was with me for twenty-one years. She won't last . . . You said so yourself. You said she was blonde and dolly-looking. No bones!'

'But why do you want him back? Don't you despise him?'

'No!' Veronica sliced lemon and dropped it into her glass. 'It is her that I despise. Men have these weak times!' She put in ice and then a large measure of gin. 'You are so extreme, Anna. Don't waste your time looking for perfection in a man.' She came to Anna and put an arm round her, embarrassing her. 'You know, I've never felt that I understood you. I always seemed to be pushing you the wrong way.'

'Oh, I'm all right.' Anna moved gently out of Veronica's way.

'Yes, I think you'll be all right now. But not with Freddie. Not for you, Anna. He is so . . .' She could find no words. Freddie treated her with an overwhelming gallantry, flattering so much it made her feel, quite rightly, that she was no longer interesting to him as a woman. 'James will have a lot of nice friends,' she said, with a playful little smile.

'James? Why should I meet his friends?'

'Anna, don't be so obtuse. Surely you can see how things are? She'll marry James this year. In the autumn, perhaps. Or September. That's a lovely month for a wedding.'

'She's not going to marry James. He is a diversion. He takes her to nice places. She's getting it out of her system . . . If you think love is important, it is Pym you must want her to have. And she will. No one, loved by Pym, could want James!' Even to herself, Anna did not sound convincing. Her hands were shaking. She thought of trying to tell Pym tomorrow, that Linden had gone. *Damn her. Why does she leave me to sort it out?*

The telephone rang, interrupting her. She crossed the room and snatched up the receiver. 'Hallo?'

It was Freddie.

'Anna, look, I'm up to my neck at the moment. I got in to Heathrow at four and I'm trying to work out some facts to cable Stephano. D'you want to come round here and wait for me to finish?'

'Yes. Of course.' And obediently she got into the little car and drove towards Brook Street. She was restless, shaken, her mind full of Linden and Pym and James and Veronica. Their actions were incomprehensible to her. Was it possible that none of them really knew what they were doing? Freddie knew. He knew exactly what he wanted. She drove more quickly. She parked outside his shop and found the door on the latch. She tiptoed up the stairs, pausing at the top and looking across to where he sat, half turned away from her at his desk, writing. The sight of his wide back and his brown head made her happy. She went quietly across the room and kissed the nape of his neck where his hair curled.

It was not at all the kind of gesture Anna normally made; he jumped and swung round to look at her. 'Christ, I thought you were someone else!'

She stood back, her face showing the hurt. 'No. Just me! You asked me to come, remember?' She hovered awkwardly, irritating him. His desk was littered with the brown folders, neatly labelled. The ashtray overflowed. He put his elbows on the desk and was angry with himself for hurting her so childishly. She was so easy to hurt there was no fun in it. 'I'm sorry.' His big mouth spread into a smile and he sat back and put out his hands. 'Thank you for coming. Is that better? Now, pour me a whisky, love, a big one, and I'll get this finished and we'll go out and have a meal somewhere.' Freddie searched under the folders for his cigarettes, lit one and leaned back in his chair. 'Stephano has gone overboard, Anna. To hell with caution . . . Mind you, it's about time he stopped teetering on the brink. And he has! My God, has he stopped teetering! His collection will be enormous! Now I'm the one who advises caution.' He laughed.

Anna put the glass down on his desk, making a wet ring on one of his folders and annoying him again. 'Who did you think I was?'

Freddie's eyes narrowed. He hated this very female habit of brooding, while appearing to listen, and then irrelevantly harping back to the imagined insult. 'What do you mean?' he said coldly.

'When I came and kissed you, you said you thought I was . . .'

'A sexy little Jewess I met a few weeks ago. She's rumoured to be the greatest thing since Cleo Lane. Jazz singer. She works in Ollie's club at the moment. Been around a few years but only just getting noticed. Surely he's mentioned her?'

'I hardly ever see him. But Linden talked about her once.'

'Well, the silly bitch has taken a fancy to me. She keeps ringing me.' He looked at Anna's round, stricken eyes. He hated to see her look like that and his reaction disturbed him. He believed his success with women was largely due to a combination of tenderness and indifference, applied alternately. He didn't want to be ashamed of that valuable indifference. He didn't want the softness Anna awoke in him, the pleasure he felt at seeing her after a week's absence; he didn't want the ridiculous feeling which he couldn't rid himself of, however much he laughed at it, that, having had no man before him, she was somehow precious; he didn't want to love the expressions which moved across her round face.

Her eyes reproached him. She looked utterly desolate. She had come here full of excitement, longing for the end of this small separation. She had come here, full of the sadness of other people in her life, wanting to be happy.

'I missed you,' he said. He stood up. He was tired and he spoke his thoughts without censoring them first. 'I would have liked you to be here when I got home. All this coming and going is absurd. Why don't you move in here?'

Anna totally misunderstood. She thought he said it merely to underline the fact that he was pursued by other women. She stood and stared at him, her silence as damning as outright refusal.

Freddie forestalled her refusal, slipping back into his normal role and covering the lapse. 'Bloody convent educations!'

'I wasn't.'

'You might as well have been. And for Christ's sake stop looking so haunted! Come on, I'll leave this and do it later!' It was an extraordinary thing for Freddie to do, and she knew it, to leave something he considered important, in the middle. 'I'm hungry and tired. We'll go and eat.' His voice was kind. He rested his arms on her shoulders, clasping his hands in the air behind her head and kissing her nose. 'You look nice. Very nice.'

'I love you Freddie,' she said, frowning the words. 'Did you mean me to?'

'Stop it, Anna. Stop digging in. I want no drama. I want laughter and food.' He tucked his arm through hers and switched off the overhead light.

'All right.' She had wanted to tell him about it all, about Linden and Pym and James, but now she put it away, pressed it all down to think of later.

CHAPTER FIFTEEN

'You're very quiet,' James said, leaning back in his seat more comfortably as the road became dual carriageway and the speed limit was raised to 70. 'Tired? Do you mind coming down to cook this week-end?'

She shook her head. Tonight she found it difficult to keep her hands still. She turned and looked at James's strong, almost Roman profile. Did the face show anything of the man? If so, here was a man to spend a lifetime with. 'I'm thankful your mother asked me.' She paused. She sighed quietly. She was beginning to want to tell James the truth. It seemed unfair that Pym should know and James should not. Also, she was beginning to be afraid of the nervous condition she was getting herself into. She longed, suddenly, to finish with it all. It would be a relief to talk it over with James. Last night she had seriously considered giving in, saying to hell with it all, loving Pym as he wanted. She had pictured herself going back to Oakfield Court and packing, pictured herself trying to instil some order and dignity into the chaos of Pym's flat. It would be an extraordinary full stop in her life, to give up James and all the dreams for Pym and the empty milk bottles, but she had to do something soon. It had never occurred to her, long ago when she made her plans, that she could be pulled in half like this.

'James,' she said abruptly. 'There is a man at Anna's art school.'

James took a glance at her. He felt quite cold, cold with tension. He showed nothing but he looked at her whenever he could. 'Go on, Linden.'

'He thinks he loves me. Well, I mean he does love me . . . But he's crazy. Oh God!' She stopped and her voice trembled and she could never, never have planned it this well if she had thought about it for half a lifetime. Her face was very white.

'And what do you feel about him?'

'Well, sometimes, when I'm with him, I think perhaps I love him too but I know it is absurd. I couldn't stand the kind of life we would live. We have nothing in common and he is so young. It's just that I had to tell you. I think I am going mad. He pushes me.'

'Linden, would you marry me?' James said.

She let out her breath in a long sigh. The car was very quiet, very little wind noise. So little sound that perhaps, she thought, he could hear her heart beating. Her brain played tricks. It superimposed on the windscreen a picture-postcard view of a small white cottage tucked into the hill with a pump outside and black-faced sheep; she saw again a great stone fireplace and smelt a damp morning through the open window and felt the slight man beside her shudder with joy as he looked at her, touched her; she saw a room in Paddington and heard his impatient voice. 'Sit still, woman. How can I draw you when you fidget like a kid all the time?'; she remembered sausages and beer and hesitant music from a guitar he plucked in a slow, beginner's way, humming the chords he couldn't find; his hands, the surprising strength of him, the way he could make her into something which scared her, uncover in her passion which she despised . . .

'Yes, I will marry you, James.'

He had been expecting, after this long silence, a polite refusal. He had been surprised how empty the thought of that refusal had made him. When she said yes, he laughed, sounding much younger, shedding the careful layers of dignity. 'You will? Really? You want to?'

She laughed, too, at his reaction. 'Well, I wouldn't say yes if I didn't.' And she leaned forward and rubbed with her flat palm at the window. She smeared away the past.

James smiled. 'Quickly, before any of Anna's art students get to you again?'

'Yes.'

'But my mother will expect a church wedding. Having no daughters, you see, she still longs for the flowers and the tradition.'

He sounded so different. So happy. It was disconcerting for her. He looked in his driving mirror and indicated left and pulled off the road. He turned off the engine and Linden moved across into his arms. He looked at her and his eyes laughed. 'You planned it all, didn't you? Mentioning this other man.'

'Not really.'

'I wish I could remember the very first moment when I wanted to marry you. The first moment I was certain. I think it was in Austria. I have never thought about it before with anyone else, Linden.' He put her back into the passenger seat, leaving her feeling vaguely lonely as he talked, talking as he had never talked before. 'There is so much I want you to know and understand . . . about my work. It absorbs a great deal of my time, and I will be away frequently. You will understand that, Linden? It was my father's brainchild, the company, but I have nurtured it. He started with nothing but determination. In 1935, after a few restless years in the Army, he was looking round for something to do. He had been married to my mother for just a few months . . .' He looked at Linden. 'Does this bore you?'

'Not at all.'

'He thought to himself: Where is there an area of dramatic growth? And he looked at the hairdressing salons which were springing up all over the country. Someone had invented the perm a few years earlier and it was really catching on. He asked himself: Why can't I use these shops as outlets? He took over a minute factory and with three girl employees he began to make nail varnish and sell it through the hairdressing salons. Then shampoo, setting lotion, lipstick. All from one good idea. I care about the company a great deal. I care about my family. My father has made himself into a very wealthy man and he has been generous to Oliver and me. The one thing that upsets me is to see Ollie on the outside . . . I wish he would come in.'

'He won't, will he?'

'No. He will never take anything from me. He would never compete. As a child he was very small for his age and I was over five when he was born. Perhaps I seemed very distant.' He frowned. 'And my mother and I have always been very close and things came easily to me. I can see that he felt shut out, sometimes, and then he would slink off to his piano. It was something none of us understood.' James laughed. 'Poor Oliver. Even now, if he becomes a world-famous pianist, we will not appreciate any of his skill.'

'Perhaps,' Linden said, 'if this thing with Freddie Monroe continues to succeed, he might feel he could come into the company from a position of strength.'

'Yes. I tried to think that. But that man makes my hackles rise. He will use Oliver for just as long as he needs the money and then he will ease Oliver out. He is not the type to tolerate a partner out of loyalty, is he? He will want to run the whole show. Luckily Oliver had the intelligence to get our lawyers to sort out the legal side! He won't be able to screw Ollie but I hope Ollie gets out before the bubble bursts!'

'Must it burst?' Linden liked to talk in this way, to discuss them all, to speculate.

'Yes, it must. How can you predict something as volatile as the art market? The stock market is bad enough!'

'You hate Freddie, don't you?'

'No. Hatred is the wrong word. I despise him. I despise his whole attitude, the way he elbows his way through life, the way he snatches any opportunity. He gives nothing away. My father also started with nothing and has made a lot of money but it has not changed him into the kind of man Monroe will become. He has no concept of the basic ethics on which the whole system of business is founded. There are permitted ways of cutting throats, ways everyone understands.' James's voice was low and cold. 'I hate to see Oliver manipulated.'

'I hope Anna doesn't go on seeing him.'

James laughed. 'I should think it's unlikely. What can Anna do for him? Anyway, to hell with him! We have so much else to talk about. Where shall we live? When shall we get married?'

Linden leaned her head back and let her hand lie under his. She closed her eyes. She let his obvious happiness – or was it satisfaction? – touch a response in her. This was, after all, exactly what she had always wanted. Above all else, she felt overwhelming relief at having made a decision.

A week later the engagement was announced in *The Times* and *The Telegraph* for all the world to see. Anna still could not believe it. Linden had telephoned them with the news on the Friday morning. Veronica answered the telephone. From her mother's voice, Anna guessed. She thought: *Pym . . . what can I do for Pym?*

'Anna will want to speak to you . . . Anna, darling, come and talk to Linden. She and James are engaged.'

Anna held the receiver in a damp hand. 'Hallo. Yes, it's me.

Well, congratulations . . . Linden, are you sure it is what you want?'

'Of course I'm sure,' Linden laughed. Anna imagined an audience at the other end, excitement.

'Don't ask me to tell him.'

When Linden rang off, Anna drove to Pym's flat. It was 8.30 in the morning. She needed to let him know there would be no week-end in Dorset. She thought, if she got that across first, the other would not be such a shock. Anna wrote a note on a page from her sketch book and put it in the letter-box.

At the Cannon he pounced on her, dragging information from her. 'Why did she go? When? What did she say? Why are you being so secretive?'

'Oh, leave me alone, Pym. Ask her yourself on Monday.' Her eyes were full of pity for him.

It was a restless and unhappy week for Anna. Freddie was extremely busy. She had dinner with him twice but on both occasions there were other people with them. On the Tuesday, Carlos Stephano. On the Thursday, two Australians. Anna could not concentrate on anything, she was so miserable for Pym.

'I went to see him,' Linden had said, her face and voice matter-of-fact. 'I thought I owed him that much. But he wouldn't believe me, Anna. I said it would be in the newspapers in a few days. He just looked at me as if I was mad.' She shut her mind to him.

Although Anna tried to get used to the idea she was quite unable to join in Veronica's excitement. She knew that she was a dampening presence but she couldn't pretend. She, after all, was the one who saw Pym every day, who saw the extent of his feelings. On Friday evening she came home and changed and drove to Brook Street, carrying *The Times* with her, showing it to Freddie.

'So she made it.'

Anna sat down wearily. 'I wish it hadn't happened.'

'Why? What makes you think you can predict the future or the way people will feel about each other? It may turn out entirely differently from the idea you have!'

'I suppose so . . .'

'And stop looking so bloody miserable. I've had a great week.

I'm happy. You always bring me luck, Anna!'

'Freddie, I don't want to go out. Could we eat here? Get hamburgers and chips and apple pie?'

He patted her stomach. 'Chips? Of course, if you like. But I told Oliver we might look in at the club later. It's a big gala night or something. We could go in around twelve.'

This is the best evening I have ever had with him, Anna thought, dreamily, lying beside him, watching him. *Staying here gives me such a feeling of permanence.* Peace. Perhaps he is right? I should be here all the time.

Freddie was day-dreaming about an office in New York, at the top of a sky-scraper. He looked at his watch and yawned. 11.30. He was beginning to feel very sleepy. It had been an exhausting week. He pulled Anna closer to him, liking the feel of her big warm body. Tomorrow, Saturday, he could sleep late. He wanted company. He wanted someone to cook him a huge lunch.

'Anna.' He rolled on to his side, supported on one elbow, looking down at her.

She smiled up at him. 'You can't be bothered to go and see Ollie?'

'I can't be bothered to go anywhere.' He wound a piece of her hair round and round his finger. 'Do you remember what I was saying when I last saw you? About you living here? I like it when you're here. I'd like you to be here tomorrow and Sunday. You're old enough to live your own life. Stay tonight and tomorrow morning we'll go and pack your things and I'll talk sweetly to your Ma. God knows why, Fatty, but I want you around!'

Anna listened, biting the insides of her mouth, thinking: *Why did he have to start it again now? On this wonderful evening.* She sat up. 'Freddie, please understand me. To begin with, I couldn't just stay out all night . . . what would she think, tomorrow, when she finds I'm not there? First I must tell her. I love you so much but I'm just not quite ready . . . I don't know . . . can't we go on like this? Please. I'll buy a bicycle and take myself home.'

He didn't smile. His first reaction was pure hurt which surprised him very deeply. Instantly he superimposed anger. Anna was meant to be completely pliable. He had never asked a girl to live with him before, let alone asked her twice. They had merely hinted and arrived. When he spoke, his voice was icy, using all the advantage that age gave him. 'Anna, I hope you aren't waiting for me to marry you? Surely one engagement in your family this week is enough? Or do you have to live up to Linden? I suppose your head is full of wedding clichés and white dresses and all that crap! Well, I'm not that sort of man. I think weddings are irrelevant and dangerous. It is how people feel and behave together that matters.'

Anna got out of bed, wrapping the quilt round her and shuffling to the window. She was beginning to be deeply unhappy in a very frightening way. Loving him as she did, she needed to believe in him, in his ideas. She tried to explain herself, turning back to him. 'It's not because of Linden. Why can't we go on as we are?'

'Because I'm tired of it. I want a woman here.'

'But I don't want to be just a woman here. I suppose I feel it is so special, what is between us, that I want you to acknowledge it, not push me down into the usual mould. Being the kind of man you are, if you wanted to marry me, it would make me different from all the others who leave their bloody health foods in your kitchen and their make-up in your bathroom! I want to be more important! I know you, I know you are not as confident as you seem. I've seen you worried. I love you . . .'

'Don't try and fit me into some woman's magazine image, Anna. I'm not worried or lonely. I like making love to you. I'm fond of you. But I have no intention of marrying anyone.'

'I didn't say you had to marry me . . . I said I wished you wanted to! Why can't you understand me? Why can't you see how much it matters to me? I want to be with you, but give me time!' Tears began to spill out of her eyes and run down her face. She stood, asking things of him, demanding a level of commitment he was not prepared to give. She was crying but her eyes were narrowed with anger.

Freddie thought how much she had changed in the few months he had known her. *I have changed her*, he thought, *from child to woman*. He took a cigarette from the packet on the dresser. There was an ugly, raw and dramatic feel about the room. He shook his head. 'Forget it. I'm going to Ollie's club. If you want to come, get dressed and wash your face.'

'Don't talk to me in that patronizing way! I don't want to come!'

'Please yourself.'

They did not speak in the car. Freddie drove too fast, stopping outside the flat so violently that Anna was thrown forward. Instinctively he put out his hand, to stop her hitting the windscreen. He changed into a leaning gesture to open the car door. He would not acknowledge the emotion that her bent head aroused in him, or the way he felt when she looked at him once, mouth stiff, eyes wide. She got out. Freddie cursed her and himself for getting involved in all this drama. Anna said nothing. He expected some kind of climb down but she didn't speak because she had nothing to say. She gathered round herself the confidence Freddie had given her to use against him. She slammed the car door, childishly, knowing how he hated to have the doors slammed, trembling because she had dared and because of his closed-up face.

Freddie drove to Billy's Basement, leaving the car outside, running down the steps and going into the smoke and the dimness. It was extremely crowded. He made his way to the bar and ordered a whisky. He wanted to be able to laugh at Anna, but he couldn't. She had hurt him. She had surprised him, because she had thought everything out and it disturbed him that he could be so upset. He drank deeply and looked across, through the layers of smoke, to the stage where Oliver sat, to the woman who was singing. Rachel. Her powerful voice was extraordinary coming from such a small body. She used her hands and her body superbly. Freddie listened for half an hour and when she had finished he found himself clapping as enthusiastically as the rest. Oliver stood up, seeing Freddie and beckoning for him to come forward to the table which was kept for performers and their friends. Freddie made his way forward. Rachel was sitting there. She smiled at him. Freddie sat down beside her.

'You were superb,' he said.

'Thank you.' She twisted the stem of her glass round and round. 'I hoped you might come.'

'I'm glad you could make it, Freddie' Oliver was saying. Isn't she great? Tonight you were absolutely fantastic, Rachel! Where's Anna?'

Freddie offered Rachel a cigarette. She shook her head. 'I've no idea,' he said.

Anna barely slept. The night seemed interminable, broken by little patches of sleep and bouts of crying. By six, fully awake, she told herself she must have been mad. What the hell had she been fighting against? In his own way, Freddie had paid her a great compliment. He wanted her around all the time. She wanted to be with him. What could be simpler? Veronica would understand. Life was different now. Anyway, she had Linden to walk the straight and narrow.

Anna got up and made herself coffee. *He knows me. He knows that I would panic but he needs to make people behave contrary to their natures, jump through hoops, love him when he is being impossible to love. Or is it merely that he never looks at anything from another point of view? Just Freddie's side.* She felt terrible but she bathed and dressed and threw some clothes into a suitcase. She wrote a note for Veronica, saying that she was going away for the week-end and would telephone at lunch time. *If Linden can leave mysterious notes, why can't I?* She took a taxi to Brook Street. It was strange in the early morning. The sound of the taxi's engine was the only sound in the street. Anna paid him and let herself in.

She carried her case up the stairs. She wanted to arrive with it; she wanted to make an entrance, to show she had come to stay. The case banged against the walls of the stairs. She started up the second flight and then stopped as the bedroom door opened and Freddie came out, closing the door behind.

'What the hell are you doing?'

'I'm walking upstairs.'

Freddie came down to meet her. He took the case and guided her down to the living-room. 'Anna . . .' He was touched yet angry. 'You don't own me, you know. I thought that, last night, you made it clear you didn't want to live here.'

'I was being stupid.'

'But convincing . . .' He looked up the stairs and back to Anna. 'I've got someone else here.'

At first she felt nothing. Just the words, *Not so soon, not so soon,* drumming in her head. And then anger and humiliated fury and the hopelessness of being a child in a world of adults.

'Well, you didn't wait long, did you?' she snarled and swung round, sobbing, dragging her case after her, banging it against the walls, running through the shop and out into the bright, bare street.

Freddie ran upstairs, pulling on jeans and a sweater. He threw open the window and looked out but the street was empty. He swore.

'Good morning,' Rachel said gently. 'Trouble?'

Hell, he thought, *in the long run it is better like this. Let her go. I'm sorry it was this way, though.* 'Good morning,' he said. 'No trouble at all!'

CHAPTER SIXTEEN

Linden and James were married on 29th July at St Michael's, Chester Square, with flowers and beautiful music and photographers outside. Anna and a seventeen-year-old cousin of James's were adult bridesmaids, dressed in long Liberty print dresses. Four little bridesmaids and two pages, wandering delightfully up the aisle, solemn and adorable, and changing at the reception, into dressed-up chimpanzees, bouncing from one rugger tackle collision with adult legs to the next.

When he read of Linden's engagement in the newspaper, her father had telephoned. He wanted, he said simply, to be there. He wanted Linden to have a big party. Linden had hesitated. Then she thought: *Why the hell not?* And Douglas was pleased and he was absurdly generous trying to recreate the feeling there had been long ago between Linden and himself. But she treated him with a distant politeness, thanking him but never confiding anything of how she felt. Nevertheless, Douglas was proud of her and of the man she was marrying. A great deal of champagne loosened the five hundred guests and the noise and laughter hung over all like an immense canopy.

Weddings, Anna thought from her corner of the elaborate reception, *are not really the smooth performances they appear from the outside. They are built up to with weeks of planning but when the time comes, it is all butterflies in the stomach and layers of crises.* Flowers had not arrived when they should and when they did come they were wrong; a great aunt had suddenly demanded to be collected from Paddington; a hole was discovered in Linden's veil; a hideous glass vase, a present from Marietta's oldest, dearest friend, slipped through Veronica's fingers and splintered into a thousand pieces. Linden, surprisingly, had burst into tears over this last disaster. But she had been unusually emotional throughout the two hectic months which preceded the wedding.

'Why must you hurry?' Veronica asked frequently. 'Couldn't you wait until September . . . it doesn't look right to hurry!'

'I'm not pregnant, if that's what you're worried about,' Linden snapped. 'He wants us to get married before all his friends go away on holiday and in August he has planned a long trip to America and we can go to the West Indies first. I've told you. I've explained. He won't wait until the autumn because he says I might change my mind.' Anything romantic that James said was frequently repeated. He said such things so rarely.

On the morning of the wedding day, Anna and Linden sat side by side in Linden's hairdresser's. They both had wet heads. It was the first time Anna had ever had her hair 'done'. The hairdresser's name was Gary. He cut off four inches and dried her hair with a hand drier until it was silky and thick and brilliant. He wound Linden's hair on to rollers . . . she wanted curls, she had decided. He talked non-stop and Anna was relieved. She had little to say to Linden. Still she had not been able to ask, 'How can you do it?' and 'Why?' It was partly because she knew there was no point in asking. Nothing would change Linden's mind now. It was far too late. And partly because her own intense unhappiness, through the past two months, had kept her apart.

The shock and humiliation of the early morning encounter at Brook Street had kept Anna away for a week. When she could stand it no longer, she went to see him, telling herself she was over-reacting. It could still be all right! He was busy. He had Mrs Hull in his office. Anna stammered and went home and cried. A few days later she swallowed her pride again and rang him. He was non-commital and rather cold. It was irritating him enormously that he missed her, that the sound of her voice on the telephone gave him a twist of some feeling close to regret; he told himself it was better to keep this new, low-key relationship going. He sensed that any big reconciliation would be something he might not be able to control. And there was Rachel . . . He took Anna out a couple of times but he made her do all the running. He hadn't thought the thing through to the end but he had decided to let it all cool down. He did not answer the invitation to the wedding which Anna had begged out of Linden.

Anna rang him, a couple of days before the wedding, trembling as she waited for him to answer. 'Freddie? It's me . . . I just wanted to ask you to, please, come to the wedding.'

'Anna, Thursday afternoon is almost impossible for me and I hate weddings and we both know James can't stand the sight of me.'

She held the receiver in both hands. 'Please come. They'll all be there, the aunts and cousins, cooing over Linden, looking at me and thinking "She always was a plain lump!" I just can't face it alone, that's all.'

'Don't be so childish, Anna. To hell with them and what they think!'

'Couldn't you come just because it matters terribly to me and not bother analysing how stupid I am?' Desperation was stretching her to the limit.

'I'll come if I can.'

'That's not good enough. Say you'll be there! At least at the reception if not at the church.'

'I'll be there if I can.'

Please, Freddie. Anna prayed in the hairdresser's, prayed in the taxi going home to a cold lunch which no one wanted. The wedding was to be at 3.30. *Please come, Freddie*, Anna prayed.

'It must be time to change,' Linden said.

'At two forty-five.'

'Well, it's two thirty now.'

'Once you've changed,' Prue said, 'you can't sit down. You may crease the dress.'

'I don't want to sit down! I can't even stand still, let alone sit down.'

'What time is the photographer coming?'

'What time is Daddy coming?'

'She won't come, that awful Tracey, will she?'

'Telegram, Linden.'

Linden opened it, read it slowly and then tore it into four neat pieces. 'I'm damn well going to change now, whatever you say!' She swept out with Veronica and Prue muttering after her. Anna bent and picked up the pieces of paper and put them together. STILL NOT TOO LATE TO CHANGE YOUR MIND STOP LOVE YOU STOP ALEXANDER.

Douglas strutted proudly up the aisle with Linden. James was absurdly tall and handsome at the altar rail and Oliver beside him was obviously nervous, snatching little glances at the congregation. So many familiar faces were altered beyond recognition by their hats. Anna had the impression of beautiful music, solemn words, Linden clutching for James's hand and touchingly, typically, giving a good performance, Anna thought nastily. Linden's voice was clear and slow. 'I'm damned if I'm going to be one of those pathetic little whispery brides.' In the vestry they were all touched with relief after the tension of the service. The register was signed, the organ exploded with sound and they swept triumphantly down the aisle and out into a radiant afternoon. One of the best afternoons of a mediocre month. Even God, it seemed, or whoever managed the weather, was under Linden's spell.

There had been no sign of Freddie in the church. *But he'll come*, Anna had told herself. She thought it again, now, on the edge of this loud reception. She had positioned herself by a table and she was eating steadily, more than she had eaten for months. She watched Linden circulate like a big, white butterfly, alighting here and there to talk and smile and then flutter on, introducing James to Hayward relatives, being introduced herself to Carrolls.

Just when I give up hope, he'll appear. Just when I'm reduced to absolute misery I will look across and see him and experience one of those flattening surges of joy.

Marietta, looking immaculate and extremely attractive in a silk coat and a little hat and a silk scarf, came and deliberately talked to Anna as if saying, 'Despite the five hundred other important people to whom I could be speaking, Anna, I have made time for you. To smooth over our first disastrous meeting.'

'You look charming, Anna.'

'Thank you.'

'Tell me, is this man Freddie Monroe here? I do so much want to meet him.'

'He hasn't come yet.'

Veronica arrived, looking beside Marietta's understated elegance over-dressed and fluffy. Her hair was lacquered into a great grey creation under a tulle hat. Anna wondered why Linden had allowed her to wear a dress which was too short and too young.

Wedding cake and speeches, Oliver stammering slightly at first and then seeming to collect himself and being extremely funny. Anna listened with a smile on her face and with a new respect. She had guessed that Oliver was a funny man behind that secret face, that his thoughts would be interesting if he had the courage to express them. Telegrams were read and then the speeches were over. Anna felt Linden's hand on her arm.

'Come and help me change, Anna?'

Douglas had reserved a suite in the hotel for Linden. Her clothes had been brought in earlier. A silk dress lay on the bed. A big, pretty hat, gloves and shoes. Linden pushed the door shut and pulled out the pins which held the veil.

'Thank God that's over!'

'I thought you were loving it.' Anna flopped on to the bed, avoiding the silk dress.

'I did. In a way. It was what I wanted.' The dress fell round Linden's feet like a huge meringue. 'What a waste of money! Just to wear it once. Perhaps I can sell it.' She kicked the dress aside. 'But it looked marvellous. We looked good, didn't we, James and I? We are a pair! We match.' She paused, lost in some private thoughts. Then she said, 'You'll come to the party tonight, Anna, won't you? I need you to be there. I need a friend there.'

There was silence in the room.

'You don't love James, do you?'

'Of course I love him. But there are many interpretations to that hackneyed word.' Linden stood straight and breathed deeply. 'We will be good for each other!' She went into the bathroom and stripped off her underclothes and splashed herself with cold water. 'I admire him and he adores me . . . he is quite different when we are alone, you know, Anna. I haven't time to bath . . . Do I smell? I sweated terribly. Usually I never do. Have you any talc? Is there some on the bed in that little red bag? Don't worry, I've found it.' She came into the bedroom, naked and powdered, looking like Peter Pan. She brushed her hair and checked her make-up and pulled on clean underclothes and the silk dress. She settled the hat on her head.

'Okay?' She turned to Anna.

Anna nodded slowly. 'You look absolutely beautiful.' She was right back where she had started, playing the elephant to Linden's gazelle. Linden crossed the few yards between them and took Anna's wrists and gripped them very hard.

'You will come tonight, Anna, won't you? You have to. It's protocol. You have to come for the best man because you're the chief bridesmaid.'

'Over-doing it a bit, isn't it?' Anna giggled, breaking the tension.

'Shut up!' But Linden laughed, too, and for a moment all the bad times between them vanished and they felt very close.

'Linden, Freddie might turn up this evening. He almost promised me he'd come to the wedding and he hasn't so if he rings me . . .'

Linden shook her head. 'Freddie is going to another party, Anna. Oliver told me, last week, when James was planning ours. Oliver was rather upset that the two parties had to be on the same night. Surely Freddie told you?'

Anna said nothing but inside she gave one great agonized sob.

The party afterwards had originally been Linden's idea. She insisted that she and James should not be banished after their own wedding, so James booked a large table at a small restaurant he frequently ate at. About thirty of his closest friends were to meet there at nine.

Anna wandered her bedroom miserably. The last thing she wanted was a large party. She put on a long brown cotton dress. It was cut low. There seemed to be too much white skin and she went into Linden's bedroom to look for some beads. Linden had left a lot of things. It had been such a rush at the end. The room seemed tidy and empty and scaring. It occurred to Anna, suddenly and surprisingly, that she would hate this flat without Linden. She had wondered what it would be like without those eagle eyes watching her each time she went into the kitchen, without Linden's voice giving authoritative opinions on everything Anna wore and said and did, but she hadn't thought that, so soon, something would go out of the place. She took a string of polished amber stones which hung on the side of the looking-glass and wound them round her neck. She went to the sitting-room to say good-bye to Veronica.

Her mother sat in front of the television. She opened her eyes as Anna came in. 'You do look nice . . .'

'I'm just off, to this party. I don't think I'll drive. I had so much to drink at the reception. I'll get a taxi.'

'Didn't your father look attractive? Do you know, I saw him as a stranger would. Funny after all these years . . . We talked for quite a time. I'm so glad he didn't insist on bringing her. I think there was a row about it. She felt he was ashamed of her. I told him that Prue and I were going away for a couple of weeks. He thought it was a good idea.'

'Yes.' Pity pulsed through Anna. 'Will you come and wake me tomorrow morning if I oversleep? It's the last day of term and I must go to the Cannon.'

'Yes. Have a nice time.'

Still Anna was pretending – 'Oh, and if Freddie should ring, tell him I'll be here tomorrow evening.'

It was like stepping into the reception all over again! Anna pushed open the door to the restaurant and saw a dozen of James's friends shouting happily at each other while Oliver and a small flustered waiter tried to move them downstairs. They surged forward suddenly and Anna followed them to the basement with its pretty, candle-lit tables and a dance floor; there were two men with guitars and one with a double bass. Linden was organizing people but they seemed to fall into natural pairs. Even Felicity, the other adult bridesmaid, had brought along a scared-looking boy-friend.

Anna met Oliver's eyes, returned his smile and thought: *We are the left-overs, Ollie and I.* She sat down next to him as instructed.

'Hallo, Anna. I haven't seen you for ages.'

'No.' She thought: *I am too tired and sad. I can't talk to anyone. I should not be here. I should be crouching on Freddie's doorstep, waiting for him to come home, waiting to ask if he would still have me?*

She rested her eyes on Oliver, wondering if he still cared about Linden. Such a kind, secret face. So ordinary next to James. Even now, when it was quite still, James's face was fascinating. But it was just an accident of muscle and bone. It occurred to Anna, in this strange mood of weariness and desolation, that the expressions which came to Oliver's face were far more complex, censored, as her own were, by shyness and hope.

He turned into her scrutiny. 'You look as depressed as I am! Weddings shouldn't go on this long, should they? Come and dance, Anna?'

She was surprised but she smiled her acceptance and went with him on to the dance floor. He was a little taller than she was and wide although he was thin. She didn't feel awkward with him. He put his left hand against her back and said, close to her ear so that she could hear him above the music and the voices, 'You are so much thinner I hardly recognized you. Has no one been buying you éclairs?'

It was nice to hear, even if he did exaggerate. The drink she had been absorbing steadily all day was making it too complicated for her to speak anything but the truth. 'It's funny, but I haven't needed to eat so much in the last few months. And painting satisfies me more. I suppose, thinking about it, I've been more alive recently. Happy and unhappy. But at least living in the real world!'

'And never before?'

'No.' She looked into his eyes, talking directly to him, not just at him. 'But there was no particular reason for my feelings. No one was ever unkind to me . . . just indifferent. I needed attention. I needed . . .'

'Freddie?' He smiled. A tiny smile but it touched her. It was the first private expression he had ever given her, the first time they noticed each other as two real people.

She nodded. Round them bodies circulated, engrossed in one another. Linden and James danced in a relaxed and married way. Oliver, who followed Anna's eyes, said, 'I can see food. Come and sit down.'

The tables were covered with plates of smoked salmon. Oliver poured Anna a glass of champagne. 'I must eat something. Do you mind? You start, too, to keep me company. I seem to have had no food all day. I've been worrying about stupid little things. Especially that speech. How I dreaded that!' He squeezed lemon and ground black pepper. He took a large mouthful of salmon and made a small, satisfied noise. He swallowed. 'Mmm, that's nice.'

Anna smiled at the way he ate. Like a child. She began to eat too.

'I'm sorry Freddie isn't here tonight . . . Not that James would have asked him! But he would have had a good time, stirring up this lot, wouldn't he? And baiting James.' Oliver laughed. 'Sometimes I think I admire his ability to anger people most of all. He knows just how far to push them.'

Anna, feeling the misery begin to seep in, put down her fork. Everyone was sitting down now. The music had temporarily stopped and a toast was proposed, to Linden and James.

'Would you like my salmon too?' Anna said. 'Suddenly I'm not hungry.'

'Sure?' Oliver grinned and swapped plates. 'It's nice, sitting here with you, Anna. You don't make me feel obliged to fill in every second.'

'Just because I gave you my food, you don't have to be kind!'

They laughed. 'I'm trying to say that I never would have thought of asking you . . . Now that sounds awful! I mean I don't consider myself the sort of man who would interest you.'

'Are you being sarcastic?'

'No. Not at all.' He frowned. 'Now you've spoilt it . . . Now you're forcing me to concentrate and I've drunk too much to think.' Oliver moved his eyes to where Linden sat. 'Is she happy?'

'Of course,' Anna said, warily.

'Why "of course"?'

'Because she intends to be happy.'

'But she is so alive. James may . . .' He broke off, realizing he should not speculate this early in any marriage. 'It was always James. I knew that. I was a stepping stone but she trod very gently. I enjoyed being used . . . But I can't understand why James took so long to move in. Unless it was just that he needed proof that she really was as attractive as she seems. He always liked second opinions.'

As Oliver finished speaking, James and Linden got up to dance, to the accompaniment of applause and cheers. Oliver looked at them and then back to Anna, dropping his chin into his hand and mimicking her . . . 'I am no longer under Linden's spell. But I enjoyed the experience.'

They stayed, looking at each other, until they both laughed. Then Anna pushed aside this easiness between them. Impossible. Not with Oliver! It was just the champagne and the mood.

The plates were taken and more plates came; bottles were emptied and replaced; the room was thick with smoke and talk and music and between the times when they danced, Oliver talked to Anna with a surprising honesty, uncovering for her some of the layers of himself, a little of the way he looked at life from his off-beat corner. They talked a great deal and very intently and were both surprised, when they thought about it, how much they had come to feel at ease with each other in this one evening when frequent previous meetings had left them almost strangers.

'Look at them,' Oliver said, indicating a couple who danced near their end of the table. 'He is in the company. He was at Oxford with James. I suppose he is James's best friend. His family live in Coventry. His father drives a bus. He is an extremely clever man but he is a man on one level. Do you understand what I mean? He does not want to bring forward anything of his childhood. He feels he has outgrown that way of life. So he behaves, all the time, the way interviewers behave on television. He has adopted that kind of relaxed, slightly superior, slightly left-wing attitude to everything. He is a man of one dimension.'

'He is like your house, then.' Anna smiled. 'He has been furnished and decorated all at the same time and by one person only. By himself. There are no interesting accidents in his personality. No antiques. No mistakes!'

'Yes, exactly,' Oliver said. And he picked up one of her hands. 'You never talked to me like this when you were painting the bathroom.' He reached for his packet of cigarettes, and offered it to Anna.

She took one. 'Of course I don't smoke, really!'

'Nor do I.' He held his lighter for her and looked at her very closely. 'I feel I've just met you, Anna.' He tilted his chair back on its hind legs and rested his arm lightly along her shoulder. The room was emptying. Linden and James still circled, slowly, in each other's arms, but when the music ended it was obviously time to leave. A little group formed round James and Linden, saying long good-byes, and when it finally dispersed James came across to the table and leaned on Oliver's chair.

'Do you feel like coming on for a drink, Ollie?'

'Sure.'

Early morning Berkeley Square. It was warm. This day had seemed as long as a week already. They went downstairs and into the night club and Anna followed Linden into the Ladies' cloakroom.

'It's late, isn't it?' Linden sat on a stool and looked into the mirror at her reflection, at the great engagement ring and the narrow gold band. 'I don't want to go back to that enormous hotel . . . I don't want today to end!' She stood up. 'Come on, Anna, let's go,' as if Anna was the one hesitating.

Oliver and James were seated at a low table in the semi-darkness. The music was rather loud and the general atmosphere unreal, if luxurious. James and Linden went to dance again and Anna sat down and yawned and smiled apologetically.

Oliver leaned forward. His face was thoughtful. 'It won't be like that for me. I refuse to marry someone who has all the right qualifications, someone everyone else wants. A prize! I shall marry a girl like you, a solemn, gentle person who means what she says.' He looked at Anna. 'Shall we see each other sometimes? See what happens?'

Anna shivered. She had a strange sensation as she looked at him. She felt that it should have been obvious to her before. 'Of course, Oliver.' Then she shook her head, convinced she was very drunk indeed and very tired as Oliver must be, to mention marriage in the same breath as her name. Marriage, which was so far out of her awkward reach. She had hardly begun being adult . . . 'I never thought of you, Ollie.'

'I never thought of you either. But then, I never plan these things!'

'It would be silly if we went out together . . . two brothers and two sisters!'

'Why? There are no rules of how you must meet. Anyway, I have always been silly. Just come out with me sometimes. Come and paint all over my house. Paint my piano if you want. I can't say more than that!' And he kissed her, shortly and formally, as if shaking hands on a deal.

'And don't worry about Freddie . . . I know it's finished between you. You and I are both at a loose end, aren't we? Freddie always talks a lot. In the beginning, when I asked about you, he said how different you were, how refreshing. But last night –' and he took Anna's hand – 'he talked all about Rachel.'

Anna's heart stopped, lurched, and began to pound. She drank deeply from her glass. 'Rachel,' she said, shivering.

'Yes. From my club . . . you know the girl.'

'I know who she is. Tell me about her and Freddie.'

Oliver frowned. 'Don't you know?'

'Yes, I know, but I've tried not to. He's with her tonight?'

'Yes . . . I knew she'd make it sooner or later but Freddie's found her a backer and she's made a record and tonight is the big party. I'd like to have gone. She seems crazy about him.' His expression was sympathetic. 'Did you really know, Anna?'

'Some of it. Did he talk about me last night?'

'Yes, he did. And he spoke as if he knew I might repeat what he said. Do you understand what I mean? The things he said were not confidences. He said you were young and you wanted all the things from a relationship that a young girl wants and he wasn't prepared to give. He can be very honest when it suits him. He said it was far better for you if the two of you stopped seeing each other. What he didn't say, but I know about him, is that Freddie loves success and, at the moment, Rachel has that quality about her and he enjoys being around her.'

Much later, back at the flat, elbows on the wooden table and a mug of coffee in front of them both, they still talked, sleepily, until just before five. The room was light. Anna knew that, when Oliver went, she would cry about Freddie but she could wait to do it. It wasn't urgent. It could wait to be felt.

'Anna,' Ollie said, pushing his chair back, 'I'm not drunk or mad or desperate but it has occurred to me tonight that I want to know you. I have an instinct about you.' He stood up. 'I must go, I suppose.'

She stood up too and they leaned forward, shyly, until their mouths touched. 'Good night, Ollie,' she said, thinking: *You pretend to have it all sorted out, don't you? But you're just on your own, like I am. I have nothing to lose if I try and love you.*

'Shall I ring you tomorrow?'

She nodded. She went with him to the door. And then she went back to the kitchen. She was afraid to go to bed because she didn't want the silence and the darkness when she would be forced to admit Freddie had removed himself from her life.

Freddie, how could you just dismiss me? Leave Oliver to make it plain? A moment of panic hit her. A moment when she knew it would be terrible to get over him. She realized with deep surprise, like someone who has just cut themselves very badly, that it was really over.

CHAPTER SEVENTEEN

In August, three weeks after the wedding, Anna went to stay at Pyecomb for the first time. Oliver had a week's holiday. His club had closed down for a summer pause and Anna left London at ten o'clock on a beautiful Friday morning, driving slowly and following Oliver's directions.

The three weeks which had elapsed since Linden's wedding had totally altered Anna's life. Oliver had telephoned her, the day after, and they had talked stiltedly, very reserved with one another, and arranged to have dinner in a few days. When he rang off, Anna wondered if two people as inhibited as Oliver and herself could ever manage to get close to one another. Who would push through whose shyness? It was one of those instinctive flashes of common sense which she should have respected. But she felt so battered and sad and he was sweet and shy. Nothing to lose, she thought.

It had been a terrible day at the Cannon. Last day of term and she went in about ten, dazed from lack of sleep, cringing at the thought of seeing Pym. She went into the Litho room but she couldn't concentrate. At lunch time she went to the little delicatessen in Church Street to buy apples and cheese.

She had felt Pym beside her, rather than heard or seen him, and turned. He looked terrible, as if he hadn't slept for days.

'When did you last eat, Pym? I'm going to buy you some sandwiches. You must have something!'

'I couldn't eat anything.'

'Have some fruit.'

He shook his head. 'A bottle of milk, that's all,' and he paid for it and wandered out, after Anna, into the brilliant sunshine. 'Come to the park? Tell me about the wedding . . . You look exhausted too.'

'I didn't get to bed till five! But I had to come in.'

'I can't bear to look at you, Anna. You remind me of her in a way you never have before. Suddenly you look like her.' Saying this, he put an arm round her shoulders to take the hurt out of the words. 'I hope she'll be happy. Isn't that incredible of me? I keep telling myself that Fate knows best and she would have distracted me hopelessly and now I have something to motivate me, whatever that means. I have agony!' He thumped his chest with mock drama but his eyes were dead.

They sat on the grass in total silence. Pym drank his milk and then rolled on to his back, looking up at the sky.

'I think about her so much. I can't eat and I can't sleep. My body seems to be stuck. I think about her until I can almost feel her, almost smell her, as if my brain is recreating her! She loves me, you know that, don't you? But she hated the idea of me. She hated me for making her feel so much. Sometimes she would push me away. She would put her hands out and force me back, her face full of fury.' He rolled over on to his stomach and lay very still and Anna knew he was crying. She had no idea what to do. She could not touch him. She moved away and sat for a few moments and then got up, very quietly, and left him.

Oliver won't come, she had thought, on the first evening he was due to take her out. *He will ring and make some excuse. It was stupid. How silly they were, the things he said. And yet it made me happy. He surprised laughter out of me. How pleased everyone would be. How suitable! So a streak of Linden runs in me too! We are alike, Oliver and I, too involved in ourselves. If he wants me at all, it is not because I'm attractive to him but because I am — what did he say? — solemn and gentle.*

Freddie's voice seemed to speak in her head. 'Sometimes, Fatty, I watch you move across a room and I want you so badly . . . especially when you are talking to someone and trying to be polite and well-behaved, trying hard like a kid. Then I want you.' It was like that for her all the time. As she desperately tried to make the idea of Oliver and herself seem credible, memories of Freddie, great, powerful, enveloping memories would sweep any thought of a replacement away and leave only a desperate panicky loss. *Anyway, what does it matter? Because Oliver won't come!*

He did come, armed with a huge bunch of flowers. Chrysanthemums with shaggy orange and yellow heads, delighting Anna. And despite the odds against it, it was a good evening and it had been followed by other frequent, good evenings. They always talked a great deal. Oliver made her laugh. They were friends.

She heard nothing from Freddie and she knew she would make no move. Never again. Especially now there was Oliver with his funny rolling walk and marvellously expressive shrug and trick of making life funny.

'I've told James I shall go on living at the mews. Hinting, you understand, that Freddie is making me a fortune. It will be a bit of a struggle but as long as James is impressed.'

'It matters so much what James thinks?'

'I'm afraid so! It matters absurdly. I carry my own examiner with me everywhere. What would James think? Would he be impressed? I know it's ridiculous. I even apply it to things James knows nothing about. Listen to these harmonies, James! Aren't they superb?'

They tried so hard to explain themselves to each other and yet it seemed they only scratched the surface.

'I loved a girl last year,' Ollie said vaguely. 'But she got tired of the unsocial hours I work or tired of me or something. But I liked loving her. It felt right, to care that much about another human being.'

'People need to be in pairs, don't they?'

'Yes . . . and you must miss Linden, after all these years.'

She nodded. 'I didn't really think I would. I thought it would be a relief not to have to provide a contrast to her any more. I thought I would get rid of my examiner. But as you say, you carry it with you! And I miss her very much. I hate her room now it is empty and tidy and light. And I worry about my mother . . . she and Linden discussed everything. I'm no good at that: I don't want to confide. I wish James and Linden would come home. Most of all I think I miss the attention Linden gave me. She was always watching me with that fierce, critical look!'

'At least you are friends between the skirmishes. Now, James and I, from the day I was born, haven't had a thing in common. It's mostly my fault as I refused to take up any of the things he already excelled in. I just couldn't see the point of being more put in the shade than I was already. All I had left was shooting, which he can't do because he has a funny eye. And the piano which nobody wanted!'

'Linden is almost tone-deaf.'

'So they have their flaws then, these super-beings?'

'But not many!'

They had laughed together like two children.

'If I had any sense,' Oliver said, cupping his hands round his wine glass, 'I would work in the great Carroll machine. I would be safe for the rest of my life. James would like it very much. He likes the idea of two brothers against the world. He is very protective of me in a way . . . and my father would be pleased. But I just can't do it. It would be so hypocritical. I have no business sense and I'd loathe to sit in an office all day and I can't stand the thought of a lifetime playing second fiddle. I see myself, at fifty, still trotting into his office when he wants me. No! Freddie is my only hope. I am relying on him to make me immensely rich and then I shall retire to a house like Pyecomb, or somewhere quiet, and grow corn and cows and play the piano for my own pleasure.'

'Will Pyecomb go to James?'

'Yes, of course. It's all part of the business. Besides, he feels it is essential for his image and for entertaining people. But really James is uneasy in the country. He is a Londoner through and through. He loves the noise and the fumes. He likes meeting his friends for lunch. He likes going out of London for a day's racing at Sandown or Fontwell but, best of all, he likes struggling back through the rush-hour traffic, cursing the favourite who didn't try hard enough!'

Anna was a little scared by the bitterness in Oliver's voice. She didn't want him to be like that, she wanted him to be gentle and without malice, laughing kindly at the world from the sidelines. Everyone else was so vicious.

'Freddie was a godsend to me,' Ollie went on. He looked up, his eyes meeting Anna's. 'Do you mind me talking about him?'

She shook her head. 'Not now. I used to . . . adore him. But it seems so long ago,' she lied. 'I was very young for my age.'

'Last month, that was,' Oliver said solemnly.

'Yes. Sounds silly, doesn't it? But it's true. He dragged me out of my extended childhood and I worshipped him for it. You know I slept with him, Ollie?'

'Yes.'

'Now the thought of even seeing him makes me cringe. He was so cold when he'd had enough of me. Absolutely brutal.'

There was a small silence while Oliver digested her words. *Is there,* he thought, *a gentle way of getting across that you no longer want someone?* He said, 'You don't still still want him?'

'Oh no.'

He smiled. 'I'm glad. D'you know, I liked him at once. I thought: This man is exactly how I would like to be. Sure of himself. Pushy. Later I realized he exaggerated it to impress me. He had me figured from the start. He was getting desperate for cash to start him off. The whole idea fascinated me. I knew Freddie was talking sense when he looked at my father's stuff . . . I'd picked up enough to realize that. And I knew James would be horrified! And I thought: At last, a chance to impress them on their own level. Now, every month I get a neatly typed statement and I feel involved! I wish I had more time to go and watch Freddie at sales.'

Anna said nothing, remembering occasions when Freddie had been impatient that Oliver telephoned or enquired at all.

'Anna, come down to Pyecomb for the week-end. I'd love to show it to you. I've taken a couple of stupid girls who hadn't got gum boots and didn't like the smell of pigs but I know you wouldn't be like that!' He sounded so sure, as if he had some special insight. Anna believed him. She bought herself some Wellington boots and set off for Pyecomb on the appointed Friday.

At the end of the journey she got lost because she wasn't concentrating. Six days earlier she had had her twentieth birthday and Oliver had solemnly presented her with a heavy cardboard box. Inside was a cassette player and four cassette tapes; two Oscar Peterson, one George Shearing, one Art Tatum. 'You must listen to them, Anna, to understand the difference. I listen to Oscar Peterson all the time and Shearing.'

She had been overwhelmed by the expense of the present and all the thought that was obviously behind it. Oliver wanted her to understand about his music.

'It's all a great search, Anna. I have to find my own identity. Sometimes, at the club, we almost make it . . . it's as if we read each other's minds and trigger off things in each other. Then we lose it again. There!' He sat forward. 'That's an open-ended block . . . the chord is carried with both hands. Isn't that beautiful? He is such a musical player.'

Anna listened, dutifully, and tried to enjoy the music, but on her own she played the things she loved. Joni Mitchell, Carly

Simon and Jackson Brown, her own personal minstrels, imprisoned forever in the little machine, ready to pour their hearts out when Anna pressed the button! And singing with them, lost in a trance, she missed the Lewes turn and got herself very lost. It was nearly 12.30 when she turned the car into the drive and drove towards the big white house, pillared and dignified and bound together with tangled branches of wistaria.

Anna was surprised and rather scared by the house. She remembered Freddie talking about it but she had expected something more comfortable, picturing old red bricks and a farmyard. She got out of the car and a big labrador came bounding out, barking in a friendly way, and behind came Oliver in jeans and a T-shirt, shouting, 'Shut up, Toby!' He took Anna's case and laughed when she showed him the shiny new gum boots. He led her through a large flagged hall and up a curved staircase, and the paintings on the wall made her want to stop and look. He took her to a spare room with two wide single beds, long lemon-yellow curtains with elaborately draped pelmets. The room was rather old-fashioned and lovely, Anna thought.

The dog came in, padding up to Oliver and pushing his nose into Oliver's hand.

'Is he yours . . . Toby?'

'My father's, but I'll do as a substitute. Come on, Anna, and I'll show you round the place.'

He showed her every inch; the galleried landing with its big skylight above and the bedrooms which opened off it, each with their own bathroom; the old nursery and the attics and back stairs and a huge modernized kitchen; a drawing-room, a dining-room and a room called the library which was shabby and comfortable; various rooms at the back for flowers and guns and sewing and coats, the stable which they had converted into garages and a huge room for parties; a swimming pool, the McKays' cottage, a walled vegetable garden and finally the farm. He talked non-stop and pride shone in his eyes and Anna had never seen him like this before, had never seen this enthusiasm. They walked back to the house through a series of meadows.

'Of course it's not as if it's been in our family for generations! They only bought the place in nineteen forty-nine, when they were getting over the war. But I was born here. Mr and Mrs McKay came with the place. They're getting on a bit now but he still does the garden, with a bit of help, and she does the cooking. Amazing woman. She really puts my mother in her place. Always has done! And yet they're great friends.'

They wandered back to the swimming pool. They sat in the sun and Anna took off her sandals and dabbled her feet in the blue water. The stone she sat on was warm. 'Where are your parents, Oliver?'

'They've gone away for a couple of weeks.'

'You could have told me! I've been desperately borrowing skirts to make a respectable impression in!'

He laughed and came and sat beside her. They grinned at each other happily. Toby panted beside them and white doves made soothing noises at one another. High up in a perfect blue sky, an aeroplane scratched a silver trail. Anna could smell roses and honeysuckle and waves of peace and contentment lapped at her. She wondered what it would be like to come here frequently with Oliver. She found herself believing she could love him. She bundled it all together, the fairy tale place and the sun and the joy of having someone interested in her again.

'I've a couple of friends coming over for dinner tomorrow night. And James and Linden are due back some time soon . . .'

'I don't have to cook, do I, Ollie?' she said, panicky.

'You don't have to do anything!'

They spent a long afternoon, swimming and sunbathing, spread flat in the heat, padding barefoot into the kitchen for cold drinks. At five, when Ollie was getting restless and said he must go down and look at his pigs, Anna said she would make a pot of tea. In the kitchen she met a tall, wide-shouldered woman. *Mrs McKay*, Anna thought and said 'Good afternoon,' very carefully because any woman who could scare Marietta Carroll had to be daunting! Mary McKay smiled and asked if they had enjoyed the cold lunch and she made the tea and put a plate of shortbread on the tray. Anna carried it out to the pool.

A quiet evening, watching the television in the library, eating with plates on their laps, hot Quiche and salad. Oliver opened a bottle of wine.

'God knows what it is . . . I know nothing about wine. It's probably something priceless of my father's.'

Knowing him reasonably well now, Anna recognized this pose of his, this disinterest in anything his family cared about. She was drowsy and yawned a lot, wondering who would sleep where. Not that she had intense feelings about it but she would have liked to be close to Oliver, to wake in the morning with him. But he kissed her good night outside the spare-room door and went down to give Toby a run. And Anna spent the night alone, trying not to think how Freddie would have laughed.

Saturday was more cloudy but still hot and they spent the day on the farm, in the morning looking at and discussing the new cow sheds, hay-making in the afternoon. It was a gentle, happy day and the smell of hay and the feel of wind reminded Anna of her childhood. At six she went up to have a bath and change, wanting to impress Oliver's friends, whoever they were, taking a long time over herself, trying her hair five or six different ways and finally leaving it loose. She was getting very freckled. Even to herself she looked well.

She went down to the drawing-room rather timidly, because the house was quiet. The room was empty, a big, cool, blue room, with the cases of porcelain lit from the inside and sofas and chairs in every shade of blue, from navy to the blue of Friday's sky. She looked at the porcelain until she heard voices in the hall and turned as Oliver entered, bringing a man and a woman.

'Anna, these are my friends, John and Felicity Loveridge. Very old friends indeed!' In his own informal way, Oliver was good with people. When he wasn't feeling shy, he could draw them out, obviously eager to hear what they had to say, laughing his deep pleasant laugh and keeping their glasses full. 'Anna and I have been working all day. I asked her down for a quiet week-end and then . . .' And he shrugged and they laughed. He stood by the fireplace, one hand loosely circling his glass, and then a pause in the conversation as everyone drank or thought or just breathed, and in the pause they all heard the sound of a car on the gravel and then car doors slamming and quick feet across the hall.

Linden threw open the drawing-room door, laughing at their surprise. 'Hallo, all of you. We're back a couple of days early. Don't tell Mum, Anna, that I didn't go straight to see her, will you?'

Linden crossed the room and kissed Anna. It was an uncharacteristic thing for her to do but she acted spontaneously, and Anna, in return, was suddenly delighted to see Linden, realizing just how much she had missed her. James came into the room, looking very sunburned, smiling rather than speaking his hallo and pouring himself a drink.

'We've been delayed and held and re-routed and diverted. But we had a very good time and I managed to see a few people, Oliver. D'you want a drink, Linden?'

'First, I'll go and change. I seem to have been in these clothes for days. Who dares to go and tell Mrs McKay that we've turned up just before dinner? Come and chat to me, Anna? I'll be very quick. I'll tell you where we've been.'

She ran up the stairs as if she had lived in the house for years, pushing open the door to one of the big bedrooms and throwing her small case on the bed. She stripped off her clothes. 'Isn't this house amazing? Like a hotel or a film set or something.' She stepped into the bathroom and turned on the shower, pulling a bath hat over her hair. 'I gather the parents aren't here? I'm glad in a way. Although Robert is adorable, James was a Mummy's boy and she still isn't quite sure about me . . .' Linden had a deep golden tan and a white skin bikini. She made a soft sound of joy as she stood under the water, letting it run on her face and down her body. 'Oh, this is lovely! How is everything, Anna? Are you seeing Ollie? I thought you got on very well after the wedding. What a great idea – you can build up each other's shaky egos! How's Mum? Are you staying the weekend or longer? What do you weigh?'

'All right, yes, yes we did, very well, the week-end and eleven stone ten!'

They laughed. Anna sat on the bed while Linden dried herself, talking incessantly about the places they had seen and the food they had eaten and the people; coral reefs and scuba diving and steel bands and water skiing; photographs and New York and . . . 'Oh, Anna there is so much in the world to see.' She took a narrow tube of a dress from the case and pulled it on. She coloured her lips with bright lipstick and her eyelids with shiny shadow. 'Okay? Not bad for fifteen minutes?'

Anna nodded, feeling ashamed of herself, of the way her contentment had vanished, feeling absurd to be staying here with

Oliver, who Linden had looked at and discarded, feeling, beside Linden's narrow brown beauty, immense and white and ashamed of that old sick-making jealousy.

Linden went towards the door and, as Anna stood up to follow, tucked her arm through Anna's. Anna felt the tension, the extreme thinness of Linden and asked, automatically, 'Are you happy?'

Linden didn't answer.

Dinner was elaborate. Places laid on delicate muslin mats. Asparagus and roast lamb and some exotic pudding made of chestnuts and meringue. Mrs McKay appeared unmoved by the sudden appearance of Linden and James. 'Although,' she said, 'if I'd known you were coming, Mrs James, I would have made a special effort!'

Linden parried this slight lunge. 'But this is special! It's so lovely to eat delicious English food again.' She talked of squid and King fish and melon and rum. The conversation was entirely dominated by Linden, nervously talkative, finding a partner in John Loveridge, who had also been to Tobago and Trinidad and the Virgin Islands. The others were content to listen. And when the meal had ended, Linden took Anna and Felicity upstairs and James poured brandy, having assumed the role of host.

'Well, how has everything been, Oliver?'

'Fine. We're just coming towards the end of our first year. Freddie is getting the figures out, I think. The profits are amazing.'

'The market is still holding, then?' John Loveridge said.

'Yes.'

'You'll never guess who I bumped into in New York! Carlos Stephano. We had lunch together. I'd forgotten what a charming man he is. He seems extraordinarily committed to this investment thing of yours!'

'Yes. He is by far Freddie's biggest client.'

'I asked him if he wasn't afraid that the bubble would burst.'

'Well, of course it will go some time,' Oliver said calmly. He echoed Freddie. 'As long as one anticipates it, it won't matter. We will have enough capital to survive a slight drop and we can change horses. Freddie thinks silver or Impressionist paintings.'

'Coolly confident?' James said sarcastically.
'Yes.' Oliver stood up. 'Yes, we are.'

The Loveridges left just after midnight. Anna stood with Ollie on the porch and watched them go. There was a huge moon, a white hole in the sky, and the lawn was dark and inviting. Anna tucked her arm through Oliver's and, acutely conscious of James and Linden inside, she was trying to behave the way she thought she should. Possessively and flirtatiously. 'Let's walk a bit, Oliver.'

'All right,' he said, without much enthusiasm, and they walked down the length of the lawn to where a post and rail fence divided it from the paddock. They did not feel natural together and it occurred to Anna that Oliver was probably acting, a little too aware of Linden. He kissed Anna dutifully. She liked the feel of his mouth but it was just that. Two mouths touching. The rest of their bodies were hardly involved. She felt Oliver's mind was elsewhere. After a short pause they strolled back up to the house.

'Go on in, Anna. I'll call Toby.' Anna thought Oliver might come and see her, perhaps just to say good night. She waited for half an hour, lying straight in her bed as Oliver lay, frowning, in his. Anna fell asleep shortly after she heard the clock in the hall strike one but Oliver was awake much longer, wondering what else James and Carlos Stephano had talked about.

All Sunday morning, they lay in the sun, ignoring the pleading of the church bells, offering their bodies like sacrifices as the day worked itself up into the eighties. By noon the sun was too much for Anna's white skin and she withdrew to the shade and lay on her stomach and read a book she had chosen from the rows of shelves in the library. A book of poems. And Oliver got up and disappeared and came back with a tray of tall glasses and a long jug of Pimms. He put it down in the shade by Anna.

'This is the first day I have done nothing for as long as I can remember.' The ice clinked coolly in the glasses. 'It's lovely. I'd forgotten about being really idle!'

James laughed and got up and came across to them. . . .

'Bloody fruit salad in a jug!' Then he poured himself a drink and one for Linden. He was trying to push down the impatience he was beginning to experience. He was restless after too long away from his office. He missed the feeling of being involved. After nearly four weeks of honeymoon, James was a little bored of playing the newly-married man. *Only one more day*, he thought, carrying the glass to Linden.

She leaned up. 'How delicious! Thank you.' She smiled up at James, wanting him to lie down again, but he pulled on a towelling dressing-gown and wandered to the far side of the pool; already she had come to know this restlessness of his, the way he became uneasy if she was too possessive, if she asked more than he thought she should. She crushed the unwelcome thoughts. It was a marvellous day and they seemed, she thought, like four close friends, enjoying one another's company. It was good, wasn't it, all this? It was what she had wanted. She needed to move and she got up and jumped into the pool, sending cascades of water to make diamonds against the sun and fleeting rainbows. She surfaced and splashed James playfully but he ducked away and sat down, out of reach.

Anna lay in the shade with her eyes closed and the book forgotten. She could hear the sound of a distant mower and a bee somewhere and smell the combination of smells which would be forever after inextricably entwined with the memory of this day. Chlorine, from the pool, and honeysuckle from the tangled mass which festooned the roof of the old stables and the smell of sun-warm skin.

She felt Oliver flop down beside her and opened her eyes and looked at him. There was a wistfulness on his face which prompted her to touch his arm and he looked down at her gratefully, like a small boy, and she knew that his expression was one she often wore herself. It was surprise. Surprise that someone noticed and that someone cared. At that moment she touched the core of Oliver, the way she had on the night after the wedding. She sat up and he put his arm around her shoulders, not because he felt he should or because she expected it, but because he wanted to. Then he stood up, to go and swim, and Anna followed, keeping her towel wrapped tightly round her large body until she was at the water's edge and she could slip in and let the blue water hide her.

Lunch in the shade. Cold chicken and salad and French bread and lemon water ice. A holiday feeling hung over them all and they said, again and again, 'Best day we've had . . . best week-end of the summer . . . remember last year?' And later they played a terrible game of tennis, with Linden and Anna, in borrowed shoes, and the temperature in the court in the low eighties and everyone forgetting the score except James.

By ten, Linden and James had left to drive back to London. They were spending a week at Peterstone Mews, at the end of which time they hoped their new house would be at least livable-in, if not at all finished.

Oliver and Anna came in from saying good-bye and Oliver wandered over to the piano and sat down and began to play old, nostalgic tunes, filling the room with music. Anna switched off the lamps and opened the windows as wide as they would go. The summer evening came into the room and she watched Oliver lose himself in the music. For over an hour she sat and listened, trying to understand herself and how she felt. There was still a great pain when she thought about Freddie but she could turn herself away from the memories now because she had an alternative.

'I love listening to you,' she said when Oliver stopped.

He seemed almost surprised to find her there. 'It's late, isn't it? I hadn't realized . . . Back to work in three days!' He stood up and closed the piano carefully, gently. He whistled to Toby.

Anna stood up and went to Oliver and took his hands. She wanted, very much, to be with him tonight. She wanted a definite ending to this lovely week-end. She wanted Oliver to stand level with Freddie.

'Ollie, please come and say good night to me? Come and see me?'

She watched him hesitate.

'Please.'

He smiled. 'Okay. When I've locked up.' But his smile and his face was wary and she thought. *Oh God, he didn't mean any of it and now he is afraid I will hold him to things he said on that unreal night after the wedding and push myself closer than he wants.*

In her bedroom she left the curtains open, washing and

cleaning her teeth very quickly in case he came too soon. She did not scrape her hair back into its usual night-time rubber band which had enraged Freddie so. She faced herself flatly in the mirror, eyes stripped of make-up, face brutally displayed, shiny and freckled. But she wanted him to see her like this, want her like this. She pulled on a cotton nightgown, years old.

Oliver knocked at the door and Anna jumped and turned off the lights and got into bed, calling, 'Hallo,' because 'Come in' sounded absurd, she thought, or like a whore. He stood in the doorway, his face solemn, wearing navy blue pyjamas. The room was lit by the moon and Oliver closed the door and came and got into bed beside Anna. He lay very still. She put her head on his chest and she could hear his heart beating slowly and calmly.

He is not excited by me at all. Something close to rage for the whole world and its lifetime of indifference burst into Anna, making her hot all through, so that she pulled herself up and put her mouth on Oliver's and held his shoulders with hands that gripped so tightly they must have hurt. He responded much too gently, deeply surprised, and treating her with a respect that only increased her frenzy. As if she were full of liquid, boiling and boiling, wanting to shout, 'Freddie would make love to me!'

As if he sensed some of it, Oliver said, 'Anna, it's not time!' His voice was low and almost angry.

'Why not? Why isn't it time?'

'Because we are not sure of anything.'

'What does that matter? I shall never be that sure.'

'Don't be so childish. Of course it matters.' He became cold, sitting up in bed, shutting her out. 'I suppose you have slept with so many men it may not matter to you!'

'No . . . no . . .' Her voice trembled and she stammered, 'Of course not. Of course I haven't.'

He sighed and pulled her against him. 'I'm glad. Anna, don't push me. Everyone pushes me; let me choose my time. You seem to look on sex as a kind of demonstration of the depth of feeling. It's nothing of the sort. And to be basic, I have no . . .' He hesitated.

'Things?' Anna said and laughed, but the mood was gone in a moment, because of the rage boiling inside her. He was right.

She did see sex as a demonstration. In her mind it was the ultimate test of attraction. 'It would be all right,' she said. 'Nothing would happen. I've only just had the curse. Oliver, I can't go on walking on the surface like this! I want to be real. To belong. I must know how it would feel between us. I won't ever hold you to anything.' And amazed at her own courage she began to touch him, at first circling her hand on his stomach, thinking how smooth it was, touching the little dent of his navel, and then pretending her hand had a life of its own, timid and curious, feeling him, feeling his excitement, his response to her hand.

He treated her so reverently, lifting off the terrible nightgown as if it were a bandage. He touched her as if she were made of glass. Anna had been trained in a rougher, earthier school. She stood back, watching from the outside, not a part of herself at all, watching Oliver as if it were a stranger she was with, feeling like a judge or an examiner, and despising herself.

There was tenderness between them afterwards when he lay and played with a long piece of her hair. After a long silence Oliver said, 'I didn't want that to happen. Not with you, Anna.'

'Why not?' She was agonizingly hurt.

'Not yet. I wanted us to know each other. Everyone does this, treats sex like shaking hands.' He got out of bed and stood by the window. 'I'm sorry if you were disappointed.' He came back and put on his pyjamas and then tucked in the bed with great care.

'I wanted it, Ollie,' she whispered, eyes full of tears.

'I know.' He bent down and kissed her and then went out, closing the door gently and leaving her far more alone than if he had not come at all. She lay awake for a long time, scared that Freddie had stamped his identity into her so deeply that she would never scrub him off. She wished Oliver had stayed to sleep the night with her, that they could have woken together in the morning. It would have been something she had never done with Freddie!

She was afraid in the morning. Afraid to see Oliver. Afraid of how she would feel, of embarrassment or, worse, of nothing at all, and while she was trying to get up the courage to go down to breakfast and face him, there was a light knock on her door and Oliver's face appeared, smiling ruefully.

'It's me. I wanted to see you before breakfast! I wanted to tell you it won't always be like last night.'

She ran across the room to him, putting her face against him.

CHAPTER EIGHTEEN

In the third week of September, Anna went thankfully back to the Cannon. She needed a framework for her days. On her own she gradually worked less and less, losing momentum without the constant encouragement and criticism. It worried her. It made her feel that she would be a perpetual student, lost at the end of her four years unless she could find herself some kind of commercial art job which would force her to work. Nothing appealed particularly and she knew competition was intense. Somehow, in the next two years, she had to find a definite identity and direction. Anna was third-year now, expected to be reasonably dedicated, to attend all lectures. No excuses. Expected to think. But Anna had never minded having claims made on her time, apart from the brief Freddie period, and with Oliver she felt entirely different.

Oliver and Anna had drifted into an understanding, a kind of wait and see phase. They needed the other to be around, to talk to, to care about; he frequently picked her up at the end of the day in the little navy blue Mini he had bought, waiting patiently in the street until she came, and they would have a few hours together before he began work. Sometimes Anna went with him to the club. She liked the atmosphere of the place and the friendly way she was treated. They kept a corner table, near the small raised dais where Oliver's piano stood, for staff and friends of staff, and she spent many evenings sitting and listening, making a couple of drinks last for hours and eating sandwiches because she and Oliver so rarely got round to having any supper. Billy's had a new girl singer now, hoping to follow in Rachel's footsteps, a small, round, blonde girl. Anna got to know them all, the barmen and the waiters, mostly students picking up some money on an evening job; the regular customers; the jazz fanatics; the spotters, cruising on the look-out for some exciting new talent in the place which had cultivated Rachel Ray. And when, in the first week of October, Ollie went with his trio to Edinburgh for two weeks to play in a club there as part of an exchange system, Anna found the evenings very dull. She missed Ollie. She missed the little blue car and his face, looking out, grinning at her. She missed his voice on the telephone.

It was strange to walk home through the park again. It made her feel guilty, as if the park were an old friend she had dropped when a new friend appeared. It was untidy and brilliant with autumn and the paths were papered with leaves, stuck flat on wet days, or in crisp and crunching heaps. Walking home like this pushed her thoughts back, made her think of Freddie, of the past. She never went near him now. She avoided the whole area that she thought of as his but she did think about him, trying to understand what had been between them and round it off in her mind. She searched the newspapers avidly to keep up-to-date on the state of the market. All major sales were covered. Freddie was frequently named and Maisie Hunter and two or three others. The sums of money involved now had become unreal. Once or twice a month, Freddie would come to see Oliver, bringing typed sheets of figures, giving a progress report. If she sensed that one of these visits were due, Anna avoided the Mews. She lived in terror of meeting Freddie unexpectedly, afraid of her own feelings and not yet sure that she had outgrown or forgotten the misery.

Pym took Anna to lunch fairly frequently through that autumn term. He would put his elbows on the table and begin to talk. He would talk until the food was eaten, until they were extravagantly drinking cups of weak, milky coffee, which they always did, and then he would pause and lean back and ask, 'By the way . . .?'

'She's fine, Pym. She spends a lot of time with my mother, comparing little squares of curtain material with wallpaper samples and those cards of paint colours and scraps of carpet. They've finished the basement, made it into a self-contained flat, and now they are living down there until the rest of the house is done. It's lovely, with huge sash windows and old boarded floors and a mulberry tree in the back garden. I hope it takes a long time because it keeps my mother happy. They try to involve me sometimes but I only annoy them.' Anna grinned.

Pym would nod his head, all the talk emptied out of him,

seemingly satisfied just to hear that she was well. He still felt one half of him had died but Jane was back with him on and off. Life was stormy but at least it prevented some of the memories.

One lovely afternoon in mid-October, as they waited to cross the street and go back to the Cannon after a lunch of stewed beef and plums and custard, Pym suddenly took Anna's hand. He had been very quiet all through the meal.

'Anna, Jane's moved out for a few weeks. To think, she says . . .'

'I heard a rumour.'

'Do you realize that, exactly a year ago today, I came down the stairs with you and Linden walked into the hall of the Cannon! A whole year has passed since then!'

'I didn't remember the exact date . . . Look, Pym, if you're on your own . . .'

'Come round tonight and cook me something?' he finished for her.

'Jane won't turn up, will she, and think anything?'

'No. She won't. I hate the idea of being alone this evening.' He grinned suddenly, a flash of the old Pym. 'Incredible how you soft-hearted birds always fall for the old sob story! Once I have you in my clutches . . .'

'Oh no, you don't! Not again! Not a whole year later! I have Ollie now.'

'Ah yes, the lucky Oliver.' He touched the inside of her wrist, making her feel wonderful, wanted, deeply sexual. 'But would he mind if you fed me? He would spare you for one evening, wouldn't he?'

'He doesn't get back for five days!'

'Good. You buy the food and I'll pay.'

Anna went home through Kensington High Street, buying onions and mince and spaghetti, tinned tomatoes and garlic. Spaghetti Bolognese was one of the few things she could cook. It was six when she let herself into the dark and empty flat. She made herself a coffee, put two pieces in the jig-saw on the dresser and ran a bath. She lay in the hot water, perfectly content. Everything would be all right. She and Oliver would stop circling one another, stop being so shy. When they came to know each other absolutely, she thought, the intricacies would make the Freddies of this world seem brash and crude and obvious. *And I am thinner, I really am, and tonight with Pym will be fun . . .*

The telephone rang and she tried to pretend she couldn't hear it, reluctant to leave the warm water. She was sure it would be Veronica, saying where she was. Twenty rings. It stopped. Anna sank, guiltily, lower into the water. The phone started again and this time she got out at once, grabbing a towel and leaving wet prints all down the hall carpet.

'Anna . . .' It was Oliver but his voice was strange.

'Yes. Did you ring a moment ago? I was in the bath.'

'Yes, I did. I had a feeling you were there. Anna . . .'

'Yes. What is it, Ollie?' Such trivial things flashed through her mind, such selfish things, that for months afterwards she would remember her priorities at that time and be ashamed. She thought, *He is tired of me*, or *something has happened to Freddie and the business*. 'Where are you, Ollie? In Scotland?'

'No, I'm at Heathrow. I got in a few minutes ago.' He paused and she could hear him breathing. 'Something terrible has happened. I can't believe it. James rang me at lunch time. It's my father, Anna. He died this morning. Very suddenly. In his office.'

After a shocked pause, Anna said helplessly, 'What can I do for you?'

'I'm on my way to Pyecomb but I wanted to tell you, to see if you were in. I'll come by.'

'I'll come to Heathrow and meet you, Ollie. I've got Mini.'

'No, it would take longer. I'll catch the bus. Or get a taxi or something. I can't think very clearly. Wait for me, will you? I'll be about three-quarters of an hour, I suppose.'

She put the telephone down very carefully as if it might break. She stayed where she was until she realized she was wet and very cold and then she wandered to her bedroom and pulled on some clothes. He couldn't be dead, that big, friendly, gentlemanly man. She had met him only a few times but they had talked at the wedding. He wasn't old. Why should he die? It wasn't fair. It wasn't true!

But when she opened the door to Ollie she knew by his face that this was real. He put his arms round her, holding on to her.

'I had to see you just for a moment. I don't expect you to understand but I know they will have each other. I need to be able to think of you, Anna.'

Anna had not been near death before. The grandparents and great aunts who had died in her family had obligingly done so when she was too young to feel more than a shiver of excitement at the adult reaction around her. They had merely disappeared. But this ghastly ritual! It appalled her to think that day after day thousands of people went through this, that everywhere people were dying and this agony burst on to their families and devastated them. It was terrifying to her that she had lived twenty years without realizing. It changed the entire perspective of life to see that this was how the end came, to see that there was an end at all. She wondered how many other enormous and frightening things she had not considered.

On the day of the funeral Pyecomb was cluttered with stray relatives, gathering before the service. At twenty past two they walked along the little footpath behind the house and through the fields to the church. It was gentle and calming, that little church, and the Carrolls had been known there, through Christmas and christening and Harvest Festival, for over twenty years; the flowers from Marietta's garden had often decorated the altar. The hymns were beautiful, the service itself, Anna thought, was all right. It was the actual burial and the hole in the ground which so horrified her. The heavy coffin was carried by six men from the village and the farm. It was lowered into the ground with a series of jerks.

Marietta, dignified and pathetic, held on to James's arm with a desperate strength, making Anna think that children could give back some of the time and the love. Older, faded people, aunts and cousins, men Robert had worked with, friends from the past, came to wonder at fate and shudder or cry or feel a secret triumph that they had escaped this time. Some of them felt nothing but merely came because they felt they should or wanted to be seen to care. Linden, solemn and still, was everything a daughter-in-law could be. So many flowers, brilliant heaps of flowers, and October sunlight, pale as lemonade.

'Hear what comfortable words the Lord sayeth . . .'

But the words did not comfort, Anna thought, looking at Oliver and reading in his face and the attitude of his body a dirty agony of loss which she couldn't bear. Forever after she could not read a book or watch a film in which death was mentioned without being repelled by the falseness, by any attempt to make it sentimental. She looked from face to face and knew death was unimportant only to the dead. She moved closer to Oliver and, as she did so, he put out his hand towards his mother. Marietta didn't seem to notice.

Oliver turned to Anna. He held her hand tightly and her sorrow for him began to be mixed with a suffocating panic. She could not meet his eyes. She wanted to turn and walk away from him, from all the things he would ask of her but he held on to her tightly all the way back to the house.

A lot of people came back, walking in small, muffled groups. They stood in the big blue drawing-room and drank whisky. They ate sandwiches. At first the idea of a gathering afterwards had sounded horrific to Anna but she realized now that many of them had come a very long way and also that, compared with the enormity of Robert's death, the details were unimportant. Marietta talked for a few moments to one or two very close friends and then made her way slowly upstairs.

Hours later it was just Anna and Oliver in the library. James was with Marietta and Linden had gone to bed, struggling to hide the unease felt about the way Marietta clung to James. A fire gave the only light in the library. Oliver had drunk carefully and massively for the past three hours but was still disappointingly aware of his surroundings and able to feel. He had the beginning of an appalling headache. He lay back on the sofa, playing with Anna's hand.

'Anna, let's get married. I'd like to marry you as soon as is decently possible. No fuss. Just the two of us. Mother will go away, probably for several months. She'll go to my aunt in Jamaica I should think. I can't stand the thought of being alone and you have no one either, have you?'

'No,' Anna said in a small voice.

'So that's settled then? In a month perhaps?'

'Do you think it should be so soon? You may not feel the same after the shock has worn off.'

He tilted his head until he was looking at her. 'I forgot to say that I love you, didn't I? It's not just my father's death, Anna, although this has made me realize how pointless it is to jog along. I must do things, not wait for events. Please, Anna.'

'I couldn't stand a church wedding. It would be like a sick joke assembling all the relatives again after today. And you and I would be just understudies after James and Linden.'

'We'll marry in a registry office and have a blessing here afterwards. But let's go back to London tonight. Now. I can't stay here. James is here if she wants him. I know she doesn't need me. I've never felt it more clearly than now. This room is so full of my father. Come back and stay at the mews with me and later, when we feel like it, we'll get married.' She was silent and he said, 'Once, before, you asked me to come to you and . . .'

'Of course I'll come with you, Ollie. I must make you some coffee first. You've drunk so much.' She took her hand away and stood up and he followed her with his eyes as she crossed the room. In the doorway she paused and looked back at him. He was very pale, his eyes looking almost black in his white face, dark hair falling on his forehead. He looked lost and terrible. Whatever it was that she felt for him tore at her, opened her up and raked through the insides of her. But she had no name for the feeling. Pity? Understanding? Sympathy? Gratitude that he wanted her? Certainly it was nothing like the feeling Freddie had aroused in her. *Forget Freddie. That is done with. Today I have grown up. I have doubled my age. I have not grown mentally since I was ten until today. Now I have leaped a huge gap . . .*

She felt a stillness and a lack of hope which she was convinced were the signs of being adult. Ollie suddenly smiled at her. The smile was slow and sweet, lighting his face. She had not realized before that his smile was so lovely. *We will be all right, won't we? He wants it so badly . . . In wars people marry hardly knowing one another. Anyway, how could I leave him now?*

Throughout that first week which Anna spent at the mews with Ollie, she watched him experiencing absolute desolation. He said he had to go back to work. It seemed to be a relief for him. Every night Anna went with him, sitting at the small table and listening to him play. Every few minutes he would look up and check that she was still there.

One part of her loved it. One part of her said, 'All my life I have longed to be part of a permanent pair. Now I have my wish.' She loved the way Ollie rolled over to her in the night. There was great joy in waking next to him, registering him and the fact that he wanted her there so badly; she appreciated the occasional, gentle times they made love; she liked making her way back to the mews after a long day's work and knowing that, as she let herself in, Ollie would come to her, put his arms round her, hold her. For those few weeks after his father's death he opened himself up to Anna as he had never done to any other human being before.

He took her back to Pyecomb. James and Linden were there. It scared Anna a little that she was so pleased to sleep in a bed on her own, that she felt panic when Oliver spoke of telling them all.

At lunch, on Sunday, he suddenly said into a silence, 'Oh, and Anna and I are going to get married quite soon. No fuss. We'll tell you the exact day when we decide it. Later on, in the New Year, we might have a party.'

No one showed any surprise. Marietta smiled, said she was pleased, and began to talk about Robert again and their lives together. She did not slink off and cry by herself. She would not make her grief secret and shameful. Her life had been destroyed. She could not face it by herself. She must talk of Robert, re-live the happy times. After the meal she got out photograph albums and turned the pages back. Pictures of herself and Robert looking very young and round-faced and happy; baby photographs and Pyecomb before it was altered; holidays and various nannies; a lot of James, always good-looking even as a little boy, with legs as thin as sticks and a huge mouth.

'We knew he'd grow in to his features. He was like a little elf. That's Rufus, his first pony.'

'Is that Oliver?'

'Oliver?' Marietta looked blank for a moment and Anna could feel the effort it was for her to pull her attention away from the child James had been. 'Yes. Oliver was very unhealthy as a small child. He cried constantly.' She turned the page and showed a small boy, solemn-faced, holding tightly to the hand of a pretty, dark-haired girl. 'That's Nanny Bye. She stayed for seven years. Nice girl. Oliver adored her. I'm sure he thought she was his mother.'

She looked at Anna as if feeling some declaration was necessary. 'I do hope you will be happy. Life is so strange, isn't it? Both of you . . . sisters . . . You know I felt, that first morning when Linden walked in the door, looking so beautiful and composed, that there was some significance attached to her. I suppose it was what they call a premonition. Life moves in such devious ways. The way I met Robert was very curious . . . I was in love with a man my mother detested. She despatched me to stay with Carlos, my cousin, and while I was there this young English Army Officer, who was on holiday and had read of Carlos's collection of porcelain, wrote and asked if he could come . . . She talked, in a low voice, recalling her first impressions of Robert, the wedding. She paused eventually and asked Oliver if she could be there when he and Anna were married. It pleased him very much. Then she went back to her memories. It occurred to Anna that in one way Marietta was lucky: there was a dignity about being a widow which would have done a great deal for Veronica.

CHAPTER NINETEEN

They were married on 23rd November. The wedding was such a slight affair. The registry office was like a doctor's waiting room and the registrar couldn't have been less interested, except in Linden. It reminded Oliver of going to court for a traffic offence, bustling in, hanging around aimlessly, finishing and feeling lost. He looked so uncharacteristically tidy and serious. He had had his hair cut for the occasion and it was too short. His ears seemed too big. Marietta and James and Linden and Veronica were all pretending unsuccessfully that, in its own way, the marriage was moving.

Anna wore a velvet trouser suit which Linden bullied her into buying and carried a bunch of pink rosebuds which Pym sent her. Tied to them was a caricature of himself, with a clown's face, crying. Her hair was middle-parted and caught back with two big slides. She was surprised, when she looked at herself, at how nice she looked. They all went on to lunch with Marietta, an elaborate meal sent up from the restaurant below, and there was a lot of champagne. Veronica took photographs. Then they all kissed and Anna and Oliver went back to the mews in a taxi.

'Should I carry you over the threshold?' Oliver said.

'God! Do you think you could?'

'I don't know, I'll try.' He picked her up quite easily, surprising them both, although it flashed through her mind how Freddie had constantly pounced on her, scaring and delighting her. He dumped her, unceremoniously, on the sofa and she could see from his eyes that he had drunk a great deal. He got yet another bottle of champagne from the fridge and opened it and the cork hit the ceiling and fell into Anna's lap. She thought it was a good omen. Oliver filled two glasses and crossed the room unsteadily, sitting down beside her.

'Getting married is something one has to do, Anna. It's part of the whole business of life. It's necessary to be married, to have children, to work, to grow old and die.'

'I don't like the sound of that much!'

The drink had made him serious. 'But we'll be okay, Anna.' He sounded as if he were trying to convince himself as well as her.

Neither of us, Anna thought, *really knows what the hell we're doing*.

'Don't look sad, Anna. It's your wedding day.'

'I'm scared, Ollie.' She spoke without thinking. It was true: little jabs of fear poked into her like nasty fingers, trying to attract her attention to the situation she was in. She stood up and took off her jacket and paced the room restlessly. It was nearly four. What could they do until it was time to go out? Go to bed? She wanted to ring Linden and ask what she and James had done between the wedding and the party.

'I've booked a table somewhere nice,' Oliver said quietly; he spoke slowly, trying to sound normal. Why had she suddenly said she was scared? 'Will you wear that thing you've got on now? I like you in that.'

By accident he pressed one of the right buttons. Anna swung round, went to sit by him, leaning back against his shoulder. 'We'll be all right, won't we, Ollie?'

'What do you mean, all right?'

'We'll be happy.'

'I don't know how important it is to be happy . . . I think that will depend on our basic natures. But I care about you, Anna. I need to be with you. Is that enough?' His eyelids, as she looked sideways at him, were heavy. He touched her face, shyly, as if he expected her to recoil. 'You won't go home sometimes by mistake, will you? You won't forget that we are married?'

She shook her head and smiled. 'You say such funny things.'

'In a few weeks, we'll go away. I've told them at the club I want a holiday but I have to give them time to find a replacement. I think they may well give me the push permanently but I don't mind. I could work with Freddie full time.'

Anna mopped the name out of her mind. She turned and put her arms round Oliver, pressing herself against him and trying desperately to suppress the feeling that she was married to a total stranger.

'We've got hours before we go out,' Oliver said. 'Perhaps we'd better go to bed?'

She nodded.

'Then you will never be able to go home, will you?' He kissed her mouth gently.

Anna had never felt less like making love. She took off her own clothes in a businesslike way, wondering why Oliver hesitated, irritated that he bothered to fold his clothes over the chair when he was normally so untidy. She got into bed and lay straight and still until she realized how daunting she must look and rolled over and pretended to sleep. She felt Oliver get into bed beside her very carefully. He put a timid hand on her shoulder. And the day was so bright through the curtains and they had never made love in daylight before. Anna couldn't bear to look at Ollie. She was too shy. She shut her eyes tightly and pretended some elaborate fantasy. She wanted to make it easy for him, to be warm and to respond but she was paralysed by weariness and food and drink and an overwhelming sadness.

A ticker tape processed through her head behind her tightly closed eyes. *We are both so raw. We touch each other and flinch. Who will push through? Who will lead? If I knew more, if I had slept with a lot of men, I could get to him. I know my shyness is terrible for him and my expectations even more crippling. He has sensed my disappointment. His instincts are razor-sharp, like mine. We will cut each other to bits trying to be kind. And it matters so much to me to have this great hungry body of mine get off the ground, inflate like a hot air balloon and take to the sky.*

Oliver looked at her. Her eyes were still tightly shut. He thought, irrelevantly, of the poem about the dormouse in the bed of delphiniums (blue) and geraniums (red). He wondered if it were Freddie who hovered behind her closed eyelids. He had wanted so badly to make this love-making special for her and it had, obviously, been nothing of the sort.

No one had told Anna how things would change. No one had ever mentioned little bickering fights over tiny things just concerned with not being private any more. In the weeks after Oliver's father's death when she had stayed at the mews they had not been relaxed enough with each other to bother about these irritations but now they assumed great importance. Oliver was sleeping very badly, owning the bed, rolling over and stripping the bedclothes from Anna; sometimes he got in at four, slept for an hour, and then woke again after some violent dream and would insist on talking about it; Anna felt she never had enough sleep. She was hopeless at running a house. She had never thought about it before.

For their honeymoon they flew to Africa. They stayed with a distant cousin of Oliver's in Nairobi for a week and then hired a car and drove down to Mombasa. The days were spectacularly beautiful, distracting them with the scenery and the wild animals and the weather. They ended up in a game park in a small chalet of their own where long-tailed lizards sat on the walls like china ducks and the night chirruped and purred and screeched and growled.

They had been away two weeks when Oliver said, 'Anna, now that we've seen the lions, shall we go home? This is costing such a lot of money and I'd love to be home for Christmas. We could get a flight from Nairobi tomorrow if we can alter the tickets. Would you mind, Anna?'

'No. Not at all.' Last night they had both got drunk and made love like two human beings instead of two actors. At last she had felt she was with a warm male animal. She had felt right. Oliver had felt the significance too because he had whispered, 'Did you like that?' in the hot darkness.

'Yes.' One of the rushes of whatever it was she felt for him, and she still couldn't analyse it except to guess it was recognition of another human being as ill-equipped as herself, made her hold on to him. They held each other all night, skin to skin, making love again in the white early morning. That hot room was kept in Anna's mind as the only night of her honeymoon which lived up to her expectations.

And suddenly, having decided to go home, they were both excited about it. They were brown. Anna had lost weight. They crammed their suitcases shut and were weighted down with bags of presents. Nairobi Airport was infinitely more exciting going home than it had been coming away. They talked to each other constantly ... 'I wonder how Linden and James are? I wonder if their house is finished?'

'I wonder how that sale at Christies went on the 14th?'

'I hope I'll be able to catch up on all the work I've missed at the Cannon. Perhaps Pym will lend me his notes.'

'Passengers for British Airways flight 362 for Rome and London please proceed to gate 6.'

They were carried home in a metal tube and they were happy

to have the honeymoon behind them, although neither would admit it to the other. London was wonderfully familiar, grey and cold and cluttered with cars. *Now we'll be all right*, Anna thought. *Now we're home!*

Oliver said they must have a party instead of a reception. Linden agreed. In fact she seized on the idea with such enthusiasm, when she came to see them the day after they got home, that Anna was surprised.

'Is your house finished?'

'Yes. Except for a few finishing touches. I gave a dinner party last week and I'm having another on Thursday.' Linden leaned back against the cushions of the sofa, restlessly turning her rings round and round. 'James and I had five days in Paris which was nice and next month I'll go with him to the States again.' She was wearing a spectacularly beautiful grey suede suit. Outwardly everything was perfect but Anna suspected that Linden was bored.

Linden sat forward. 'Why don't you have your party on New Year's Eve? It always has such a good atmosphere. You could send out invitations now. Why don't you have some live music? If you put all the furniture in the garage you'd have room.'

'I don't want anything so elaborate,' Anna said firmly. 'Just people and cold food and wine. That's all!'

'How ordinary!' Linden said tartly. 'Unless you have a huge joint of beef and really nice salads and a cold fish thing and . . .'

'It all sounds very expensive!'

Linden raised an eyebrow. 'Does that matter? It's not as if you'll do it very often and Oliver isn't poor, is he?'

'No. But . . . Perhaps I should ask him what I can spend.'

'Doesn't he give you money? For housekeeping?'

Anna shook her head. She could not bring herself to ask Ollie for money and he was always forgetting. She spent her own money instead, steadily diminishing the amount she had built up from the allowance her father had given her. She also spent money changing the house. She wanted the house to express more of Oliver and herself. She had pulled Oliver's piano into the middle of the living-room to make it seem as important as possible because even in the times when he seemed a total stranger, when he retreated into a shell through which she could not reach him, the music would touch her and try and explain.

She had had no idea of the complications that made up Oliver until she found herself living with him permanently. He had no middle stage between normal humour and rage. Tiny things infuriated him. Being extremely untidy he lost things constantly and searching infuriated him. But his rage was against the world in general and himself, not Anna. If he shouted it was at the object he couldn't find or to hurl streams of abuse into the air. Anna watched helplessly. She was simply not required in these scenes. If she ran forward, trying to be helpful, holding out the thing he was searching for, he would be disconcerted, ashamed.

'I don't mean any of it. I don't mean to be so childish. Just leave me alone when I'm angry,' he said, again and again.

But to Anna, anger like this was an outward sign of something wrong. She hated to leave him alone because it meant that she, in turn, was by herself. The way she hovered, the way she became upset, made Ollie feel more ashamed and he would go out or play the piano, withdrawing from her. Sometimes it seemed the music apologized to her. Almost made love to her . . .

Almost as disconcerting as his rages were his bursts of happiness, crazy, incredibly funny moods when he could reduce her to hysterical laughter. Life for the two of them was like a clumsy dance, each coming forward towards the other, touching, being surprised or held or rebuffed and then retreating. It was impossible to form an opinion of their lives together.

Linden came, the week before Christmas, to organize. 'We must have a lot of lists. They make me feel safe. Lists of lists. You will need flowers and paper napkins. Or I could lend you some of our linen ones; Marietta has given me dozens.' Linden loved these old-fashioned examples of comfort and wealth. Linen and cut glass, softly yellow with age; silver, heavy in the hand, and books. 'And have you decided what you will eat and have you enough glasses?'

Anna, rather restless now the Cannon had closed its doors for the Christmas pause, found that she enjoyed her new life more when Linden was there. She was reminded of games played years ago in the big nursery, when dolls were arranged in rows and meals set out. The planning had been much like this, Linden organizing, Anna agreeing.

'Who have you asked?' Linden said, when they were shopping for wine and the food that could be bought in advance.

'Oh, Oliver has asked a lot of his friends. And people from the club although some of them will have to leave long before midnight because they're opening that night. And I've asked people from the Cannon and Janey and Martha and Hilary and Pym of course.' She paused and thought, *Oh, how stupid I am! Of course! Why should she care so much about our party? When will I learn to see a manipulation coming?*

They unloaded the wine and candles and nuts and crisps and glass jars of salad. Huge tins of fruit juice and rice.

'Coffee?' Linden said, plugging in the kettle. Anna sat down. She was tired. She put her hand up to her forehead and a sudden wave of nausea made her shiver. She shut her eyes until it passed.

'What is it?' Linden said.

'Nothing. I felt sick, that's all. Sometimes, recently, the sight of food makes me feel sick. Isn't that amazing? The constant mouth, shut!'

'You are quite a lot thinner,' Linden said. 'Are you ill?'

Anna shook her head. There was a thought in the back of her mind which she had been avoiding. She spoke it, surprising herself as much as Linden. 'I wondered if I might be pregnant.'

'Not already!'

'It is much too soon, isn't it? I don't think it can be true. I take the pill now but, before, after Robert died, there were times when we didn't think. Back in October.'

'How stupid of Oliver!' Linden said crisply.

'Why Oliver? It's half my fault. I said it would be all right.'

'How careless of you!'

'Don't be so self-righteous!'

Linden's eyes blazed and then she sighed and sat down. 'All right, I'm sorry. But it's so like you . . . so hopeless. Why don't you think what you're doing? And for God's sake, find out if you are or aren't. Have you missed the curse?'

'I'm very late but that's nothing unusual. I keep hoping it will go away. I don't want a baby, Linden. The whole idea terrifies me. Sometimes Oliver and I are not at all happy.'

'Well, you've only been married a couple of months. Give yourselves a chance.' Linden dropped her chin into her hand. 'I always thought it would have been better if you'd just gone on living together quietly until you both grew up a bit. How is Ollie? Is he happy?'

'I don't know. I thought I knew him. After his father died we seemed very close. I got near him but I've never got inside him. He is so secret. He is unpredictable. He'll come back with a chocolate cake for me, or a magazine or a book and if it's something that I don't want, he'll guess and his eyes will sort of cloud over just because I show my surprise. I never get a second chance. If I hurt him or disappoint him, however unintentionally, he hides it and shuts me out.'

'He sounds exactly like you.'

'He keeps telling me how important it is to get on with life. He bustles round to see Freddie, goes off to the club in the evenings. Sometimes I go and sometimes I stay. He makes love to me about twice a week. I count the days. I think, three days since he's touched me so I lie stiff and waiting. It must be awful for him! I wish I could touch him first, start things, but once I did and afterwards he said he wished it hadn't happened.'

Linden giggled suddenly. 'Your marriage doesn't exactly read like the Kama Sutra, does it?'

There was a surprised silence and then Anna laughed too, with enormous relief, and found herself thinking how Ollie would laugh if this were about someone else.

'It's my fault, isn't it, Linden? It's because I'm so self-conscious and I think too much and I have always longed to have someone of my own! I expect too much.' She began to drink the coffee. 'Are you and James. . . ?'

Linden put her head a little on one side. 'James is good at everything. He takes great trouble. I am sure he has read all the right books about marriage and sex and how to make it work. He makes time for sex! In bed we are fine.' She raised her eyes to Anna's face. Her eyes said, 'And yet . . .'

'Pym?' Anna said very softly, almost mouthing the word.

Linden said nothing. Her shoulders drooped, her face relaxed and it was as if she allowed herself to sink into a dream. She controlled herself after a moment. Her voice was low. 'If you ever breathe of it, to anyone, I'll kill you. I understand myself. I know it takes time to forget. It was unreal with Pym and I resented the way he could make me feel. I hated his power over me. He could make me into someone quite different, without control, without ambition. I hated him for it.' There was a long silence. Then she said, 'Give yourself time, Anna. Ollie is so sweet underneath his complexes. You'll be all right, you two. It's not as if you were exactly happy out in the world on your own, is it?'

'No,' Anna said truthfully, 'but I did have a choice still. I had potential in my own mind.'

Linden stared at Anna, her face stripped of all expression except a terrifying desolation. 'How is it that out of the clutter of your brain come such exact thoughts? Potential. Plans and dreams. You can live your whole life for them. I didn't realize how it mattered. I didn't realize how much I needed the excitement. It's rather frightening, Anna, to have achieved your ambition. I suppose that's why people like James and Freddie will keep pushing until they die.'

Christmas was brief and disappointing. Oliver had only three days off and Pyecomb was subdued. Everyone felt Robert's absence strongly and Anna was glad to come back to London, to prepare for the party.

On New Year's Eve, when everything was done, she lay in the bath and tried to project herself forward a couple of hours, imagining that silent, tidy room downstairs filled with noises and people. Anna washed herself. She squeezed soapy bubbles on to her hard round stomach. It had never been hard before. Always fat and soft. Her mind shivered away from the knowledge that she must do something, ask somebody, find out. But until she was certain she could pretend it wasn't true.

She heard the front door and voices downstairs.

'Anna?' It was Ollie. He always called like this, urgently, with a slight undertone of panic, reminding her how he said, 'Some day you'll go home by mistake.'

'I'm in the bath.'

'What time is everyone coming?'

'Nineish.'

'Okay. Freddie's here.'

Freddie. She sank lower into the bath for safety, hating the way she reacted to his name. It was six months since Anna had last seen him – it had been before Linden's wedding! She had tried very hard in that time to clean him from her mind. *It all seems long ago,* she thought, getting out and drying herself. She put on careful eye make-up. She brushed her hair back, caught it with two slides. A new dress, bought under Linden's supervision, black and dramatic. The result was good and yet Anna was afraid to go downstairs, afraid to see him. She made excuses to herself but decided, at last, it was better to see him now, alone with Oliver, than to be shocked by him at the party.

Freddie watched her all the way down the stairs. Two weeks ago when he got the invitation, written in Anna's distinctive handwriting, he had held it and stared and remembered, feeling a wave of nostalgia, remembering her as he might remember a good holiday. At the bottom of the stairs she looked at him quickly. He saw that she was half-proud of herself, of the way she looked now, half-scared. He had forgotten her vulnerability. Or had he thought marriage would have changed her more? He stood up and came and kissed her cheek, in a way that was friendly and brotherly and utterly meaningless.

'You look lovely, Anna. It's so long since I've seen you . . . Marriage agrees with you. But then, you always thought it would!'

She ignored the jab but inside, secretly, was pleased that he bothered. 'Shall I get you both a drink?' Her hands trembled but she was telling herself, *It's all right. All right. I feel nothing for him.*

'I'd love a beer, Anna,' Oliver said.

'Yes, so would I.' Freddie sat down again. 'Well, Ollie, at least think about it.'

'Think about what?' Anna asked, handing them a can each, a tankard each, looking at Freddie properly for the first time, testing herself and remembering.

Freddie didn't answer. Oliver ripped the metal ring from the top of his beer can and poured it carefully. 'Freddie wants to buy me out of the business, Anna.'

'We've had a fantastic run of success. It's been far better than my most optimistic forecasts. But it's time to settle down and establish ourselves on a wider base. We must offer alternative investment opportunities. We must expand. There's a small merchant bank, which I doubt you will have heard of, Anna, which is scouting around for set-ups like ours. They want in . . .'

'I can't see the hurry,' Oliver said. 'After the January sale . . .'

'If the market wobbles, Ollie, they won't want us. They like the way we're looking now. But Japan is having money troubles. Real trouble over there will mean we might have the famous disappearing Jap trick! They could vanish as suddenly as they appeared. No more discerning little men with big cheque books. If that happens we won't look nearly so good!'

'Why can't the market survive without them?'

'Well, it can and it may. However, it only needs a few people like Stephano to get nervous and the whole set-up could collapse. I'm seeing three of my clients tomorrow. They are having a sudden attack of cold feet. I have to reassure and convince them that the year ahead will be better than the year behind.'

Anna said, 'Why don't you tell them the truth?'

Freddie laughed. 'The only reason they trust me with their money is that they naively believe I am psychic. If I turn round and ask them, "Shall I or shan't I?" I put decision back into their hands. They hate that. They pay me to worry about decisions. They can blame me if things are not as good as I say.'

'But why have things changed?' Anna said.

'They haven't changed. It's all a question of keeping several jumps ahead . . .'

They had temporarily forgotten Ollie. It was like those evenings, months ago, in Freddie's big white room, with the brown folders and the smoke from his cigarette, talking about it all. The smoke from the cigarette he held now reached out to Anna and the past reached out and she felt suddenly and violently sick. She spun round and lurched into the kitchen, gulping cold water.

'Are you all right?' Freddie said, leaning into the kitchen, and he said it in the tone Oliver should have been saying it in and all three of them knew it. Freddie stood aside, letting her come out.

'It's nothing. Excitement.'

'Bun in the oven already?' Freddie said archly, and finished his beer. 'Things could get expensive, Oliver. You'd better get out now on these good terms!' Then the joking was gone. 'Seriously, you made it all possible. I'm warning you that the next twelve months could be risky. I want you to be left with a worthwhile amount of money, if only to show James that I'm not the crook he takes me for!'

Oliver stood by the piano, one finger pressing out the same sad note. 'It's very considerate of you, Freddie. Such good terms too! If you like, I'll tell James of the offer, just to set your mind at rest. But I don't want to get out. I'd rather spend more time involved in it all. I like the feeling of risk. I want it to be all or nothing. I enjoy the way James tut-tuts at me. I like having a reason to snatch the newspaper from the doorstep. In short, Freddie, whether you wanted to or not, you've hooked me!'

Freddie stood up slowly. The anger was well concealed. It was a hard knot in his stomach and a stiffness in his face. He changed his approach. 'As you wish . . . but perhaps Anna can persuade you to change your mind. You talk to him, Anna. He has been extremely shrewd in the past. He has proved to the people who, frankly, may have considered he was not exactly cut out to make any great mark on the world, that they are quite wrong. They have under-estimated Oliver.' Freddie's brown eyes were round and sincere. 'Especially James. I am sure he knows the judgement required to withdraw at the right time is far more skilled than the judgement required to begin!'

Anna looked into his face, down to his restless hands. *Bastard*, she thought coldly.

Oliver hated the way they stood and looked at each other. 'I'm going to change. We'll talk about it again tomorrow, Freddie!' He went up the spiral stairs three at a time, making the whole structure shake.

'How are you, Fatty?' Freddie said very quietly. He moved across the space between Anna and himself, putting his hands each side of her jaw, caressing her neck with his thumbs. In her imagination she had lived this scene a hundred times. In reality she was afraid. She couldn't bear it. She dipped her head out of his hold and went into the kitchen, consulting the list Linden had left on the fridge. Neatly typed instructions. '7.0. Turn on oven. 7.30. Turn on warming cabinet, put potatoes and quiches in oven.' She heard Freddie behind her and, his hands on her shoulders, he turned her round. His mouth was warm and firm as he kissed her, parting her lips with his tongue. Her carefully collected indifference cracked from side to side. She put her arms round his neck and her body against his and she was filled with a sense of loss. Freddie drew back. He gave a small, thoughtful sigh, crossed the room and let himself out.

Anna stood with her head bent, teeth clenching her lower lip, shaking inside until Oliver's voice cut, angrily, through the quiet.

'Anna . . . there aren't any towels!'

She went slowly upstairs, smearing at her mouth. But what did it matter? What did a kiss matter? How childish to feel such guilt! Ollie sat in the bath, hair wet and sleek against his head.

'I'm sorry I shouted. But there are no towels and there's no lavatory paper either. You may well trap someone in here!'

Anna didn't laugh. She sat down on the closed loo. 'I'm sorry. I'm sorry I'm so hopeless. I'll get some.'

When she reappeared he was standing in the bath, water streaming down his body. She thought how good he looked naked, far better than clothed. An excitement, a longing for Oliver she had not experienced before, touched her. 'Shall I dry you?' Instinctively she tried to move closer to him – to blot out Freddie.

'No thanks.' He splashed her getting out. His face was closed up. What was it? Jealousy? Irritation? Worry?

'Don't look like that, Anna,' he said softly, seeing her face in the steamy mirror. 'It's just that Freddie has disorganized me. I am beginning to see how absurd I was in my hero-worship of him. I am beginning to think I have been most skilfully used and am about to be discarded now that fatter fish are interested. We have all been used, haven't we, Anna?'

She flushed, meeting his eyes in the mirror. 'Only as much as we wanted to be, Ollie. Freddie is no magician. He has not forced us to do things.' She stood up. 'Ollie, please get out of it all. You don't need him now.'

'No. I want to stay in. The fact that he wants me out makes me feel I should definitely stay in.'

'Please.' Her voice became shrill. An instinct, all through her, screamed that they should finish with Freddie. Cut the ties and get out now. 'Let's be free of him!'

'I am quite free,' he said coldly.

When Freddie left the mews he was extremely angry. The strength of his anger was out of all proportion to events. He rationalized. *Okay. So Ollie wants to play hard to get. I'll up the price. If I go carefully, I can handle him . . . Anna on my side would help.* The traffic lights turned red, suspending him for a few moments, in stillness, in a feeling of loneliness that was quite new to him. Six months had changed her considerably. She still had an overwhelming air of gentleness about her but her expression was braver, more in touch with real life. Marriage to Oliver, Freddie thought grimly, would not be a bed of roses. *Why the hell did she do it? Why did she marry Oliver? Why did she rush? Panic?* Instead of going straight home he drove to Rachel's flat. If she was going to the party he would take her.

They all brought presents, something Anna and Oliver had not expected. They heaped them on the table by the front door until it looked like a stall at a church fete. Flowers, bottles of wine, kitchen things, sheets, towels, table cloths, a set of tiny oval engravings, even a teddy bear! And at first they circled each other, Anna's people and Oliver's people, until the alcohol blended them and gave them a temporary interest in one another. Anna found she was enjoying herself, moving from group to group, watching Ollie and seeing that he, too, was happy. She didn't see many people arrive. Most of the time the door was opened by whoever stood nearest to it. She would just become aware of people in the room. At about ten she saw Freddie with a small, fascinating-looking woman whose black hair fell to her waist and whose dress showed a lot of creamy bosom. Oliver greeted the girl warmly. When Anna asked who she was he looked surprised. 'That's Rachel,' he told her.

At about ten-thirty they began to eat. Music from Oliver's tape deck spilled out of the open windows into the mews and evaporated into the night.

Veronica arrived. She had said she would just look in but all sense of time had deserted her. Before she left she had had two or three drinks to make her feel better. The silence of the flat, without Linden or Anna, was depressing her terribly. Prue kept going on about the change of life and hormones and alcoholism and a good woman doctor but Veronica didn't want to be taken in hand. She knew perfectly well what made her drink. She was lonely and she wanted her husband back!

At one point, standing half way up the stairs, Anna looked down on them all like God and thought how little they had changed. She decided it was a good party. She felt proud and also empty, withdrawn from it all.

Pym came just after eleven. The front door had been left open to release heat and smoke. He stood on the edge of the party until his eyes found Anna, half way up the stairs with a plate on her lap talking to no one. He saw things had not really changed for her and he was sorry. He waved. Anna didn't see him but Linden did. She pushed across the room towards him, putting herself in front of him and then leaning forward to kiss his cheek. She had almost given up . . . 'Hallo, Pym.'

He shrank back. He had thought about seeing her so often and for so long, through dozens of restless and broken nights, that to be presented with her, to be touched by her in this meaningless, social way, was overwhelming. 'You look well,' he said awkwardly.

'Thank you.' She was smiling and he saw that, for Linden, she was almost drunk. She was altered and blunted and made crude by the drink. She tucked her arm through his. 'Come and have something to eat. There is still some food left.'

He took his arm away gently. 'No, thank you. I've eaten. I want to talk to Anna.' He wanted to hurt this caricature of Linden who was treating him so superficially. 'I came to see Anna.' He moved across the room to the stairs, touching Anna's foot to get her attention.

As she watched him go, it seemed to Linden that the whole room narrowed round him, sucked inwards to leave only a path where he had walked. A very narrow path. The voices round her went far away and her ears sang.

'Are you all right?' someone said.

'Hot,' she murmured, and went out of the front door, taking deep breaths of the cold night air. *I am losing my touch*, she thought wearily. *I should have done far better than that. Far, far, better. I should at least have arranged it so that he danced with me, so that I could touch him again . . .*

When midnight came they stood in a big, ragged circle, hands linked, shouting *Auld Lang Syne,* dragging themselves forward and backwards and then darting from person to person, kissing, wishing 'Happy New Year'. Ollie sat down at the piano and began to play Beatles songs and Rachel leaned on it and sang, playing with the melodies and the words. *Yesterday,* and *Can't Buy me Love,* and *Eleanor Rigby* and *Hey, Jude.* And people danced, swaying in unsteady couples, leaning against one another, feeling each other's bodies with uninhibited drunken hands, mouths pressing mouths; some of them went home, calling 'Good night' and 'Happy New Year' and reeling unsteadily down the mews; someone sat under the table for hours, feet sticking out and quite still, heels together, toes apart; the door to Anna's painting room was locked for hours; and Freddie, temporarily without Rachel while she was singing, watched Anna and knew, in the raw truthful early morning, that he still wanted her.

'Lovely party, Anna,' Richard Cannon said. 'Hilary, can I run you home?'

'It's kind of you, Richard, but you look tired and it's a good twenty minutes to Wimbledon, even at this time . . .'

'Perhaps you're right. Can I drop you at a taxi rank?'

'James, how nice to see you again after all these months,' Freddie said. 'I'm so sorry I didn't get to your wedding . . .'

'That's quite all right. Oliver tells me how very busy you have been. Very, very busy!'

Freddie smiled noncommitally, determined not to be drawn. But the back of his neck was cold when he stood too near James. James wore his dislike so openly. Rachel leaned on Freddie's arm as he turned to Anna, kissing her cheek and giving her a shock of pain as she thought of the earlier kiss. She looked into Rachel's black eyes and then down to the small hands which gripped rhythmically at Freddie's arm.

'Thank you for singing,' Anna said dully. 'It made the party.'

Now the room was almost empty. Pym had left much earlier, just after the year turned, hugging Anna, whispering, 'Bye bye, Fatso! I'm off. I can't take it tonight . . . not in the mood. You know?'

'Yes,' she had said, understanding. Now she looked round the room. They had come and filled it and eaten and drank and talked and danced and kissed and gone home. James and Linden were the last to go and Linden said she would come round in the morning and help with the clearing-up. It was just after three-thirty when the door closed after them.

Oliver lay full length on the sofa, arms thrown back over his head, eyes closed. 'Went all right, didn't it?'

'Yes.' Anna came and sat on the floor by him, pleased that he was pleased, feeling an unexpected tenderness for him. She laid her head on his tummy against the blue Shetland sweater which smelt of the airing cupboard. Half asleep, he stroked her hair.

'Anna, don't ever cut your hair, however much you may hate me.'

'What a stupid thing to say!'

'Promise me?'

'I promise.' She yawned. 'Let's go to bed and leave all this mess till the morning.' She got up and pulled Oliver to his feet and they went slowly up the stairs, switching off lights, dropping their clothes on the floor like children, washing and cleaning teeth automatically and falling thankfully into bed. *Make love to me,* Anna willed, half asleep. *Now, in the New Year . . . such a good way to start a year.* But beside her, Oliver was almost asleep, trying to blot out of his mind the expression he had seen on Anna's face when Freddie kissed her good night.

CHAPTER TWENTY

By the beginning of February, Anna could no longer pretend she wasn't pregnant. She couldn't fasten any skirts or jeans round her waist. She was buying bigger bras. Reluctantly she rang Linden for advice and Linden came round with the name of a doctor.

'He's Marietta's doctor. Very nice and fatherly. Very understanding.' She yawned. She sat, rather wearily, on the sofa. 'Every night this week we've been out somewhere or taken someone out! It's always like that . . . It's strange for us to be in the house alone together.' She left the sentence unresolved.

'Why did you see this doctor?' Anna asked, shrewdly.

'James is eager for a family. Lots of great clever sons to run things.' She rested her head against a cushion and closed her eyes. 'But I refuse to start yet. I must have a breathing space. So I went to him just before we were married and got myself fixed up. I don't trust James.'

'What do you mean? That he would let you get pregnant, before you want to? No one would do that.'

Linden lifted her head up, opened her eyes, and sat forward. 'I'll tell you something, Anna. Both you and I are extremely naive. We haven't been very long in the real world. We tend to judge people by our own standards. We run around inside ourselves, thinking we are making great plans and manipulating people but in fact we are doing nothing of the sort. I am beginning to understand how very subtle, how delicately cruel, people can be to one another when they live together.'

'You're always so dramatic. What does that mean?'

Linden shrugged. 'Nothing, I suppose. It doesn't mean that I'm unhappy! Not really . . . Anyway, ring this man and make an appointment. Now, while I'm here!

He was, as Linden had said, the classic Father figure. Tall and narrow-shouldered with thick greying hair. Firm and gentle hands, feeling Anna's stomach. She had brought, as she had been instructed, a specimen to be tested. He said he would telephone her in the afternoon. She walked back to the mews and now that it was real, now that she had faced the problem, she was acutely nervous.

At four, when the telephone rang, she snatched it up.

'Mrs. Carroll?'

'Yes. Yes.'

'I think you had better start knitting. The test is positive.' He said a lot more about making her an appointment with a gynaecologist. She hardly listened. She was trying to make herself believe that the idea which had nestled secretly inside her was true. Confirmed. Alive. She answered the doctor, yes and no, wrote down a telephone number, thanked him. She walked the room carefully, feeling entirely different from the way she had felt before the phone call and the dread inside her was changing, gradually, to exhilaration.

But Ollie? What will he say?

He came in at six, slamming the door, calling to her. Anna was waiting upstairs with no idea of what to say or how to tell him. She had tried out a dozen different approaches in her mind. She had forgotten that Oliver was completely unaware of the possibility of her being pregnant. She answered him and came down the stairs and on the bottom step she blurted out, 'Oliver, I'm going to have a baby. In July. Or August.'

He stood absolutely still and stared at her. 'Jesus!' He pushed his hair back impatiently from his forehead. 'How did that happen?'

She laughed nervously. 'Well, really, Ollie, surely you know what causes it?'

'I mean when? How? I thought you took the pill.'

'I do. But obviously once or twice I didn't . . . and after your father died . . .'

'Oh God!' Oliver said and he sat down heavily. His first reaction was one of pure panic.

Anna came down the last step. She clasped her hands in front of her stomach as if she could hide it. Her teeth were chattering.

'That ruins everything, doesn't it?' he said. 'We can't have a baby here! We'll have to move. Oh, my God!'

'Why can't we have one here?' she said, amazed.

'Don't you know anything? They have to have somewhere to be. In a pram! To lie out . . . you couldn't leave it in the mews and you'll be sure to fall down these stairs with it and the traffic would wake it. It would be hopeless here! In a couple of years, when things are settled, it would be so much easier. I suppose . . .' He looked at her and then darted his eyes away.

'Don't say it. Don't ask if we have to have it!' Her mouth started to shake. She was filled with pity for this thing no one wanted. 'I didn't want it to happen either. I've tried to pretend it would go away but it hasn't!'

She watched him make an effort, summoning up the sort of attitude he thought he should adopt. 'Look, Anna, I'm sorry, but I had no idea! A baby is about the last thing we need.' He was silent for a few moments. 'Now it's happened, it's happened.' He stood up and smiled stiffly. 'Have you thought of some names?'

He couldn't make it right that easily. Not this time, not just by laughing. She was deeply hurt. She was still shaking inside and her voice was cold. 'I went to this doctor of your mother's. He's sending me to a gynaecologist. It's all private. I expect it's very expensive. Can we afford that?'

'I don't know.' He hated her like this, so organizing.

'Well, think! Tell me!' she shouted, tears springing into her eyes.

'Yes, we can afford it,' he shouted back. 'James made me take out some kind of medical insurance years ago. I don't know if they pay for babies but, anyway, with the interest from Freddie, we can pay.' He came and stood in front of her. 'Anna, I'm sorry. I don't mean to react as I do. It's just that you seem to thrust things at me without warning . . . I never thought . . . Anyway, now I've had a chance to register the idea, well, it's not so awful. In fact, I'm rather pleased.'

She nodded, knowing that he didn't mean it, turning away and trying to be grateful that he was at least trying.

From that night onwards, Oliver did not touch her very often. He lay in his own half of the bed. The things he felt were very complicated and confused. He was afraid of hurting her, afraid of the future, afraid of the baby inside her. If she rolled towards him, timidly reaching for him, he would wrap himself more tightly into his own side of the bed. When they made love it gave little enjoyment to either of them. Anna made comments about 'people who are afraid of responsibility' and 'people who couldn't grow up!' In return, Ollie treated her with a consideration and politeness which only increased her loneliness. But underneath, deep inside himself, he was afraid he had lost her to the baby before he even fully knew her. He thought of the relationship between his mother and James. He was desperately afraid of being dispossessed.

London, in the spring of that year, while Anna and Oliver drew farther and farther apart, was bright with flowers and the trees were a pale and brilliant green. The shop windows were full of pretty dresses. Flower shops displayed tempting boxes of petunias and geraniums. By May the evenings no longer slammed down early, mornings were light.

Anna, walking slowly and heavily, sensed that she was alone. Her hand explored the bed timidly. A cool and creased space where Oliver had been. Last night, through the intense sleepiness which attacked her every evening around nine, she was aware that Oliver had talked of leaving early, of going to see Freddie. He had talked of the take-over idea finally falling through ... She wondered, with her eyes tightly closed, if Oliver had kissed her as she slept? She thought it was doubtful. For the past few months they had seemed to be two strangers merely sharing a house. They slept and woke at different times. They lived in different worlds.

Anna pulled herself upright, the great round bulk of her stomach moving with a reluctant jerk, making her grunt. She saw herself reflected in the long mirror opposite which tormented her so. She lumbered out of bed, swinging her feet heavily to the floor. Swollen feet. Nearly three months left but already this child had taken over completely, invading every portion of her, fattening, slowing her down, bringing this constant sleepiness.

She stood up, arching her spine and putting her hand into the small of her back in an age-old gesture of pregnancy. Her nightgown was stiff with her stomach. She went down the spiral stairs with care and made herself a cup of tea. Coffee sickened her. Wine and cigarettes revolted her. She was totally changed in all her tastes. There was no sign of Oliver having had breakfast. He seemed to ask less and less of her, and of the house. She hated the way he was so independent of her now, taking meals out to save her trouble, he said. He treated her with such agonizing politeness, as if she were dying. She thought of him coming downstairs, letting himself out, whistling perhaps because the morning would have been cool and clean.

She sat and stared at her feet as she waited for the toast to pop up. She thought: *I wanted someone of my own. So did he. What's happened? It wouldn't be so bad to be invaded like this if Ollie was eager for the child but however much he pretends he is scared, trying not to look at the little white clothes Marietta keeps buying, trying not to answer when I ask him where we should move to!* And yet, underneath, Anna almost understood the situation she and Oliver found themselves in. Too many difficulties, too soon, but it could be all right. It could be. As she worked at the Cannon, painting a pale self-portrait, lunched with Pym, went shopping with Marietta, she still thought that it could be all right.

Linden was a frequent visitor, watching Anna with fascination, pacing the house and talking, raving about James and Marietta. 'He lunches with her once a week; come hell or high water! He makes time for her! Why doesn't he use that time for me? Why am I not asked? It enrages me, Anna. He does just what she asks! The great James Carroll, tycoon!' She turned and stared at Anna, almost with repugnance. 'Surely you won't feed it yourself?'

'Yes, I will. I want us to be a team. It and me!'

Linden wrinkled her nose. 'Well, I know it's supposed to be a good thing but it will make you sag and, honestly, Anna, with a bosom as big as yours, what on earth would you look like?'

'Who cares what I look like? I want to feed it!' She spoke bravely, trying to pretend that this lump, which kicked and fluttered, would really turn into a small human being.

In the kitchen on this bright May morning she sat and drank her tea and ate her toast. Today she was due to visit the gynaecologist. She enjoyed these monthly visits. She liked the way he believed in it. He would put a small metal ear trumpet against her stomach and listen to its heart beat. He talked to her about the baby. He told her severely she was putting on too much weight. She always left him feeling happy and optimistic, resolving to eat less, rolling down the street, vast and imposing, with her hair streaming behind her. She found people were very kind. Strangers smiled at her and made jokes. She realized it was because, being pregnant, they instinctively felt she was harmless and good. At the Cannon they treated her with affection. She was the centre of attention, the only married mother they had ever had. She went to pre-natal classes, at first repelled at the sight of nineteen other women, all pregnant, but finding after a while that there was a great mutual interest and complaints to share. The woman who took the classes was brisk and kind, teaching them relaxation, teaching them about their bodies, asking them to encourage their husbands to come. Sometimes she would pause and look at them all with a sort of tolerant pity as if, Anna thought, she knew what was coming and wondered if they would all survive. Not merely the birth of the child but all of life was included in that compassionate look.

'You may find, especially as you near the end of your pregnancy, that sexual intercourse is uncomfortable and the idea is unpleasant. Naturally this may be hard for your husband to understand. You can expect patience and consideration but you cannot ask them to give up all interest in sex for a period of months!'

One girl raised her hand and put into words exactly what Anna longed to ask and couldn't. 'It's the other way round with us. I feel like it and he doesn't!'

'Have you talked about it?'

She shook her head. 'I think he finds me repulsive . . .'

'I wish my husband found me repulsive . . .'

The discussion took off. It was far the most animated class they had had. Anna sat and listened, not able to join in, but thinking how night after night and day after day, as she rested in the afternoons, sometimes even as she walked in the street or lay in the bath, her body clamoured and ached but she dared not touch herself for some primitive fear of hurting the baby.

It was after that class that she went home and walked over to Oliver, who was sitting at the piano. She bent, awkwardly, and put her face against his.

'Oliver, why don't you make love to me any more?'

'I'm not supposed to, am I? I thought it made women miscarry in the beginning and that you wouldn't enjoy it now.'

'No. It doesn't hurt.'

'Oh . . . Well, you might have told me. Why didn't you say anything before?'

'I just thought you didn't fancy me fat.'

'Well, Anna, you've always been fat!'

Each time she remembered that conversation Anna cringed. Thinking of it now, as she got up from the table and went to dress. By ten-thirty she was ready to leave and as she approached the front door it burst open and Oliver came in, his face pale and furious.

'What is it, Ollie?'

'That bastard, Freddie! He's trying to throw me out. Not in the open. He doesn't say that. But he makes decisions without even mentioning them till months afterwards. He . . .' Oliver paced the room.

Anna had never seen him so angry. She stared at him helplessly.

'Why do you stand there, looking at me like that? As if I were mad or something? You are just like he is. You don't ask me. You never asked about the baby. You just did it! My family never ask, they just command!' He lit a cigarette. 'They want me to sign a year's contract at the club. Before I do, I wanted to see Freddie. I was seriously thinking of chucking Billy's and working with Freddie full time. But I find he has already employed someone. Without even giving me the chance!'

'Well, perhaps he needed someone who knew a lot about porcelain?'

'He wants me out, I can see that!'

'Ollie, I'll miss my class. I must go . . .'

He controlled himself with difficulty. 'All right . . . shall I drive you?'

'No. I'll walk or get a bus. I need exercise!' She let herself out, escaping from Ollie and all his problems and making the gulf between them even wider.

They looked for a new house in sporadic bursts, at first searching Surrey and even Sussex, until Oliver decided that it was too far for him to drive every night. They came back, depressed and exhausted after looking at houses in Kingston and Barnes and Blackheath. When they grew very disillusioned they would give up for a while but in June James had a very good offer for the house in the mews which he accepted and the panic began again. Sometimes Anna would wake in the night, hot and with a dry mouth, wanting to go to the lavatory, terrified that she would be left without a home when the child was born. A lot of primitive instincts rose to the surface. She needed to nest. She wanted to make a room for the baby, to prepare herself.

She was sent the particulars of a house in Parson's Green and she went to see it with Pym. Three floors, big rooms, a space for a car and a garden at the back. It also gave the impression, on the hot June morning when they looked round it, of being airy, of being removed from the frantic centre of London.

'What do you think, Pym?'

'I like it. I like the big windows and the kitchen and the garden will be great for it to crawl around!' Pym, avowed child-hater, was the one most concerned with this baby. He was determined that it would be a girl.

'No, I won't have a girl, Pym. I couldn't stand it. I'd worry for her and she'd be like me, massive and plain and miserable. A boy is altogether a simpler thing.'

'Anna, you will have an enchanting little girl, as feminine as you are, with bright orange hair!'

'And Oliver's eyelashes?' She sat down, thankfully, on the low wall in front of the house. 'I like this place.'

'Well, that's settled then!'

The estate agent, who had been waiting by his car while they took a second look, cleared his throat.

'I like it very much but I'll have to bring my husband to see it. Could I keep the keys until five?'

Oliver said, 'It seems okay. Do you want to live here, Anna?'

'Yes.' She was wary, now, of taking any decision without letting Oliver feel it was his. 'But of course it's up to you.'

'For God's sake, Anna, I know nothing about houses. Just because I have had a few childish outbursts lately, don't treat me like a high court judge all the time!' He dug his hands into his pockets. 'Bought you a present.' He pulled out a bag of crisps and Anna took them and smiled.

'It's freehold,' she said.

'Yes. And expensive. But I've asked Freddie to pay me back some of the money I have with him . . .'

'But you didn't want to do that, did you?'

'It's only part of it and it seems sensible to buy a house that is big enough to last us for some years.'

She nodded, thinking, *How amazing that he has long-term plans for us, that he believes we will survive together for some years.*

And so they bought the house in Dora Road and Linden swept in with her little squares of colour and was scathing when Anna said she wanted the whole house painted white. 'Except the baby's room which will be apple green, like Granny Smith apples, and I shall paint pictures all over it of things babies like. Rattles and teddies and ice-creams and things.'

Through July the days were crammed with activity and yet they crawled, seeming longer than normal days.

'First babies are always late.'

'Obviously a girl. You're fat all round.'

'Must be a boy, you're so out in front!'

'William? You can't call it William!'

'Aren't you huge? Have you gone off Matthew?'

'I thought you had it weeks ago.'

'You don't look well.'

'You do look well.'

'I think we'll induce you, Mrs. Carroll . . .'

'Thank God! I can't go on lumbering round like this. It's so hot and at night I wake up with my feet burning and I can't go to sleep again and we're moving into a new house the day after tomorrow!'

'Well, come in the following Monday then. If you haven't started labour on your own beforehand, that is!'

She told Oliver that evening that she was to go into hospital on Monday. He was in the bathroom, cleaning his teeth, and she looked past him at her reflection in the mirror. She looked quite extraordinary now, with a lump stuck on to the front of her and her ribs rather thin for a change. Her bottom and thighs had grown vast. Her hair tormented her, it was so long and hot and thick.

'And Linden and Mother are coming tomorrow to help with the last of the packing.'

He nodded. He met her eyes in the looking-glass and smiled. She wanted to say, 'Soon it will all be over. We can start normal life, with the baby, and care about each other again.' But he smiled at her so thinly, as if she were a stranger, and she was too tired to want anything but sleep.

On the morning of the move, while everyone else did the packing and the removal men removed, Anna said good-bye to the mews and quietly and wickedly lumbered up to Chelsea Green to the hairdresser she had last visited on the morning of Linden's wedding.

'Could you please cut my hair? Quite short. Cool. Like a boy.'

There seemed to be yards and yards of it and it lay in an orange mass on the floor round her chair, making her think how much her life had changed through the years that hair had been growing. She looked up, out of her thoughts, at her face in the glass and was deeply surprised. A slender neck appeared and the shape of her head and her face, hollowed out by the past months, looked almost fragile.

Gary was full of enthusiasm. He ignored Anna's request to cut it like a boy. Instead he parted her hair at the side, cutting it thick and blunt and into a point at the nape of her neck. It was soft and it moved and he dried it with a hand drier and said what a beautiful colour it was.

When he finished, Anna was delighted. She took a taxi to Dora Road where Linden was organizing the unloading of the first van. 'My God, you look marvellous . . .' Linden almost skipped round her. 'I always said you would!'

Veronica liked it too. And Marietta, who called to see the house for the first time on the worst possible day. And James, who came to collect Marietta and take her to lunch. And Pym, who called in at tea time.

Only Oliver said nothing. He stared with disbelief and then tried not to look at her. He couldn't recognize her. Her action underlined the gulf between them.

That evening they sat in the big bare kitchen with the back door open on to the garden. 'I know I promised, Ollie, but I was so hot. And I just needed to be different! I'm sorry. If you really mind, I'll grow it again.'

'It would take years,' he said dully.

'We haven't got years, have we?' It came out quite calmly.

'No, I suppose not.' He turned to face her.

'What are we doing, about to have a baby, moving into a new

house, when we are so unsure of each other? Why aren't we happy?'

'Happiness isn't important. Unfortunately we make each other unhappy. I planned it all so differently.' He stood up and went to the open door, looking out into the garden. 'You seemed so gentle. So exact and sensible. I thought, with the success of Brook Street and you and I looking out for each other . . . Well, I had been so lonely and so had you.'

'We still don't know each other, that's what it is. We haven't had time. It's not even nine months yet!'

'No.'

'I'm sorry about the baby,' Anna said stiffly.

'It wasn't your fault. I should have made sure. I am supposed to be managing things, aren't I?' He felt, as he had done for the past eight or nine months, like a man caught up in a series of frightening events, swung against his will.

'What happened at the sale today?'

'It was a fantastic success. Some things fetched double the amount that was estimated. I sat at the back . . . Freddie was selling about a dozen pieces for Mrs Hull. Not a single Japanese dealer in sight and yet these huge sums of money being thrown about the room as if they were playing monopoly! Freddie was wrong when he thought it all depended on the Japanese. He says himself that he was wrong.' He turned slowly to look at Anna. 'Do you mind me smoking?'

She shook her head.

'We'll jog along for a while, shall we?'

She nodded and tears began to run down her face.

'Please don't cry, Anna.'

'I can't help it. I feel so alone. I am afraid. I shall have this child to look after for ever . . .'

'You never seemed to be afraid. You never ask me for help or anything. You don't let me drive you anywhere, come with you, choose anything, discuss anything. Like all the other people in my life you appear to ignore me most of the time.'

'But you didn't want it. I thought you would rather not be involved. I tried to stop beating you over the head with it!'

Oliver said, very softly, 'Is that the reason, Anna? Is it my child? How did Freddie know, long before I did? That day of the party, New Year's Eve. He knew then.'

'Of course it's your child,' she screamed at him, appalled. 'Freddie just guessed. Oliver, how could you think that?' And all the implications came to her, one after the other. 'Did you think I still saw Freddie after we were married?'

He was standing in front of her, very stiffly. 'Is it mine? Really?' All the agonizing uncertainty, the insecurity, was plain in his face.

Anna shook her head helplessly. She felt dazed, light-headed and lost. 'It's your baby. It's yours!'

He put his hands each side of her face. 'Anna. Anna, swear it.'

'I swear. I swear.' She stood up, clumsily, and they moved close together, holding on to each other and feeling an extraordinary closeness. They slept all night in each other's arms, despite the heat and Anna's bulk and her restlessness. And each time she woke, as she did frequently, because of the baby moving or this new room without curtains, she would find Oliver awake and every time his hand rested possessively on her stomach.

On Monday morning Oliver drove her to the hospital. It was already a very hot morning and the traffic roared outside her little room on the first floor. She got undressed and into bed, feeling absurd to be undressing again at nine-thirty in the morning and Oliver sat on the end of the bed, smiling at her sometimes. There was a clumsy sweetness between them, a nervousness and excitement about the baby which delighted them both although they hardly believed it. After all these months of pretending, of ignoring the other, of separating, somehow they were both aware that the other cared.

'What happens now?' Oliver asked.

Anna shrugged. She looked lost, sitting in that white bed. Despite the vast lump of her stomach she looked fragile for the first time in her life. 'I wish I had some knitting.'

'Can you knit?'

'Sort of.'

'I'll go and buy you some. A pattern and some wool. What else? Knitting needles? You can knit me a sweater . . . knit me a baby!'

She smiled and watched him go and when he had gone and she was alone she was afraid, looking down at the lump of her stomach and hoping she and the child would separate easily. It was a boy. She was convinced of that. A boy without a name because they had not been able to discuss anything through these past difficult months. But last night Oliver said he wanted to call it David because it was a name utterly unconnected with anyone in his family.

While Oliver was away, they came to examine her. The small grey-haired doctor tut-tutted and said her blood pressure had risen and they would have to wait for a day or two. They could not induce the baby until it went down. Anna must stay in bed, stay quiet and still. The world was abruptly reduced, by this sudden and unexpected development, to the oblong window and this tiny room. When Oliver returned she told him the news. He stayed for an hour and then left, promising to come back later in the day.

CHAPTER TWENTY-ONE

Freddie sat with his elbows on his desk, drawing a complicated and aimless pattern on the back of an envelope. He had been working all afternoon and he was tired. He pulled at the neck of his shirt, undoing another button. The big sash windows were open but there was no breeze in London today. Just flat heat and the noise of traffic and the occasional angry horn. At four o'clock Penny came up and poured him a cold beer. 'Waste of a beautiful day,' she said, carrying her glass down the stairs. 'Who needs money, anyway? Can't we shut up shop?'

'At five,' Freddie said. He was doing one of his periodic appraisals of the whole situation, balancing his clients, checking if one could benefit another. *In October*, he thought, *we will have been going for two years. Very, very successful years. But still it is not fully mine!* He rapped the pencil thoughtfully against the desk. Damn Oliver and his lawyers and his control! Even with the money Oliver had withdrawn, he still held the major part of the company. *That was a bad miscalculation*, Freddie thought, *not reckoning on Oliver being stubborn. Why wasn't he scared off months ago?*

Freddie got up and walked to the window. Now that he had employed Patrick Jones, a knowledgeable and intelligent man quite capable of correctly assessing the merit of various pieces of porcelain, a considerable load had been taken off Freddie. He had more time to plan his expansion. He wanted to open an office in New York. Above all else, he wanted total control!

Last week, Freddie had actually allowed himself three days off. He had taken Rachel to Paris. Three comfortable days in which he thought, as he had frequently thought over the past year, how well they suited each other. They were strong enough to stand up to each other. She was frequently away, working all over the world, but she always came back to Brook Street. She had a key. She had her own flat where she kept her vast wardrobe of clothes and where she could go after she and Freddie had indulged in one of their violent quarrels. She was perfectly happy with the arrangement. She had no intention having children . . .

'Freddie.' It was Oliver, making Freddie turn from the window, startled.

'I didn't hear you. I'm sorry. How are you? A father yet?'

'No. I don't understand the hold-up! She's been in there three days. I don't know what to do with myself! Tell me more about the sale last week – I still can't believe it!'

Freddie nodded and lit a cigarette. 'I got what I wanted because I stayed out at the beginning while the bidding was low and let Maisie and a couple of others do the hard work and then I came in at one hundred thousand pounds.' He paused, remembering the tension, the steady pulse of his heart. There was absolute quiet in the room as the figures rose and rose. The auctioneer's voice was more expressionless than usual. Freddie always bid, with a brisk nod of his head. 'It was knocked down to me for one hundred and fifty thousand pounds. And that comes to one hell of a commission!'

'Jesus!' Oliver said.

'But I don't like it. I don't like such an enormous collection being in the hands of one man.'

'I thought this was for Stephano's woman friend. What's her name?'

'Maria Ricardi. Yes, but she acts entirely on his advice. Perhaps I'm looking for trouble unnecessarily. Do you want a beer, Oliver?'

'Thanks.' Oliver sat down. 'By the way, I was talking to James the other day about all this. I didn't go to see him about it – it just came up. He seems to think your merchant bank was pretty undesirable. Although, at the time, he advised me to sell out! He still does. Endlessly.'

Freddie looked down to hide the anger. 'I did look into it myself.'

'I know you did but James has access to a lot of inside information. He could be very useful if it ever happened again.'

'I'll bear it in mind,' Freddie said, coldly.

'May I ring the hospital?'

Freddie nodded. 'I'm sure you don't need to worry. Anna is built for having children, isn't she?'

Just lately he had taken to making this kind of remark. Oliver picked up the telephone and looked at Freddie. 'She is afraid,' he said simply.

Freddie ran his finger thoughtfully round the edge of his glass. He thought of Anna in this room, solemnly watching him while he worked. Anna in his bed. Anna laughing and crying. Anna afraid? He didn't want her to be afraid. He looked at Oliver's back and his face was full of contempt. It was so absurd that she should be having Oliver's child. Why the hell had she done that? Damn her and damn Oliver!

Anna lay in her white bed, dreading the coming of night. It came so early in the hospital, the quietness beginning to fall shortly after 7.30 when they removed the supper trays. This was her third evening and already she knew each detail of the routine. The silence of the evening was broken occasionally by calm but purposeful footsteps in the corridor outside or the shrill call of the telephone. Oliver had left at nine. She moved restlessly and her back was aching uncomfortably. Anna rang the bell.

A face looked round the door under a white cap. There were so many different uniforms and caps and faces. Which was this? Staff nurse? Sister?

'My back aches terribly,' Anna said. 'I was wondering if I could have something stronger to make me sleep?'

'Just let's have a look at you, Mrs. Carroll.' She lifted the bed-clothes and put her hands on Anna's stomach. 'Well, well, I think you're in labour.' She left and came back and took Anna's blood pressure and temperature.

'But I have no pains.'

'Your back ache . . . It can start like that.'

Anna lay back. The light was on over her head. The thin flowered curtains hid the night. Shiny grey walls. High ceiling. A room crammed into a corner of this vast old hospital. She didn't want to be alone and she picked up the telephone and asked for Oliver's number. While she waited another dull pain attacked.

'Oliver?'

'Yes . . .' His voice was blurred with food. He was obviously eating a quick meal before leaving for work.

'The baby has started. Could you come? Please? Just for a

bit.'

'Sure. I'll ring the club.'

A young doctor arrived. He was Australian and he listened and took her blood pressure again. They turned out the light which shone in her eyes and she wanted to go to the lavatory and Oliver arrived.

He was serious, wide-eyed and trying to be helpful. 'Try and remember all that breathing they taught you . . . Does it hurt much?' It was nearly ten o'clock.

'No. I can't think why people make so much fuss,' Anna said. gaily. She breathed as she had been taught. Someone brought Oliver a cup of tea which he drank merely to be polite.

'I think it will get worse,' he said carefully.

Anna wasn't aware of any one contraction being stronger than the last, just that the pain became more difficult to cope with. It began to surprise her. Physical pain like this was something entirely new to her. As contraction followed contraction they lasted for longer and became stronger, bewildering her until, even by midnight, she could not cope with her breathing. She was so shocked by the power of the pain. Oliver sat near her and his voice kept coming through, telling her to breathe, breathe. And they moved her and touched her, and listened to the baby's heart until she screamed 'I'm going to be sick!' and they brought her a tin bowl and she wanted to die.

I will die, Anna thought. *It will all end here. I shall be destroyed, torn into pieces.*

The doctor came back, asking Oliver to go outside for a few moments while he examined Anna. Oliver left obediently.

Now Anna fought the agony of the doctor's hands, trying to push him away, while they told her in soft voices to be sensible. Like being raped she thought, as he put his hands inside her and the agony made her scream and she felt a sudden warm rush of water. The pain was so enormous now it was tearing her in half, each time attacking her before she had recovered from the last time, catching her, rolling her like an enormous wave.

Oliver was back, she realized, and grabbed for him. She was doing it all wrong, forgetting the breathing, cringing inside herself, shouting, waiting to be sucked down into absolute madness. They gave her pethadene. It did nothing for the agony but it drugged her between contractions so that she dozed through the short periods when she might have been preparing herself and woke only to the pain. Oliver crouched near to her, his face next to hers, trying to be in it with her, unable to reconcile the calmness of the nurses with Anna's obvious agony. 'Please, Anna. Try and remember what they taught you.' He thought, *God, I wish I had gone with her, heard some of it! God, I wish I could help her!*

There was nowhere for Anna to go. The force which occupied her body was unbelievable. She was swamped and broken by it and she said, 'Will I die?' and a nurse smiled and shook her head. 'But it is destroying me,' Anna shouted, and she experienced absolute despair. There was no time. There was no climax. It was endless and overwhelming and suddenly it was as if she was waking from a nightmare. She seemed to feel a corner to the pain. It turned. No less but different. It seemed to have a point to it.

Mr Stern, the gynaecologist, looking younger in the early morning, bent over her. 'Hallo, Mrs Carroll. Well done . . . not long now. I'll go and scrub up and see you in the delivery room.'

'Are you coming, Mr Carroll?' they asked Oliver.

'Yes.'

Suddenly Anna felt the need to push they all talked about. The need to force down. But she looked and her stomach still bulged enormously. They gave her gas and air to gasp at through a black rubber mask. On to a trolley. 'Don't push yet, dear . . . not yet. Pant instead. If you push now you'll slow things up. Keep over it. Good girl . . .' Blessed, dizzying gas. Down a corridor. A new room. Voices. 'Don't push yet.'

God, what is happening? God, this pain is so big. It's so big! Oliver sat beside her head, his eyes wide above the white mask. Eyes she had not looked into for months. Mr Stern in a white bath hat; a new nurse explaining quietly and kindly why Anna must not push. They put her in a sitting position and made her hold her legs . . . Mr Stern was strong, calm, efficient. Oliver's bewildered eyes. 'Now push. Good. Stop. Pant. Long deep push. Got to get the head round the corner.' And it was happening on its own, threatening to burst her head and body. And Anna felt something round and hard and then a slithering wetness and there was a cry and Mr Stern's triumphant, 'Yes . . . Yes. A little girl.'

He held up a mauve, white-encrusted bloody thing, the cause of all the agony. Anna lay back, eyes full of tears, finding it impossible to believe it had come from her body. It was attached by a lumpy blue umbilical cord and the crying was a sawing sound and they handed Anna the baby, wrapped in a piece of clean cloth, and she held it with deep amazement.

She looked at Oliver and he stared back and neither of them could say anything. Oliver took Anna's free hand. He lifted it to his lips. It was incredible to him that he, Oliver Carroll, who had never had the slightest influence on anything, could have been partly responsible for this. He stayed, holding Anna's hand while the after-birth came and they stitched the cut they had made to allow room for the child's head.

A sweet-faced Irish nurse bent down and took the baby to be washed, 'Well, hallo there,' she said in a thick brogue. 'And it is very welcome you are.'

A little pink-mauve face. Eyes open. Hands weaving angrily through the air. Anna lay in blood and sweat, watching the baby go, and was still unable to believe that the pain had ended, that the baby was hers and that this was Oliver beside her, holding on to her with such an expression of shock and pride on his face.

CHAPTER TWENTY-TWO

The fringe on the pram canopy danced in a little wind and Anna sat and watched it, wriggling her bare feet against the wooden steps which led down into the garden of Dora Road. She had watched clouds and birds in the one tree in their garden. A newspaper lay, unopened, on her lap, the headlines screaming of the Middle East war and of a threatened oil crisis! But Anna was indifferent to the news or the soft, watery October sun. She sat thinking of all the things she should be doing. She sat, knowing that her life was limited to a small area directly surrounding that navy blue pram. It was no longer her life at all. It was the baby's.

Anna was so tired that her anger was muted. She sat in the garden and looked back, almost apathetically, over the time she and Oliver had been married. *We married out of pity, on impulse. We didn't know each other. We shrank away and hurt each other. We were scared and far too immature to have a child. But we did have one and it fused us together in an extraordinary way and I thought, 'Now it will be all right.' As I think, periodically and quite wrongly. But then I had no idea I was to be imprisoned.*

Rosie was her gaoler. She had held the keys ever since the morning, some seven weeks earlier, when the monthly nurse departed. Rosie was an exceptionally demanding baby. Every few hours her zig-zagging cry cut through the house, demanding attention, reassurance, love, food. If it wasn't Anna's actual presence she demanded, it was Anna's time. Time to wash nappies and clothes, make shopping lists and always, always, time to be fed. The house, unthought about, looked like a slum.

Frequently Oliver asked if they couldn't employ a daily woman more than two mornings a week, as he struggled through the heaps of drying nappies, the washing-up, as he lay on the unmade bed. 'You have too much to do, Anna.'

'No. Not yet. I don't want anyone. I want to find my own way!' And so she stubbornly struggled to be the sort of mother she had wanted to turn into and constantly failed. The white walls of the house gave her a frightening feeling of unreality as did the knowledge that Rosie was utterly dependent on her. Even now, while the baby slept quietly in the pram, Anna could feel the invisible strings.

She had not really conquered the first disbelief. She still found it hard to accept the continuing presence in her life of this small, loud baby with its thick tufts of orangy hair, its funny little face, rather squashed up under the eyes, its pointed chin and the mouth, always a little open, always hopeful that it might latch on to a passing nipple. The feeding had been successful from the start, surprising Anna more than anyone. And parallel with this constant surprise she felt fear. Fear when the baby cried and fear when it was quiet. She was scared of carrying it, scared of hurting it, scared of doing things wrong.

Oliver, by complete contrast, was like a child at a circus. At first he had just come, again and again, to stare reverently at the baby. He would put out his hand and tuck one finger into its starfish hands. He watched Anna feeding, the constant curling and uncurling of those little hands as the baby sucked contendedly. And gradually he dared to hold the baby, and relaxed and began to talk to it, carrying on long and quite adult conversations.

At first, coming on them together like this, Oliver and the child, Anna would be filled again with an overwhelming gratitude towards Oliver as if he had saved her life; she had never considered him a strong man in the way she thought of strength. Brutally strong like Freddie. Coldly strong like James. But when she had needed him so desperately, when she had called for him in labour and thought she would drown in her own private agony, he had been there. More than that he had been what she needed.

Once she asked him, 'Oliver, did I look terrible at the end, when she was actually being born? Was it awful?'

'I don't know. They tactfully sat me up by your head, remember?'

'I never thought you'd stay with me. I never even thought it was worth asking you.'

He had come to sit beside her. Since Rosie's birth he had become far more demonstrative. He had put an arm cautiously along her shoulders. 'I couldn't get away, could I? Anyway, I wanted to help you. I was suddenly ashamed that I had taken so little notice.' His hand touched the sharpness of the bone in her shoulder. 'You're thin, aren't you?' he had said casually.

It was true. Anna was thin. The child, her gaoler and tormentor, had given her, by way of an afterthought, a gift she had longed for throughout her entire life. She was thin. She had lost thirteen pounds in hospital and over the last three months when she had not wanted to eat very much, she had continued to lose weight steadily. She was occupied with the baby and she forgot about eating. Her life was full and strange and she forgot about eating, forgot the complicated relationship between food and happiness and hunger and life. She was tired and the mouth inside her was shut. The scales, unbelievably, told her that she weighed just over ten stone.

For the first time in her life she could enjoy buying clothes. Any clothes, however old, looked all right. She could walk down a street without fearing the shop windows. Sometimes people she knew passed her in the street without knowing her and she would turn, swinging the pram like a battering ram, and give chase and make them look at her.

'Anna, I didn't recognize you! You're so thin . . .'

She would laugh, loving every longed-for moment.

Oliver and Anna had never functioned to a routine. Suddenly it was required of them that they organize their day round the baby. They had to eat at more regular times, go out at times made possible by the baby's sleeping patterns. They took to visiting Pyecomb at week-ends, leaving London in the early hours of Sunday morning when Oliver finished at the club and getting back Monday evening, in time for him to play again. These week-ends became Anna's islands of freedom. Marietta loved the baby, pushing her round and round the garden in a pram she had bought specially, nursing it, talking to it, attending to it in a way she had never attended to her own children. She had not had time for them. Now she had all the time in the world and Mary McKay was always on hand to change nappies and soothe and bath. They genuinely enjoyed caring for the baby and Anna loved handing it over.

There were occasions, on those drives to Pyecomb, when the night was black and late outside the car and Rosie slept in her carry-cot, when music from Anna's cassette player sang to them sadly with mock disillusionment and gentle repetition about life and love, when Anna was at peace. At these times she could look at Ollie, perhaps reach out and touch him, sensing his tiredness and think, as he might well have been thinking, that this was a beginning for them. A difficult time in the life of a very new family.

There was a night when he suddenly pulled off the road into a lay-by. 'Anna, I must sleep for a while.'

'Shall I drive?'

'If you want to.' But he leaned his head on her shoulder and he slept almost at once and she hated to disturb him. She felt and heard the rhythm of his breathing. She let him sleep against her for nearly half an hour until she ached with sitting still and moved and woke him. They changed places and Anna drove the last thirty miles and accepted now that, however crookedly it had come about, she did love Oliver.

There were very bad times, too, especially when Anna knew the autumn term at the Cannon had started and a restless longing to be back there filled her. She missed the work desperately. She tried to keep painting on her own but she seemed to have no direction. She knew she had to put her own life away for a while and give her time to the child but it didn't stop her struggling, standing sometimes by the little gingham-lined crib Marietta had bought and staring at the baby and being clenched with spasms of guilt. The guilt was not for what she had done but for what she might do and sometimes she felt an emotion close to hatred for this tiny human being who lay, clean and sweet-smelling after a bath and drowsy with food, saying as plainly as if it could speak, 'I need you. I require you all the time. It is in your power to destroy me, to make me miserable or so nervous and lost that I will never be able to function as a complete human being.'

'I didn't want you. I don't want you now,' Anna hissed more than once through clenched teeth. 'Why couldn't you have come later, when I had found myself?' But still she would let no one else care for the child. Her guilt demanded that she give Rosie all her time.

Pym came to see her frequently. He began coming in October,

pealing importantly on the bell, coming in and sitting down and talking as much as he had always talked, bringing fresh gossip from the Cannon which Anna seized on hungrily and asking her things about herself she didn't want to answer. He told her about his forthcoming exhibition. He asked, 'Are you happy, Anna?'

'Yes, I suppose so. I don't know. I am trapped and restless but Ollie and I seem okay. Or perhaps having the baby has blunted me so that I no longer need to be wild with joy. We care about each other. He still flies into his rages occasionally, as if underneath the big problem is still there. Something I don't understand which makes it necessary for him to explode. But not so often. I think it is tied up with Freddie. Oh, Pym, marriage is so different from what you think.'

'Only from what you thought, Anna,' he said gently.

'I suppose you're right. I only wish I had thought more. I wish I was back working with you all, feeling myself to be stretched.'

Pym folded his arms and looked at her shrewdly. 'You say that, Anna, and yet if you really wanted it you could arrange to be free for at least half the day. I think you are happier than you will admit to yourself. I think you should give in . . .'

She stood up, sharply.

He changed direction, seeing she did not want to hear any advice. 'I'd like to take you out, Anna. I'd take you somewhere and we'd talk all night and I could find out about you again, find if you are still spinning out of control. I could walk you home and kiss you good night, and be proud that other men wanted you.'

They laughed. It was a game but she loved it. She needed so desperately to be admired, to be flirted with, to pretend life was not this white and chaotic house with dirty windows, dusty rooms and Oliver's chaos colliding with her own. And she had become so preoccupied with herself that she did not see the change in Pym. How he was calmer, quieter and patient at last.

Linden came to see Anna once or twice a week, occasionally with Veronica but more often alone, coming through the wooden gate at the side of the house and in through the kitchen door. She looked so perfect now that Anna found herself brushing dust from chairs, re-washing cups before she poured coffee. Linden looked unreal, as if poised to be photographed.

She came into the garden on this October afternoon, carrying a newspaper under her arm, wearing a simple cream suit.

'Hallo, Anna. Have you read all this about the war? James thinks it's extremely serious. We were due to visit the Middle East in a couple of months. Let's hope we won't go now.'

Anna made a non-commital noise.

Linden sat with her face tilted to the weak sun, eyes closed, talking and talking; about which of James's stupid friends was sleeping with which other friend and a proposed visit to Europe and how she was starting to beat people at backgammon. Anna listened, turning her attention away from her own problems just enough to recognize aimlessness in Linden for the first time.

When Linden paused, Anna said, 'A year ago you would have snarled at the mention of backgammon. You would have dismissed it as a ridiculous and trivial game played by people who needed to pretend. It all sounds so empty, all this going everywhere, and talk of James's friends. They don't seem to be real people. I remember you laughing at that cousin of James's, Anthea or Annabel or something, with the very trendy clothes. You said she just sat there, thinking how fantastic she was and the pathetic thing was that no one but you read the magazines! No one realized. They thought she was quiet and dull and looked awful.'

Linden stood up. Her voice was a hiss. 'Sometimes, Anna, you are so boring I find it hard to believe, even having known you all your life. You sit here, playing mothers and babies, in all this chaos, looking terrible although at last you are a reasonable size, and harping back to something I once said! People change. I change. How dare you tell me I am aimless! The things I do matter to me!' She slammed the gate behind her, leaving Anna surprised and rather shaken at the vehemence of her outburst. It also occurred to Anna that it was strange how Pym and Linden never accidentally met at her house.

Linden got into her car and slammed that door too. She made a furious sound, an explosion of her feelings. *Bloody Anna. Sitting there . . . Casually telling me my life doesn't matter*! And then she dropped her forehead against the steering wheel and felt the wetness of tears on her hands. She let her body go. Her shoulders drooped and her breath came out in a long shivering sigh. She must be fair. She had chosen James . . . She sat up straight, wiping the tears away, started the car and drove to his offices in St. James Street. She abandoned the car to the porter and stood in the lift, tapping her fingers restlessly. When the doors parted she walked past the receptionist, smiling slightly, and through two sets of doors into James's office.

James looked up with surprise, automatic anger at being disturbed coming to his face first. He replaced it with caution.

'Hallo, Linden.' He began putting into a neat pile the various papers spread on his desk but Linden, coming to stand behind him, picked some up irritatingly and read. 'Monroe Antiques . . . what's this? Surely you're not going to invest with Freddie as well?'

'Certainly not. Could I have them back, please?' He held out his hand. 'I am curious about Freddie, that's all. I try to keep well informed about him.'

'You spy on him?' Her voice was sharp.

'No. I keep a lot of information about a lot of companies.' He put the papers back into the folder. 'To what do I owe this visit?'

She sat on the desk. 'I just wanted to see you, that's all. This morning I was reading through my diary. In the ten months of this year you have been away, alone, for fifty-four days. We have been at Pyecomb, with various friends, for seven weekends. We have been out, with other people or to other people, on one hundred and twenty evenings and we have been at home, alone, just you and me for ten evenings. That means that if we are married for fifty years . . .'

'Stop being so dramatic,' James said. 'What has suddenly brought this on?'

'I'm lonely.'

'You knew how it would be.'

'No, I didn't. You told me but I didn't know. And I hate the days you lunch with Marietta!'

He came and stood close to her. He was wearing the expression he always wore when she was asking too much. A kind of mask. 'We should have a child, Linden,' he said gently.

She clenched her hands. She narrowed her eyes and turned

away. 'Not until it is right between us. I am not that weak. I won't hide behind pregnancy and fill my life, temporarily, with a baby. I married you, James. Now, take me out for a drink. I want to talk to you. Alone. Just us. Not with Mr Wong and Mr Kung Lee and old Uncle Tom Cobley and all in attendance!'

'All right.' He pressed an intercom button. 'Jenny, I'm going out for about half an hour.'

'Half an hour?' Linden said.

'An hour then.'

At whatever time of the day or night Oliver came home, he would go in and look at the baby. He did it in the way some men take off their coats or pour themselves a drink. If Rosie was awake he would talk to her, teasing a series of excited nonsense sounds from her and making her pat the air wildly with fat little hands. He would crouch down and look at her through the bars, sending her into cascades of lovely baby laughter, the laughter which he thought should be recorded and played to anyone who was unhappy or lonely. It was irresistible, that laughter.

At first, Oliver had found it impossible to believe that the child was anything to do with him. In the beginning, Anna had scared him. Much as he loved her and wanted to express it by making love to her, he could not get Freddie out of his mind. He was convinced that Freddie must be superb in bed. He cringed at the thought of how Anna must compare them. And her sudden, terrifying pregnancy and the irrational conviction that the child was not his . . . But gradually, as the baby grew, as it became a fact in his life and he came to believe this was his child, he rose in his own estimation. Anna had given him something she had never given Freddie. They had created this life. The three of them were a small, compact unit. Anna and the baby needed him. For a man who spent his entire life in a family he felt did not require him at all, it was a revelation. He began to think seriously about the future. He began to make plans.

There were times when, hovering outside the door and listening to Oliver and Rosie, Anna felt desperately shut out. She was cut off from this new and adult Oliver, cut off from the child, by her own stubborn reluctance to give in and love them. They were two strangers. She didn't know either of them.

By December, Rosie was beginning to become a person with definite likes and dislikes. She loved to be held and attended to. She would sit on Anna's lap, lying back against Anna's arm and gazing dreamily at the world with round and curious eyes; she loved food, her body contorting with joy when the bottle or the spoon approached and she loved the feel of warm water and hands. But most of all she loved Anna.

'She is just imprinted, that's all,' Anna would say irritably when the baby, crying with loneliness or anger or some incomprehensible fear, would go to no one but her mother. Anna resented this unasked-for partiality but Rosie couldn't care less. She appreciated Oliver's adoration but, for the moment, Anna was her sun.

They were to spend this, their second married Christmas, in London. Ollie could only get two days off and Anna, thinking back to the last sombre Christmas at Pyecomb and knowing that Marietta would not go through that again, suggested that they stay in London. 'It would make the house seem really ours, to celebrate in it.' Oliver seemed quite happy with the idea. He bought a small tree and Anna decorated the house with cards and holly. As they had guessed, Marietta announced she was going to spend Christmas with her sister, in Jamaica, and that left James and Linden at a loose end and they invited themselves for lunch on Christmas day. And then there was Veronica and Prue and somehow the Christmas Anna had planned, with just the three of them, turned into a family party.

In the morning they went to church, leaving the turkey in the oven, and Rosie sat happily on Anna's lap and was surprised by the singing. And they came home to a house that smelt good and exchanged presents and for some unfortunate reason Rosie was scared of the huge teddy bear Oliver had bought for her. Oliver looked so crestfallen when the baby cried that Anna snapped, 'Oh, for God's sake, she doesn't mean it as a personal insult! She's a baby!'

Oliver shrugged. 'I know . . . I know. It's just that I took a very long time trying to pick something she would like.'

'Why do you care so much, Ollie? You care too much about everything. Everyone pretends! Everyone lies! Everyone says, "Oh, just what I've always wanted," and then gives it away the next day. You expect too much of people!'

He shook his head. 'No, I don't, Anna. Not any more.'

They ate an enormous lunch and drank champagne which James brought and Christmas Day moved heavily past, restrained and traditional and uneasy, Anna thought, hating the grey rain on the window and remembering a Christmas when she had wished hopelessly for snow and Freddie. She turned from her window and watched them all fussing over Rosie, who lounged contentedly in a slanted canvas chair which she could rock a little. *Funny*, Anna thought, *the way people fuss over dogs or babies when there is a lull in the conversation or in their lives.*

Veronica and Prue left at six o'clock, their arms full of presents. But Linden and James stayed on, sitting at opposite sides of the room. Anna kept hoping she imagined the great wall of indifference between them, the way they did not refer to one another, enjoy any present with one another. James was exceptionally quiet. When Anna came down, having put Rosie to bed, Linden said, 'Shall I do some cold supper or something? Do you mind if we stay?'

'Of course not,' Anna said.

James stood up and stretched. 'Come out for a walk, Ollie? I need fresh air,' and the two men left the house. Anna went back upstairs, running herself a hot bath, hearing Christmas carols from the television and slight sounds from the kitchen.

She climbed into the hot water and lay and dreamed. She felt sad that Christmas held so little for her now. Once the excitement had begun weeks before! Once it had had a deep, if childish, religious meaning for her. Now she was as muddled over religion as she was over everything else. Growing older, it seemed, was just a shedding process. The more you learned, the less you could hold your dreams and illusions and even ideals. People varied only in the amount of child they kept in them . . . Ollie, she thought, still had a great deal, searching in his music, enraged that he could not please people as he wanted, laughing at the world from the sidelines. *He refused to try and get to know me! Somehow I disappointed him. The baby was not what he wanted but now it is born he is different. We have been married one year and one month and for most of that time we have made each other quietly unhappy. Or is this the way things are? Do most people feel so stiffened? So lonely?*

She got out of the bath, rubbing the back of her hair dry. She went into her bedroom and put on the dress Freddie had bought her, seemingly a life-time ago. It was far too big now but the colours were so beautiful she couldn't bear to give it away. She lifted the material to her face and the smell of it weakened and softened her as she remembered.

Freddie had spent Christmas day with his parents. It was something he had not done for years. In the months before Christmas he had been working extremely hard, preparing himself for catastrophe. He had expected the oil crisis to have an immediate and disastrous effect but nothing had happened. He had expected the market to peak out in November and start sliding down, but it hadn't! It was now a peculiar situation. It seemed that he and Maisie Hunter, who had some insatiable source behind her, kept the market going between them! Maisie bought and bought. It was comforting to know that she was there, Freddie thought, if he got nervous, if he felt he should sell. Stephano was constantly on his mind. His holding was so immense! Occasionally, as Freddie and Maisie faced each other as they had done at the end of November, at a sale where the prices were record-breaking, so immense that they were mentioned on the national news, he wondered if she felt about him as he felt about her. That the other would always be there!

It was not possible to ignore Christmas in Freddie's acre of London and his mother telephoned frequently and wistfully. He stalled. He tried not to think of a long day in that hot little house and his father trying to make conversation. His father was seventy now! Freddie spent an afternoon with his lawyers, working out an attractive offer to put to Oliver yet again. He bought Penny a Hermes scarf which pleased her, and Rachel a bracelet which he thought should guarantee him a good Christmas. She opened it, thanked him, kissed him and told him quite flatly that she was going to be tied up throughout Christmas week.

'I've met this man who will be extremely useful, Freddie. I know you'll be understanding, because you do the same thing yourself!'

'Not quite the same thing.' He smiled. 'And it doesn't mean I like you doing it! You don't need any favours. I was looking forward to spending some time with you. I am giving myself a short holiday; I don't want to spend it alone!'

'Well, I'm in cabaret on Christmas Eve . . .'

'I see.'

'Freddie, I can't understand why you are being so odd! You can't expect me to jump when you snap your fingers. The reason we work so well together is that we both have a life of our own. You can't expect me to sit around . . .'

'Lie around, don't you mean?' Freddie said nastily.

'For Christ's sake! Shall I give you the damn bracelet back? You try your luck elsewhere!' Her eyes blazed. She looked lovely, Freddie thought, disliking her.

'It wouldn't suit anyone else.'

He left her frowning, wondering whether it was an insult or a compliment.

On 21st December, Freddie was thirty years old. He rang his mother that evening and said he would be coming down for Christmas Day. He stopped regretting the various invitations he had turned down while he still thought Rachel would be with him, when he heard how delighted his mother was.

But on the actual day, his satisfaction because he was pleasing her wore off after the second drink. He dutifully ate as much as he could. He talked about his business in general terms. His father fell asleep in the chair he had slept in for years. He seemed, to Freddie, to be a strange old man. Freddie forced himself to stay for tea. He left at 5.30, promising to come again soon, driving back towards London very fast and hating the idea of the empty evening ahead. On impulse he left the M4 at Hammersmith and turned down towards the Fulham Road. He wanted to wish Anna a happy Christmas.

Anna came out of her bedroom. The house was absolutely quiet. No television carols. No sound from the kitchen. No sound from the baby. She hated the silence. She wanted, suddenly, to be with people. She called and no one answered. She ran down the wide stairs, feeling panicky as she had as a child. She pushed open the sitting-room door and went in.

Freddie stood on the far side of the room. His back was towards her. He was holding something in his hands and he turned as he heard her. Anna stood quite still. Her cheeks flamed. Caught unprepared like this, seeing him quite suddenly after all these months, she had no way of censoring her feelings. She was filled with that old joy, that inner sigh of relief that he was still, at least, in the world.

Freddie's face showed nothing. 'Come and look at this beautiful thing, Anna. I didn't know Oliver had inherited these.' His voice was soft, drawing her across the room. He held a small jar. 'Look at the shape of it, the rightness of it.'

Anna stood a little way from him. She struggled to feel indifference, to cover up that first, wicked joy.

She looked down at the jar he held. 'Pretty pattern,' she said dully, wanting to irritate him.

'Prunus mume. Early flowering plum. Painted on this ground which is meant to be cracked ice. These were given as New Year presents, filled with something delicious and edible and, when it was empty, the jar was often returned to the giver. The Chinese New Year coincides with spring, hence the blossom and the breaking ice. Very logical. Very beautiful.' All the time he spoke he had been watching Anna. Now he turned and put the jar back, very gently, on its shelf. 'That little jar was responsible for the conversation Oliver and I had at Pyecomb two years ago now. The conversation which started it all!'

'His father left Oliver all the porcelain. Most of it is still at Pyecomb.'

'You look lovely, Anna. So changed I hardly know you.' He stood very still. 'You have blossomed under Oliver's gentle care. Or is it motherhood? Anyway, I came to wish you all a very Merry Christmas! I have been to my parents and I come home this way.' He took cigarettes from his pocket. He could not read her expression. There was a long silence.

'Would you like a drink?' Anna said.

'Yes, I would. I was trying to think when I last saw you . . . It was one day when you were all pink and pregnant, billowing down towards South Ken. I was in the car and I hooted but you didn't see me.'

She poured whisky into a glass. Her hands shook a little. She didn't want to turn towards him because she could not keep the excitement from her body or her face. She felt that she had strayed, accidentally, after months in a nursery, into the real world.

He was coming nearer to her. He touched the sleeve of her dress. 'You still wear it?'

'Why did you come here, Freddie? How did you get in? Where are they all?' She looked at him, holding out the drink.

He smiled. 'I came to wish you a merry Christmas. I've had an awful day, trying to pretend I was enjoying myself, and I suddenly wanted to see you. I frequently feel like that. Usually I do nothing about it. Today I had time.'

'Time. You were always talking about time.' She smiled and let the memories run, seeing them in his eyes too, thinking: *What will I do if he touches me?* and not knowing the answer.

'So I rang the bell and nothing happened. But the gate at the side was open, as was the back door. I walked in.' He moved up close to her. 'Happy Christmas,' he said, very softly, putting his lips on her mouth and sending a shock of feeling through her.

She swung away. 'You know, you are like Linden. Now that you both have your big ambition achieved, you begin to regret the little things along the way.' A strange triumph was making her hard and brave.

Freddie gave one of his harsh bursts of laughter.

There were voices in the hall. James came into the room and Anna jumped guiltily. 'Freddie is here,' she said unnecessarily.

James nodded. 'I'm glad to see you, Freddie. I keep meaning to find the time to ask you if everything is really as amazing as Oliver makes out.'

Freddie nodded. 'Yes, it is.'

James poured himself a drink. 'But you had ideas of a takeover some months ago?'

'Yes. Unfortunately Oliver was not at all keen. I stalled. The moment passed. I imagine he asked your advice?'

'Yes, he did mention it. I told him I thought he would be extremely wise to quit while he was ahead. I advised him to accept your offer immediately!'

Freddie smiled but his expression and the stiffness of his body expressed intense dislike. 'How very unfortunate! It seems he has a mind of his own after all!'

'Damn you both!' Anna exploded, coming between them, eyes narrowed. 'Why do you talk about Oliver like that? How dare you! You have never given him a chance. He knows

262

exactly what he's doing in his own way.' She amazed them both and herself. They made soothing, surprised noises. Freddie drained his glass. He said his good-byes. He moved into the hall and met Oliver. They stood and talked for a few moments and arranged to meet in the week.

Anna watched Freddie go, watched his back, and her anger slipped through her fingers. She tried to stay angry. It was better to feel rage than the emptiness that came after, when the door closed after Freddie. She closed her eyes. All her instincts told her to go after him, go with him, find out what she was now and what kind of woman she had become. She controlled the ridiculous longing and opened her eyes. But perhaps it was still in her face.

James took her arm, surprising her deeply, turning her to face him. 'Anna, that man is poison. If you have any influence with Oliver at all, persuade him to get out. Now.'

Anna stepped back. 'Why don't you let Ollie do what he wants? Your concern and interference weaken him. You have always treated him like a simple child!'

'And you, Anna?' James said quietly. 'How will you treat him? Are you really as concerned and loyal as you seem?'

Anna shivered. She said nothing. She was afraid of James then in the primitive way she had feared certain school teachers and policemen.

'Perhaps,' James was saying, as Linden came in, 'like your sister you are not always what you seem!'

'What am I interrupting?' Linden asked. She came up to the fire. 'I'm frozen. I went for a walk of my own, on my own.' She sat down, rubbing her arms. 'I looked for you and Ollie, James. As always, I couldn't find you.'

The evening was uneasy. Ollie was restless and he left them, going into the room which held his piano, settling down to play. His music strayed across the hall and into the room where the others sat round the fire, not wanting to eat the meal Linden had laid on to trays. At ten o'clock she stood up and carried the things out to the kitchen and Anna followed. Linden closed the kitchen door.

She began to pace backwards and forwards like a small caged animal. 'Tomorrow we go to Pyecomb for two days. James must have his injection of the country. I wish you and Ollie would come, Anna.'

'We can't. Ollie has to work. Anyway, I don't want to go there . . .'

'I don't blame you. Nor do I. It is eerie at the moment.' She began, instinctively, to stack plates, to organize, while Anna sat in one of the kitchen chairs, watching, thinking about Rosie's next feed. 'What are you going to do, Anna?'

'Me? What do you mean?'

'Well, when you are tired of serving out this prison sentence you have imposed on yourself. When are you going to admit that you need to get back to work?'

Anna shrank from the inquisition. 'I'm all right. We're all right.' She didn't want to be drawn into a spate of confessions she might regret.

'Lucky you!' Linden said, sarcastically. 'You are really going on this latest wild goose chase of Ollie's then?'

'What?' Anna frowned.

'This Welsh idea. These boats! He was talking to James about it earlier in the evening, when you were putting Rosie to bed. James was being infuriating. Patronizing and fatherly and, "what will you do with your life, my boy!" He asked Ollie, yet again, if he was really going to spend his whole life in Billy's Basement! And Ollie said, No, he was thinking of going back to the first idea he had ever had. The boatyard thing. It was booming and now that his capital had been virtually doubled by Freddie, he could buy himself in. He said a lot about you and the baby and the quality of life. It was rather sweet, really.'

'Has he really thought it out, then? Seriously?'

'Hasn't he told you?'

'He's mentioned it. I didn't really listen. He mentions so many things.' She took a cigarette from the packet on the table. 'Somehow, Linden, we've bounced off each other. I don't know what's happened. I seem to be only half alive. I live with two strangers, Ollie and the baby . . . In the beginning, when I tried so hard to get close to him, and all the time I was pregnant, he was a stranger. He had trained himself to be self-contained. Oliver and the music. Sometimes when he gets home from the club he'll sit down and play for another hour, two hours, chasing something I can't begin to understand.' As she said it, she was surprised how much of Oliver she had absorbed without realizing it. 'He doesn't want to play acrobatically, although I believe that he is technically very good. He knows he'll never be a really great jazz pianist but he wants to find his level. Perhaps, if he's talking of Wales, he's achieved it.'

'Perhaps he's tired of trying?'

'I don't know. He doesn't tell me very much . . .'

'Don't go, Anna,' Linden said suddenly, coming to sit down. Her eyes filled with tears. 'I couldn't bear it . . . I have to be able to come here, to see you.' She laughed, embarrassed. She sniffed. 'Do you know how I feel with James now? As if he is a windmill, turning in a slow, steady wind, exact and smooth, and I am just some useless piece of fluttering cotton stuck, by mistake, on to one of the sails. I saw that once, on holiday. A piece of bright red cotton stuck to a windmill. It fluttered and fluttered but it didn't come off . . .'

'Stop it!' Anna hissed. 'I don't believe in the things you say. I don't believe you feel. You talk yourself in and out of things. You talked yourself into James, built him up in your mind into what you wanted and now you are talking yourself out of him. He is the same man he has always been. He is quiet and clever and reserved and you used to find that fascinating. You said you'd like to disrupt him, remember? Now, because you're bored for some reason, you've changed it all and the parts of him which you liked have become bad things.'

'I loathe you when you lecture.'

'Why don't you listen? Doesn't James count? Doesn't he have feelings? You are like Freddie . . . You dismiss people unless they shout and wave their arms and push and scream. You think we deserve to be hurt, because we are not so brilliant as you are.'

'You can't put yourself and James into the same category, Anna. Nor can you pair Freddie and me . . .'

Anna drooped her shoulders, all anger gone as suddenly as it had come. 'I am in the jelly category. Shout at me and I quiver. But I'm trying, Linden. Can't you be happy with James, if you try?'

Linden held her mouth stiffly, like a child's. 'If I saw him, perhaps I could. I never do see him. All his stimulation, all his emotional satisfaction come from work. All day he works. In the evenings there are people to entertain. At week-ends we take people to Pyecomb. He reads till one in the morning. I am tired when we get in from these endless dinners. I go to bed and I sleep . . . I know I am a terrible disappointment. I was a bad investment. I am not content to sit on the edge of his life, like some accessory. James is a robot.' She stood up. She paced the room. 'Sometimes, Anna, when he is sitting, thinking, frowning over the latest idea that intrigues him, I go and stand in front of him and ask him what it is. What he is thinking about. He looks surprised that I want to know and then he makes an effort to explain. He has a certain look on his face. I can't bear it. It's a mask to cover the annoying waste of time. My mind wanders. He says, "You're not listening," I lie. "Yes, I am!" So he goes on talking and I sit and remember how it used to be. The days when life was full of uncertainty. The thrill of the chase.' Her eyes shone. 'I suppose I became addicted to excitement, Anna.' She stood still. She faced Anna. 'What shall I do?'

Never in their lives had Linden asked Anna for advice. Anna was silent, shaking her head, unable to answer.

CHAPTER TWENTY-THREE

When Anna answered the telephone and his voice said 'Anna?' she knew it was Freddie at once. She realized at the same moment that she had been expecting this ever since Christmas. Some contact. Some word. 'Hallo, Freddie.'

'I'd like to see you. I'd like to talk to you. Is Ollie working? Could you make dinner?'

'He will leave in about an hour. I could try for a baby-sitter,' she said, quite calmly.

'I'll collect you around nine-thirty. Look, don't mention it.'

'No. No, I won't.'

She rang three baby-sitters. The third agreed to come. A married woman who worked for a friend of Veronica's and lived in the Fulham Road. 'Nine,' Anna said. 'Just a couple of hours . . .' She put the telephone down. The guilt she felt made her very restless. She went upstairs and had a bath and Ollie came in and announced that he was leaving. He hesitated in the doorway and Anna couldn't look at him because she felt quite weak with the deceit.

'You haven't been to the club for ages,' he said. 'Will you come, one evening, soon?'

'If you like.'

'I would like it.'

'Will you be late?'

'Probably. Shall I sleep in the spare room?'

'No,' she said, very quickly, and hoped suddenly that he would collide with the baby-sitter and she would have to explain. She could not bear the idea of building a great castle of secrets. Not with Ollie. If she needed to talk things over, it should be with him! She shut her eyes.

'You sound funny, Anna. What is it?' He came into the room, looking down at her. 'I know you're not very happy. I keep meaning to talk to you. About this idea of mine. About getting right away. Starting again. In Wales. We can afford to buy the sort of house I would love to live in. But I am afraid to start talking about it in case you don't want to come.' He frowned. 'It would mean pulling right out of Freddie's thing. You want that, don't you?'

'Can I think about it? Can we talk about it tomorrow?'

'Sure,' he said, a little hurt, and bent and kissed her forehead and went down the stairs. She heard the front door close. It was a good fifteen minutes before the baby-sitter came.

Freddie sat in his car outside her house for quite a while before going to ring the bell. He sat and tried to work out exactly what he was doing and why. He knew he would need to be absolutely sure. It had always been his ultimate weapon, this planning beforehand. In the three weeks since that impulsive Christmas Day visit, he had found himself constantly thinking back, remembering, sorting memories. He had found Anna intruding into his concentration and his work and that was too much. He would see her, test his feelings when he was alone with her, see how she felt. And if she wanted him, despite all the complications, he would have her. Oliver, he thought grimly, had interfered far too much in his life already!

She opened the front door. She wore a black dress. She looked scared. He studied her, assessing her now that she was a woman, and he saw that, out of the fat, white cocoon she had been, had come a tall, striking-looking girl. There was no beauty in her face but it intrigued and appealed and above all it was still so gentle. Her face was not surprised. Her voice on the telephone had not been surprised. She had been expecting him, he realized.

Each time Freddie touched her, accidentally, Anna's skin reacted with a shock which made her shrink away from him primly. But sitting opposite him at the small table, she had the impression she was being touched, somehow, invisibly, all the time. They talked very little at first. They studied the menu and ordered and smoked. And Freddie watched her constantly and she was acutely aware of his concentration, framing her, flattering her, making her every movement a considered thing. She felt perfect. She felt adored as she had never felt in her life before although he said nothing.

The waiter bought them their drinks and Freddie leaned forward and took Anna's hand. He turned it over and opened it up. He stared into her palm until she couldn't bear it and she had to clench her hand shut, clench her thighs together. It seemed all the parts of her body were confused. His scrutiny of her seemed so intimate it should not be seen. Unbearable and yet she could bear it. She looked into his face, absorbing each line of it, the hard brown eyes and the mouth. She looked back at him from his own level.

Freddie suddenly smiled. 'Yes. You have a question?'

Anna laughed. 'What did I say? I said nothing, didn't I? I was so scared of you. So fascinated by you, from the moment you came into that studio. What a long time ago! I was going to be a painter then. I thought I was adult but I was all child. And none of it had happened!'

'It still hasn't happened, has it? It isn't finished?'

'No,' she whispered. 'It isn't.'

'I have been more restless these last few weeks than I have been for years.' His face was wide open and honest. 'I hope you realize how important that makes you. I had a lot of good reasons for asking you tonight. I was going to tell you that it was because of Oliver . . . But now it seems pointless. Now you're sitting here I just want you to know that I had to see you, to test my feelings. To test yours. I can't quite understand what went wrong, Anna. I met you, I cared about you, you showed more independence than I wanted in a woman then, especially someone I thought of as mine, and suddenly you were gone. Someone else's. Oliver's, of all people! And then you are having a child and you are put away from me. It should not have happened.'

'But it did. Oliver exists. And he has become a part of me. Even now, when he's working, I can picture him. He has been exceptionally involved lately, listening to his tapes for hours. Getting angry with himself. As if he is approaching some kind of climax.'

'You seem to understand him very well.'

'I don't understand him at all but we are married, Freddie. We spend a lot of time together . . .' A wave of disloyalty passed through her.

'But you are untouched. Quite uncommitted. You do not belong to Oliver and the child. You could be a virgin still.'

She flushed, ashamed for herself, for Oliver. 'Well, sex has never been right with us. Never. At first I thought it was not important to Ollie but it isn't that. It's too important. He is such a hidden person, he has so much to bring forward. I think, to be a good lover, you must be shallow, concentrating on the surface, just getting on with it. Not thinking too much.'

'He lets you think too much,' Freddie said impatiently.

Her eyes were full of tears. It was herself she was talking about. 'I would have given up, got out of it all, right back at the beginning if I hadn't been pregnant. The pregnancy was terrible but after it we had something. We still care . . . Oliver loves the baby so much and between them they have me trapped. I cannot take what I need from them but I cannot leave.' She bent her head. 'Why did you make me talk about it? I'm going to cry and embarrass you.'

'I'm not interested enough in other people to be embarrassed. Tell me, Anna, what do you want? Do you want to see me, frequently, so that we can work out how we feel? Or would you rather I went?'

'You care enough to ask?'

'Yes, I do.'

She looked into his face again. She thought of his body. She wanted to be with him, if only once, aching to let her body go, to know how it would feel.

'Can I have some more wine, please?'

'What does that mean?'

'Let me get drunk and a bit happy and then take me home and . . .'

He gripped her wrist until it hurt her. 'You cannot live your life like that. I will not be left to chance! Know what you want, Anna.'

She pulled her arm away. 'Stop putting it all on to me,' she snapped. 'Do you want a written declaration that I won't blame you later if things go wrong?' And her mood suddenly changed and she leaned towards him, some instinctive wickedness bubbling through her, putting a little smile on her mouth, making her eyes dance. 'Tell me how you feel about me, Freddie. Over and over again.'

Neither of them was aware of the people eating at the other tables, of the circling waiters, of the glass door to the street The door opened and three men came in and the man who entered last was James.

He saw Anna the moment he looked across the room. It seemed to him that he paused as he recognized Freddie but perhaps it was his imagination. He made himself move forward, smoothly, so as not to attract attention. The two men with him, both from Nottingham, were impressed with the place. The head waiter greeted James, led him and his guests across to their table. It was against the wall, a long way from Anna. There was no reason that she should see him as he sat with his back to the wall. The room was dimly lighted and James settled his guests, laughed at a joke, ordered their drinks. And all the time he was trying to think of an innocent reason for Anna to dine with Freddie Monroe, to lean over the table and take his hands, to accept the caress of his fingers on her face.

James recommended dishes from the complicated menus. The waiter hovered politely, pencil in his hand, explaining specialities. James could not stop watching Anna and Freddie although he was afraid his scrutiny might somehow attract their attention. He watched them as if they were two unknown lovers. There was that air about them, even across the room, that air of being totally involved in one another. *I might never have seen them,* he thought, *if it wasn't for Anna's hair. Hair like a flaming flag.*

Pity knotted his stomach. Old, familiar pity for Oliver and a kind of shame. Why? Even since the beginning, why had it been like that? Why had Oliver shrugged away from help and gone his own, ineffectual way? A dozen little scenes flashed through James's head. And always they were Oliver's defeats and Oliver refusing help. As a child he had had an expression, a tightening of his mouth, a narrowing of the eyes, which meant he was determined not to cry. James had never been able to bear it. 'Mother, look, Ollie's fallen down again. Look. But she had never looked. Not really. Why, now, should Anna carry on where Marietta had left off? The pity in James was beginning to be something else. A cold fury. Monroe. That bastard! He was the one.

'Well, James, this is a nice place you've brought us to!'

Surprising how easy it was to talk to these men and yet watch Anna and Freddie. And think. And plan. And even talk about the events of the day and the factory at Nottingham. James was used to functioning on two levels at once. He glanced at them once more. He saw that Anna's face was alive with a glow he had never seen before.

'She never stirred, Mrs Carroll,' the baby-sitter said.

'Thank you.' Anna paid her and she let herself out, glancing curiously at Freddie who smiled and wished her good evening. The front door closed.

'I must look at the baby,' Anna said and she ran up the stairs to Rosie's bedroom. Rosie slept deeply, one hand curled up beside her face. Anna went down to the kitchen, finding Freddie sitting there. She kicked off her shoes and plugged in the kettle. 'Coffee?'

'All right. If you need a pause . . . Why the sudden panic?'

'I just had to look at her.' Anna stood on the far side of the room from him. 'Freddie, please, have a coffee and then go home.'

He stood up and came to her, switching off the kettle, standing behind her, his hands closing over her breasts. He put his mouth against her neck and made her tremble violently. He took her hand, pulling her gently up the stairs, opening, with some instinct, the door to the spare room. 'You don't sleep here with Oliver?'

'No.'

'Good. It's cold though.'

'The bed is made up. Ollie sleeps here sometimes, when he is very late. But I can get another blanket if you want . . .'

She fetched it and a song ran crazily through her head. 'Then up she went to her grandfather's chest, and bought him a pair of the very, very best. . . .' And she threw the blanket on to the bed and sang, 'Soldier, soldier, will you marry me?' all the guilt vanishing as quickly as it had come, the wickedness and the joy in control.

'You're quite mad,' Freddie said comfortably. 'I always thought you were,' and he drew the curtains and closed the door and switched off the overhead light. She stood and watched him. Then he came and stood in front of her and his expression was gentle and he began to undress her, the way he had the very first time, his hands moving against her body as he removed each piece of clothing until she was trembling so violently that she had to lie down.

'I've thought about this so much, Anna. And about you. You were so closed up. Prim and white and wide-eyed. You never made it with me, did you?'

He made her feel like a butterfly pinned to a board, pulsating to escape and yet not wanting to, pinned by her own will until all her instincts rose up through the hard shell and smashed through and flooded her, rolled her, surprising her with the simplicity of it all. She was aware of Freddie's voice, encouraging, loving, and afterwards, holding on to him, she kept putting her mind back and spasms of remembrance flickered inside her.

'So it's true. Everything they write about sex. How important it is. How it controls people's lives. I never knew.'

Freddie laughed. 'Thank you.'

'But don't you feel like that? That this is what matters, what you were born for? Only this. Above everything?'

'No. At the time, yes, but I know how much the outside world matters and I also realize that this feeling is a combination of instinct and insecurity and optimism and love.'

'But it matters to you?'

'Now it matters who. Very, very much who . . .'

'Of course. I meant that. I want it to be you Freddie. I always did. Just you.'

'That is going to make things difficult, isn't it?'

'I don't know . . . yes, of course.' She yawned, stretching her arms above her head, tightening her body all through. 'I know nothing. I adore you. I have begun again.' Words bubbled sleepily from her. Warm weariness. Peace. Exhaustion.

She was aware of Freddie's going, of his voice telling her to go back to her own bed, of his mouth, starting all the feelings again, gathering her up. But he went and she stumbled sleepily to her own bedroom.

'Linden.' James shook her gently. 'Linden, wake up! This is

important.'

'What is it?' She pulled herself up, wearily, on to one elbow. She had thought for a moment that James had come to make love to her. There was a savagery about these late sessions when he came in and found her asleep and woke her, which, although exciting for both of them, underlined the enormous gulf between them. Linden felt that he was thinking, *At least I can still have this from her, if nothing else!* But the light was on, a sudden light which made her hide her eyes. She had been dreaming of a small white cottage and sheep with black faces.

'Do you remember, at Christmas, how Oliver kept talking about Wales and that absurd boatyard idea? About selling out of Freddie's company? Do you remember?' For James, the voice was very excited.

'Yes, I remember, vaguely.'

'Well, has he or hasn't he?'

'I don't know! Why don't you ask him? He doesn't confide in me!'

'If I could ask him, I wouldn't be asking you. I want you to find out for me, Linden. Tomorrow. I want you to go and see Anna and find out, very casually, if Oliver has released his money from Monroe Antiques.'

She lay back against the pillows, watching him with an apathetic expression which enraged him.

'Bitches! Both of you!' He stood up, as if he could not bear to be so close to her. 'I don't want Anna to know that I am asking. Do you understand?'

'What do you mean? Both of us? Bitches? What is all this? Suppose I don't want to crawl around, spying on my own sister, just so that you can pull off yet another bloody deal!'

The expression on his face scared her. 'All right, I'll find out.' He went towards the door. 'James,' she said, 'I never intended any of this, you know . . . I didn't mean this to happen between us. Stay and talk to me. Let me tell you . . .'

He paused in the doorway. Linden rolled over, face in the pillow. 'Don't go away. Listen to me. A long time ago, when you asked me to marry you, I told you about a man at Anna's art school. You thought I said it to force your hand. I wish to God I hadn't said it! We might have taken more time . . . Anyway, what I am going to tell you I am saying because there is still time. If you will only concentrate on me occasionally. Just enough for me to feel that you know who I am! A couple of months ago, this man came to see me again. I hadn't thought about him seriously for some time. He just arrived and rang the doorbell. He had been to see Anna. They had talked about me. It was early December. I asked him in and gave him tea. He asked how I was. I told him about the Australian trip and things and I asked, eventually, why he had come and he said he was just checking. He wanted to see if he had stopped loving me. He decided he had not.' She lifted her head, and turned and sat up. The doorway was empty. She began to tremble.

'He comes to see me often,' she went on, to the dark empty doorway. 'Always in the late afternoon. Tea time, he says, is safe. He sits and talks and I tell him the small things about my life which are destroying me. How I loathe the men you work with letching and pawing at me, and how I feel you expect me to respond to them up to a point; how I feel I am merely a pretty but useless corner of your life; how all my energy and strength are turned inwards, eating me away; how you should never have married anyone. Between your mother and the company there is not enough left for anyone else. How asking me to marry you was the only impulsive action in your entire life! Having him to talk to makes my life bearable. He tells me I am shallow and I find it reassuring. He says I have never extended myself, tried to learn more and expand. He says I have a lifetime ahead of me and nothing to do. He never touches me and I never touch him. In June, he will take his degree and be finished with the Cannon. . . .' She got off the bed and went to the door. She looked down the stairs to where light spilt from James's study into the dark hall.

'James, what the hell has happened? Why are you only half alive?'

James sat at his desk. He took out writing paper. His anger rose up again, almost singing in his ears. Anger at Anna but most of all at Freddie.

He was aware of Linden's voice. He began to compose a letter to his cousin, Carlos Stephano. Linden's voice went on. He had not been able to stay and listen to her. He did not want to. He detested these late-night dramas. It was hard enough to write this letter anyway, without Linden's voice . . . He got up and closed the door.

From her place at the top of the stairs, where she sat hugging her knees, Linden watched the square of light on the carpet in the hall below narrow to a strip and then disappear.

Anna woke at 6.30 because Rosie was crying for her early feed. Oliver was a heap in the bed beside her and Anna got out carefully, trying not to disturb him, and went to the baby, lifting her, cuddling her, changing her nappy. She was ashamed and afraid for the child.

Rosie smiled. Her hands patted at Anna's face and she drank from the bottle hungrily. Anna sat by the window, listening to the sounds in the darkness of their garden. The first mutterings of birds, distant traffic from the Kings Road. All round her, her house slept peacefully but she was divorced from it. The bottle was empty and Rosie obligingly brought up her wind. Anna laid her back in the cot, thinking how impossibly clean Rosie's skin was. She touched it. She needed to register such things and store them: the child, the house and this time of her life. Because she felt it was, already, over.

CHAPTER TWENTY-FOUR

Anna was living now, had lived for the past two months in a state of unreality, of wild extremes. Like the little mermaid, she walked on knives. She expected disaster and was surprised, each night when she finally closed her eyes and tried for sleep, that she had somehow come through another day without the violent explosion of truth she was waiting for. And her unlikely accomplice in all this, her baby-sitter who made it all possible, was Prue.

Anna had rung her, in desperation, the second time she wanted to go out with Freddie and Prue had come round at once although, as she said on the telephone, 'I don't know one end of a baby from the other!'

'It's obvious, I assure you,' Anna had laughed, constantly surprised that she could laugh over such small things when her life was balancing on a knife-edge.

'Anna . . . my God, you look terrible! What the hell is happening?' Prue said bluntly when Anna let her in.

Anna sat on the stairs and told Prue, quite simply. She watched Prue's face soften and she realized that, without thinking, she had picked on the one person she knew who would not tell her to be sensible, to pull herself together. Veronica, for all her romantic ideals, would have been appalled.

'I never meant to tell you but it's such a relief. I can't justify myself. I feel awful. I can't sleep. But I have to go on seeing Freddie. It was never resolved before. I must work it out this time! I married Ollie with my head in the sand!'

'Yes,' Prue said briskly, 'you do need time. You'll need to see him. I'll come whenever I can and that's fairly often but if I bump into Ollie, you must do the explaining. Don't ask me to lie to him. I never was a good liar . . .' There was a silence and Anna knew that Prue's life story hung on those words. But there was no time for other people's pasts when her own present was so frantic. She kissed Prue. 'Rosie needs nothing. If she cries, just change her nappy. Can you do that? Copy the nappy she has on now?'

Prue nodded.

'I won't be very late,' Anna said, awkwardly, and took her bag and coat and ran out into the street to use the precious hours while Oliver worked.

If she thought she knew Freddie before, Anna now realized she had been entirely wrong. Now, on a level with him, she saw the man he was. She saw that he had courage, shouldering his way into a world that didn't want him and admired none of his talents and making it take notice. He would not hide. Defiantly he insisted on taking her to the restaurants he liked. Having adopted a certain way of life and come to like it, he said, he would not give it up.

But little of their time was spent eating. They talked and they made love. He told her that he was gradually moving his clients from porcelain to silver, reducing the size of their holdings. He told her that Stephano would not budge, that he claimed he cared for the collection he had far more than he cared about money. He told her that Oliver had approached him about selling out.

'Yes,' Anna said quietly. 'I am encouraging that. I feel I must get you separated. I listen to the Wales idea. I pretend to like it. I feel hypocritical and terrible but I want him to have it so badly. To know he has that!' She smiled. 'Everyone persuades him to take his money out. Even Linden was asking me.'

'Yesterday we ironed out some of the details. We virtually agreed to go our separate ways. I shall pay him back his original stake, plus about the same again. Ironically, it is not at all the time I would have chosen. It means paring myself down to the bone and it leaves me far more vulnerable than I like. If you didn't feature, Anna, I'd make him wait. But if he needs this money to get himself set up in Wales, I want him to have the money too. And this time, he won't take you!'

It seemed to Anna she would never, never get enough of their love-making. It seemed that in her own pleasure she was proving at last that they had all been wrong, all the people who had ignored her through the fat years. Each time Freddie touched her she would look back and cancel out one more small occasion in her past when she had been untouched. Each time her body coiled and tightened and then rose and exploded into orgasm, it was as if she said to Linden and the frightened lump she had been, 'You see. You were wrong! Wrong! I can be loved. I can feel like this.'

'I want you to be happy, Anna,' Freddie said. 'I think I must always have wanted that but I couldn't allow myself to go off course to achieve it. I must have been mad. I should have kept you then. Right from the beginning, underneath those terrible clothes, you had something. You are more real than other women and nothing leaves you unmarked. You were too delicate for me then, Anna. Too much trouble. You asked for time I didn't have.' Freddie enjoyed nostalgia, playing the part, quite sincerely and with great relish, of the lover.

'Do you have it now?' she whispered, loving every word.

'Yes. I do. I asked you before, Anna, and I'm asking you again now. Two years later. Are you ready yet?'

She sat up. 'I want to be with you, you know that, but how can I undo it with Oliver? I can't just walk out!'

'But when he and I go our separate ways? Then?'

She shivered. 'Yes. When he has somewhere to go.' She wrapped her arms round herself.

'God knows why I agree with you,' Freddie said. 'I am sure he would not use the same delicacy with me!'

'He would,' Anna started to say, but she was learning that Freddie hated her to defend Oliver. Freddie, she thought, did not know Oliver at all.

'Is it possible to love two men at once?' she said, suddenly.

'No. Come here. I don't want you to talk like that.'

He was the lion again, reassuring her that he knew, that he was sure about her, about everything.

It was the best hour of Anna's day. Between six and seven, when Rosie was safely in bed, Anna could sit in the kitchen and be quiet and dream of the time when it would all be over. She heard the front door open and Oliver call, the way he always did. 'Here,' she answered, stubbing out the cigarette. She seemed to smoke constantly now, picking up these half-used packets of Freddie's without thinking.

'Hi,' Oliver said, coming in. 'Smells good.'

'Curry.'

'I meant to be home much earlier but I finally got round to telling Jack I am definitely leaving. Where's Rosie?'

'Asleep... Ollie, don't wake her.'

Again and again, Anna built up her courage for some kind of showdown but never achieved it. Oliver vanished, two at a time up the stairs and into the little bedroom, leaning over the cot and looking down at the child hopefully. But she did not stir and after a few moments he went down to Anna again.

He sat on the edge of the kitchen table, taking a cigarette from the packet. 'Anna, I've been meaning to say I've got a couple of weeks off. Rachel is coming to the club with her trio. Big feature. And I want us to spend the time in Pyecomb. It seems so long since we were out of London and it's beautiful there in April. I want to talk to you, tell you about Wales and this house. I feel you haven't quite made up your mind. I want you to be sure.'

'Is your mother there?'

'No. But Mary McKay will come in and cook and help with Rosie. It would give you a rest.' He looked down at her, at the narrowness of her arms and wrists. She was so thin, so jumpy. She never picked up a pencil or a paint-brush. She was totally unlike the girl he had married, physically and in every other way.

'Laugh, Anna.'

'What?'

'Laugh. You know, open your mouth and make that odd noise human beings make sometimes. Think of something funny. Me, changing a nappy. Freddie, thankful to be rid of me at last. He gave me a cheque today! Perhaps, now that I'm out of it all, we should ask him down to Pyecomb for the week-end, just to make him feel we will still be friends. What do you think?' He picked up the empty cigarette packet and crushed it into a little ball. He watched Anna closely.

And Anna did laugh but it was a humourless and frightened sound.

She expected to be desperate during those two weeks at Pyecomb. She was utterly wrong, as it seemed she was so often wrong about herself. They arrived on 21st April and Oliver insisted on turning on the swimming-pool heat. Anna shed Rosie, thankfully, into Mrs McKay's care and realized, with amazement, just how much she liked this place. It was wonderful to have time on her own, to have an hour or two to walk and think. To watch spring in the country again. To smell and see. She felt like running everywhere. She was alive in a normal way, not constantly shivering inside. She found, to her deep surprise, that a lot of the feelings Oliver had about Pyecomb had rubbed off on her. She liked the feel of the house, the garden and all the preparations which were being made for the year ahead. She watched the birds which had nested in the wistaria and the vines and realized, sadly, now it was too late, all the things she and Oliver had in common which she had never bothered to consider. She felt so easy with Oliver that it disturbed her terribly. She had hoped for emptiness, to make her going easy. She had hoped to be miserable. Instead, she found she was happy here and she realized that she was not yet twenty-two, that she had been married only one year and five months!

At the end of the first week, walking in the garden on a lovely morning, she heard the cuckoo and ran back to the house to tell Oliver. For years he had kept a graph in the library of the date when it was first heard at Pyecomb.

'He's taken the little girl down to the farm,' Mary McKay said. She smiled. 'He really loves that child!' Like all women of her generation, it surprised her to see a man show such interest in a young child.

'Yes.' Anna smiled back, and she went out again, towards the swimming-pool. It occurred to her that she had not thought of Freddie all morning. She had thought, instead, of Oliver. She had not looked at him for so long. She had decided, months ago, that he was 'inadequate', that they were 'unhappy' and had not looked to see how much he had changed. Until now.

Anna found an old bikini, faded with use, clean and cotton-smelling and she put it on and took a towel from the changing-room cupboard and went and stood at the edge of the pool with the sun on the back. Then she sat down and dabbled her feet in the water, watching the sun make patterns on the surface of the pool. She thought of how angry Freddie had been when she said she must come here. Angry in a hurt way which told her she dictated now. But he could not stop her from coming. It was the last time, she had said. She needed this pause and this ending very badly, needed time to tell Oliver. Needed it the way she had needed, years ago, to see her father and round things off. But now she was here, it didn't seem like an end. Did she want it to end? She knew that Oliver would survive without her. He would, after all, have Rosie. Thinking this, she shrugged off her towel and slipped into the water. She lay on her back, looked up at the sky and then rolled over and dived to the bottom of the pool, touched with a sudden joy which was unrelated to anyone but herself.

When she finally came to the surface, gasping for air, dragging it into her lungs, and opened her eyes, she saw Freddie. He was standing on the edge of the pool. The first thing she thought was 'No!' She was terrified. 'Why are you here? What's happened?'

'I've come to see Oliver.'

'He's not here. Why have you come? What's happened?'

Freddie didn't answer. Her teeth chattered as she looked at his heavy shoulders, his flat stomach. She wanted him. And yet she resented his intrusion into her rare moment of peace and private joy. She pulled herself out of the water and huddled into the safety of her towel, sitting down, arms crossed round her knees.

'I had hoped for a more enthusiastic welcome,' Freddie said coldly. 'Has this little holiday changed anything?' She could see now that he was desperately angry. 'Do you know who visited me this morning, Anna? At nine-thirty? Stephano. He wants to sell everything. He estimates there is just time to put the whole collection in the June sale at Granbury's!'

His hands closed round her arms, dragging her upright. 'They're out to get me, Anna. The bastards. Stephano's panic is entirely due to a visit from your charming brother-in-law. Now that his precious Oliver is sitting pretty with a fat cheque of mine, already cashed I might add, James sees no reason for me to continue to prosper. Even to continue to live! If Carlos sells his entire collection, and drags that woman with him, the market will fold. I've told him that it is only held up by faith anyway. Faith and Maisie Hunter. Once word gets around that so much is being sold they will all panic. There will be no one buying, a vast proportion will remain unsold and the whole idea of investing in antiques will appear to be dangerous and risky. So I've come to see Oliver. If he has any influence at all with Stephano he must use it. This is it, Anna. Whose side are you on?'

All the violence had left him. 'I shall need you, Anna, if I have to start again. I'll make it again. I can do it. But I must know where you stand.'

They were facing each other, when Oliver came round the side of the house.

'Hallo ... saw your car, Freddie.' The closer he came, the more obvious was the tension between them. There was a long silence and Anna thought they must hear her teeth chattering.

'James has buggered things up, Ollie. I should have seen it coming perhaps, I don't know, but I have not been concentrating these past few months as I should have been.' Both men looked at Anna. 'Now that you have taken out your money and your profits, James has put the wind up Stephano and he wants to sell everything and now!'

Oliver frowned. 'Why the hell did James do that?'

'Because he hates my guts. And because he knows about Anna and me, I suspect.'

Anna's eyes, wide and terrified, went to Oliver, watching for his reaction, bending herself down a little and thinking she would not be able to bear it if his face showed that expression of disbelief and pain he had worn sometimes after his father's death. She had lived this moment over and over again, picturing horror and disgust, picturing everything but this blank lack of surprise.

Oliver was very pale. 'I hoped it wouldn't ever have to be said ... I don't know when I first guessed but it was some time ago. Did you really think, Anna, it was possible to live with someone as much in love as you have been, and not know? You are transparent. And all the little things. The cigarettes. You are not a great actress, Anna. You haven't been to the club since last year. I just hoped it would all blow over, I suppose. I thought you needed time to get through Freddie. I thought, if we once got to Wales . . .'

'I did not come just to tell you that,' Freddie said. 'I came to ask you to see Stephano. He's here for a few days. Persuade him for his own sake, and mine, and yours if you are still selling your porcelain, to go easy.'

'You expect me to help you?' Oliver's voice was quiet but his eyes and face were full of disgust.

'Yes, I do. Because I believe you felt the same kind of pride as I did in our success. Because it can and does work. And because, if it comes to James or me, I think you'd rather see me proved right!' It was very hard for Freddie to keep his face so calm, to control the longing he always had to smash Oliver's indifference, or outward indifference. 'But Anna is coming with me!'

'Are you, Anna?'

She heard a small, terrified sound which must have come from her own throat as she swung away and ran through the big party-room in the old stables and into the changing-room, slamming the door behind her. She stood shaking, staring at herself in the long mirror, going close and seeing a set of features in a white face. Her mind somersaulted back to the glass in her parents' bedroom, a diamond split in lily of the valley wallpaper. Anna, at eleven, staring at her face, like a face drawn on a boiled egg at Easter, she had thought. She could still feel that surge of despair. It was as if she still occupied that solid child's body with fat knees above grey socks and big feet in brutal brown sandals.

'But I don't. All that is over.' She began to cry as she hadn't cried since childhood. It was loud, terrifying and convulsing, and it went on and on, because of herself and Oliver and the agony they had made, two people trying to love each other, to be kind. She didn't hear the door open. She was unaware of Freddie until he turned her round and she cried against him. He held her until she was quiet.

'Wash your face.'

She didn't want him to see her face. She knew it would be terrible. He went to the basin and ran the cold tap, dipping a towel in it, handing it to her. It was rough and cold against her hot eyes.

'Go and pack, Anna. You can't possibly stay now.'

He was right. She stripped off the wet bikini and dried herself, dimly aware of Freddie despising Oliver out loud because

Oliver was so passive. 'Jesus, in his position!' She crossed the courtyard and went up to her bedroom, packing at first without thought, merely throwing things in the case, but she slowed down and began to fold them. She folded a blouse she had never particularly liked with ridiculous care. She lay the sleeves across the chest, as if laying out a dead body, packing as if it were just the end of a holiday when in fact it was the end of a whole section of her life and the end of a marriage that never really began.

As she shut the case, she looked up and saw Ollie in the doorway.

'You're going?'

She nodded.

'If only James hadn't interfered . . . we would have gone to Wales, wouldn't we, Anna? A few more weeks.'

'You'll go anyway.'

'Yes. And I'll take Rosie. You're not having her.' He stood straighter and his eyes narrowed and she was afraid of him for the first time in her life.

'I don't want to take her away from you. She's far more yours than mine.'

Oliver came into the room. 'I'll do what I can with Stephano, for all our sakes. Stay with us, Anna. You belong with us.'

She said nothing. She was aware, as she picked up her case and her coat and started towards the door, that Oliver's mood was changing. All the way down the stairs she heard him, shouting with agonizing and impotent sarcasm, shouting after her as she ran out to Freddie's car.

CHAPTER TWENTY-FIVE

Anna was silent in the car as they drove back to London, sitting with her eyes half closed, finding, when she breathed in, the breath was shaky, sometimes like a sob. The journey seemed endless. She ached and her stomach churned nervously.

It was extraordinary to follow Freddie into Brook Street, to go upstairs with him and take her things to the bedroom and try to make herself believe that this time it was different. It had finally happened. The split. The end of herself and Oliver. Desperately she searched herself for conviction, for deep emotion, for relief. She felt nothing. It had been so sudden.

She sat on the bed and put her hands over her face. She thought: *I must tell Ollie about the cuckoo* . . . and then realized that, of course, she could not. She thought about Rosie and swerved her mind away. But what would happen? What were the rules? She must, surely, be allowed to see Rosie sometimes? *I haven't thought about it properly,* she realized.

'Anna . . .' It was Freddie, shaking her shoulder almost roughly. 'I need help.' His voice was hard. He looked down at her, shrewdly, sensing her thoughts. 'I've a hell of a lot to do. I must go through Stephano's file. And Maria Richardi's. I must know exactly what they have. And there are some smaller people I need to check. Coming back in the car it suddenly occurred to me that there might be a way out of this mess.'

Anna said nothing. She sat, looking up at him.

'Come on . . . I'll get you a drink but then you must work.' He pulled her to her feet and kissed her, and then went down the stairs. Anna followed as if too tired to contradict, and obediently drank the whisky he poured her. He threw her some papers. 'This is what I want you to do . . .'

They worked for nearly four hours. Anna ran down to Penny with sheets of paper to be typed, ran back up again, made coffee, checked figures slowly and laboriously; Freddie had incessant telephone calls and the shop was busy downstairs; he rang a rather dubious acquaintance and discussed the possibility of a substantial loan; he rang Stephano, asked to see him that evening and was told, 'Tomorrow morning.' Carlos was polite but cold. 'I am dining with friends this evening.' The room was full of cigarette smoke and Anna opened the windows looking down at the street, on the people. They seemed small, aimless, rather pathetic.

'Anna . . .' It was Freddie, calling her back to work.

She slept fitfully that first night. She kept waking and imagining she heard Rosie crying, half sitting up in bed and taking a few seconds to realize where she was and remembering that Rosie was miles away. Who would hear her? Would Mary McKay take Rosie to her cottage when Oliver's holiday was over? Did she sleep heavily? Would there be times when she would not hear? The night was a patchwork of disturbing dreams. When, at last, she did go into a deep sleep, it seemed only minutes before she was aware of Freddie beside her, rolling over to kiss her. He was smiling as she opened her eyes. 'Happy?' he said.

She nodded but it was quite untrue. She felt a lot of things. A strong fascination for his face, for his body, relief because he was sure, excitement because he wanted her here; she loved the things he said about her body and her face, things which Oliver had no way of expressing. Things she carried off, quietly, to relish later. But she also felt a deep unease . . . Where was the exhilaration? Why wasn't she sure she had done the right thing?

'Do you regret it?' Freddie said. 'Talk to me, Anna. I expect you to feel lost, at first. Do you regret coming?'

'No . . . but I feel I was hurried.'

He smiled. 'If I hadn't come to Pyecomb you would never have got round to telling Oliver.'

She knew it was true. If he hadn't come, would she ever have left Ollie? Or would she have gone to Wales? Perhaps she would have come to look back on Freddie, on this whole short, intense time in her life as just a digression. Freddie leaned over her, occupying her body, convincing her in his own way.

A week passed. Unreal as it seemed to Anna to be at Brook

Street, day followed night, a gradual routine built up. Freddie was intensely busy, responding to tension, as always, with exhilaration and increased energy. He watched Anna and guessed when she was feeling lost, unsure, and he would pounce on her, hold her, quite sure he could imprint his will and his absolute confidence on to her.

Each night, Freddie lay in bed and watched Anna as she stood and stared at her naked body, doing a slow pirouette, checking herself minutely in case, from somewhere, the fat had come back.

'It's not vanity, is it?' he said. 'You get no pleasure from what you see . . . You are more like a diver, checking his life-support system. You still can't believe what you see, can you, Anna? As you still can't believe you are here, with me.'

When he read her mind like that it scared her. It made her want to draw back, hide herself. She did not want to be understood so thoroughly.

A letter came from Oliver. He had received much the same reaction from Stephano as Freddie had had. Carlos was adamant. Apart from twelve pieces which he particularly loved, he wanted to dispose of the entire collection. So did Maria Ricardi. Reluctantly Freddie put the wheels in motion. It was all to be offered at the 6th June sale at Granbury's. In number, the pieces were not great. In value, or cost value, they were extraordinary.

Oliver, too, had put some of his porcelain in the coming sale. His friend was enthusiastic at the idea of Oliver joining him, becoming an equal partner in his boatyard, and Oliver found that he needed more capital to buy his house. *A house to stay in*, he thought. *A house for Rosie* . . .

It was long and white and it stood on the side of the steep hill which sloped down towards Milford Haven, a couple of miles from the mouth of the estuary. Even if Oliver had not wanted to raise money, he would have sold the porcelain. He could not bear to look at it. It filled him with despair and disbelief. Only now, when Anna had actually gone, did he realize how much he wanted her.

Those weeks of May were unreal for Oliver and very lonely. He left Rosie at Pyecomb and worked out his contract at Billy's; ironically there was a resolution and a maturity about his playing, now that he was giving it up, which had never been there before. He put the house in Dora Road on the market. He avoided all his friends. He went to the club every evening, around seven, and sat, eating sandwiches and drinking beer and waiting to work. He could not stand the silence of his own house. He could not bear to think of Anna, only a few miles away, in the same city.

He had one evening with James and Linden. They asked him to dinner. They sat in Linden's immaculate dining-room and ate a perfect meal off beautiful plates and the atmosphere was icy cold. James talked a great deal about Freddie's coming downfall, about people who manipulated others, about ethics. He sat at one end of the oval dining-table, his attention wholly on Oliver. His eyes glittered when he spoke of Freddie. 'When I saw that bastard, sitting with Anna . . .'

Linden, at her end of the table, was as silent and pale as a ghost.

'Well?' James said.

Oliver looked up slowly. He felt recently that he had been slowed down in all his actions. All the emotion in him had been taken away and replaced by an enormous sadness. 'Don't expect me to share your rejoicing over Freddie's defeat. I detest Freddie, but I feel no gratitude towards you. I feel a deep resentment that you have, yet again, interfered in my life but I now realize it has always been my own fault. I have let you run everything. I have let you, indirectly, take Anna away from me. Once and for all, James, leave me alone! Let me run my own life!'

He stood up and walked to Linden's end of the table and bent to kiss her. She stood up and went with him into the hall. She took his hand. 'Ollie, I didn't know how it would be or what he would do, when I asked Anna if you were finished with Freddie, when I spied for him. I haven't been thinking clearly . . . I should have guessed.'

'Don't worry. He would have found out anyway.' He smiled at Linden. They both registered affection for the other. 'What about you? Why don't you get out and start again? You will never be happy with James.'

'Soon,' she whispered. She looked up at Oliver, stepping back. 'Anna is so wrong . . . If I can, I'll tell her how wrong.'

Oliver opened the front door. 'That's what I keep telling myself. That I must try and see her . . . all I care about is getting Anna back.'

Through those last weeks of May, as the sale grew nearer and the tension increased, Freddie felt more alert than he had ever been before. He felt this was the climax he had waited for all his life. He was nervous but he was ready. He talked incessantly. He paced that white room, slapping his fist into his hand, planning, thinking. Anna was unusually still and watchful and silent.

'If I come through this, Anna, if the market holds and I pull it off, I shall be right where I always wanted to be. I'll buy another house. Somewhere in the country, so that work does not intrude into week-ends . . .'

'No,' Anna said suddenly, vehemently. 'What would we do? I'd hate it. I can't imagine you doing nothing. I like it here. I don't want any more changes. I love this building. It's yours. You seem to be here even when you are not. I don't want to go anywhere else.'

He stroked her hair. 'But don't you want more space, Anna? I want room for some beautiful furniture. All my life I have looked at other people's beautiful things. Now I want my own. I want a dining-room . . .'

She stared at him in disbelief. 'Are you serious? What does it matter about rooms and furniture and things, however beautiful? Look at Linden. Look how meaningless she has found it. I don't want trappings. I want you. I had all the rest . . .' She found there were tears running down her face. 'I keep wanting to ask you. Did you know, when you came to Pyecomb, that Oliver had guessed about us? Or were you really prepared to descend, with no warning, and destroy his marriage?'

'I had no idea what Oliver had guessed. I never considered Oliver. Everyone in this world is responsible for themselves and I didn't destroy Oliver's marriage. He did. He wasn't enough.'

He was right, wasn't he? She needed to believe that he was right, that she loved him, that the loss she felt, the longing at odd times of the day, in unoccupied moments, to see Rosie, would pass. But still she was so scared of the letters, scared that one morning there would be a white envelope from some solicitor. The thought of being separated from Oliver by written words and strangers horrified her. *And yet,* she thought, *I have lived here almost a month, away from Ollie and Rosie,* and could not believe it was true.

Veronica came to see her, nervous and distressed. She kept saying, 'Well, I suppose you must know what you're doing . . . I'm going away for a couple of weeks – would you like the car?' And Prue came and sat while Anna talked, pouring out her uncertainties, and then said, 'Anna, I wish I could help you but no one else can tell you what matters more, Freddie or Oliver and Rosie.'

There it was, put into words, quite simply.

Linden did not come. She telephoned frequently, sounding very strange, distant and brittle. She kept saying, 'I'll come round . . .' But she didn't.

On 1st June, Freddie brought home a catalogue. He read it, cover to cover. He drew in his breath. 'This is the most valuable collection of Chinese porcelain ever to be auctioned at one time . . . it's quite unprecedented.' He pulled his shirt open at the neck and lit a cigarette. 'Oliver's prunus mume jar,' he read quietly. 'How I would love that! Just out of pure sentiment.' He looked across at Anna and his brown eyes were hard. 'It's going to be a hell of a morning, Anna. I want you to come. I need you there to bring me luck. I need you there if nothing sells and the vultures gather to pick at my bones.'

All the myth was gone. She knew the man now. Utterly. The strength and the weaknesses.

'I don't want to come. I don't think I could bear the tension. I'll wait here. At the end, I'll come.'

'No!' he snapped. 'I want you there all the time. You must be involved, Anna.' He sprang to his feet and paced the room. 'Five days,' he said. 'Five days, Anna, that's all.'

Five days, in which Anna became more still, in which she did more thinking than she had ever done in her life, in which Freddie, intensely busy, for once was not watching her, did not see her thoughtfulness. Now, at last, she appreciated something of how Linden had felt when she tried to weigh Pym against

James.

She could not sleep on the night before the sale. It was very hot. Freddie had made love to her with all the strength and nervous energy that was stored in him. Afterwards she could not stop her body reacting. Freddie slept at once. It amazed her that such passion and emotion could leave him so quickly. His breathing was deep and even. Anna was alone. *A few moments ago our bodies were combined, giving the other almost unbearable pleasure and now it is as if it never happened. How temporary!* It depressed her and she stared at the skylight and her thoughts went back to Pyecomb, to Rosie. She could almost smell the child, almost hear her laughing . . .

Anna got up as quietly as she could and went down to the sitting-room. Much cooler here. She lay on the sofa. She began to think, clearly and calmly. It was two hours before she crept back to bed and finally slept.

Freddie woke early. He opened his eyes. *This is it,* he thought. His watch said it was just after seven. The room was light and, beside him, Anna slept deeply. For half an hour he lay and thought and then he got out of bed as gently as he could and went to have a shower, standing under the water for a long time. When he turned and reached for his towel, Anna was standing in the doorway, watching him, her eyes wide and tired. He went across to her and kissed her, making her face wet. He put his arms round her and held her, making her nightgown wet.

'Please come back to bed,' Anna said. 'It's so early . . . I want us to make love . . . Please.'

'Anna, I can't. I have a thousand things to do. Make me some coffee?'

She put her hand up, appealingly, against the side of his face. He put his hand over hers and gently pulled it away. He went to the basin and began to shave and still Anna stood, watching him, feeling a panicky longing to be in bed with him, hiding against him. She turned abruptly and forced herself to go down to the little kitchen, standing with bare feet on the cool floor and waiting for the kettle to boil. *Odd, how I know the song of his kettle, the way it starts with a tiny whisper and gradually builds up until it is as impatient as a train. The kettle at home has a lighter, more breathless sound.* She wondered, as she silently rebuked herself for still thinking of Dora Road as 'home', how many other useless things her brain had hoarded, squirrel-like, without her consent. She carried two mugs of coffee upstairs to the bedroom, putting Freddie's on his chest-of-drawers, climbing back into bed with her own.

Freddie came in, sliding back the doors of the long built-in wardrobe. It was full of his clothes. His morning ritual was elaborate. He paused, deciding what to wear. Which tie with which shirt? Anna had watched him, morning after morning, shaking the clean shirt from its cellophane envelope. The crackle of the paper, the smell of clean cotton as he slid his arms in and buttoned it across his wide chest . . . *Oliver treats clothes merely as a means of covering his body, of keeping him warm and dry. I always loved the way he got up in the mornings, making small, resigned noises, swinging his legs out of bed, sitting for a few moments with his hands in his hair and then putting on whatever happened to be lying on the floor by the bed where he had dropped it the night before.* . . . Anna shut her eyes. She was being pulled in half.

Freddie finished dressing, drank his coffee and came across to the bed. He bent to kiss her. 'Don't be late.' She could think of nothing that was worth saying. 'Good luck,' sounded pathetically inadequate. She heard him go down the stairs, gather papers from the room below. She heard the telephone. For a long time she could hear his voice.

It was just before nine when Freddie left. Anna could hear him speaking to Penny, heard the bell on the showroom door, and she sprang out of bed and went to the window and watched him walk down the street. He moved fast and deliberately. He surged through the world. She watched him until he turned the corner but even then she stayed, where she was, at the window, absent-mindedly pulling small weeds from the window-box, where she had planted geraniums a few days after she arrived. Her attention was attracted by a taxi drawing up outside and she was surprised to see Linden get out, unloading suitcases on to the pavement and paying the driver.

Anna swung away from the window, listening to the voices, hearing Linden call. Linden ran up the flights of stairs and burst into the bedroom. The face was very white, eyes enormous, mouth shaking. It was frightening to see her like this. Scared. Bird-thin. She came towards Anna.

'Thank God you're here! I thought you might have left

early.'

'What is it? Whatever's wrong?'

Linden paused, twisting her rings nervously. Rings which James had bought her.

'I'm leaving James. Well, I've left!'

Anna said nothing. She stood and waited as she had waited so often before.

'I have to,' Linden said simply. She spoke as if she were very tired and at the very end of her resources. 'I was wrong about him. I have been wrong about everything but it's not too late. Not if I go now. He left the house early. I've got everything I want from London but I must go to Pyecomb. I have a lot of things there. I will collect them and go and never see James again. Not trouble him or ask anything from him.'

Still Anna did not speak.

'Please, Anna, take me to Pyecomb. I must go this morning. Now, I must go now!' She gripped Anna's hands. They so rarely touched.

'Borrow the Mini and take yourself. I have to go to the sale. It's this morning . . .'

'I know it is! My God, I've lived with nothing else for months! I can't drive. I couldn't drive any car. Please . . . I must talk to you anyway.'

Anna moved into the bathroom, turning on the taps. Linden followed.

'I rang Pym this morning. He's been asking me for weeks, seeing how things were. He will pick me up at Pyecomb tonight and we'll go to his home for a few weeks, to think. Anna, please. I can't be alone this morning. If you've known how hard I've found it to do this. I have been paralysed . . . I've never found it hard to make a decision before but this time I kept thinking, "Wait a few more weeks . . . things may change." It's so easy to hang on. Terribly hard to go. To break. But I must. James is a shell. He barely sees me. I love him in a way, but the thing I love is a photograph, an idea in my own head.' She paused. She was trembling.

'Go and make us both some coffee,' Anna said, almost unkindly. 'You look terrible.'

Linden, surprisingly, turned obediently and went down towards the kitchen. And when she had gone, Anna picked up a towel from the corner, a damp heap where Freddie had dropped it, thinking: *How typical of me to leave one untidy man for another who is almost as bad*, and was scared then that she could think about it all so lightly.

The smell of Freddie was everywhere. The smell of the soap he used and after-shave. A spicey, sexy smell. She buried her face in the towel and the smell enveloped and weakened her. He would be so furious if she took Linden. He would see it as a betrayal. She raised her head, folded the towel over the radiator and took off her nightgown. She rubbed a hole in the round, steamy mirror and looked at herself, wondering, even now, why he wanted her. Such an unimportant face, she thought. And she remembered Oliver, shouting down the stairs at Pyecomb . . . 'You are convenient and flattering. Just one more thing ticked off his list. And more desirable because you are my wife and he likes to use my things.' She cringed as she remembered. Oliver's wild and vicious sarcasm had made her, at the time, deeply ashamed, as if she had caused a normally gentle human being to change completely. Only now did it occur to her that he must care a very great deal.

The bath water was very hot. It made her white skin instantly pink. She snuggled into it and lay still in the curling steam and the warmth and when she relaxed her hold on herself she thought of Oliver and Rosie. Probably having breakfast at Pyecomb, side by side in that big kitchen, the high chair close to Ollie's chair; Mary McKay, frying bacon. Oliver talking to Rosie, seriously, as he always had. *Has she forgotten me yet? God, how I wish I was there with them, savouring the thought of a long, empty day, getting to know them both again. I wish I was the kind of woman who could be happy with Oliver. Could I take the part of me which craves Freddie and destroy it? Sterilize myself? However intense life is now, and wild and stirring and violent, it does not seem to balance the past. We have been through so much together, Ollie and I. Just days and nights. Time when we barely knew each other, Robert's death and Rosie's birth* . . .

Linden stood in the doorway. 'Why are you crying?'

'Because I am being pulled in half. It hurts. It makes you cry.'

'Once Pym said, "Take a decision, any decision. You will feel immediate relief. Take two decisions every four hours if necessary!" But lately he has stopped talking like that. Lately we all seemed to have stopped laughing.'

Anna smiled. She could hear Pym saying it. She sat up in the bath and took the coffee.

'I'm sorry I was so long. I couldn't bear to make that instant rubbish.' Linden spoke tartly. Anna watched her making an enormous effort to behave normally, watching her take deep breaths and summon up her strength. Linden smiled shakily. 'I can't believe it is nearly over. Resolved. We have been so good, Pym and I, through all these terrible months. Sitting and talking. Sitting and holding hands . . .'

'Linden, this sale is vital for Freddie. He's been expecting disaster ever since the Middle East war. There is far too much being offered today. The market is only held up by faith. I must go. I said I would.'

Linden's mouth curled. For a moment she looked quite normal. Her voice was acid. 'Surely Freddie isn't worried? I thought he could always make people do exactly what he wanted? That's his big thing, isn't it? Making you jump when he pulls the string. As I used to be in that line myself, I always liked to watch him. Watch an expert at work! Look at the way he used Oliver. Picked him up, kept him until he'd got what he wanted and then calmly removed you! What a magician! Storming down to Pyecomb and manipulating some big dramatic scene. "You can't stay now, Anna." He knows you so well. And what about Ollie? He owes Ollie everything and he never even gave him a thought!'

Anna stood up, water streaming down her body. 'People don't behave like that. Not so calculatingly. They do things because they can't help it, because they feel.'

'Not Freddie!'

'Well, James precipitated the crisis anyway!'

'And Freddie was so ready when it happened!' Linden threw Anna a towel and she shrank into it. When she was dry she put on mascara and lipstick and pink blusher on her white cheeks and the scent which Freddie said was lucky. 'You never liked him, Linden. You never gave him a chance. I know he can be ruthless but, Christ, you've schemed enough yourself!'

'I suppose the difference is,' Linden said dryly, 'that Freddie is rather more successful than I am.' She followed Anna into the bedroom, watched her put on a cotton dress and belt it tightly, wedge-heeled sandals, a string of beads.

Linden went to the bed and sat on it. 'Anna, are you going to take me? I know, in the past, I have asked you for things, to do things. One more time, Anna? I must get away. Now.'

'Why can't I take you after the sale?'

'It would be too late . . . if it's gone well you'll be caught up in all the celebration and if it hasn't, you certainly won't want to leave. Please, Anna. It will take a few hours at the most. I must get away, now, while James is occupied!'

They stared at each other across the room. Anna struggled, not only against Linden but against herself. 'You don't know Freddie. He wouldn't forgive me. He would always say I had let him down!'

'You'll be back before he's even realized you've gone . . .'

'You know that's not true!'

Linden sighed. 'Yes, I suppose I do. I need you to help me, Anna. If I could drive myself, I would, but I can't explain how I feel . . . I couldn't drive.'

There were so many arguments and alternatives in Anna's mind, so many things she could have suggested. A train, a hire car, to ring Pym and wait here for him . . . But she said none of them. She was silent for a long time, her eyes on Linden's face, and she gave in, as Linden had known all along that she would, had planned that she would, because she wanted to. Because, underneath everything, Anna wanted to run.

'I must go and explain to Freddie. I'll be as quick as I can but I must tell him I won't be there . . . Then we'll take the old Mini. I hate driving Freddie's car.'

Linden lay back, fitting her slight body into the chaos of the unmade bed. 'Please come back, Anna. Don't change your mind.'

'I'll come back,' Anna said, smiling a little. 'Haven't I always done what you wanted?' She ran down the stairs and exchanged good mornings with Penny.

'Is your sister all right? She looked terrible!'

'She's a bit upset. She's going to wait upstairs till I get back.'

Anna stepped out into the hot June morning, walking swiftly down the street, putting on her sunglasses. Everyone she passed was carefully dressed, looking into shops, assessing and being assessed. *I've had enough of it!* Anna thought, with surprise. *It's just a game that people play in city streets.*

In the bedroom at Brook Street, Linden opened a lot of cupboards until she found a suitcase she recognized as Anna's. She began to pack Anna's clothes, quickly but neatly. She put shoes into a carrier bag. She collected Anna's books and radio. There was not a great deal. She took the case downstairs. Penny was on the telephone and only glanced up briefly as Linden carried out the case and managed to get it into the boot of the Mini. She went back for the carrier bag, putting it on the back seat under a newspaper. She put her own cases in and then she straightened her back and rubbed her hands. She began to feel alive again, energetic again. Exhilarated. She was planning again. She was going to be all right.

She ran back up to the bedroom, picking up the telephone and checking that the line was free. She rang the Cannon. She waited hours. Someone answered. 'I must speak to Pym MacDonald. I realize he will be in class but this is an emergency.' They found him surprisingly quickly.

'Hallo?'

'Hallo!'

'Where are you?' he said gently. 'What are you doing?'

'I'm making it all right. Everything. I've done it. I've left James. Anna is taking me to Pyecomb. Will you collect me tonight? Can we go to your home like you said?'

He let out his breath in a long sigh. 'It's taken you long enough . . . nearly three years!'

'I never act on impulse!'

They laughed, for a long time, and then there was a silence. 'I'll have to tell a few people, pack a few things, give the car a transfusion . . . I'll be there around nine if you tell me where it is!'

CHAPTER TWENTY-SIX

The hall of Granbury's was quiet and cool. Anna found the contrast rather bewildering after the brilliant sunshine and flamboyance of the street. A different world. She paused and took off her sunglasses. Automatically she bought a catalogue.

The long hall was crowded with people viewing paintings for a forthcoming sale. Anna progressed slowly towards the sale room, frequently held up by the number of people. In one of these pauses she saw herself reflected in an oval glass. She looked at the image curiously . . . Nothing showed in her face. Just a face under bright red hair. Some shadows under the eyes which she rather liked. They seemed to her to be hints of fragility, underlining the fact that after all those years in an awkward and over-weight body, she was finally free. The people parted and she moved on into the auction room, a high-ceilinged room with a boarded floor. It was just after 10.30 and although the sale would not begin until 11 o'clock, all the chairs in the centre of the room were taken.

She saw Freddie almost at once, sitting at the green baize table leaning forward on to it, and for a moment she experienced the feeling which had touched her that very first time. Not plain fear but fear of being across a room from him. An instinct that she should be close to him, sheltering, not apart like this and vulnerable. Freddie turned, looking across the room and finding Anna. He studied her for a moment before he smiled his approval of the way she looked. He never slackened. Not even on a morning like this! He blew her a kiss and her courage evaporated. Most of all she had feared one of his sudden displays of tenderness.

Anna sat down on a chair which was angled towards the auctioneers' table, towards Freddie's wide back. Blue-coated porters moved past her. Hard to believe Freddie had started like that. The room was full of separate sounds, like a tuning orchestra. People began to fill the remaining chairs as if it were a children's game they were playing and the music had suddenly stopped. Interesting people, ordinary people, strangers and familiar faces smiling at Anna. She looked, anxiously, for the vast figure of Maisie Hunter. 'They must all be there today!' Freddie had said.

A pretty brown-haired girl took her place beside the auctioneers' table, tapping a pen lightly against her lower lip, her eyes resting on Freddie. *All I have to do*, Anna thought, *is to get up and cross the room and whisper to him that I can't stay. That Linden needs me, desperately; he must understand that, despite all the jealousy and the competition and hurt and neglect, we have always been there for the other. Always.* But she knew he would not understand, would not even try. He would expect, more than that, he would demand that Anna put him before anyone else today.

Perhaps, now he has seen that I am here, I could slip out . . . And as she thought this she moved her eyes across the room and saw James. He was staring straight ahead. She saw the long straight nose, definite chin, dark sleek hair. So unlike Oliver. He sat absolutely still, long legs crossed. *Why is he here? To watch Freddie go under?* Anna sat forward in her chair, her nervousness growing, and as she did so James sat back a little and she saw, beside him, Carlos Stephano's white head.

The room was very crowded now. People were standing at the back. Tim Granbury appeared, making his way to the auctioneers' table, brushing past Anna's chair. She had met him a couple of times with Freddie . . . *I must go now, before it begins. I will go because she has implored me, despite the fact that Freddie needs me to be here and that he is the person I have twisted my life around.* She watched Freddie, trying to calm herself, but he was restless in his chair, tapping his pen against his knuckles. Tension seemed to have clamped an iron collar round Anna's neck. She wished, absurdly, that she did not know Freddie so well, that she hadn't come to know the part of him which wanted her to be here. But she had sensed that part right from the beginning. *And Freddie will survive*, she thought, and knew it was true. *No matter what, he'll survive. But Linden well might not.* She stood up. Tim Granbury sat in his chair. Anna went forward to where Freddie sat and touched his shoulder.

He looked round, surprised, frowning at her expression and the tight grip of her hand. She swallowed and then bent and kissed his mouth.

'Good luck,' she whispered.

He stared into her face. He put up his hand and touched her cheek and then took one of her hands and held it tightly.

'Freddie . . .'

'Lot One,' Tim Granbury said, and Freddie turned his head to look at the auctioneer and as he did so Anna backed away, hurrying towards the door, through the standing people. 'I have to go, Freddie. I'm sorry.' She ran down the steps, thinking how this building reminded her of the Cannon. Same air of left-over concentration. The blazing street and the noise and cars shocked her. She paused, and shaded her eyes, and then started back towards Brook Street.

When Freddie turned round again, to look for Anna, she was not there. For a few moments he searched the rows of people. She would have been easy to see with that brilliant hair. He knew that she had gone. He would not let himself go on looking. He turned back, drawing black lines on his catalogue.

This is what matters in my life. This room and this stillness. There is a degree of tension here I have never felt before in all the years I have been involved. How did they make her go? Why?

He felt a deep, twisting hurt. He contained it. Later. Once again he looked round but this time to check that the people who mattered had come. They had! Every one of them. Maisie was near the front. Freddie looked sideways and met James's eyes.

So it was just the two of them. The lesser people were irrelevant. It was to be Freddie or James, as they had known from the beginning. Freddie looked back to Tim Granbury. The early bidding was sticky and slow. He would not know for some time which way it would go. Freddie controlled his restless hands and settled down to wait.

Linden was standing in the street, leaning against the roof of the dusty little car, quite oblivious of the effect the dirt had on her pale cotton dress. 'I thought you weren't coming. What's happened?' She stood back, opening the door. Anna stared at her small white face, at the creased, dusty dress, and she was suddenly desperately glad that she was doing this.

'It's just started. It's packed. I'll take you to Pyecomb but I must come straight back!'

'Of course,' Linden said, her voice low and docile. 'I've got all my things in.'

The traffic was thick in Park Lane and Anna changed direction, intending to go out of London over Hammersmith Bridge. She turned on the radio. She looked at Linden occasionally but Linden appeared to be asleep, head tilted back uncomfortably, hands folded in her lap rather pathetically, as if she were dead.

'I must be quite mad,' Anna said aloud. 'What am I doing? Why am I taking you to the one house in the whole country I don't want to visit? I know when I get there I shall want to look at Rosie and I'll go into the cottage and Mary McKay will stare at me with those terrible stern eyes and say, "She's asleep right now. You'll not want her woken, will you? We had a bad night." Hinting at the hundreds of things I don't know about my own child because I'm not there when she cries in the night or laughs in the day. As I won't be there to watch her change . . . I do want to be at her birthday, Linden, I want that so much. And suppose Marietta is at Pyecomb? I couldn't face her.'

'Nor could I,' Linden said quietly.

Anna reached for the packet of cigarettes, half full, familiar and crumpled, one of the hundreds Freddie had discarded since she had known him. She lit one and then hated it. She wished Linden would talk, would distract her from the silent lunges of her conscience. 'You know, Linden, I have never really reasoned anything out. I just reacted, took to places and people like an animal does . . .'

They sat, side by side, in the small car and both had their thoughts wound up in the same, interlocking story. They sat, for a long time, in silence.

'What a beautiful day!' Linden said at last, sitting up, arching her back. They were well out of London now.

Anna was startled out of a complicated memory. 'I'd almost forgotten you were there . . .'

'What were you thinking about?'

'Life.'

'Mine or yours?'

'Mine, of course, but they seem to run parallel. I was looking for the obvious mistakes but there are so many and I don't know where to begin.'

'How about the morning Tracey first looked at our susceptible father across the office and gave him a wink? Or the day I rang Marietta and wangled an interview? Or the day you walked up and down Brook Street and stood with your nose pressed against the window of Freddie's shop?'

'Or the wedding . . . Oliver and I, neither of us knowing what the hell we were doing! I thought marriage was like the pearly gates and once you scrambled through, no matter who with, it was happy ever after. And Ollie thought it was just one of the hurdles on the way to becoming level with James!'

'You were both too young,' Linden said vaguely. 'Not just in age but in everything.'

'What about you? You and James weren't too young?'

Linden shook her head, violently, as if she could not bear to talk about it. 'What did Oliver say when you left?'

Anna sighed. 'I didn't tell him . . . Freddie did. It just happened. Another thing I never planned. Ollie has so many layers. Impossible layers. Freddie is easy to touch. Hard and dirty and plain. I thought I would never be afraid of hurting Freddie. I thought, "He will shout back." If I hurt Ollie he just went away.'

'Why is it so sudden?' Linden said, wrapping her arms round her knees. 'The end comes with no warning. Like the end of a holiday or dying, I suppose. You think the sun and the feeling of waking in the morning with nothing to do but enjoy yourself will last for ever and quite suddenly someone points out that it is over. Time to go home. And you think, "But I haven't written my postcards yet or visited the ruins or said my prayers." Too late! Time's up!'

Anna shivered. 'That's just how I felt when Freddie came to Pyecomb. I thought, "Not yet. Not just yet." All this has happened because I didn't think enough!'

'It doesn't help,' Linden said, very quietly. 'I thought and I thought. I have been doing it all my life. And it should have worked with James. I would have loved him in my way but there isn't enough of him and through these last months he withdrew what little I was allowed in the beginning. He has been obsessed with destroying Freddie. The first time I tried to tell him that Pym was back he was writing his letter to Carlos

. . . that was the night he saw you and Freddie together. He wouldn't listen to me. He closed the door as if I were a rather noisy child! And as I became more and more unhappy I became more extreme and dramatic and I seemed to repel him. He was not available to me. And Pym was.' She sat forward restlessly. 'Perhaps if you and Freddie had chosen another restaurant that night . . .?'

'And Pym? Will you be all right with him?'

'I hope so. We've both changed a lot but it's still there, between us. It's funny, Anna, to walk around behind a face like mine. It gives everyone the feeling they have a right to make an instant judgement. Most women dislike me. Nearly all men will do anything for me but they do not see me as a person. Except Pym. For some reason he has always known me.'

'I told you, didn't I?'

'Yes.' Linden smiled. 'Some things are constant. This old car and you, Anna, plodding on from disaster to disaster. And Mum . . . Guess what? After all this time our wandering father is having second thoughts about Tracey! They don't get on as well as they did. She's twenty-six now. She's turned into a human being as dull as the rest of us!'

'Will he go back to Mum?'

'Yes, I really think he will. It will have to be gradual, to keep his pride reasonably intact. That's why Mum's gone away, I think. To give him time.'

'So we have all been marching around in a pointless circle?'

'Not all of us. If this sale is the disaster that James foresees, Freddie won't survive.'

Freddie! Anna had not thought about him, had forgotten the sale. She felt quite detached, as if talking about someone she hardly knew. 'Nothing will keep Freddie down. He will start again, somehow.'

'And what about you?' Linden said, very quietly.

Anna did not answer. The big roads had given way to smaller lanes, achingly familiar. She drove more slowly with her window open. She crept through Lewes and turned on to the Pyecomb road. Ten more minutes to the gates of the house and Anna took her car round to the back and switched off the engine. She saw Oliver's Mini, the roof rack packed with suitcases.

'Come in,' Linden said.

Anna shook her head. 'It will be over now, one way or the other. I must go back . . .'

Linden looked up at the clock over the old stables which was always slow. 'It's been over for quite a while,' she said gently. 'Thank you, Anna. Or perhaps you should thank me? Go and see Rosie.' She got out, turning and lifting her cases from the back seat. She left them beside the car. She crossed the yard towards the house, walking slowly, and then suddenly raising her hands above her head, stretching like a dancer, spinning on her heels in a wild, expressive circle of delight. She laughed and waved to Anna as she went in.

As Anna stared at Oliver's car she remembered how he had spoken of Wales when he was trying to infect her with his enthusiasm . . . 'This house, Anna, you'll love it. It's on the side of the estuary. It's white. It's a bit rambling with big windows. It's old and it's lovely. It needs doing, of course. The garden is on a series of flat terraces. There's a boat-house and a marvellous attic with huge north-facing windows. It would make a wonderful studio.' Anna curled and uncurled her fingers. Once she had believed she could paint. Not so long ago. Could she? Her hands now were so clean. No paint stains. No black charcoal smudges. She sat back, trying to make herself start the car but she could not. She didn't want to . . .

Anna got out of the car and walked through the yard, passing the McKays' cottage. She pushed open the door to the walled vegetable garden and then closed it behind her. This garden was made of oblongs and stripes of green; soft circles of strawberry plants; currant and gooseberry bushes; brilliant green lettuces and bright yellow poppies and, against the old brick walls, fig and pear and peach trees. There was a shady corner full of large flower-pots and Anna went and sat down on one, eyes fixed on the door, heart thumping in her mouth as she waited.

It was a few minutes before she heard the latch on the door, felt the hesitation on the other side, saw Oliver come into the garden. He looked thinner, his hair shaggy, and he was browner than she had seen him before. Anna almost held her breath, waiting, as he pushed his hair back from his forehead and then seemed to make up his mind and come towards her.

He stopped a few feet from her.

'Linden said you were here . . .' He stood with his back to the sun.

'Yes. I drove her down.' Anna tilted her head, shading her eyes so that she could see his face. She talked quickly. 'She came round this morning . . . almost hysterical . . . I had to bring her. She and James have . . .'

'I know. I said so, didn't I, at the very beginning?' Their eyes kept meeting and then moving apart. Oliver came forward, sitting down on a large upturned flower-pot.

'Yes, yes, you did.' She was deeply surprised. 'How amazing . . . I thought it was all our fault. Hers and mine. I thought there was something wrong with us. I suppose it was James, after all.'

'Of course it was,' Oliver said impatiently. 'But it's taken me years to realize it. He ran my life. I allowed him to. But what he did with Stephano finally made me see . . . At last I'm on my own! I shall probably make an appalling mess and waste my money and achieve nothing, but at least I am doing what I want! I like Colin. I know we can work together. I'm taking Rosie with me. If I leave her here I know she will be beautifully cared for but that's not enough. I was beautifully cared for . . . I think it's better she should take her chance with me, don't you?'

Anna nodded, full of an icy despair, shut out of their lives.

'Shouldn't you be at this great dramatic sale? I did my best with Stephano but he wouldn't listen. I reckon Freddie knew he wouldn't! But once Carlos was thoroughly panicked by James and I, Freddie coolly stepped in and offered to buy almost half his collection prior to the auction at very low prices. He pointed out that to wait for the sale could be extremely risky. He pointed out that Carlos had obtained the pieces very cheaply . . .' Oliver laughed. 'So Freddie stands to make a fortune today!'

'Or lose one. The Impressionist sale on Monday was a disaster. And where would he find the money to buy these things from Carlos?'

'Well, he's borrowed it, I suppose. So, if the market has collapsed he'll be in a bad way.' Oliver looked at his watch. 'It must all be over now. My guess is that, somehow, Freddie will come out of all this far richer than he went in. In an extraordinary way, I hope he does!' Oliver turned and looked at Anna. 'Why aren't you there? Don't you enjoy the excitement?'

She shook her head. 'I didn't know half of it. He didn't tell me.'

'But you're happy with him?' Oliver said, stiffly.

She didn't answer. They were both looking, deliberately, out across the garden. In the silence they turned their heads.

'Did you ask Linden to bring me here?'

'No . . . but she said she would try and do something. I have been trying, Anna, wanting to come and see you and talk to you. I didn't know how to begin. But I wasn't going to Wales without asking you, once again, to come with us. I can't bear it without you. There is no point in anything. Please, Anna, come with Rosie and me.'

'Do you really want me? After all this . . . I can't keep on changing and changing.'

'Why not? I've changed enough. Rosie has changed me. I know I was impossible in the beginning but later you never gave me a chance. You decided it had been a mistake and you never looked at me again. But it counts for so much, all the things we've been through together. How can you wipe it away?'

'I have been pulled in half these last weeks . . . but all the time, it was stronger: the longing to be here. I couldn't bear the thought of missing Rosie's birthday. Can I really come with you?' So many tears in her eyes that the garden danced in front of her and she was aware of Ollie, beside her, shaking, and she saw that he was laughing until there were tears in his eyes too.

'What is it? What's funny?'

'It's just so silly, the two of us, on these flower-pots like a couple of garden gnomes!'

They stood up, arms round each other, rocking each other, laughing, and then walking towards the door. Ollie was saying, 'Come with me today, Anna. Now. I'm driving down to see the house . . . It's mine but there's no furniture yet. I want to see what I should need. I was going to leave Rosie but if you're coming, we can all go, can't we? The three of us. At last.'

'Yes,' Anna said. A deep sweet happiness came with the word.

As he sat in the crowded saleroom, entirely at the mercy of the people who surrounded him, his future life depending on what they had read in the newspapers and what they believed and the actions of the incomprehensible men who controlled the oil, thousands of miles from this room, Freddie Monroe was afraid. Fear was new to him. *Ironic*, he thought, *that the end should come here at Granbury's where I began*! He stared down at his hands. It was still early in the sale but lots were selling slowly and for only slightly over their reserves. There was a heaviness in the room. He thought of Anna. He would not forgive her for leaving him. She had known how much he wanted her to be here. She probably knew him better than any other living soul and he had needed, very badly, to have one sympathetic presence in this hostile room. He was a superstitious man. A sentimental man. A part of him closed down against Anna. *Once before,* he thought, *I let her come too close. Weakened myself.*

Unimportant pieces, merely padding, wasted time, built up tension. It was very, very quiet. Freddie's throat was dry. He looked at Maisie Hunter's florid face. Was she buying or selling or merely spectating? Lot 50 failed to reach its reserve. Freddie found his mouth was very dry. He glanced at James and saw that he was smiling slightly. Carlos Stephano sat nervously, curling his catalogue. Fear made Freddie very cold, very still.

So they have got me, he thought. *The market will fold. I shall be left enormously in debt, not merely back where I started but far, far more badly placed.* For a moment a wave of absolute despair touched him.

'Lot Fifty-one.'

It was Oliver's jar. The jar which had started it all. The porter put it into the hands of Paul Allen, who sat next to Freddie. He examined it and passed it on.

Oliver's jar. Freddie cradled it in his hands. He felt softened. He felt a sudden peace. He remembered why he had started all this in the beginning. There was more in him than the ambition. He loved the beauty too. The jar fitted his two big hands. It was not immensely valuable, merely exquisite. Reluctantly he handed it to the man on his left and, as he did so, Freddie knew that he had to buy it.

What the hell difference is a few thousand pounds going to make in the long run? In a couple of hours it will all be over, anyway. For a little while, I'll own it!

The bidding started, slow and depressed. Freddie came in

right from the start. It was quite unlike him. His voice was loud and held a most unusual urgency. He rarely bid in words. His normal technique was a brisk nod of his head. But now he spoke out, loudly, into the silent room. And Maisie, a few yards from him, eyed him shrewdly and then came in too, admiring Freddie's courage. Her voice was determined. Just the two of them. The price rose steadily, soaring well over the value of the jar as Freddie and Maisie competed for it, fought it out, in a last, ritual battle. And the buyers who had been hesitant, almost ready to go home, and the people who had come to watch the market collapse, were surprised by the determination in the voices and by the vast and unreal prices and began to think, 'Can it hold? Can it go on for a few more months? It has stayed all this time, against all odds.' And catalogues were reopened and nerves were calmed and when Tim Granbury knocked the jar down to Freddie for an absurd price there was an excited buzz of comment in the room which, a few moments earlier, had been almost dead. A reporter at the back ran to find a telephone.

Tim Granbury rapped for silence. 'Lot Fifty-two.' He felt the extraordinary change, the eagerness, the recklessness. The bidding began almost at once. It was another of Oliver's pieces. And Freddie, getting up slowly and going to write a cheque for his jar, could at first hardly believe it. He turned and looked down the room. He watched them all, fighting over this second piece of Oliver's. He stared at James and he thought: *Christ Almighty, I'm going to make it.*

Linden, waiting for Pym that evening, sat in the library at Pyecomb, curled on the sofa with her feet tucked under her, and watched the nine o'clock news on television. And towards the end, after the normal casually recounted disasters, they showed Granbury's saleroom and one of the last lots being auctioned. They talked of the enormous prices, about inflation and investment and the extraordinary way the Chinese porcelain market had lasted when so many other fields of the art market had collapsed. They even interviewed Freddie, as they had done several times before. He looked sleek and confident. He said a few things about the indestructable quality of beauty.

He said, 'There are still, thank God, a lot of people in this world who value this kind of exquisite craftsmanship and beauty more than they value making a quick buck!'

Linden rocked with laughter, hugging herself, talking to herself. 'Oh, my God, he's done it! How incredible! He would. Freddie, you hypocrite!'

She was still laughing some minutes later when she heard the distinctive chug of Pym's Volkswagen and its wheels on the gravel. She ran to the back door and looked into the warm night for him. Above her head the lantern was attacked by dancing moths.

Pym opened the car door and got out slowly. He stretched. He wanted to savour the moment he had waited for so long. In the doorway Linden hesitated but for a different reason. She was trying to believe that it was, at last, all done with. That all the waiting was finished.

He came across to her, putting one hand each side of the door-frame, leaning forward, putting his mouth on hers. 'I've booked us a room in the pub,' he said. 'You won't want to stay here and it's so late to start tonight. Okay?'

He carried her cases to the car and she shivered a little, with excitement, with relief, as she looked back at Pyecomb for the last time. In the car beside her Pym found it hard to drive. He needed to touch her. He swore because of the need to change gear, to steer. Then he laughed, telling himself there was nothing to fear now. No hurry. No need to steal time. They might have gone the long way round but they had, finally, arrived.

HEYWOOD BOOKS

TODAY'S PAPERBACKS
– AT YESTERDAY'S PRICES!

Heywood Books is a new list of paperback books which will be published every month at unbelievably low prices. It will range from up-to-date contemporary women's novels to exciting romantic thrillers and the best in historical romance, from classic crime to nerve-tingling horror and big adventure thrillers, presenting a superb list of highly readable and top value popular fiction.

Look for this month's new titles:

HAMMERSTRIKE	*Walter Winward*	£1.75
GOD OF A THOUSAND FACES	*Michael Falconer Anderson*	£1.50
MUCKLE ANNIE	*Jan Webster*	£1.75
THE WINDMILL YEARS	*Vicky Martin*	£1.75
QUICKSILVER LADY	*Barbara Whitehead*	£1.50
THE WINNOWING WINDS	*Ann Marlowe*	£1.50

MUCKLE ANNIE
A vivid saga of bitter poverty and hardship – and the triumph of undying love

Jan Webster

In spite of her family's wealthy past, Annie McIlvanney has only known deepest poverty. When she is insulted and cast out of work, she at first loses hope, but is saved from the depths of despair by her love for Hector, the laird's son.

Annie follows her Highland love to Canada, enduring the discomforts of a bride ship. On the dreadful journey she hand-rears a baby whose father begs her to marry him. But Annie's heart belongs to Hector and she is determined to find him, even if it means braving the dangerous Indians, bitter weather and the grinding hardship of the goldfields.

QUICKSILVER LADY
Sequel to THE CARETAKER WIFE
Would she make a 'good' marriage or marry for love?

Barbara Whitehead

Arabella was eager to go to London to taste the delights of fashionable society. Disappointed in love, she hoped that the distractions of the city would sooth her aching heart. At the advanced age of twenty-one, she hoped to find at last the man of her dreams.
London welcomed her with balls, masquerades, theatres, eligible young men – and trickery. Seeking fashion, wealth and the advantages of a great match, she found instead that she too must follow the dictates of her own heart.

THE WINNOWING WINDS
Death and danger lurk in the snow-clad mountains

Ann Marlowe

Deirdre Sheridan hoped that a teaching post at an expensive school in glamorous jet-setting Gstaad would help her forget a recent tragedy. But there is danger and the threat of death even in the idyllic peace of the Swiss mountains. Among her pupils is the heir to the oil-rich sheikhdom of Qaiman, an obvious target for kidnappers and assassins.

But Deirdre is captivated by Prince Haroun and his two motherless young sisters and when one near-fatal accident follows another, she becomes increasingly worried about their safety. In her anxiety, there are only two people she can turn to: Sadiq, the children's enigmatic but attractive uncle; and the father of another pupil, who has gone out of his way to befriend her. But as the peaceful Alpine resort becomes a setting for violence and conspiracy, she realises she cannot trust even them . . .

HAMMERSTRIKE
The secret plan for a mass breakout of German POWs

A great war thriller from
Walter Winward

In Skiddaw POW camp, imprisoned Luftwaffe officers plan their escape. Back across the Channel, the war is going badly for Germany. In a desperate bid to tip the scales, Goering has masterminded Hammerstrike, a daring plan for the mass escape of German POWs in Britain. But, unexpectedly, the key man in the plot, a senior Luftwaffe officer, is shot down and interned in Britain.

To save the plan, an ex-SS officer must do the impossible: before the British can discover their prisoner's true identity – and the secret plan called Hammerstrike – he must penetrate British defences and spirit the general out of Skiddaw or, failing that, make sure the secret dies with him.

HEYWOOD BOOKS

FICTION

One Little Room	*Jan Webster*	£1.50
The Winnowing Winds	*Ann Marlowe*	£1.50

SAGA

Daneclere	*Pamela Hill*	£1.75
Making Friends	*Cornelia Hale*	£1.75
Muckle Annie	*Jan Webster*	£1.75
The Windmill Years	*Vicky Martin*	£1.75

HISTORICAL ROMANCE

The Caretaker Wife	*Barbara Whitehead*	£1.50
Quicksilver Lady	*Barbara Whitehead*	£1.50

THRILLER

KG 200	*J. D. Gilman & John Clive*	£1.75
Hammerstrike	*Walter Winward*	£1.75

HORROR

The Unholy	*Michael Falconer Anderson*	£1.50
God of a Thousand Faces	*Michael Falconer Anderson*	£1.50

NAME ....

ADDRESS ....

....

Write to Heywood Books Cash Sales, PO Box 11, Falmouth, Cornwall TR10 9EN. Please indicate order and enclose remittance to the value of the cover price plus:

UK: Please allow 60p for the first book, 25p for the second book and 15p for each additional book ordered, to a maximum charge of £1.90.

B.F.P.O. & EIRE: Please allow 60p for the first book, 25p for the second book, 15p per copy for the next 7 books and thereafter 9p per book.

OVERSEAS: Please allow £1.25 for the first book, 75p for the second book and 28p per copy for each additional book.

Whilst every effort is made to keep prices low it is sometimes necessary to increase cover prices and also postage and packing rates at short notice. Heywood Books reserve the right to show new retail prices on covers which may differ from those previously advertised in the text or elsewhere.